My Letters to You

by Dale Denney

PublishAmerica
Baltimore

First printing

ISBN: 1-4137-5291-8
PUBLISHED BY PUBLISHAMERICA, LLLP
www.publishamerica.com
Baltimore

Printed in the United States of America

To My Juanita

Best wishes

Dale Denney

Foreword

I don't feel that I had a life before I began writing letters. I was just there, a kid too little for his age who had a passion for reading.

I couldn't wait to get to our little home town library after school let out. It was a small house on main street they'd converted into a library. Slanted roof. Porch. Paint peeling.

Mrs. Rader was our volunteer librarian, an elderly lady with her graying hair pulled back tightly and fastened in a bun behind her neck.

She sat at a small desk to the right when you went in. She'd smile. Nod. She'd know you—at least know what family you belonged to. Too many families had too many kids to remember them all individually.

My name was on my library card. Dale Denney. But she always called me Don, my next older brother's name. People always seemed to remember Don. I didn't mind. I was comfortable with who I was.

What I loved about Mrs. Rader was she understood readers. She was kind enough to leave me to my own thoughts as I browsed the shelves. She sat at her desk looking out the window over her reading glasses, sometimes humming a hymn softly to herself. I'd browse, and browse, and browse before making a selection, take it to Mrs. Rader, respond to small talk as she rubber-stamped the due date, and carry my prize home.

I read the ten-cent pulps, too—discarded ones, borrowed ones, and the ones I found in the back room of the library.

My favorite pulps were westerns and one called the G8 Series, which were about a pilot (known only as G8), and his adventures in the Great War. ("The War" then was World War I because World War II hadn't happened yet.)

Sometimes I'd make sure Mrs. Rader wasn't looking and read the romance pulps too. They told you what it felt like to kiss a girl. And be in love.

Ah, to write something, anything, which would bring as much joy to a reader as I got out of the books and magazines in our little library on Main Street.

Writing a book would be nice, I kept telling myself. It would have dignity and a long life. Once completed, it would last forever.

I made many starts—westerns, sea adventures, a love story.

But something was missing. I know now what it was—a reader. A book simply wasn't what I wanted to do. It was merely a logical choice, a commercial reason for doing what I loved to do.

I missed Mrs. Rader and that little nondescript library more than anyone or anything else when I left home after graduating from high school. Home, my parents, and what few friends I had simply disappeared from my mind.

I was lost. I wandered about aimlessly, suspended in time. My job was just a job. I had no future. I missed going to school and its disciplines toward learning.

Although I had secret dreams of being in love with a girl, I had serious doubts that it would ever happen.

Then it did happen. I met Nita. Beneath all the silliness of youth, the longing, the denials, the crushing misery of rejection, I fell in love with her immediately after only a casual introduction.

I was too shy to ask for a show date, or even to suggest buying her a cherry Coke at the drug store.

While I didn't know it was love, I did know I had a deep yearning to know her better. When we were together in groups, my inner attention was always on her: what she was doing, what she was saying, and wondering if she even knew I existed.

Then war broke out and I left to enroll at Oklahoma University. One of the first things I did was write Nita a letter, even apologizing for doing so because we were not friends, just acquaintances.

After mailing the letter, I was both frightened and filled with a sense of power I'd never felt before. Just imagining her reading my words, thinking about me, a virtual stranger, elevated my emotions to new highs.

Making it even more exotic was the fact I would not suffer personal rejection. If she didn't bother to answer, the letter would be gone, disappeared from existence forever. Nobody would be offended, nobody would be hurt.

That's what happened. She didn't answer.

I had other new friends to write to. I did, but it wasn't enough.

I simply had to write Nita again. I pretended to be hurt because she hadn't taken the time to answer a friendly letter.

This time, after dropping it in the mail box, I didn't dwell on it as much. If she answered—fine. If she didn't—forget it.

At least that's what I kept telling myself. But the day I pulled her reply from my post office box and saw her name as the return address, it was like a first kiss. I wanted that moment to last forever.

I don't remember what she wrote. It didn't matter. Something any careful sixteen-year-old would write: What are you doing there? I didn't know you had left town. What subjects are you going to take at the university? That sort of thing.

Going to a university was a big thing and I was proud doing it. I hoped she would be impressed.

I returned home one weekend and asked her for a date. We went to the Saturday night preview and saw *Dr. Jekyll and Mr. Hyde* with Spencer Tracy. I walked her home.

That first good-night kiss wouldn't happen until several months and several dates later. Just being able to hold her hand and have her willingly clasp mine was much, much more than I expected. I can still relish that wonderful feeling in my mind sixty-some years later.

I wrote to my folks while attending the university, also my brothers, my sisters, my friends, to anybody and everybody I could think of.

But Nita's letters were always special. She didn't know that. She knew I was writing to other kids and probably thought she was simply one among many.

But when I'd come in from classes to find one of Nita's letters on the little hall table in my rooming house, I'd rip it open and read it running up the stairs to my room.

All too often her letters were short, sometimes only one page of a small writing tablet. But each word was precious—and thrilling because they were coming from her to me.

I'd spend the rest of the evening answering her letter—not writing constantly, of course. I would spend several minutes between sentences, rereading what I had just written and wondering what she would be thinking when she read those words.

Would they make her happy? Would she be sad? Would she be able to see in them that I thought she was special—yet I didn't want to be too bold and frighten her away.

My letter-writing reached new heights when I was in the army writing to Nita and members of my family and friends. By then Nita and I were very much in love, and writing her a letter every day was not only a must, but a joy.

Of course, receiving answers to my letters were important. But I honestly believe the greatest delight in receiving a letter was knowing that now I could answer it. And, as soon as possible, I would begin the next letter, especially to

Nita.

I even proposed to her in a letter by telling her I intended to propose to her in person the next chance we had to be together. I did, and she said yes.

My love for writing letters influenced my decisions when I returned to classes at Oklahoma University after being discharged from service. I selected those courses which would lead me to a career in writing.

I learned all about the business of writing, about book publishers, agents, characterizations, plots, scenes, dialogue. One assignment was to study the advertisements in a magazine. That will tell you quicker than anything, our writing professor said, who reads that publication. Always know your reader when you write.

I worked hard at it. But, in reality, what I was trying to do subconsciously was just hoping to make money writing so I could spend time doing what I loved to do most—write letters.

All too often I'd shove my class assignments aside and write a long letter to a friend, a brother, a sister—anybody.

I stuck with my lessons, however, long enough to earn a degree in literature. I didn't even know what that signified, or what I could do with it to go out into the world and earn a decent living.

I simply could not see myself as a member of the academic world: advance degrees, a professorship perhaps. So when a prominent businessman in my home town offered me a deal to become an instant editor, I took it. He'd purchased our weekly newspaper after its owner died to keep it from going out of town to a nearby competitor. He offered it to me for $25 down and $25 a month.

I bought it with visions of revolutionizing the weekly newspaper business with my style of writing.

My love for writing overrode the frustration and hard work that went into pulling together and printing a weekly newspaper. It was exciting being able to publish my own "stuff." Best of all, I knew every one of my subscribers, and I always tried to imagine what old so-and-so was thinking when he was reading what I was writing. Each article, in essence, was a letter to a friend.

Oh, I had a career—of sorts. Writing and editing big-time magazines. Public relations work for everything from car racing to serving time as a public relations officer for the U.S. Army Corps of Engineers.

But I drifted back to writing what I wanted to write when I retired. The home town paper was pleased with my material—which were, in my mind, simply letters to a friend.

That's what I do best, and I love doing it.

So—what has it gained me?

First: the most precious thing in life—a loving wife.

And because of her, a son any father could be proud of, a wonderful daughter-in-law, and a granddaughter full of happiness and delightful surprises.

What more can a man ask for?

And it came because of my love for writing letters.

Now I have the joy and honor of writing these letters to you.

Section I

The CAT Scan

"You've got cancer," he said, the man in the long white coat.

Me? No way. Somebody made a mistake. I've worked in a hospital. Technicians make mistakes all the time. That was it. Somebody made a mistake.

He kept talking, seeing I was taking it so well. I glanced at Nita sitting in the corner. I could tell it hadn't registered with her either.

I had agreed to have a biopsy made of the lump on my neck just because she had kept insisting.

The man in the long white coat acted confident. I could take my chemotherapy there—

In this dinky hospital? I thought.

I asked if he'd mind if I got a second opinion.

Not at all, he said. Then proceeded to caution me not to put it off too long.

"The kind you have—Non-Hodgkins Lymphoma—doubles every thirty days..."

That scared the hell out of me. Dad pulled a fast one on me once. He told me it took thirty nails to shoe a horse. And if I were a blacksmith and charged $10 to shoe a horse, which would I rather have: double $10 for shoeing a horse, or one cent for the first nail and doubled for every nail after that?

I said I'd take the $20. He laughed. Then I spent the rest of the day figuring it up. I quit at one million dollars.

Then suppose I got a second opinion and that doctor said I didn't have cancer? I decided then and there that I'd rather be treated for cancer if I didn't have it than not treated for cancer if I did have it.

"All right. What do we do first?"

He scheduled the chemotherapy treatment first, followed by a cat scan of my complete body to follow.

Nita pretended it wasn't all that bad, that they'd cure me. Her faith gave me confidence.

I reported for my first chemo treatment. I asked the oncologist what caused cancer.

"We don't know what causes one of our cells to suddenly start growing wild," he said. "Some think it's our environment. Some think it's a genetic thing."

Even after the treatments send it into remission, the biggest fright is: Will it come back?

When I returned for my CAT scan the young X-ray technician running the machine was nice. She handed me a hospital gown and led me to a cubicle with a curtain hanging in the opening. She did a very pleasant job explaining in detail how many clothes to take off, how to put my hospital gown on, and to call her when I was ready. And when I was ready, she kept reassuring her aged patient (me) not to be afraid as she led me to the table I was to lie on.

"Here, let me help," she said, taking my arm.

"I can do it," I told her, disdaining her assistance.

Being treated like an old man hurt my feelings because I never thought of myself as being old—just a young man trapped in an old man's body.

She politely backed away as I climbed awkwardly upon the table, trying not to fall and trying to keep my fanny covered at the same time. She stood over me, smiling, and patiently explained the process, what the giant machine was going to do, how the table I was lying on would move me in short increments through the machine, that she would be repeatedly telling me when to hold my breath and when to breathe.

"Just lie quietly and follow my instructions," she said.

I wanted to reassure her by telling her I wasn't frightened, that I had been an X-ray technician during the war. But she probably would have asked, as most young people do, "Which war?"

As usual, I remained quiet—just listened politely to her instructions—another lost asset of my generation, politeness.

As she prepared me for being ratcheted through the CAT scanner, I would have liked to have told her, for comparison, about one German who tried to escape from the Prisoner of War camp where I worked as an X-ray technician. He was meaner than all get-out. Had fought for years with Rommel's vaunted African Desert Korps.

A guard shot the guy as he was running away. The slug lodged in his pelvic area. They brought him to X-ray to operate.

I did my best to keep the blood from staining my nice clean X-ray table, swiping it up with a bloody sheet. When the captain was ready, I rolled the X-ray tube into position and lowered the fluoroscope plate down over the patient's pelvic area so the captain could see what he was doing probing for the slug.

The brave German's eyes bugged when I pulled the fluoroscope screen down against his belly. He panicked. It took six of us to hold him down. My German helper explained: He thought we were going to burn a hole in him with the X-ray machine!

But why tell the nice girl at the X-ray controls all that? It was so long ago and so far away.

She gave me a reassuring pat on the arm and stepped into the radiation-proof operator's booth.

"Don't breathe," came her soft voice through the speaker as the giant machine began to whir. Then she'd say, "Breathe."

I felt the machine ratcheting the table I was lying on an inch farther into the machine.

This was going to take a while. Unlike the German prisoner of war, I knew what the machine was doing. It was taking cross-section pictures of me—like a meat cutter slicing baloney in a grocery store.

When I was a kid, I loved watching Howard Tippin slice the baloney I'd ordered. He'd be standing ankle-deep in sawdust behind the meat counter catching the sliced meat in his bare hand. When his hand was full, he'd hold it up and ask, "Is that enough?"

Yes, I'd nod.

He'd wipe his other hand on his bloody apron and rip a piece of wrapping paper from a heavy roll nearby and spread it over the scale. He'd drop the sliced baloney on the paper, check the weight, and fold the paper noisily over the meat. He'd tie it with twine string that came off a cone over by the wall, up across the fly-specked ceiling through eyelets and dangled down over the meat counter.

Then he would scribble a price on the paper and I'd take it over to his brother, Kie, who would be standing on his crutches behind the cash register where the white paint had been rubbed off the counter from customers sliding things across.

"Don't breathe," came her soft voice. The machine whirred. "Breathe."

She didn't have to tell me now. I was ahead of her. Knowing what the machine was doing, I fell into rhythm with the automatic ratcheting of the machine, my thoughts drifting.

Was that where I got my cancer? From Tippin's Grocery? Could be. Besides handling the meat with his bare hands in an unsanitary situation, Howard would roll up his apron and tuck it around his waist when he carried cardboard boxes

14

out back to burn them. He'd stand in the smoke and stir the fire until it was burned down and come back in to slice more baloney.

Don't breathe. Whirr. Breathe.

Yes. The destroyer cells could have gotten into my system from Howard's apron, or the sawdust, or the smoke from cardboard boxes made of who knows what and from who knows where. Maybe they came from the lead in the paint flecking off the counter next to the cash register.

Or how about the polluted streams in the oil fields where I grew up?

My friends and I had fun rolling up our overalls and wading in a creek heavily polluted with salt and oil spills, sailing homemade boats down the riffles. Sometimes we'd have to skim off the crude oil where it had gathered on the top of the water in still pools. We pretended these pools were "oceans" which we had to sail through to get to the next riffle.

One time we set fire to the layer of oil on top of the water to make it more exciting for our flotilla to battle its way through.

The fire we'd started for fun caught the dead grass hanging over the edge of the water and went racing out of control across acres and acres of pasture land. We forgot about our burning fleet and ran to get away from the scene. We watched from afar as oil field workers fought hard to save two oil wells from being destroyed by the rampaging blaze. Served them right, I thought, and proclaimed it was one of the more exciting afternoons of my life.

Or maybe the cancer got into my system from eating half-raw meat. We used to tramp the sand rock hills along the Cimarron River, hunting.

When we got hungry at noon, we'd clean whatever we had—a rabbit, even meadow larks—wash them in a pool of water collected in a rock depression, and roast them over a fire. We'd be so hungry that as soon as the meat got charred good on the outside, we'd gnaw into it. If we killed enough meat for lunch, we'd call it a successful outing.

Or could it have come from the months I spent in the army taking X-rays, being careless about my own radiation exposure. Maybe that German prisoner's blood on my hands gave it to me. Hadn't he been on duty in the desert in North Africa two years before being captured? No telling what he could have picked up in the deserts of North Africa fighting a war.

Don't breathe. Whirr. Breathe.

How about breathing the fumes from melting lead in a newspaper print shop, lead used to cast pages for my paper?

Don't breathe. Whirr. Breathe.

Or it may be like the cancer specialist said—a genetic thing. From my dad's ancestors? Or from Mom's side of the family? Or did it come from a blending of both? Or my environment? What mattered now? All these things are a part of my life, and irrevocable.

Don't breathe. Whirr. Breathe…

Life sure is strange. We keep trying to manipulate ourselves through it, knowing all the time there is only one inescapable ending. The overriding thing about being diagnosed as having cancer at seventy rather than at thirty is that you are able to enjoy the beautiful sunsets of your past.

While at thirty you may be excited by the glorious sunrises ahead, so many turn out to be like Oscar Wilde's *Picture of Dorian Gray*—only illusions. And when our dreams disintegrate, they leave us filled with bitter disappointment.

For those of us in my generation, we've come to know it's time to enjoy the sunsets of the past, pick and choose, enjoy the good, forget the bad. It'll make the few sunrises we have left even more beautiful, for out of many, there'll be a few precious ones we can yet store away in our rich bank of memories.

"We're finished," the nice lady said.

My thoughts shut down with the X-ray machine. She hurried to help me get off the table, taking me by the elbow, guiding, steadying my stagger. I accepted her help this time.

Perhaps I am an old man after all . . .

The Poetic Chicken Thieves

Elzie and Alfred Montrose were brothers. Both were red-headed and freckled-faced. Elzie was tall and skinny. Alfred was short and fat. They always seemed to have money. And everybody knew why.

They stole chickens. And wrote poetry.

About once a month they'd raid a hen house. They always left this message:

We steal from the rich
We steal from the poor
We leave you a hen and rooster
To raise some more.

Everybody knew it was Elzie and Alfred who were stealing our chickens and leaving their poetry behind.

But nobody tried too hard to catch them because everybody liked Elzie and Alfred. The boys' daddy was a poor sharecropper who housed his large family in a small two-room clapboard shack down by the river. If he knew what his two oldest boys were up to, he never let on.

Once in a while, Elzie and Alfred would help their daddy work the farm, gathering corn, or something like that. But mostly, they slept late and their mother would keep shushing the younger kids to keep them quiet.

But darn it! people complained. Times were hard and chickens were chickens—meat for the table, eggs for cooking, and feathers for mattress ticking.

One reason we were so certain Elzie and Alfred were the ones stealing our chickens was because they always seemed to have plenty of money. They would buy high-priced Beech Nut chewing tobacco and pay cash for it. Nor were they chinchy with it. They'd dig into the package with a finger and thumb and pull out the gosh-awfullest wad of shredded tobacco you ever saw and stuff it into one side of their mouths.

Then they'd pass it around. Even we younger kids'd take a shot at it, filling our mouths with the sweet-tasting stuff.

Your teeth would sink into the wad and your mouth would fill with the tangy juice. It was very difficult to keep from swallowing—until you learned the hard way not to.

The time I learned not to swallow tobacco juice was just after a couple of friends and I had sneaked some green apples off Dad's prize June apple tree.

I don't know of anything that makes you sicker than tobacco juice mixed with green apples. It all came up in a hurry. I thought I was going to turn myself inside out.

When I was through and was standing there gasping for breath with tears in my eyes, Elzie, laughing, held the Beech Nut package out to me and said, "You lost it, kid. Want some more?"

I shook my head, then said quickly, "It was them green apples." I didn't want him to think I was too young to chew tobacco.

Every time somebody lost his chickens, he'd complain to the city marshal, who'd have to call the county sheriff, because most of the hen houses were out of the city limits and beyond the city marshal's jurisdiction. The sheriff would come and get the local marshal to go with him to investigate the site where the crime took place in hopes of finding something they could pin on Elzie and Alfred.

The closest they ever came was when they ran into Elzie and Alfred coming up the river road toward town carrying a gunny sack full of something. The sheriff slammed on his brakes and jumped out.

"What you boys got in that gunny sack?" he demanded, one hand on his gun butt as if he expected them to drop the sack of chickens and make a run for it.

"Well, we don't rightly know," Elzie said. "We met a man down the road a ways that give it to us. Said he'd give us two-bits if we'd tote it to the feed store for him."

"Here, give me that," the sheriff growled. He snatched the gunny sack, dug out his pocket knife, slashed it open, and peeked in.

Suddenly he had a face full of fluttering, squawking chickens. He dropped the sack and began flailing both arms fighting them off. Then he tried to catch one for evidence. The marshal joined in. They ran every which way trying to catch a chicken. But they all got away.

Furious, the sheriff came back to where Elzie and Alfred stood. He snatched up the gunny sack. A lone feather fell out.

"A man gave it to you, huh?" he blustered.

"Yeah," Elzie said.

"What was his name?"

"Never thought to ask. Two bits is two bits."

"Yeah," Alfred said. "Now we won't get our two bits. Who's going to pay for this?"

The sheriff turned red, then spluttered, "You boys think you're funny. I'll catch you yet. Just you wait and see. Come on, Marshal."

The two officers climbed in the car and left.

Elzie picked up the gunny sack and showed it to Alfred.

"Why'd he have to go and cut it like that? Just ruined a perfectly good sack. Why couldn't he of untied the string?"

Alfred was staring after the car disappearing down the road in the dust.

"Forget the gunny sack. We'd better hurry if we're going to catch all those chickens."

But the sheriff was bound and determined to catch Elzie and Alfred. He organized a Catch-Elzie-and-Alfred-red-handed committee, made up of the more prosperous farmers around. They drew a map of the area and put the date on all the hen houses when the chickens got stolen.

They came up with a pattern…of sorts. After arguing over it, they decided that the Williams' was going to be the next chicken house hit that month.

Mr. Williams said, "We'll help, sheriff. We'll post guards and catch them coming out."

"I don't need any help," the sheriff fumed. "I'll teach them a thing or two about stealing chickens and writing poems. I'll fix me a bed in your chicken house. Have my loaded shotgun handy."

The others thought shooting the Montrose boys would be taking things a little too far. They insisted they could lay for them in the dark and catch them without anybody getting hurt.

"Then you can put a little scare in them, sheriff," they insisted. "Maybe lock them up a few days. You can let them out in time for them to go back to the farm and help their daddy do the plowing.

"To heck with that," the sheriff snorted. "They'd be right back at it again. I say give them a good dose of bird shot in their behinds. That'll put an end to chicken-stealing around here once and for all."

The others gave in. The sheriff carried through with his threat. He fixed himself a bed in the Williams' chicken house. But it was such a good bed that he went to sleep. Mr. Williams' old red rooster woke him up at sunrise the next morning, crowing in his ear. He sat bolt upright and grabbed for his gun. It was gone. Pinned to his chest was this piece of paper with writing on it. He ripped it off and read:

We steal from the rich
We steal from the poor
We came for your chickens
But your shotgun is worth more.

And since it *was* worth more, it was almost a year before anybody lost any more chickens.

Most of the people around about thought it was a pretty good trade.

Dad's Day

"Who are we going to vote for?" Nita asked as the nightly newscast was drawing to a close.

I told her. She didn't comment. I hoped she would vote for my guy. But she's got a mind of her own and I knew she'd use it.

One thing for certain, I wasn't about to try and influence her one way or the other. I'd learned my lesson on political philosophy early in life.

Dad—everybody called him George—was a devout Republican. Mom—all her lady friends at church called her Lula—was a die-hard Democrat.

Why, how come, or where Dad was converted to his political doctrine, I don't know.

My brothers and I assumed Republicanism was rooted deep in the hills of Kentucky where Dad was born and raised. But that didn't make sense, because Mom was born and raised there too. In fact, Dad and Mom had attended the same backwoods school that offered only eight grades.

And Dad didn't even finish his final year. He went to Pennsylvania to work in the oil fields.

Oil booms excited him. On his way to the Oklahoma boom, he swung through Kentucky and asked Mom to marry him. She'd had a crush on him ever since the 1st grade, and he her.

Apparently they didn't check one another's political persuasion before getting married.

Dad was a big man, physically active, and strong. He could do anything, it seemed to me.

When there wasn't any work in the oil fields, he'd turn to farming to feed us. He could make furniture, half-sole our shoes, even help us make the toys we played with.

Mom was a diminutive woman with premature graying hair which she kept pulled back, braided, and always coiled in a beautiful bun at the nape of her

DALE DENNEY

graceful neck.

Over the years, she gave birth to a new baby every couple of years, scrubbed clothes, kept a neat house, and was always inviting a neighbor in after church for a Sunday dinner of biscuits and fried chicken.

Mom loved the principle of the secret ballot. She would never say how she voted, but Dad knew. How he knew, I was never able to figure out. He'd argue that by her voting Democrat, it only canceled his vote.

"We might as well not bother to vote," he grumbled.

Mom blithely ignored him, refusing even to discuss politics. Dad stomped away, growling his protests over her stubbornness to listen to reason.

But sometimes one of us boys would tease the secret out of Mom when Dad wasn't around. We'd run down the list of candidates and when you hit on hers, always a Democrat, she'd stiffen and declare, "I'm not telling!"

We thought their differences were a joke until they got older and more crotchety. We began worrying that their marriage might yet break up over their politics.

Especially one election when Dad got up early and hiked down our dirt lane into town to vote. Later, some of Mom's lady friends—Democrats—came by to pick her up.

They wheeled the car around and went speeding down the lane, almost running over Dad. Probably would have if he hadn't dove for the ditch. The ladies thought it funny, giving him a gay wave as they flew by, leaving him scowling at them through the swirl of dust.

That night at the supper table, Dad roused from his deep, angry silence and asked Mom, "I suppose you canceled my vote again, didn't you?"

Mom pretended she didn't hear as she continued feeding the baby. Her cool silence made Dad angrier.

"You voted for that Democrat, didn't you?" he said, spitting out the hated word as if it were profanity. Mom stiffened.

"I'm not telling!" she snapped—a sure giveaway.

Dad jumped up from the table and stomped out of the kitchen. I felt the floor tremble. I heard him outside on the porch banging and rattling milk pails around until he found the one he wanted.

Mom returned her attention to the baby, a tight, determined smile of triumph on her face.

I hated to see them fight, especially over something I didn't think was worth fighting over.

Then things seemed to swing in Dad's favor the next election. It rained for

22

a week before time to go vote. Our lane to town was impassable. Only high-centered oil field trucks could make it through the muddy goo.

We all knew there'd be no Democrats coming to pick Mom up that day.

With a knowing, exultant look on his face, Dad pulled on his rubber boots the first thing that morning and took off down the lane, stomping through the mud in high spirits all the way to the polls.

"Gimme that ballot," he demanded gleefully. "At long last, my vote is finally going to count."

The Democrat poll workers knew how he'd vote, and he knew they knew, which increased his sense of pleasure. Inside the polling booth, he whammed the elephant stamp on the ballot so hard, it made the Democratic poll workers wince.

While Dad was gone, Mom's friends had somehow made it up the lane in their car and honked at the gate. Mom flung a shawl over her shoulders, cautioned us older kids about watching over the younger ones, and splashed her way across the yard to the car.

The ladies turned the vehicle around and went slipping and sliding down the lane. About halfway to town, the wheels dropped into deep ruts, burying the car up to its axles.

The driver tried to get free, gunning the engine, spinning the wheels. She was unable to budge an inch, hopelessly stuck.

"Oh, my! What'll we do?" the driver moaned. Then she saw Dad coming down the lane, sloshing his way home after voting. "Look!" she shouted. "Here comes George! He'll help us out!"

Mom said nothing as Dad approached. The driver rolled down her window, smiled sweetly, and said, "Are we ever glad to see you, George. We're stuck. Would you go get your shovel and dig us out?"

Dad frowned, and eyed the car filled with women. His glare settled on Mom. She never batted an eye.

He said, "If you ladies think I'm going to help a car load of Democrats get out of the mud and go vote, you're crazy!"

And he sloshed on his way, his rubber boots flopping. The ladies stared after him in stunned silence. Just as Dad turned in at the gate, I saw him glance over his shoulder at Mom watching him through the rear window of the car.

He seemed to wilt inside. He trudged to the barn, got his shovel, and ordered all of us older boys to follow him. We went back down the lane to the immobile car.

We worked for over an hour digging the vehicle out, with Dad working the hardest. He was covered with mud from cap to boots before we were able to push them free.

Dad leaned on his shovel, wiping the mud from his face as he watched the car go slipping and sliding toward the polls, still slinging mud at us.

We could see Mom staring out the rear window until they turned the corner and out of sight.

That night at the supper table, Dad announced—proudly—who he voted for. Then he waited, finally demanding of Mom, "Who'd you vote for?"

She kept her face averted, saying nothing.

Dad, more exasperated than usual, grumped harshly, "I suppose you voted for that Democrat and canceled my vote again, didn't you?"

Mom's eyes swung on him. I saw no anger in her face, nothing but a softness in her eyes.

"I didn't vote, George," she said, her voice soft, loving.

Dad's mouth fell open. His eyes misted. Obviously embarrassed, he looked down, tried to continue eating, couldn't, then got up from the table.

"I better go milk the cow," he said, having to clear his throat to get the words out. He slipped quietly out of the kitchen, found his milk bucket, and headed for the barn.

Mom smiled contentedly as she watched him walking across the barnyard, happily swinging the empty milk pail.

The only thing stronger than political persuasion is love.

Old Man Lyle's Gold

"Hello, the house."

Old Man Lyle's raspy-voiced call startled us all—Mom, Dad, and us six kids sitting around the supper table. He never knocked, even when he came to plow the garden every spring. He always stopped a discreet distance from the front door and called out, "Hello, the house."

We looked at one another, wondering: What in the world?

But not me. I was scared. My best friend Henry and me had hitched a ride on the tail gate of Old Man Lyle's wagon that day, strictly against Mom's rules.

Not that she had anything against Mister Lyle, she said. It was——. She never explained. But I knew. It was because of the way Old Man Lyle talked to himself all the time, even when he was plowing our garden.

Plus the fact that when the plowing season was over, he drove his mule team and wagon all day up and down the sandy roads in the Cimarron River bottoms, digging a new hole every day—sometimes two or three.

Folks said he was looking for gold that Jesse James was supposed to have buried around there somewhere. It was as good a reason as any.

My friend Henry and I didn't bother Old Man Lyle none. We just had fun riding the tail gate of his wagon and pulling this piece of wood with a rope behind us and watching it bounce this way and that. We pretended it was one of Buck Rogers' space ships firing ray guns at space ships from the evil Ming's empire.

Now he was out there, in front of our house. My fertile imagination went into high gear, telling me to say we knew for a fact that Old Man Lyle had found the Jesse James gold that day. We had watched him digging this hole out on the river hill and when it got so deep it was over his head, we sneaked up to the edge of the hole and saw Old Man Lyle opening the chest full of gold.

Then he covered it back up and——

By then Dad was getting up to go see what it was Old Man Lyle wanted.

I slid quickly out of my seat. I felt I had that right—the right to be present when Old Man Lyle accused me of—of whatever it was grownups accused ten-year-old boys for doing when they disobeyed.

"Hello," Dad greeted, going down the steps from the porch to the front sidewalk.

I tried to keep Dad between Old Man Lyle and me. He was a gaunt man with a drooping, graying moustache, and frowzy black-white hair which you never saw until he'd take his old felt hat off to wipe the sweat from his face on his shirt sleeve.

"I come by to ask if your misses had seen my Nellie, seeing as how your misses and my Nellie did a lot of church doings together."

"Not that I know of, Mister Lyle." Dad always called him Mister Lyle to his face. Fact was, so did everybody else.

"But I'll ask," Dad said, turning to go back in the house. "You're welcome to come in and ask her yourself."

Old Man Lyle smiled but shook his head, keeping his self-designated respectful distance from our house.

I thought this would be a good time to smooth things over the best I could before the world caved in on me.

"I'm sorry, Mister Lyle, if me and Henry bothered you riding on your wagon all day. We didn't mean no harm."

His sad gaze fixed on me.

"You weren't no bother, boy," he said.

I felt a whole ton better and blurted, "We didn't pay any attention to what you were saying, Mister Lyle. Honest."

He tried to smile, but I saw the tear form in one bleary eye and race down through the white stubble on his cheek. It was such a sad thing to see that I had to start wrinkling my nose to stop the sting of my own tears trying to form there.

Mom came out with Dad and stood on the front edge of the porch wiping her hands on her apron.

"No, Mr. Lyle. I haven't seen Nellie since last Sunday morning. Is anything wrong?"

"No, ma'am. I don't think so. I mean I hope not. She wasn't to home when I got in tonight. She hadn't even fixed no supper. That's not like her. Not like her atall."

Mom's brow furrowed. "No, it's not. Maybe she's gone out somewhere visiting with the neighbors. You want the men to get up a search party—"

"No, ma'am. I don't want to put nobody out. It's just…"

His voice trailed off as he turned to climb up onto his wagon seat and drove away—talking to himself.

We all went back in the house and finished supper, each of us speculating where Old Man Lyle's Nellie might be.

My over active imagination jumped into high gear again. Pirates got people to help them dig holes on beaches to put their gold in. Then they killed them and buried them on top of their chests of gold. You don't suppose—?

No. No. Of course not. Just because he talked to himself all the time didn't mean he was crazy enough to kill his Nellie.

On the other hand—.

Me and Henry started playing detective then, trying to solve the crime. We found a lot of answers; the most likely, we decided, was the one Sammy Hudspeth told. He'd seen Nellie get in the bread delivery truck from Tulsa and they drove off together.

Knowing Sammy, it wasn't much to go on. So after a few days, when Old Man Lyle went back to driving the bottoms again and digging holes, me and Henry followed him, dashing from tree to tree and boulder to boulder.

The fact that Old Man Lyle didn't stop digging for Jesse James' gold was proof enough for some folks that maybe, just maybe, that Sammy's story wasn't so far off after all.

But the Christian folks wouldn't stand for talk like that. They knew Nellie Lyle. Why, she'd give you the shirt off her back, they said, and meant every word of it.

We were trailing Old Man Lyle the day he stopped his wagon on the bank of the Cimarron and stared long and hard at something out on the sand bar near the water.

He got down and started walking across the sand bar. I jumped from behind the bush to follow. Henry grabbed my arm.

"Don't let him see us—"

I shook loose because I'd seen what Mister Lyle had seen. I ran across the sand bar to catch up to him just before he got to where the neat pile of women's clothes were. And I saw the same thing Mister Lyle saw: the barefoot tracks leaving the pile of clothes and disappearing into the water.

He reached out and laid his arm across my shoulder. A sob choked up through his long neck.

"Oh, my precious Nellie."

I reached up and squeezed one of his gnarled fingers.

"Bless you, boy," he mumbled.

After a long search, they found her naked body down the river a ways where the current had pushed it under a brush pile.

That fired up a million more stories why Nellie Lyle drowned herself.

But the one I liked best was the one I told Henry.

Old Man Lyle told me that day he found her clothes on the sandbar that it was all his fault. You see, he really did find the wagon load of gold Jesse James had buried, but didn't tell anybody but his Nellie.

Being a person who went to all the church doings, she wanted to share the gold with all the people around town. But he said everybody'd get in a fuss over it if they did that. He wanted to sell the mules and their house and go off somewhere to live like rich folks for the rest of their lives.

But Nellie didn't want to go, see. And she didn't want to betray her husband, so she just went down to the river and drowned herself.

I really didn't think Henry would go around telling his and my secrets like he did. But he did.

That's why so many of my home-town folks started going up and down the Cimarron River bottoms digging holes where Old Man Lyle had dug, hoping to find that wagon load of gold.

Only they didn't call it Jesse James' gold anymore. They called it Old Man Lyle's gold.

The Pirate's Oath

Bessie was my summer friend.

She was a tow-headed, freckle-faced kid who lived with her family down by the river. Her Dad worked for a big land owner who paid his help by giving them shares of the crops harvested.

Bessie was somewhere in the middle of a whole passel of brothers and sisters. During the summer, she wore her big brother's overalls turned up at the cuffs.

But she had to dress up for school. Her mother would rummage up an old dress from somewhere and redo it for Bessie. It made her look worse than her wearing overalls, I thought.

Evidently, other girls at school thought so, too, because none of them played with her much. So she spent most of her time standing alone watching us boys play marbles.

I didn't have much to do with her at school either. We had an understanding. She knew that come next summer we would be wrestling one another like always, or building a tree house in the woods, or playing pirates.

She made a dandy pirate leader. She'd roll one overall pant leg up higher than the other, paint a moustache on her upper lip with mud, make a patch to hang over one eye, and order her crew (me) to take the pirate's oath: One for all and all for one. Which meant, she said, we'd all fight to the death for one another.

Then she'd stand on the prow of our make-believe ship and yell orders for all hands (me) to board the king's ship which we'd come along side of, and fight all the king's men with our wooden swords.

And she was good at sword fighting because she had such strong hands and arms that came from helping her mother do the milking. She could beat me at wrestling or just about anything—including shooting marbles.

She could flip a taw so hard it put nicks in my marbles. So we didn't do that very much. I needed all my marbles for school.

It was a shame she couldn't play marbles at school just because she was a girl. But that's the way it was and that was that.

Besides, even if she could play, she didn't have any marbles. A sack of maybe twenty marbles or so cost a dime.

Our principal had banned playing marbles for keeps. We played for keeps anyway, just to make it interesting. But at the end of the day we'd all go through our marbles and give back the ones that weren't ours because we all knew what marbles cost.

Even though I wanted to be like the other boys, I didn't enjoy playing marbles at school because: (1) I wasn't a very good shooter to begin with, and (2) it bothered me seeing Bessie standing not far away watching us play.

So I turned my back to keep from seeing her.

I didn't try to change things at school, nor did she—until Junior Christi came to town. He was a big guy with a pug nose and blonde hair too stiff to comb.

His folks had money, and Junior wore a clean shirt to school every day. The front pockets of his wool trousers always bulged with marbles, and we soon learned why.

He was good. Darn good. Nor would he give us back our marbles at the end of the day.

We tried to tell him playing for keeps was against the rules. He called us sissies, taunting us so much that we couldn't take it. We all lost our marbles to him trying to beat him.

The guys grumbled. Our marble game came to a screeching halt. Christi pranced around with his two front pockets full of marbles, daring anyone to play him a game.

That's when I got this idea.

"Hey, guys," I said. "If you all chip in and help me buy a new sack of marbles, I'll win all our marbles back from Christi."

"You?" one scoffed. And they all laughed.

"If I don't win, I'll double your money," I boasted. "If I do win, I get half of all your marbles."

It was an offer they couldn't refuse. By chipping in a penny here and a penny there, we managed to come up with enough to buy a new bag of marbles.

The next day I challenged Christi. He accepted. All the guys gathered around as we marched to the marble-playing circle in one corner of the school yard.

Christi shed his jacket and started emptying his pockets, placing all his marbles in a neat spot near his jacket.

I turned and went to Bessie.

"I want you to shoot for me," I told her.

She shook her head.

"You got to," I said. "I can't beat him. We'll lose everything."

"I have a dress on," she said and turned her back. I grabbed her arm and spun her around.

"I don't care how you're dressed. I know you can beat him."

"If I do, will you let me play marbles with you from now on?"

I held up a hand. "Pirate's oath."

She smiled and said, "Okay."

I grabbed her hand and led her to the marble ring.

"Bessie is going to be my shooter," I announced.

All the guys rolled their eyes and groaned. Christi snorted.

"I won't play no girl," he said.

"I got a right to pick my shooter," I argued. "You either play or give us all your marbles."

He laughed. "All right. You asked for it. Load the ring."

Some of the guys threw up their hands and walked away. But the crowd didn't diminish any because by then the word had gotten around and all the girls on the playground came to watch.

Christi and I placed our first batch of marbles in the center of the ring. Then we lagged to the line with our taws. Christi's taw stopped right on the line.

He laughed, picked up his taw, huffed on it, kneeled at the circle's edge, and fired away.

He sent marbles flying in all directions. His taw stuck right in the middle of the circle. According to the rules, you get to keep the marbles you knock out of the ring, and you get to keep shooting as long as your taw stays inside the circle. So Christi went to work popping marbles out of the ring one by one.

I began to sweat. I glanced at Bessie. She didn't seem at all perturbed.

Christi cleaned the circle except for one marble. He was so overconfident that he missed. It didn't phase him. He stood, sneered at Bessie and said, "Your shot, girlie."

Bessie tried to kneel properly to get in position to shoot, but her dress tail got in the way. She backed up to me, bunching up her dress behind, exposing her legs.

"Tie it up," she said.

"Bessie—" I cautioned, embarrassed for her.

"Just tie it up in a knot," she insisted.

I gathered the material and tied it in a knot, my face hot as fire.

Bessie dropped to one knee, her bare skin against the hard clay. She took aim and popped the lone marble out of the circle, making her taw stick near the center.

According to the rules, Christi and I loaded the center again, each putting in the same amount of marbles. That was all we had. If Bessie lost—

Bessie's taw was near enough that when she broke the bunched-up marbles, it knocked almost all of them out of the ring with that one single shot.

All the guys and girls clapped. Christi scowled.

Christi never got another shot. Bessie won that round, and the next, and the next. Soon Christi was out of marbles.

"I want my marbles back," he shouted, furious. "You said it was against the rule to play keepers here."

"You changed the rule. Remember?" I fired back, getting a little mad myself.

"I'm going to tell," he said.

Red faced and sputtering, he stomped away to go complain to the teacher that we had stolen all his marbles.

The teacher told him that we all knew that playing marbles was against the rule. Therefore, he deserved losing all his marbles.

I shared my winnings with Bessie. And from then on, we let Bessie play marbles with us.

Of course, you had to wear overalls to be properly dressed to play marbles.

And without any of them having to take the pirate's oath—as far as I know—a lot of the other girls started wearing overalls to school because Bessie did.

On second thought, maybe there is a secret pirate's oath which all kids take on how to dress for school.

The Bike Rider

It was a summer to remember—the best of my life up to that time, the worst in my state's history.

One of the first things Billy Jack said to me when he got out of their car was, "I got a new bicycle."

I stared in disbelief at the wide grin on my cousin's freckle face. Was he spoofing me?

His eyes danced. There was just a hint of red in his curly brown hair. Besides being cousins, we were good friends.

Billy Jack and his parents had come to pick me up to go spend two weeks with them. I was ready to go. Mom had already packed my clothes in a large brown paper sack.

"Honest?" I had to be certain I heard right; my palms were already beginning to feel wet just thinking about riding a bike, a real bike. The only problem was, I didn't know how.

He nodded, his grin widening.

"It's a red one." Then he described how it had white streaks on the fenders and down the sides of the front forks. "And it has a horn."

I couldn't believe what I was hearing. I'd seen such a bike on the bicycle pages in the Sears, Roebuck & Co. catalog, but I'd never studied them real close. Seventeen dollars for a bike was beyond the realm of the faintest hope.

Besides, even if I'd had one, there was no place to ride it. The road that ran in front of our house had ruts in it six inches deep, left by cars slipping and sliding up and down it when it was muddy. The ruts stayed there, the summer sun baking them hard and dry.

One kid who lived down the lane from us had a used bike once, and every time he got off the road with it, he'd run over a patch of goat heads that punctured his tires in so many places it'd take a whole box of his dad's tire-patching stuff to fix it up.

33

I knew Billy Jack's announcement implied that I could ride it. I began to fret. What if I crashed it into a tree or something?

It was a good hour's drive over the gravel road to Stroud, Oklahoma. I didn't want to sound too anxious during the trip, but I managed to ask enough discreet questions to hear about Billy Jack being able to ride anywhere he wanted in town because Stroud had paved streets and had sidewalks everywhere.

"Just stay off Main Street," Uncle Cecil cautioned from the front seat. "That's Highway 66, the most traveled highway in the whole country. There's so many old cars without brakes on it these days, you'll get run over."

Aunt Ruby and Uncle Cecil went on talking about the cars streaming though town, all heading west. I didn't pay much attention to what they were saying, something about dust storms and the drought causing people to lose their farms. Everybody said there was plenty of work in California, picking peaches and things.

The sun was going down when we got to their home in Stroud. Billy Jack ran to the garage and got his new bike to show me.

The setting sun glinted off the shiny new spokes and gave the red a deeper hue. Billy Jack swung on it and pedaled up the driveway and back, grinning. The tiny squeeching and scrunching sounds told how new it was and thrilled me to the bone.

"Get on. I'll pump you down the street and back."

I slid onto the bar in front of him, letting my long legs dangle off sideways. He started off, having to waggle the front wheel a lot until he got going. I was too heavy for him. I just knew we were going to fall over. I hung on, gripping the handlebar with all my might.

My heart pounded and my blood raced as we picked up speed. The huge elms along the sidewalk flashed by. It took my breath away. I glanced down. The sidewalk was whizzing underneath us. I tightened my grip, scared to death I'd fall off.

He was unable to pump me going back uphill to his house. I ran alongside, both delighted to have ridden such a fine bike and fearful that I'd never be able to ride it by myself in a thousand years.

Since it was getting dark, we had to put the bike up and go in. I couldn't sleep that night. I lay awake, reliving my very first bike ride in every detail. I could still see that front wheel below me, its shiny spokes flashing as it turned over and over, carrying me so fast that the wind blew in my face.

Billy Jack offered to let me ride by myself the next morning, but I refused. I was afraid I'd fall over and scratch the paint. He said he'd run along beside me holding me up until I got the hang of it. I was still afraid to try.

Luckily, Billy Jack's friend, Cornelius, who lived over on the next block had an old bike. He always left it lying in the driveway behind his Dad's car, hoping his Dad would back over it so he could get a new one.

Billy Jack asked Cornelius if I could learn to ride on his bike. He was tickled to death to let me try. Every time I fell over or ran into a tree, he would jump up and down and swing his arms wildly. The faster it got tore up, he said, the sooner his Dad would get him a new one.

I did all I could to help him achieve his goal. My knees got banged up, my knuckles got skinned, and I had a big knot on my forehead.

I was on the verge of giving up ever learning how when it just seemed to happen all of a sudden. I couldn't believe it. One minute I was struggling, waggling the front wheel like mad, and the next minute I was sailing down the sidewalk as smooth as you please.

I leaned my face into the wind, enjoying the way it cooled my skin by carrying away the sweat that dampened my hair and made dirt rings on my neck.

I'd never enjoyed such a sense of personal freedom in my life. I pumped harder and went faster and faster.

The bike's wheels began to sing on the sidewalk. I was so enthralled that I didn't realize where I was until I was there—riding on the sidewalk right along Highway 66.

A string of rickety rackety cars was going by. People with sad faces peered at me out of the windows. I panicked.

Uncle Cecil had warned me not to go near Highway 66 and the old cars headed west.

I slammed on my brakes, jumped off and pushed my borrowed bike up a side street as fast as I could run.

Safely away, two whole blocks, I just stood there trembling and shaking. But I just had to see—one more time. I pushed the bike back to the highway and stood there watching.

It was the look on the kids' faces that broke my heart. I simply couldn't even imagine having to move, let alone having everything we owned piled on an old car heading west.

It took all the fun out of riding the bike. I pushed it all the way back to Billy Jack's house.

"What's the matter?" he asked.

"Did you break it?" Cornelius asked hopefully.

"No," I said handing the bike to Cornelius. "I just got tired, is all."

But the fun came back the next day when Billy Jack let me get on his new bike. Since I was the biggest, he sat on the support bar in front of me while I pumped.

We even rode downtown, right along Main Street, despite Uncle Cecil's warnings.

But by now I was having so much fun riding the bike that I didn't pay any attention to the cars on Highway 66 heading west.

I wanted the tow-headed kids staring at us out of car windows with mattresses on top to see me riding on a brand new bike. A red one, with a real light on the front fender.

Riding on a new bike made me completely oblivious to the fact I was witnessing one of the greatest migrations of human beings in history.

It was one of the best summers in my life—the time I learned to ride a bike.

And it was the worst summer in Oklahoma history—when the word Okie was invented to describe us.

Our Old Red Rooster

I guided my pickup where the yellow lines told me to go to get to the take-out window of the place where they specialized in chicken and stopped at the huge, colorful plastic menu. I hurried to make my choice before the voice from the little square with the holes in it asked me what I wanted.

"May I take your order, please?" the young voice said, coming so fast the words ran together.

As usual, I panicked. I'm never ready when the fast voice in the box asks me that. I get the feeling the entire chicken cooking operation inside has come to a standstill, waiting impatiently for me to make up my mind.

"A couple of Senior Citizen's dinners," I blurt. It's the easy way out.

I pulled forward. Each car ahead of me took its turn at the window, arms reaching out of it to take stuff from arms reaching out the window handing it to them.

What a simple way to get a meal, I thought to myself. Chicken has come a long way—truly a world food, easily produced and easy to market...

Dale, I heard Mom's voice coming at me from over half a century away. *If you're not going to go to Sunday School this morning, then you have to kill a chicken and get it ready for me to fix for dinner.*

I knew she was trying to blackmail me. But I was just as determined as she was. Church was for old people and kids. I wasn't either one. I was almost fourteen—well, I would be in another ten months.

"Aw-w-w, Mom," I groaned.

"Be sure to scald it good like I showed you. And be sure to get all the feathers off."

I hated picking feathers off—almost as bad as going to Sunday School.

"Which one?" I asked sullenly.

"That young rooster. The red one."

I could have guessed that. I'd learned the young roosters were the first to go, long before the plump pullets. And I'd also just recently learned why—they contaminated the flock. Neighbors always swapped young roosters with neighbors to improve the blood line.

Mom had never explained it that way. It was one of those things you just sort of figure out by yourself.

"After you wring his head off, make sure he bleeds well before —"

"I know. You don't have to explain *everything* to me a thousand times, do you?" I grumped.

Mom was fifty years ahead of the times. She believed all her boys should at least learn the rudiments of cooking and caring for themselves, and all her girls learn as much as they could about the business world.

Mom gave me one last warning look as they all went out the door. I didn't budge from my "mad" chair until I heard the car start and pull out from the driveway. Then the house got so quiet I couldn't stand it. I decided to go find the young red rooster and take my mad out on him.

I'll swear to this day, the young rooster knew he'd been "chosen" that fine Sunday morning. He began trying to find a hiding spot the minute I opened the barnyard gate and stepped through.

That made me even madder. Instead of trying to shoo him gently into a corner somewhere and grab him when he tried to get by, I went right at him.

Now that he knew for sure I was after him, he let out a loud squawk and ran into the barn. I used some of the new cuss words I'd learned, real mean ones, and ran into the barn after him. He turned, eyeing me with a frightened look on his face.

He tried to prove he was beyond the frying stage by acting grown up. But his "cock-a-doodle-doo" was so weak it was almost comical. He reminded me of me, the way my voice was changing.

"Now, I got you," I growled, and closed in, arms outstretched.

I lunged. He squawked and attacked, flying right up into my face with his wings flapping and feathers flying.

I back-pedaled, fighting him off, and fell over the milking stool. The rooster landed on my chest, squawked in my face, and flew out the door.

38

I jumped up, so mad now I could hardly see, and lit out after him. He set up such a row that he had all the chickens in the barnyard squawking and running for their lives—all of them probably shouting in chicken language, "The sky is falling! The sky is falling!"

Our little Jersey calf thought we were playing and joined in the fun, kicking up its heels and bellowing moos happily. His mother thought I was hurting her baby and came at me with her head down.

I ran for the gate, the cow's head not six inches from my rear. I sailed over the gate in one mighty bound—I thought. Only I caught my heel on the top rail and tumbled to the ground.

It hurt. Furious, I found a garden hoe and went back into the barnyard, beat on the cow, and sent her and her calf off to the far end of the pasture.

I tossed the hoe aside and started chasing the young red rooster again. He got weaker and weaker as I chased him up and down the fence row.

He ran out of gas before I did. I finally got my hands on him and, smugly content, I headed for the house with my "prize" cradled in my arm. He started making a pitiful clucking sound, as if he were trying to beg his way to freedom.

"Look, fella," I tried to explain. "This is the way it's gotta be. It's either your independence or mine. I hope you understand."

Back at the house, I refused to listen to his pleas any longer—just determined to get it over with as fast as I could. I wrapped my fingers around his neck.

I didn't bother making sure his beak was wedged between two of my fingers, like Mom always told me, to keep his head from turning in my hand. I thought I was strong enough and mad enough to wring his neck anyway.

Gripping his neck, I spun him in the air, like cranking a car. His head wouldn't come off. Instead, all his neck feathers came loose and I lost my grip. He slipped out of my hand, smacked me in the face, flopped to the ground, and, with a hoarse squawk, regained his footing and headed, bare necked, for the barnyard in a long lope.

I started after him, then stopped. I couldn't go through it again. Besides, I told myself, if you hang a man and the rope breaks, he's entitled to go free, ain't he? Sorrowfully, I brushed his neck feathers off my hand and returned to the house.

I had fought for my independence and lost—to a young red rooster!

When the family got home, I was back in my "mad" chair, but I wasn't mad any longer. I was ready to do whatever Mom wanted. She sensed the change and didn't say a word.

I earned my independence after all, sort of. Mom never got after me about going to Sunday School after that. But since all the girls my age went, I developed a deep need to go, and went anyway.

The young rooster? Well, I think Mom guessed what happened when she saw one of her Sunday dinners running around with no feathers on his neck. She let him mature. No one had ever seen a rooster without any neck feathers. The neighbors thought he was a special breed of some kind. He wasn't, but became one because they all wanted to "use" him, thinking he would improve the blood line of their flock.

And he and I got to be real friends. He'd literally come running and jump into my arms when I went to get him, and would cluck contentedly on our way to someone else's barnyard for another one of his short "visits."

When it came my turn to pull up to the drive through window, I handed the girl a twenty, she gave me change and a couple of sacks full of chicken and all the fixings.

Nita and I enjoyed our chicken dinner that night.

It's all so easy—especially when someone else does the killing for you.

Buried Treasure

It was a family affair. I got in the food line in the kitchen, filled my plate and wandered into the living room where the others were, chit-chatting about this and that.

I settled into the rose-colored easy chair, balancing my paper plate on my knees just as a screaming and yelling bunch of grand kids, grand nephews, and grand nieces came running pell-mell into the room. They fought for sitting spaces in front of the big screen television.

The oldest nephew commandeered the remote and clicked it on. The raucous sounds of the cartoon filled the room. One of the many young mothers began snapping her fingers at them.

"You turn that thing off," she commanded. "Can't you see we're eating in here?"

She answered the chorus of moans and groans with a plea, "Go outside and play."

"There's nothing to do out there," the oldest boy said, reluctantly clicking off the TV with the remote. Then the boy added—as if it was some juvenile divine right—"We're bored."

The mother pointed. "Outside. All of you. This minute."

They filed out, still protesting.

Bored without the TV on? How can that be?

I picked at my food, recalling one summer afternoon before there was such a thing as television.

My friend Junior and I were sitting on a porch swing one hot summer afternoon. His big sister Frances sat between us reading Robert Louis Stevenson's *Treasure Island*.

I felt cold chills, the way Frances made the characters come alive. I could see the pirates fighting, hear the creak of the ship and the booming of the cannons. I actually shuddered when she mimicked Long John Silver's parrot screeching, "Pieces of eight! Pieces of eight!" Junior's eyes got so big I thought they were going to pop right out of his head.

Frances finished the story, closed the book, and went into the house.

"Let's play buried treasure," Junior said, hopping off the swing.

That sounded like gobs of fun.

"Okay."

As usual, Junior took over as captain (Long John Silver). First thing, he said, we needed a treasure chest. We sneaked a coffee can with a lid on it from his mother's kitchen. It didn't have much coffee in it, so he just dumped it out.

I hated being a party to such a wasteful act. But they would never miss a little coffee. Just run to the grocery store and get more. Their dad had a job. They had credit.

We each agreed to contribute to the treasure. We found lots of stuff—bent safety pins, even some shoe strings.

I wasn't very good at shooting marbles and I didn't have too many. But I put in what I had.

But that wasn't enough. Junior said we had to have "pieces of eight."

He said he had two very rare Indian head pennies his dad had given him. He went to get them. "These will be our pieces of eight. That makes it a real treasure."

I didn't feel quite right about him donating real money, but since his dad had a regular job, I figured that evened things up.

We headed for the creek to find a sandy beach where we could bury our treasure, like they did in the book.

When we passed a neighbor's place where a whole bunch of kids lived, the two oldest sisters we played with a lot came running out and asked where we were going.

"We're going to find a place to bury our treasure," Junior said, then added importantly, "It's got real pieces of eight in it."

"What's pieces of eight?" the younger one asked.

"That's real money, dummy."

"Wow," the older one said, "Can we go?"

"Nope," Junior said. "We're pirates. Girls can't be pirates."

We started on. They followed. We threw clods of dirt at them to make them go back. They stopped out of clod range, but refused to go back.

We turned and ran as hard as we could deep into the woods. Every once in a while we paused to listen to make sure the girls weren't following, and could hear only our own deep breathing.

Junior spotted a tree nearby, its top broken off by a storm. It appeared to be hollow. We climbed up to investigate.

It was a perfect place to hide a buried treasure. We set the can down into the hole and covered it with dead leaves.

Next came the best part of all. We returned to Junior's house to make a map showing where our buried treasure was.

We found a piece of paper and a pencil. Junior drew the dotted trail down the road to the woods, along a creek, over a hill—in fact all over the map.

"That's so nobody won't find it even if they steal our map," he explained.

That made sense, I thought, watching him fold the map and stick it in his pocket. Later, when we were playing hopscotch with the two sisters, Junior couldn't stand it any longer and blurted, "I bet you don't know what I got in my pocket."

"A piece of candy?" one of the sisters asked, wide-eyed and hopeful. Bought candy was a rarity in all our lives. And they knew Junior could get anything he wanted on credit at the store.

"Nope," Junior boasted. "A treasure map."

I gasped. I couldn't believe he was revealing our secret. Not only did he boast about it, he pulled out the piece of paper and showed it to them.

They didn't seem interested. I thought that strange. Instead, they just looked at one another and smiled. We went on playing hopscotch.

After the game, Junior and I decided to go "find" our buried treasure ourselves, since the girls weren't interested.

Although we knew exactly where our buried treasure was, Junior insisted we follow the dotted line on the map. I had to admit to myself it was more exciting that way.

Eventually, we wound up beneath the dead snag and were shocked to find the coffee can on the ground and all our good treasure scattered about—all except the two Indian head pennies.

While I was secretly happy to get my marbles back, Junior was furious. He turned on me.

"You did this, didn't you?"

I was so stunned that he would accuse me of such a heinous crime that I was unable to speak which, of course, Junior interpreted as a sign that I was guilty.

He kicked the can with all his might. "That's the last time I'll ever play buried treasure with you," he shouted and stalked away.

Still angry, I trotted after him.

"If it was me, I'd of took my marbles then. Since the only thing missing are the two Indian head pennies, it was you."

He stopped to stare at me, disbelief all over his freckled face.

"It wasn't me. I swear it wasn't me."

"Well, don't go blaming me," I said. At least I had him on the defensive, which was where you hardly ever got Junior.

Then his eyes widened. A sign of a brilliant idea. "Come on," he said, motioning.

"Where we going?"

He didn't say a word all the way to their grocery store. He ordered two penny suckers, commanding that they be put on their grocery bill.

Then we hurried back down the road to where the two sisters lived. As soon as we got there, Junior took out the suckers and handed one to me.

I didn't know what to do with it. He calmly began unwrapping his.

"Can we have a lick?" one of the sisters begged.

"Nope," Junior said and threw me a wink. "But we'll sell you ours for two cents, won't we?"

I got the message. I nodded.

The sisters looked at one another for just a second before the oldest one ran into the house and came back with two pennies. She handed one to Junior and one to me. We gave them our suckers.

As they eagerly removed the wrappers, Junior and I examined our pennies. They were both Indian heads. I gave him the one I had.

And we were all happy—Junior got his two Indian head pennies back, our friendship was saved, and the two sisters were busily licking on their suckers. They even shared licks with their little brothers and sisters.

I clicked off my mental TV and returned to the kitchen to drop my soiled paper plate into the trash can. I glanced out the window. The kids were moping around in the shade of a tree beside the swimming pool—looking, indeed, very bored.

Someone had stolen their buried treasure—their imagination.

Class Photos

I love to walk through our museum. As I stroll through, I try to imagine real people cooking on that particular stove, sleeping in that bed, swinging that scythe.

And as I stand back and look at the World War II uniforms, I think: Can it be that all of us were that slender and that trim?

Looking at some photos on the wall, I saw one of a country school. It was dated 1933-34. I counted twenty-three students.

I couldn't help but compare that 1933 school class photo with the ones I have at home.

I was lucky. My school was large enough that each class usually had more than twenty-three students.

I grew up in an oil field. I thought there were oil wells all over the world—and the water in all creeks everywhere were like ours—salty with a light scum of crude oil floating on top.

But the oil economy did give us good schools; a grade school, a middle school, a high school—all heated, three-story brick buildings.

Every year a photographer would come. Each class took turns marching out to get its picture taken. The photographer would shuffle us around for a few minutes, stick his head under a black piece of cloth behind his camera, come out, and tell us to smile.

Then, click, and it would be over. We went back to class.

After seeing that photo on the museum wall, I returned home and began browsing through my own class photos. That's when I realized I had another plus. Most of us went through all twelve grades together.

I also noticed for the first time that every girl in the front row of our first grade picture was wearing long cotton socks wrinkled at the knees.

And I remembered that my own mom made me wear a pair of those one time. Me! A boy! I thought I'd die. Fortunately, my overall legs came down over them so nobody could see.

Moms did that because folks of her generation still remembered how so many people all over the world died from the flu epidemic during World War I. They bundled you up good to keep you from catching the flu.

In the second grade photo, only three of the girls in the front row have on long cotton socks, wrinkled at the knees. Three have rolled their long cotton socks down, making a huge doughnut at the ankles. Girls did that at the school grounds after they got away from their moms.

There on the back row was Raymond Butler. I'd forgotten what he looked like. But his image in the photo stirred up old images in my head. Yes, I remember now. He was blond haired, always smiling.

What would he—Raymond—have become if he hadn't got killed? There were many versions of how it happened. The one I remember is that a man—or was it two men?—went in the Butler Drug store with a shotgun. They demanded money. When Mr. Butler refused, the man with the shotgun took aim. Raymond shouted, "Don't shoot my daddy!" Just then the gun went off, killing Raymond instantly.

By then Mr. Butler had his own pistol out of the drawer where he kept it and began shooting. The men ran off.

Rumor was they tracked the blood trail to a house out east of town.

And there the story ends.

No telling what Raymond might have grown up to be.

In the third grade, I'm wearing white striped overalls, my dress-up ones. We usually saved our dress-up overalls for Sunday School. I suppose Mom made me wear them that day because we were going to get our picture taken.

I'm standing next to Labebe. We were good friends until we got into a fight. I was chasing some girls, making them scream. We were having fun. Labebe tried to make me stop. Jealous, I suppose. We fought. I got in trouble. He didn't. Probably because I whipped him.

In the fourth grade, all the girls in the front row are wearing long cotton socks again, wrinkled at the knees. Evidently it was a cold day and their moms made them put them on. Yes, it was a cold day, because I'm wearing a sweater. My shirt is buttoned at the top.

I played a lot with Billy Joe that year. He teased me by making up a rhyme, "Dale Denney, Dale Denney, Ain't worth a Penny!"

I'd chase him. He was easy to catch because he always wore big heavy shoes.

Oh, wow! I made it to the front row in the fifth grade, along with six other boys.

That was the year when we first got the big green geography books with pictures in it of Chinamen on the other side of the world working in their water-covered rice fields, big oxen pulling plows. What a wonderful adventure it was reading that big green book.

That was the year I learned there weren't oil wells all over the world like I always thought there was. In fact, I was surprised when our teacher told us that our little oil patch in one corner of Creek County was only about five miles wide and twenty miles long.

Yet it produced almost one third of the oil it took for the Allies to win the Great War in Europe. They didn't call it World War I then because there wasn't a World War II yet.

We drew moustaches and goatees on people's faces in the big green geography book.

Also that year was when the Alford twins began singing publicly. They entertained us in our school assemblies every week. I was always fascinated, not by their singing, but by wondering how did one twin know she is not the other one?

In the sixth grade photo, the front row was all girls again, except for Jackie Hermanstaffer. He was shorter than anybody. But I liked him. He wore calf-length, lace-up boots. I thought they were neat——his boots, I mean.

I have no seventh grade class picture. That's just as well. It was a bad year for me.

My friend Jackie had gotten a magic book from sending in box tops. He read how to do magic tricks. We'd been playing magician before school took up. In class when Miss Jackson had her back to us, working a math problem on the blackboard, Jackie twisted around in his seat and showed me a small paper wad in the palm of his hand.

"Watch me make it disappear," he whispered and began his adroit hand movements.

Miss Jackson turned and saw him.

"Jackie. Dale. You two boys go see the principal right this minute. I'm not having anyone playing when they should be listening."

I was innocent. I swear I was. And to be branded a criminal in front of everyone in my class was one of the low points of my life.

The principal was Coach Wilson. He was big and had the meanest looking eyes I ever saw. Jackie, with tears running down his freckled cheeks, pleaded for mercy. I was too scared to say anything. Coach Wilson marched us out in the hall, made us bend over and grab our ankles, and whacked our butts so hard you could hear it all over the school.

Not only did Miss Jackson send me, who was completely and totally innocent, to get a humiliating paddling from mean-eyed Coach Wilson, she gave me an F in math for my first six weeks grade that year.

I got another switching from Mom for bringing home an F on my report card.

The seventh grade was a very bad year.

The photographer got real artistic when he took our eighth grade picture. He made all of us boys kneel in the front row. I notice how the flap over my overall bib pocket is sticking out. Come to think of it, that flap always stuck out. I never knew why.

That was also the first year Mom let me go to the carnival by myself when it came to town. I rode the ferris wheel. Pitched pennies. Tried to win a prize throwing a baseball at a stack of wooden milk bottles.

I had one last nickel and went into the Penny Arcade, trying to make up my mind on the wisest way to spend it.

Since I loved movies, I decided to get a picture of my favorite western star, Ken Maynard, out of one of those photography dispensing machines. I read the directions carefully. You place your nickel in a slot, the directions said, push in the lever, make a selection, pull a knob, and out comes a card with your selected picture on it.

I followed the directions, except I unknowingly pull the wrong knob for my selection. Out came the card. It was a picture of a beautiful girl with dark hair.

Stunned, I stared at the picture, overwhelmed with grief over wasting my last nickel and not getting a Ken Maynard picture.

I read the card anyway. It was a fortune telling card. It said this is the girl I will marry. We will have eight kids.

My face got hot. I glanced around to make sure nobody I know is watching. I read the card again, slower this time.

The girl was beautiful. I think: I wouldn't mind at all marrying someone like her.

And I knew all about how you get eight kids. I thought about her a lot for several days after that. It was a lot more fun than having a Ken Maynard picture.

You can have lots of fun looking at old photos…

A New Pair of Tennis Shoes

There wasn't but one thing left to do—pray.

Dear God, I prayed, if you only knew how bad I wanted a new pair of tennis shoes you'd find a way to get them for me.

There.

I lifted my head and opened my eyes. It still hurt to see all the guys running around the school yard wearing tennis shoes.

I couldn't play tag with them or anything because there was no way you could outrun a boy in tennis shoes and you with high-toppers on.

That night I decided to put God to the real test. I asked Mom if I could have a new pair of tennis shoes. I even threw in what I thought would be a beyond-all-doubt convincing argument, which was: All the other boys in my class were wearing them.

She sighed, saying, "Summer'll soon be here. You can go barefoot."

I could see God was having a tough time with Mom. He needed help.

"But, Mom—"

"We don't need to be spending money on a pair of those worthless rags."

She didn't understand. Tennis shoes were NOT worthless rags. Of course their high tops were made out of canvas, but they were supposed to be so you could run faster.

They had rubber soles that left pretty patterns in the dust. They had long enough laces that you could make big bows that flopped when you walked.

To counter Mom's protest, I showed her the soles of my high-toppers.

"These are wore out—"

"Are worn out," she corrected.

Mom always wanted to be a school teacher. If our teachers wouldn't do the job teaching us right, she would. The same went for switching, especially when we brought home low grades or tardy marks on our report cards.

"Yeah. Worn out," I agreed. "And too little."

I threw that last in just for good measure—in case God forgot to tell her.

That got her attention. "Come here and let me see."

I went to her, sliding my toes as far down in my shoes as I could. She stooped to feel.

"They're not too little. Your father can half-sole them. You can get another winter out of them."

"But they hurt my toes," I argued.

She turned her back. I thought she was angry until I heard a soft sniffing sound and saw her make a motion with her hand like you would do if you were wiping away a tear.

It must have been God working on her, because that night when Dad came home, she talked it over with him.

He argued that paying ninety-eight cents for a pair of tennis shoes was just throwing money away.

Then God lit in on him, too, and he finally agreed to take me to town that Saturday and buy me a pair of tennis shoes.

The man at the shoe store brought out a pair of white ones.

Dad shook his head. "Brown ones would be better. They don't show dirt."

"It's the only pair we have left," the man said.

Thank you, God, I whispered.

Dad let me try them on. They were a couple sizes too big, but I kept insisting they fit perfectly and Dad gave in. I could tell he'd been got to by God.

I was so proud of my new white tennis shoes. I couldn't keep from looking down at them when I went to school the following Monday.

All the guys noticed. Some even said they wished they had a pair of white ones like mine.

And the way the girls were looking at me, I couldn't help prancing as we all lined up and marched to our respective classrooms in the large red brick building.

I was so proud that I kept peeking at my new shoes instead of paying attention in class. Miss Jackson noticed and demanded harshly, "Mr. Dale Denney, I'd like to know what you have under your desk that's so important?"

Shocked at being called down, I stammered, "N—nothing."

"If you don't pay attention, I'll have to send a note home to your mother."

Oh, lordy! Not that. I sat up stiff as a board and folded my hands together on the desk in front of me and tried my best to forget about my shoes and pay attention.

But as soon as she let school out, I lit out for home, anxious to run in my new white tennis shoes. I was ecstatic. It was almost like being barefoot.

I tried everything—jumping, skipping, even running backwards.

I was so happy with my new shoes that I made up my mind to give Mom a big hug as soon as I got home for letting Dad buy them for me.

She was standing in the doorway when I got there. I ran to give her a big hug, but before I could say anything, she scolded, "What in the world are you doing home?"

What was she asking me *that* for? I *always* came straight home when school was out, just like she had always taught us to do.

"Sch—school's out," I stammered.

"It's only afternoon recess time," she said and jabbed a finger in the direction of the school. "Now you get back there this minute before classes take up. If you get a tardy mark on your report card, I'll—"

I didn't hear the rest of what she had to say. Panic stricken, I was already flying back down the road like the wind. I'd never been late for a class in my life.

The school ground was empty, so eerily quiet. They'd all gone inside. My heart sank.

I didn't know how to go in when classes were going on.

I could run away, I told myself. But I had nowhere to go, except to grandma's and grandpa's. I knew they would protect me, but I would be getting them involved in my crime and I didn't want to do that.

I turned to God again in my time of need and prayed that Mrs. Jackson would be writing things on the blackboard and have her back turned when I slipped in.

She turned and caught me sliding into my seat.

"And where have you been, young man?" she demanded.

I felt hot all over and knew my face was red as a rusty iron post.

"I—I had to go home," I said. My voice sounded strange, as if it were coming from somewhere far away. "My Mom's not feeling too good. I ran home to check on her."

I could tell she knew I was lying. But what else could I say—that I wanted to run in my new tennis shoes so bad that I forgot it was recess? The whole class would laugh at me for telling the truth.

For the rest of the day, I kept my new white tennis shoes under my desk where they were supposed to be and prayed to God that if He loved me at all He wouldn't let Miss Jackson make a tardy mark on my report card or Mom would switch me good.

When Miss Jackson handed out report cards a few weeks later, I didn't see a tardy mark on it anywhere.

I was so happy that I didn't even think about thanking God for answering my prayer.

On my way out, Miss Jackson stopped me.

"I didn't mark you tardy," she explained. And then went on to say how she didn't believe me about my mother being sick. But she had run into my mother at church and asked her how she was feeling.

Miss Jackson paused, a mysterious smile on her lips as she finished with, "Your mother wanted to know why I asked. I told her about you running home during recess to check on her. She looked surprised at first. Then she remembered and said she had a cold that day but was feeling better. I thought that was nice of you to be so thoughtful of your mother. I decided not to give you a tardy mark."

And she reminded me to make sure my mother signed my report card before I brought it back.

I moped homeward, my oversized tennis shoes flopping.

God, I prayed. You got me in this mess, now get me out.

Mom signed the report card without saying a word about me telling the teacher a lie. And I didn't say a word about finding out that she had to lie to cover up my lie—because she loved me.

Thank you, God, I prayed, for teaching me not to lie—ever again.

The Dime Story

I was so afraid to ask Dad if I could get some nails out of his tool box that I came close not asking at all—just going ahead and getting some when he was at work.

But that was the same as stealing. So, desperate, I caught him on his way out the door and asked him. He stopped, stared, frowning.

"Nails? What ever for?"

I couldn't tell him. If I said I wanted to build a wheelbarrow to haul iron in and sell it to the junk man to get a dime to go to the show on, that would be the end of it. He couldn't tolerate "giving money to that show man."

Even if it was a new John Wayne movie.

I understood. Dad worked hard to keep us fed and clothed. A dime to him was a lot of money, always had been, always would be.

He was a big man, strong from years of hard work. I never thought of his age; he was over fifty.

But I had a lot of him in me; I was determined.

"Just a handful, is all," I mumbled, trying desperately not to beg. Don't ever beg, he always taught. It worked. I could see it in his face. He waved a gnarled hand toward the storage shed.

"Just don't mess it up," he grunted, meaning, I knew, not to mess up his tool box.

You catch Dad just right, I thought as I hurried toward the storage shed, and he's an old softie. The thought made me love him even more.

It was an honor just to be allowed to lift the lid on his tool box. When the oil well drilling, which was what he liked to do, played out, he hired out as a rig builder. And, naturally, had a reputation of being one of the best. He kept all his tools clean and each in its proper place.

I snatched up a handful of nails. I had already scavenged together everything else I would need to make a wheelbarrow—an orange crate box, scraps of lumber for handles, an old water well pulley for a wheel.

My excitement grew as I worked, sawing, hammering—I could already feel the cool air inside the theater and see John Wayne standing up to the mean guy in the black hat.

The short piece of broom stick I used for an axle was too small for the hole in the pulley. I shrugged it off. So what if the wheel wobbles? This was a one shot deal anyway, wasn't it?

I nailed the broomstick ends in place, quickly flipped my homemade wheelbarrow over, grasped the handles, hefted it. Perfect. I took off.

Mom caught me heading for the front gate and demanded to know where I was going.

I searched frantically for what to say. Mom and Dad's marriage was rock-solid. They never kept secrets. But maybe Dad wouldn't ask her. That wouldn't be a secret then, would it?

"To find some junk and sell it," I finally said, keeping it simple.

Mom set her fists on her hips, her way of waiting for more explanation. A curt, "No, you're not," would end it all right here and now.

"You get ten cents for a hundred pounds of plain old iron," I finally confessed. "I need a dime to go to the show on Saturday. It's a new John Wayne movie."

She shook her head, doubting, probably.

"You be careful," was all she said.

I took off down the dusty road, the pulley wobbling this way and that and squeaking on its broomstick axle.

The squeaking noise brought Dub, my best friend, out of his house when I went by.

"Where you going with that thing?" he asked, falling in beside me.

"It ain't a thing. It's a wheelbarrow. You blind, or something?"

"I got a red wagon," he said.

I glanced at him. I didn't like his grin and boasted, "I'm going to get some iron and sell it to the junk man uptown. A dime's worth. I want to see that John Wayne movie Saturday."

His grin faded. "Can I go?" he asked.

"Sure. Get your wagon and come on. There's lots of old iron out there."

He high-tailed it back to his house and caught up with me again as I was crossing Salt Creek, his little red wagon bouncing behind him.

I began picking up pieces of iron around the first oil well. The more pieces I found, the deeper my wheelbarrow wheel dug in. It got harder and harder to push, the wheel wobbling and all.

I went from well to well, picking up pieces of iron. Dub ran alongside, his red wagon bouncing empty and rattling, except when we came to a hill. Then he'd hop in and, laughing, coast down it and wait for me at the bottom.

The sun made me sweat. The orange crate's sides bulged. My hands blistered, gripping the handles. The pully-wheel dug deeper and deeper and squeaked louder as it flopped from side to side on its broomstick axle.

By the time I figured I had a hundred pounds, my blisters had broken open and my palms stung like fire.

I asked Dub once if we could put some of my load in his wagon.

"No!" he shouted. "It'll make dents all in it."

Then I was mad at myself for even asking him in the first place. I stacked on some more pieces just to be sure I'd have over a hundred pounds, because everybody knew the junk man would cheat you.

I turned toward town, praying my wheelbarrow would hold together, its squawking wheel protesting.

Dub ran along side, his empty wagon bouncing. He did most of the talking. I was gasping for breath.

We made plans to meet at the theater up town Saturday afternoon. His Dad gave him dimes to go to the show on, he said. I knew that—without envy. Some kids are lucky. But there was no need for him to boast that his Dad sometimes gave him an extra nickel for popcorn.

I knew that, too, because he never shared his popcorn. He couldn't keep you from smelling it, though.

He stopped off at his house. I staggered on to the junk yard up town.

The junk yard man had me push my load onto his scale. I tried to read the weight, but he kept blocking my view.

"Ninety pounds," he said brusquely. "Deduct ten for the weight of the wheelbarrow. You got eight cents worth."

I wasn't going to let him cheat me. Without another word, I seized the wheelbarrow handles and headed for the door.

"Hey. What're you doing, kid?"

"Taking my iron back home."

"Tell you what. I'll give you a dime for the whole shebang, including your wheelbarrow."

I had no more use for my wheelbarrow. None. But he was still trying to cheat me. I shook my head.

"All right. All right. A dime for the load. That wheelbarrow ain't no good no how."

I dumped the load of iron and held out my hand. The blisters had started to bleed a little. He dug a dime out of his pocket and laid the precious coin in my palm.

I slipped it in my pocket, grabbed the wheelbarrow handles, and headed for home.

Squeak. Squeak. Even the pulley wheel sounded happy now.

But I wasn't. I still had to figure out how to dodge Dad about going to the show. I was so worried, I wasn't even thinking about what I was doing when I parked my wheelbarrow in plain sight out behind the storage shed.

But my stupidity came back at me with a spine-chilling rush when I saw Dad inspecting it that Saturday. I braced for his questions. I searched frantically for lies. But lies were worse than stealing. I was in a mess.

And when I saw him talking with Mom, I knew I'd never see that John Wayne movie, because Mom and Dad never kept secrets from one another.

Sure enough, here came Dad with that deep scowl on his face.

"Your Mom told me about you selling iron. Did that junk man cheat you?"

He caught me off guard.

"No—no, sir. He tried. I wouldn't let him."

He stood proud. "You did a good job making that wheelbarrow."

He dug in his pocket, pulled out some change and handed me a nickel.

"It's for popcorn," he said, grinning.

And I ran all the way to town, holding my money in a tight fist in my pocket so I'd be sure not to lose it.

It turned out Dub's Dad didn't give him a nickel for popcorn that day.

But that was okay—I'm sure he enjoyed smelling mine.

The Roadhouse on Highway 66

Uncle Alvin shocked everyone in the family when he signed a lease on a roadhouse, and located on Highway 66 of all places.

The surprising thing was that Uncle Alvin was not a business man. He was a meek, gentle soul. He had a middle-age paunch—caused from, as Aunt Hattie put it, drinking "that beer all the time."

She was a big-boned woman with a perpetual frown and a raspy voice. Uncle Alvin had handled Aunt Hattie's continual griping for forty years, so he didn't pay much attention to what she said. Besides, as he truly felt inside, he didn't hurt anybody having a beer once in a while.

He'd walk to town, moving along gracefully with that slight shuffle of his, and would come home the same way, his pale blue eyes peering out at you from each side of a large red nose.

The only way you could tell he'd "had a beer—or two" was that his red nose would be a little redder than when he left.

"If he hadn't of been beered up," Aunt Hattie apologized to the family, "he wouldn't of never done it. A roadhouse, of all things!"

People from Chicago and everywhere else back east traveled Highway 66 going to Los Angeles and everywhere else out west. America's Main Street, people called it. There'd be no way of knowing who'd be stopping at the roadhouse.

Oklahomans were excited because a good chunk of that road sliced through our state. Everyone was talking about how the new transcontinental highway would be an economic boom for all our towns and businesses.

Uncle Alvin was always looking for a way to get rich quick. This was it, he said fussing back at Aunt Hattie. Not only was there a service station in the deal, but it had a dance hall addition behind with a beer cooler in it.

As a side bonus, there were also three one-room cabins for rent, presumably for weary travelers. But everybody knew roadhouse cabins were used mostly by couples from nearby towns, which added to the shame the family had to endure.

My mom had a hissy fit when they came to get me that summer for my annual two-week visit with them. There was no way she wanted her thirteen-year-old baby boy exposed to…to…she couldn't even speak the words to describe the awful things I'd be exposed to.

But Aunt Hattie promised Mom she wouldn't let us go in the dance hall. Besides it was the 4th of July, she said, and a lot of other members of the family with their kids would be there.

Since Billy Jack was my favorite cousin to play with, and Mom knew it, she finally let me go.

Going home with them was the first time I ever got to ride on Highway 66. It was hilly, and with a curve every whip stitch, because they had built the road wherever building a road was convenient.

Sometimes you had to follow a truck for hours before you could pass. Your best chance to do so would be to ease up close behind them going up a hill. Then at the top, you stepped on the gas and raced the truck to the bottom to get around.

But curves and hills didn't bother you much. Your biggest worry traveling was danger from flats and blowouts.

Uncle Alvin bought Billy Jack and me a package of firecrackers. And some torpedoes, too. These were little silvery balls about the size of a big marble which made a loud bang when you threw them down on concrete.

Uncle Alvin showed us a trick we could pull on motorists with our torpedoes. You could put them on the concrete highway. When a car ran over them, they'd go off with a loud bang. The driver would stop and get out to see what was wrong.

That was fun. When the cars ran over the torpedoes, they would go off and the driver would wheel into Uncle Alvin's station. Uncle Alvin would help them inspect the tires and look under the hood. While there, they'd buy gas or a bottle of pop or something.

We soon caught on to what Uncle Alvin had put us up to and went back to the station.

Uncle Alvin let us pump gas. When a car stopped, Billy Jack and me would pull and push on the long handle. The red liquid would gush up into the glass container on top where the gallons were marked off. Then Uncle Alvin would remove the hose and drain the liquid into the car's gas tank.

Five gallons cost nearly a dollar.

Sometimes the man would take Uncle Alvin aside ask if one of the cabins happened to be empty.

Uncle Alvin would say, "Yep. That'll be a dollar and a half, please. In advance."

Many times the couple wouldn't stay all night. They would stay only an hour or two, then get in their car again and go on. Billy Jack and I were both old enough to know what was going on, and we just looked at one another and snickered about it.

When the crowd, mostly coming from nearby towns, started gathering for the 4th of July dance that night, Billy Jack asked if we could go inside and help make record selections on the jukebox.

The music machine was a wonder to watch. It would swing a record out, a whirling plate would come up and hoist the spinning record to the top, where a needle set down on it and the music started coming out.

And there were all kinds of bubbly lights around the front of jukebox that were fascinating to watch.

Aunt Hattie said no, positively no. We kept begging until she gave in and said we could stand on the side porch and watch through the window.

Uncle Alvin fixed up a wash tub full of ice and pop and set it on the porch. He told Billy Jack and me we could sell the pop for him.

People slugged the jukebox. After each dance, they would go stand in front of the big fan in the back window where they could cool off, the men mopping their foreheads with big handkerchiefs and the women fanning their faces and necks with limp hands.

Some of the men came out on the side porch to cool off in the night air. A few bought pop from us. But most of them slipped small flat bottles with brown liquid in them from their pockets and tipped them up to their lips to take a swig or two.

They threw their empty bottles into the darkness before going back inside to find their partners and dance even more vigorously than they did before.

Billy Jack and I hopped off the porch and searched for the bottles they threw away. When we found one with a smidgen of the brown liquid in it, we'd take a taste and pretend like we were drunk.

Uncle Alvin got into the beer box and swigged a few. Soon he was asking pretty girls to dance.

I was surprised at how well Uncle Alvin danced. He'd spin his partners around and around, or hold them close, or sometimes did little solo jigs. The others would gather around and watch, whooping him on.

Aunt Hattie charged in and got him. She pulled him outside. We could hear her giving him the holy what-for. It was lots more fun than putting torpedoes on the highway and watching cars run over them.

That put an end to Uncle Alvin's dream for fame and glory. Aunt Hattie told him to give up one or the other—the lease on the roadhouse or her.

Since Aunt Hattie made the best biscuits in the world, Uncle Alvin chose her. He resumed his old habit of shuffling to town twice a day and coming home with his red nose all lit up.

And the family was glad. They liked Uncle Alvin just the way he was. In a few years his rash venture was forgotten.

But not by me. The roadhouse is gone now. Even Highway 66 has grass growing up in its cracks. But I still remember Uncle Alvin's dream of riches running a business on what many called the Main Street of America.

It was at Uncle Alvin's roadhouse, at the tender age of thirteen, that I learned all about the sins of dancin', drinkin', and other stuff.

The 9/10ths of a Cent Law

When the price of a gallon of gas jumped from eighteen cents to twenty cents, we decided to get into the business ourselves, gathering gasoline and selling it for half price—only ten cents a gallon.

By "we," I mean my older brother Don and his friend Jake. Jake was big for his age, with his thick blond hair always uncombed. He was forever brushing it forward with one of his hands until it hung down almost to his eyes.

We had to do a lot of planning. Jake was against adding on the 9/10th of a cent like all filling stations advertised, but Don said we had to. When Jake asked why did we have to, Don said it was probably a law of some sort, else why did all service stations charge 9/10th of a cent on whatever the cost of a gallon of gas was?

So it was decided—to make our sales legal—that we'd charge 10 and 9/10ths of a cent for each gallon of gasoline we sold.

Jake continued to grump about it because it was lots easier to figure up the cost by multiplying 10 cents time gallons sold.

Don insisted we had to add on the 9/10th to make it legal.

"Since we'd be stealing the gasoline in the first place," Jake argued, "We'd be illegal anyway."

They finally reached a compromise. Jake would charge 10 cents a gallon when he was dealing with a customer and Don would charge 10 and 9/10ths of a cent for his customers.

None of it made sense to me. Nobody ever paid any attention to the 9/10ths of a cent on a gallon of gas that I knew of. In the first place, the filling station owner worked a long lever back and forth to pump gasoline from an underground storage tank into the big glass containers on top of tall metal stands.

The glass containers held ten gallons and was marked like kitchen measuring cups—a stripe for each gallon.

When you pulled in and ordered, say, two gallons of gas, the filling station operator poked the gas nozzle in your gas tank and squeezed the throttle. The gas ran down out of the glass containers by gravity. The operator had to keep a close eye on the markers. It was impossible to stop exactly on the mark, let alone knowing what to charge figuring the 9/10th of a cent.

So everybody just ignored the 9/10th of a cent. And people were happier when the cost went up to 20 cents. If you ordered five gallons of gas, the station operator watched the level in the glass container drop down five marks and shut it off.

Five times 20 cents made a dollar. You handed the station operator a dollar and he poked it down in his overall pockets.

Nobody ever paid any attention to the 9/10th of a cent.

That was Jake's argument, especially since we didn't have one of those glass containers. All we had to store gas in was a fifty-five-gallon drum we found in our barn.

We checked it out. It wasn't too rusty inside. We poured some water in the bung hole and rolled it around in the barnyard for awhile, scaring the chickens, then dumped the water out. It wasn't too rusty looking, so we decided it would do.

We found a short piece of rubber hose we could use to siphon the gasoline out of the drum with—but first we had to gather up the gasoline by running drips.

"Drips" were containers oil companies placed at all low places in pipe lines carrying raw gas from the oil wells to refineries. The raw gas inside the pipe lines would form a condensate, especially in cooler weather. The condensate would drain to the low spots in the line and stop the flow of raw gas if you didn't install a container for it to drip into.

It was the pumper's job to keep these drips emptied. First he had to shut the valve off at the pipeline. Then he'd open the valve at the bottom of the container and let whatever liquid that had accumulated run out into a bucket.

Most pumpers would use the drip gas in their own cars, especially if it was clear. But sometimes this condensate would be of such poor quality that if you tried to use it in a good car, it'd gum up the engine so bad you'd have to have it overhauled.

However, Model Ts would burn anything that smelled like gasoline. Model As would run good on drip gas too. So you had a big market for drip gas, especially for 10 and 9/10th of a cent, compared to 20 and 9/10th of a cent at the filling station.

If the pumper thought the drip gas couldn't be used for anything, he'd simply pour it into the nearest creek.

And all creeks emptied into the Cimarron River. Since the Cimarron flowed through the salt flats in western Oklahoma, it had so much natural salt in it that fish couldn't live in it anyway, so a gallon or two of not very good drip gas dumped into it didn't hurt anything.

This raw gas was considered a by-product from oil wells, more of a headache than anything of value. Sometimes oil companies didn't even bother about piping it to market—they'd pipe it ten foot or so into the air and let the gas escape into the atmosphere.

Some pumpers would have the company pipe the raw gas to their houses and stick a match to the gas escaping into the air. These flares burning day and night made dandy night lights.

One of our first decisions was whether to put all the gasoline drained from drips into a single barrel, or to have separate barrels for different grades of gas.

But since we had only the one fifty-five-gallon drum in our barn to keep the gasoline in, we decided to just put it all in that one drum, "And stick with the one ten-cent price," Jake said.

"Plus the 9/10ths of a cent," Don added.

Don planned to be a lawyer some day, and he insisted on doing things according to the law, and surely to God there was a law, he reasoned, that every gallon of gas sold had to have 9/10th of a cent added on, else why did everybody do it?

So we went out that very night to commence running all the drips we could find. We got almost a whole five-gallon bucket full.

Word got around pretty fast. People started coming to our barn to buy their gas, especially the people with Model Ts and Model As.

I'd never tried to siphon gas since Jake and Don both were so good at it. They'd stick one end of the rubber hose down in the fifty-five-gallon drum and stick the other end in their mouth and start sucking on it until they got the gas going.

There was a trick to it—you had to know when to jerk your end of the rubber hose out of your mouth and poke it down into the bucket or you'd wind up with a mouthful of gas.

The first time I tried doing it, I got a mouthful of gasoline and spit and sputtered for an hour trying to get the taste out of my mouth.

Jake thought it was hilarious. Brother Don decided I wasted too much gas to do any selling. That suited me just fine because I'd made up my mind I wasn't even going to try it again—ever.

Our business kept picking up until the richest man in town came out in his new Buick and bought a tankful of our 10 and 9/10th of a cent gas.

When he had to take his new car back to the dealer and have it overhauled to get it running right, he complained to the oil company officials.

They called the sheriff to come shut us down, even though we were legal, Don said, by charging the 9/10th of a cent on every gallon of gas we sold.

That argument stumped the sheriff. But he ordered us to stop selling drip until he checked it out.

Nobody ever knew for sure if the sheriff checked on whether or not charging 9/10th of a cent on every gallon of gas sold was a law like Don said.

But most folks agreed that surely to God it must be a legal requirement to add 9/10th of a cent to every gallon of gas sold...

Why else do they all do it?

The Stolen Hymnal

The only dishonest thing Harve ever did in his life was steal a hymnal from the church.

It was the only way, he decided. He was a big, barrel-chested man, deep blue eyes, balding, hands calloused from years working a rocky piece of land along the Spavinaw Creek bottom. His wife, Euline, existed elegantly on her sparse frame, was strong-willed, and was always humming. Her favorite was "Sing Praises Unto the Lord." They had six kids: four strong girls who took after Harve in build and character, and two boys who were fine and delicate like their mother, which was always a puzzle to Harve.

My religion just ain't right, Harve concluded. Something's wrong. He was always questioning in his mind what the preacher said, or he was always puzzling over different passages in the Good Book that seemed to contradict one another. Maybe it's because I can't sing praises unto the Lord like it says in the Good Book, he admitted reluctantly to himself one day.

It wasn't that he didn't want to. He simply couldn't. It bothered him. He didn't feel his religion was a real religion, since he couldn't sing praises unto the Lord. Was the good Lord trying to send him a message, having Euline hum that tune all day?

They came to church every Sunday, rain or shine, driving up in Harve's old brown Model A Ford. One back window was broken and Harve, always good at solving a problem practically even if it didn't look good cosmetically, had found a piece of clear oil cloth to tape over the opening, which to his way of thinking, was as good as a piece of glass, except you couldn't roll it down. He'd stand with Euline in church, head down, gripping his side of the hymnal, mumbling what he thought were words to a song. Euline's fine voice would be spilling out into the congregation all around, drawing glances of approval of joy from those standing nearby—even catching the attention of the pastor up in the pulpit on occasion.

When Harve felt full of the spirit, especially after a fine sermon, he'd rare his head back, pull the hymnal up closer to get it into better focus of his bifocals, and open up a bit more. Completely off key, of course. Euline's eyes would keep flicking up his way, trying her best to will him to quiet down a bit. And men all around them would try to keep from showing rudeness by smiling too much.

One Sunday night Euline actually tugged the hymnal from him. The display of disgust angered Harve. He folded his arms and sulked. That's when he decided to steal the song book.

During the dismissal prayer, he shuffled the hymnal into his left hand with some other papers and paraphernalia he was carrying for the kids and simply walked out with it, making his way through the front door on the far side of the crowd from the pastor so he wouldn't get caught.

"Well, would you look at this," he said when the family got back home. He was a poor liar, had always been.

"Harve!" Euline said, stiff and accusing.

But he toughed his way on through it with, "Must be the Lord's work—"

"Harve!"

"I've been wanting to learn how to sing. I 'spect He fixed it up so I could learn." He ignored Euline's withering look and added, "We'll just take it back next week. No big deal."

He'd already figured he could learn how to sing in a week. That's the way it'd always been for him, seemed like. He learned more from studying books in school than he did from the teachers. He never asked anybody how to fix anything on the farm. He'd figure it out himself. The same with singing, he thought. Nothing to it.

Somewhere in his eighth grade education he learned there were only eight notes: do, re, me, fa, so, la, te, do. A man ought to be able to master the sounds of eight notes in a week, shouldn't he? Although it always puzzled him why there were two "dos" and one was higher than the other, he did know you could always check to see what line it was setting on whether it was a high "do" or a low "do." Then there were the little flags, the eyebrows, the tic-tac-toe boxes, and all that stuff. But if a man stuck to the simple things, he figured, he didn't see why he couldn't soon be singing praises unto the Lord. The refinements he could fit in later as he went along.

He began that very night, sitting in front of the wood stove in the living room practicing the scales. He cocked his head back, peered through his bifocals, started patting his foot, and began in a loud, strong voice, "Do, re, me—"

The kids who were scattered about in the house in various beds covered their heads. Euline had it the worst because her and Harve's bed was in the same room where Harve was practicing his scales. She lay there shaking her head with a grim smile on her lips. Night after night, she'd call softly every so often, "Harve? Harve? It's getting late. The kids have to get up in the morning and go to school." Sometimes, Harve would quit, sometimes he wouldn't. The kids would crawl out of bed to close the bedroom doors, even though it meant shutting themselves off from the heat in the living room. But they could still hear through the walls their Dad's strong voice going, "Do, re, me, fa, so, la, te, do!" and his foot patting the floor in time with his "music."

When the kids started showing up for breakfast red-eyed and draggy every morning, and Euline had become a bit sharper than usual, Harve decided to do his real "word" practicing when he was alone in the barn milking.

He chose "How Great Thou Art." He began clearing his throat repeatedly when he sat down on his milking stool and washed Betsy's udder and teats off good. As usual, their old black and white tom cat that lived half-wild in the barn came sneaking up close to sit down and meow for a milk meal. And as usual, Harve palmed a heavy teat and shot the first squirt of milk old Tom's direction. The cat opened his mouth for the direct hit, then licked the splattered milk off his lips happily as he settled down to wait patiently for the next flow of manna from heaven.

Harve took a deep breath, palmed a teat in each huge fist, and started belting out the words in a strong lusty voice. Unconsciously, he began keeping time as he milked, the jet streams of milk singing merrily against the bottom of the pail.

Squirt, squirt.

Then he broke out into song.

When my so-o-oul gets to heaven...

His lusty voice reverberated off the barn's tin roof.

Mooo—Betsy joined in, turning her head to look at Harve with straw hanging out the corners of her mouth.

Old Tom meowed and the chickens outside joined in the cacophony.

How Great Thou art... How Great Thou art...

Moooo.

Meeoow.

Cackle, cackle, cackle.

Squirt, squirt, squirt.

Even the rooster crowed, but he sounded off-beat—just like Harve did in church.

Harve was quite pleased with himself by the time he was finished milking. Betsy had given more, old Tom's sides were bulging, and the chickens seemed to be clucking more contentedly with the rooster strutting around like he'd been the cause of it all.

Euline was suspicious when he skipped practicing his scales that night. She watched, her curiosity growing, as he trimmed the lamp before huffing it out and climbing into bed. After a long moment of silence trying to fathom the mystery, she had to ask, "Have you decided to quit trying to sing?"

"No," he said, and reached over to pat her arm gently. "I found out I already know how to sing. It's the sound of it that counts…and that depends on who's doing the listening."

Harve returned the hymnal that next Sunday, thanking the good Lord for making his religion whole.

The Corn Cannin' Caper

It was a good year for crops in Oklahoma before the drought hit in the mid 30s and the wind began blowing dust from Texas to Kansas and back again. Dad's once well paying job as a carpenter dwindled to almost nothing. He refused to sign up for WPA work. Didn't think it was right. Instead, he put all his energy into our little acreage at the edge of town. That year he had planted too much corn.

When the tall stalks matured and the heavy ears began standing straight out, Mom complained—in joking wonder—at the supper table one night, "What in the world are we going to do with all that corn?"

She could handle a big garden, always had; canning vegetables, storing potatoes and turnips in the cellar. Nor would she back off canning corn. But two acres—?

They made plans. Mom and Dad. They'd spent their years working together as a team, trying to do a decent job sheltering, feeding, clothing, and educating us six kids. Each respected the other's familial rights and responsibilities.

They knew it was hard times, because they had known better. We kids didn't. We grew up in it. We didn't know how it had been before, and the future was yet to come. The way it was was the way it was. You found fun in little things.

To solve the surplus corn problem, Mom and Dad decided to have a corn cannin', invite Aunt Hattie and her family to come help out.

"What we can't put up, we can let dry on the stalk," Dad said. "Feed the rest to the hogs."

As an afterthought, he said, "Me and the boys'll cut the corn stalks and stack them in shocks. The kids'll love playing in them this fall." Then he looked at Mom and grinned. "Remember how we used to do that?"

The way Mom blushed, I guessed Dad must have stolen a kiss or two from Mom inside a shock of corn when they were young. I loved them a little more, thinking that.

Aunt Hattie and her large family lived only thirty miles away. She was known for her bossiness. Dad said invite them anyway, that we were going to can corn, not boss people. Mom wrote her a postal card, said to bring the kids. We were going to have an old-fashioned corn cannin'.

Aunt Hattie came in their old brown Model A Ford coupe. There wasn't room for the whole family, only her and the older girls. Ruby, Mabel, and Evona.

Aunt Hattie started right off trying to boss everybody, but Mom's firmness wore her down. She assigned Aunt Hattie the job at the stove, scalding canning jars and lids and cooking the corn. Mom said she and the girls would do the cleaning and cutting. Dad, my brothers and I would gather the corn.

We had to fight our way through the corn patch, pulling the ripened ears off the stalks. It was hotter than all get out. The sharp edges of the leaves sliced our arms and neck. Sweat got in the cuts and stung like the dickens.

I was glad when I filled my gunny sack and could get out of the corn patch, out where the wind would cool me off a little as I carried the sack of corn to the house.

Mom had stationed cousins Ruby and Mabel and my older sister Mazie on the back porch. They sat in chairs near wash tubs. When they ripped the shucks from the ears, it made little squeaking sounds. They dropped the shucks and broken ends of the cobs in the tubs. After fingering away the long strands of silk, they gently placed the glistening ears in large dish pans and carried them into the kitchen.

Mom and cousin Evona sat in the kitchen by the south window where they could get what little breeze there was. They had the job of shaving the corn off the cobs with sharp knives, filling big aluminum pots. After they had cut off all the kernels, they would scrape the cobs. The milky juice would squirt onto their arms and into their faces. It got in their hair and on their eyelashes. They looked funny. But they didn't seem to mind, continuing their chatter as they dropped the stripped cobs into a number 3 wash tub.

Aunt Hattie would lift the pots full of corn to the stove and adjust the flame to get them boiling. She kept dabbing with a damp towel at the perspiration beading on her forehead, cheeks, and neck as she stirred the mix in the pots with a large wooden spoon. She joined in the talk, too.

At what she thought was the right time, she would plop a wide-mouth funnel into a still steaming glass jar and pour it full of bubbling corn. Sometimes, she'd pour too fast and the corn would run over the top of the funnel and sizzle on the hot stove.

I was surprised at Mom's lack of concern over the mess the corn cannin' was making on the back porch and in her kitchen. No person in the world was more neat than Mom. She always worked hard at keeping our little frame house spotless. There wasn't a morning that went by that she didn't "run over the house" after doing up the breakfast dishes. First she'd sweep the pine flooring then polish it with an oiled dust mop. If you held the screen door open too long going out or coming in, she'd sentence you to do time with the fly swatter. And you couldn't go free until you killed the quota of flies she assigned you, depending on the flagrancy of your crime.

But all the time the corn cannin' was in progress, Mom never seemed happier. Just having company had a lot to do with it, talking about all the members in our extensive family, their ailments and accomplishments, the marriages and impending marriages, the births, the soon-to-be births, how those who lost a loved one recently were getting along.

When we broke for our noon meal, Mom didn't even bother to clean up the mess. Evona asked me to at least help her carry out the wash tub full of corn cobs, but Mom said, "Leave it be. We'll just dump all the left overs from the meal into it and carry it out later."

Among other things Mom had planned for dinner were, naturally, roasting ears. We all found places around the table, buttered our ears of corn, sprinkled them liberally with salt and pepper, and began eating.

One of my little sister's neighborhood playmates, who was about five at the time, came in. She was unaware how busy we'd been canning corn. She stood politely just inside the kitchen door, waiting for us to get through eating so my little sister could come out and play.

Dad, who never passed up an opportunity to pull a sly joke, noticed how the little girl seemed fascinated by the way we were all busy gnawing corn off our roasting ears. He hurried to finish his ear of corn first. Then without warning, he nonchalantly tossed the cob over our heads toward the tub full of cobs on the other side of the kitchen. It rattled against the side of the tub and fell onto the pile.

Mom was so shocked by Dad's uncharacteristically rude behavior, she sat in stunned silence glaring at him, speechless for once in her life as he snatched another ear from the stack on the platter in the middle of the table.

The little girl's eyes bulged as she glanced from Dad to the wash tub full of cobs, then back to Dad again and said, her voice full of surprise and wonder, "You sure must like corn."

Dad's silent laugh made him shake all over. Then we all got to tittering when we realized what he'd done. Mom tried her best to keep from smiling, but did a poor job suppressing it.

The rest of the day went easy. Anytime anybody complained about the heat or hard work, all somebody had to say was, "You sure must like corn," and we'd break out with laughter. Even Mom.

At the end of the day, we loaded Aunt Hattie's car trunk with their share of the canned corn and sent them on their way. We carried a zillion jars of the stuff, it seemed, to our cellar.

Unfortunately, the family corn cannin' that summer was a total failure. Nobody knew why, whether it was the cob scraping, the way it was cooked, or how Aunt Hattie did the canning. Every few days, Mom would make a trip to the cellar, gather up an armload of jars with spoiled corn spewing from under their lids, and carry them out to feed the hogs.

Dad came up behind her one day when she was emptying the jars into the pig trough. As they watched the pigs gorging themselves on the spoiled corn, Dad put his arm across Mom's shoulders and said, "They sure do like corn, don't they?"

They stood there laughing together. Mom and Dad. They never had much. Just one another. I guess that's all they needed to raise six kids and instill in them the moral values they would need to take on a world yet to come.

Saturday Night Bath

The Saturday night bath. We laugh about it today. A bath only once a week? How shockingly unhealthy that would be.

Yet how often would we take a bath today if…

At our house, when you wanted to take a bath—usually on Saturday night because you put on clean clothes Sunday when you went to church—you had to select one of the washtubs from several hanging on nails on the side of the house.

You'd set your favorite tub under the well spout and start pumping water.

How much water to pump into the tub was always a tough decision. You liked to have a lot to take a bath in, but three inches of water in the bottom of the tub would be about all you could carry into the kitchen and lift up to set it on the stove to heat.

Once it was heated, you had to lift it off and set it on the floor. In the winter, you'd place it as close to the kitchen stove as possible. In the summer, you'd set it by the south window where you could get a little breeze to help cool you off when you got out.

Since the kitchen door had no latch, before closing it, you announced to the rest of the family you were getting in the tub so there'd be no surprises. Then you'd undress, toss your clothes over one of the kitchen chairs, and climb into the tub.

When you were younger, you could fold your legs and get all of you in the tub. When you got older, you had to ease your rear into the hot water and leave your legs cocked over the side with your feet on the wood flooring.

This brought up another problem. You knew you'd have to mop up all the water you splashed out so you had to be careful washing your legs and feet without getting the floor wet.

To do this, you had to grasp a foot and pull it into the tub with you. After scrubbing that foot and leg good, you had to wring all the water out of your wash cloth and use it to wipe the excess water off before returning the foot and leg to their proper positions outside the tub. That minimized getting the wood flooring any wetter than you had to.

You repeated the operation with the other leg.

You had to use the same care to keep from getting too much water on the floor after you finished bathing. That was why you had your towel on a chair or bench within easy reach. You'd place your hands on the rim of the tub, lift yourself out and snatch up the towel as quickly as possible to start drying off before too much water drained off you and onto the floor.

You had to dress completely after bathing because you had to clean up the mess you'd made in the kitchen. You had to carry the tub outside and dump the water. And it had better be far enough away from the house as possible to keep from making a mud hole near the kitchen door.

If you thought you could get away with it, you'd skip pumping more water in the tub to rinse away the soap scum. But that depended on the whereabouts of Mom. If she caught you not rinsing the tub you used to take a bath in, you were in trouble.

Then you had to hang your washtub on its proper nail on the side of the house to drain and dry. Your final responsibility was to get the mop and mop up all the water you'd spilled on the floor.

So…how many baths per week would we take today if we had to go through that procedure each and every time?

Was it unhealthy taking a bath only once a week? That's arguable. There didn't seem to be as many weird diseases then as now. Was body odor prevalent? No. If everybody smells the same, there is no odor.

Actually, taking a bath once a week was a sophisticated habit. Many people didn't even do that. It depended on the water supply. We were lucky having a water well on the back porch just outside the kitchen door.

Things even got better as our little country town continued to grow. We eventually got water piped into our homes and sewers connected to carry away our wastes. Even so, we still didn't think about bathing every day.

You thought: How nice it is that you don't have to pump water anymore and heat it on the stove. When Saturday night came, all you had to do was run a tub of hot water, take your bath, and pull a plug. The sewer carried away the soap suds and crud you'd washed off your skin.

Old habits didn't change overnight.

Once-a-week bathing carried over to my life even after I left home and found a job in another city called Jay. The building where I roomed had no bathing facilities. A nearby laundry provided shower services for fifteen cents. Once a week, I'd roll my clean clothes into a tight bundle, walk up the street, pay fifteen cents, take my shower, roll my dirty clothes into a tight bundle, and walk back down the street to my room.

Of course, during the summer, we boys went swimming every chance we got in a creek about a mile from town. But I didn't think of that as bathing. It was such a fun thing to do.

The water was so clear you could see bottom even where it was ten feet deep. And when you happened to get any in your nose or mouth, you didn't think anything at all about swallowing it because it was pure enough to drink.

Sometimes I'd take a bar of soap with me and soap myself good after we finished playing and would rinse off with creek water. But when I'd watch the soap suds float away, I'd feel bad about what I was doing to that beautiful stream of water.

I didn't worry too much, however, for I was only one person washing myself off and the creek could handle the waste from my body without any trouble. A few steps away you would still be able to drink it and never notice the difference.

I don't think I ever started bathing every night until I was drafted into the army during World War II.

I'm not real sure I did then, for it was a lot of trouble where I was first stationed. Several barracks shared the same bath house. You had to strip to your waist, gather up your soap and towel, and trudge down a board walk to the communal bath house.

It wasn't all that bad for me because I still wasn't having to shave every day— maybe only once or twice a month I'd have to scrape the fuzz off my upper lip.

That was another thing World War II brought to backwoods USA—the daily bath. Country boys like me learned a lot being thrown into a barracks with big city boys who bathed every day whether they needed it or not.

I suppose the daily bath is progress of some sort in personal hygiene. Anyhow, I'm not the one to argue the point.

But I do know the once clear stream you could drink out of where I took baths is no longer clear. Nor would you be caught dead drinking any of it.

Because we have washed our body wastes into it. Population is what pollutes our water—the greater the population, the more pollution we have.

Progress? Or are we only shifting our personal pollution from one point to another on this old planet?

The Adult Ticket

Mrs. Martin was such a nice lady that I hated myself for cheating her. She always had a sweet smile on her round, wrinkle-free face. It was her soft blue eyes that made me uncomfortable—they looked like they could see right into your very soul.

Maybe it was my conscience that made it feel like that.

I hung back from the boys I ran around with all the time when we'd stop horsing around on the street Saturday nights and they'd hurry to box office window to buy their tickets to the show.

Adult tickets, that is. We'd all turned twelve long ago—two years at least for most of us.

But I hadn't grown an inch since then and could still get in the show for a dime. When it came to ticket-buying time I didn't want Mrs. Martin to see me running around with the older crowd.

I'd try to keep from looking up into her eyes when I'd slide my dime through the hole in the window. I always made sure I had the exact change. And I always held my breath, afraid she'd say, "Dale, it's time you started buying an adult ticket, isn't it?"

This time she seemed to hesitate just a second before taking my dime. I felt a sense of panic and glanced up, forcing a nervous smile. But Mrs. Martin only gave me that sweet smile of hers as she ripped a purple ticket from the roll and slid it under my trembling fingers.

I took the purple ticket and hurried through the swinging doors, handed my purple ticket to the always scowling Mr. Martin—at least my guilty conscience told me he was always scowling, and was probably wise to my little cheating game.

But I was in! One more time!

Into that wonderful world of make-believe.

Of Tarzan swinging through the trees in a jungle full of apes and lions and elephants and natives with painted faces and carrying long spears.

Of a sweet faced girl I was secretly in love with, dancing and singing her way deeper into my heart.

Of hard-riding cowboys wearing big pearl-handled guns, chasing black-hatted mean guys and roping them and tying them up until the sheriff got there.

And you always had to find out how the girl and guy got out of that locomotive steam engine before it blew up and the sonorous voice intoned, "Be sure not to miss next week's episode of this thrilling serial."

I found my friends and sat down in the cushiony seats, enjoying the feel of the nice cool air floating down on me from a big vent in the ceiling.

The high anticipation rose even higher as the house lights dimmed and a shaft of light shot out from a tiny hole far overhead and lit up the big screen up front, filling it with dancing figures and lilting music coming from you never knew where and overpowering us into silence.

One thin dime changed my world every Saturday—except for having to worry about next Saturday.

I'd started carrying an extra dime in my pocket—especially on the Saturdays when there was a show I just had to see—just in case Mrs. Martin made me buy an adult ticket.

This one Saturday night I didn't have an extra dime and it was a Ken Maynard movie. He was my favorite of all the cowboys.

It would just be my luck that Mrs. Martin would make me buy an adult ticket, I figured. So I decided to join the slip-in bunch.

I saw them huddling up under the street light at the corner. Soon, I knew, they would slink into the dark alley and sneak into the theater's fire exit door.

I hurried to join them. Jack, their leader and a darn good football player, pushed me back, growling, "Not you, Denney. There's too many of us now."

But an unseen friend in the darkness whispered huskily, "Aw, let him come. One more won't hurt."

Jack glowered down at me a long moment, then gestured for me to follow.

The guys had set up a military operation slipping in. One of the older guys, usually Jack, manned the door. He'd wait until the sneaker-inner had time to make his way through the store room behind the screen, through the inner door, and into a seat down in front of auditorium before he let the next guy go.

It made sense. The chances of not getting caught were better when you went in one at a time.

All the whispering and shushing going on scared me. I was wanting to change my mind. It wasn't right, especially so many of us. I hung back, hoping Walt or

Mrs. Martin would catch us and come out and chase us away.

I was still trying to hang back when somebody pushed me forward, whispering, "You're next!"

Jack warned, "Don't mess us up, kid."

He opened the door, whispering, "Stay low when you open the inside door. If you walk to the seats standing up, they can see you from up front."

Then he gave me a shove. I stumbled into the eerie darkness. The room was filled with broken seats, mops, and brooms. My foot slipped on popcorn kernels spilled from a freshly opened sack. I grabbed for something to keep from falling. My hand hit the wall with a loud thump.

My scalp crawled when I saw what appeared to be a huge man lurking in the corner. I was about to surrender until my eyes adjusted to the dim glow and the huge man turned out to be a tall, pot-bellied coal stove. I jumped at the sound of gunshots from the movie on the screen high above me. Voices without bodies came from every which way.

Lookout! The window! (the sound of glass tinkling, followed by a thud, then a grunt.)

Bill!—you're bleeding!

Yeah, they got me good (a heavy sob.)

Then there were the bad guys speaking,

Mac, you circle around. We'll smoke 'em out!

Music suddenly filled the room, loud violin music. Violin music meant the scene had shifted back inside the besieged shack where the main guy and main girl were holed up, their lives in jeopardy, their love true to the end.

I inched toward the inner door, and cracked it so I could see into the auditorium. My heart bounced up into my throat. The light from the screen reflected off every face. I thought everybody was staring at me.

I quickly closed the door, holding my breath. My heart finally settled back in place but still kept thumping hard.

What to do? If I went back, I'd have to face Jack. I'd be ridiculed the rest of my school days. And if I didn't hurry on in, the next sneaker-inner would be on his way in. I'd be cursed for causing a traffic jam, messing up the entire night's operation. I had no choice. I had to go.

I eased the door open again. The loud music faded to a whisper. The door hinge screeched. I panicked. But just then the gunfire erupted again. The noise from the screen covered me. I opened the door wider, slipped through, bent low and scurried for one of the front row seats.

I was miserable during the entire show. Every time I heard footsteps coming down the aisle, I just knew it was Walt or Mrs. Martin coming to get me and drag me out by the ear.

I felt a great sense of relief when the show was over and the house lights came on. I got up and ambled—nonchalantly, I hoped—toward the front with everybody else.

As I passed Mrs. Martin in the lobby, she gave me that pleasant, knowing smile.

I knew then that she knew I had sneaked in. I thought she was such a grand lady for being so sweet about it. It made me more miserable than ever.

Next time I went to the show, I slid two dimes through the box office window like I was supposed to. Mrs. Martin was already reaching for the roll of children's tickets when she saw the two dimes.

Without a word, she gave me that sweet smile and tore off an adult ticket for me.

I felt more grown up. I relaxed and enjoyed the show.

Grandpa Jack

Grandpa Jack was furious coming down the lane. You could tell he had revenge in his mind by the way he was wearing his wide-brimmed hat—set squarely on his head instead of back at a rakish angle, and by the way he totally ignored Grandma humping along two steps behind trying to keep up.

I could just barely see Grandma's wrinkled face hiding in the shadows of her blue speckled bonnet, but I could hear her giving Grandpa Jack the what-for even before they got to our front gate. It didn't help matters any when he pushed on through ahead of her, not even bothering to hold the gate open for her like he usually did.

Grandpa Jack was doing a magnificent job constraining his anger as he dutifully gave Mom, his devoted daughter, a loving hug. Then, tugging angrily at the ends of his moustache, he acknowledged Dad with only a curt nod.

Dad simply gave him one of his friendly how-are-you smiles.

Nobody, and I mean nobody, had beaten Grandpa Jack at checkers for years until Dad did it last Sunday.

I didn't see the game because we boys had gone down to the creek to wade in it barefooted, chasing minnows.

But I heard about it in school that week. The defeat by his own son-in-law made Grandpa Jack the laughing stock of the town, after he'd boasted all these years about being the checker champ of Creek County—the world for that matter, if anybody would dare to come to Creek County and take him on.

One of his more historic games everybody liked to talk about was how he had taken on two ace checker players at once one day and whipped them soundly.

Everybody knew it was showdown time this Sunday—a repeat match, winner take all, a battle to the death.

But he would have to wait until the Sunday dinner was over. It was Mom's rule—no checker games to be played before dinner.

Grandpa Jack ate in silence sitting at his usual place at one end of our long kitchen table. Dad settled into his chair at the other end and joked merrily during the meal, teasing us kids about what games we planned to play that afternoon.

Grandma sat to Grandpa Jack's left, surreptitiously handing him a towel each time he needed to clean his moustache. And each time he'd glare at her like he didn't need to clean his moustache, then he'd do it anyway.

Mom's two brothers, Uncle Leonard and Uncle Leo, came with their families just as we were finishing our traditional summer Sunday meal of fried chicken, mashed potatoes, and roasting ears.

We kids started romping about the house so rambunctiously that Mom shooed us all outside so the grown ups could talk in peace.

We scattered every which way—the girls chalked hopscotch boxes on the sidewalk, and we boys raced for the barn to romp in the hay loft and climb trees.

"Don't disturb my setting hens," Mom called after us. She knew she was throwing her cautioning words to the wind and shrugged in mock disgust as she turned to go help Aunt Hermenia and Aunt Edith who were already busy ridding up the table.

After a suitable time had elapsed, and seeing as how Grandpa Jack was about to pull his moustache out by the roots, Dad reached up to slide his home-made checker board from its shelf.

Without a word, he headed for the shade of the big elm out by the water pump. And without a word, Grandpa Jack followed, tugging with even more determination at the free ends of his moustache.

Uncle Leonard and Uncle Leo exchanged questioning glances. Then they, too, eased from their chairs and followed the combatants outside.

I sidled away from the others at the barn and drifted back to the watch the battle.

The women pretended not to notice what was going on as they kept plunging the dirty dishes into a big pan of soapy water on the stove and toweling them dry before they placed them clattering into the proper places in the cabinet.

Dad set the checker board gently on a tree stump. Uncle Leonard and Uncle Leo acted as the dueler's seconds. Uncle Leonard dragged up a yard chair for Dad, and Uncle Leo did the same for Grandpa Jack.

Dad had tried and tried to teach me the finer points of the game of checkers, how you sacrificed one man to get two, how you set traps for your foe, sometimes even as far as three moves ahead.

"The trick is get to your opponent's king row first," he sermoned over and over. "Then when you're crowned, you can wheel around and attack your enemy from behind."

I wanted them both to win.

Grandpa Jack had every right to his title as checker champion of Creek County because he'd earned it fair and square.

Although Dad respected Grandpa Jack's talents, he didn't set a great store in winning. Playing us kids, he'd laugh when he beat you and laugh with you when you beat him. You never really knew, however, whether you actually beat him or he manipulated his own men to let you win.

Now he and Grandpa Jack were facing off—again. Dad dropped his red checkers (the previous winner always got the reds) onto their places on the board.

Grandpa Jack smacked his blacks down with fierce determination.

That was the first time I ever really saw Grandpa Jack's face. I mean really, really saw it. I'd grown up with him always being old and accepted that fact.

But now I noticed how much his wrinkled, sunken cheeks sagged, dragging down the flesh beneath his eyes so much the redness showed. His large thin nose looked even thinner. Even though you couldn't see his lips—come to think of it, I never had—you knew by the way his moustache twitched whether or not he was smiling.

Now he was smiling. He smiled even more when Dad (the reds always moved first) reached up and slipped one of his men in the front row forward.

Dad had always cautioned me about moving that particular man first. But he did it anyway. Maybe he had something else in mind. You could never tell about Dad.

Sure enough, and to my complete amazement, two jumps later, Dad had punched a big hole in Grandpa Jack's front line of defense, landing one of his men in king's row.

"Crown me, please," Dad said, not as a demand but to tease Grandpa Jack about him being in a heap of trouble with a slash-and-burn king at his rear.

That brought all violent action to a screeching halt as Grandpa Jack reluctantly topped Dad's checker with another. Then he leaned back to finger his moustache, slowly and deliberately this time, to try and figure a way out of the fix he'd gotten himself into.

The laughter of the girls playing hopscotch didn't seem to bother his concentration. Nor did the wild flurry of the boys returning from the barn to pump the well nearby and get themselves a drink of water, cupping their hands to catch the flow.

Dad seemed torn between wanting to watch the kids having fun and keeping his mind in the game.

Then I saw Grandpa Jack's moustache twitch. I knew there was a slight smile underneath as he leaned forward to shove one of his soldiers directly into the path of Dad's king.

Dad took one quick look, then grunted, "Uh-oh."

Grandpa Jack's moustache twitched even more. His watery eyes gleamed.

Dad sighed, leaped the soldier Grandpa Jack had sacrificed and made a give-up gesture with his hands.

Grandpa Jack attacked. Wham. Wham. Wham. One of his black soldiers killed Dad's king and took along two more of Dad's reds with it.

He chuckled as he removed Dad's dead men from the field of battle.

"Give up?" he asked.

Dad laughed. "Do I have a choice?"

Then I knew it was over. Grandpa Jack was champion once again.

There were smiles on my two uncle's faces.

And when Grandpa Jack and Grandma went home, his wide brimmed hat was set back on his head at a jaunty angle, his back a little straighter, and, I noticed, he held the gate open for Grandma like he always did.

She smiled sweetly up at him from beneath her bonnet and murmured a polite thank you as she swept through the gate.

I glanced back at Dad. He had a sparkle in his eye, too, and I knew then who had won the game.

Seven Lessons

I was at the age when girls changed—they changed from being playmates to being people you couldn't understand. They didn't want to wrestle anymore, or play right field (they still liked to bat, but they resented being stuck out in right field where we always put girls), and when you played tag with them, they'd get mad if you tagged them too hard.

And I'd get mad when I argued with them and my voice would suddenly shift to a higher pitch for no reason at all.

I knew something strange was going on, but I didn't know what.

That's why I decided to hide behind the couch that Sunday when my older sister Mazie told the family at dinner that Berle was coming to visit her that afternoon and for Mom to keep us boys out of the living room and not let us sneak up under the open windows and listen.

Just knowing Mom was put on the alert was enough to make you stay away, for she was a stickler for proper social manners.

But I was desperate to find out things I didn't understand.

Long before Berle got there, I slipped away from the gang of boys outside and sneaked into the living room. I hunkered down behind the couch. I had to "hunker" because of the way the couch was positioned against the wall. I pulled myself into a ball, half sitting, half lying, with my knees tight against my chest.

I was cramped and I was hot. But I knew old Berle wouldn't stick around long because Mazie didn't like him, which brought up another perplexing question: Why was he so determined to come courting?

Berle and his family lived down the lane not far from us and Berle had to pass by our house every time he went to school. I thought he was a nice guy, a real gentleman. And good-looking, too—a tall, blond boy who seemed to be sun-tanned the year around. He played every sport the school offered and was good at all of them. Seems as if every girl at school thought he was something special—except Mazie.

I'd watched Berle and Mazie play the game of cat and mouse all through high school. He kept trying to pass our house just as Mazie was leaving so he could walk to school with her. Then she started leaving early and Berle looked so sad having to walk to school with us younger ones.

When he started coming by early, Mazie would be putting on some last minute make up or something and wouldn't leave the house until it was almost time for class to take up.

I thought Mazie must be weird, and I wanted to find out what the heck was going on between them. Maybe it would answer some questions I had about myself.

So there I was, hunkered behind the couch, hot and sweaty, but determined to fill in the blanks of my social education.

"Why, Berle!" I heard Mazie exclaim when she went to the door to let him in. "You're early, aren't you? I wasn't expecting you until—"

"You said two thirty," Berle said, being real gentle.

You could tell by the tone of his voice that he was right and that Mazie was just being difficult.

Lesson, No. 1—Be gentle, no matter what they say.

"Well, perhaps I did," Mazie said. "I've been so busy helping Mom with the Sunday dinner dishes that I simply didn't realize it was getting so late. Here. You sit on the couch. I'll sit over here in this chair until I cool off a bit."

Lesson No. 2—They'll lie to you, tell you anything just to stay out of reach.

I felt the couch move as Berle sat down. I could just picture him sitting there, his hair slicked back, his trousers creased so sharp you could cut your finger on them, and his white shirt so stiff with starch it kept his head propped straight up.

Just when was it girls didn't want you to touch them? No, that wasn't right. They wanted you to *want* to touch them, only they wouldn't let you. It was all so confusing, my head was in a whirl.

I honestly don't believe that either one of them paid a lick of attention to what the other one was saying. When Berle said something, I could hear Mazie's chair rocking. And when Mazie said something, I could hear Berle crossing and uncrossing his legs as he squirmed around by himself on the couch.

I heard my brothers and the guys outside, lollygagging around in the shade. I was beginning to wish I'd stayed out there with them. Hiding behind the couch was no fun at all. It was like sneaking in to see a movie only to find out it was Charles Boyer standing around all the time doing nothing but talking to some girl.

Then the voices of the guys outside faded away. I knew they would be heading for the creek to go swimming or the ball field to play ball or something that was fun.

My legs began to ache so bad I couldn't stand it. I bit my lip to keep from groaning out loud.

I had to do something to relieve the pain before my knees got locked in that position and I'd be a cripple for life.

I could stand it no longer. I simply had to stretch out. I calculated that Mazie's rocker was far enough to the left that she wouldn't see my legs. No matter, I had to chance it.

I didn't make a sound as I stretched out my legs, extending them beyond the edge of the couch.

Ah-h-h, I sighed to myself. I'd never felt anything so good in my life.

What I didn't know was that Mazie saw my legs slowly folding out into view. But instead of yelling for Mom to come get me and switch me good, she started being sweet to Berle.

That mystified me.

Lesson No. 3—Never, ever count on a girl being the same from one minute to the next.

"Well, I'd better go," Berle finally said, polite and gentleman-like.

Oh, boy! I thought. I'll soon be free!

"Oh, don't go, Berle," Mazie said as sweet as you please, jumping up from the rocking chair. "I made some cookies this morning. I want you to taste them."

Oh, my God!

Lesson No. 4—They just lie and keep on lying. Mom made those cookies—yesterday. I suppose Berle will eat the dried-up things and tell Mazie what a great cook she is.

When Mazie got behind the parlor door jamb where Berle couldn't see her, but I could, she turned and stuck her tongue out at me.

Then I knew I was in deep trouble, and I understood why she was being so sweet to Berle. She was keeping him there on purpose to torture me.

Lesson No. 5—They'll figure out how to torture you, one way or the other.

I debated long and hard about surfacing and fessing up to Berle, man to man—counting on him understanding why I was doing what I was doing.

But I just couldn't do it. He was such a nice gentleman and he thought he was making great progress with Mazie after all these years. He would be devastated if he found out. He didn't deserve that.

I decided to suffer it out.

When Mazie came back with a plate full of cookies, she sat down on the couch beside Berle.

While Berle was bragging on Mom's dried cookies, Mazie was being sweet and hanging her arm over the back of the couch and crumbling dried-up cookies in my face.

If you've never tried to keep shaking cookie crumbs off your face without making a sound, you don't know what misery is. And when a crumb got up my nose, I had to fight like the dickens to keep from sneezing.

I raised my head slightly to blink the crumbs out of my eyes and saw Mom beyond the parlor room door scowling fiercely at me.

Oh, Lordy! Mazie had told her what I was doing.

Lesson No. 6—Never trust a girl. They'll tattle on you every time.

Berle wasn't gone five minutes that afternoon before Mom sent me out to the mulberry tree to get her the longest, toughest limb I could find for her to switch me with.

Lesson No. 7—You always get what you deserve.

The Great Candy Store Robbery

I have forgotten everything I learned in the seventh grade except the agony of stealing candy from a candy store.

An old man ran the dinky sweet shop half a block from the school. He wore glasses so grimy you wondered how he could see through them. He had watery eyes, a large nose, and a tiny moustache, and he talked funny. We thought he was German.

His name was Mr. Zeihe. We called him Mr. Z. And when we boys drew airplanes in a dog fight—American Spads against three-winged Fokkers— instead of doing our arithmetic, we'd snicker and say we were going to show our artwork to Mr. Z.

But we never did. He was really a nice man. We all liked him. Sometimes he'd throw in an extra jawbreaker when we bought a sackful of candy.

That's all he sold, candy. The sweet smell overwhelmed you the second you stepped inside the front door. Not only was his seldom-cleaned glass showcase filled with all kinds of candy, wrapped and unwrapped, he placed open boxes of candy on top.

Nothing cost more than five cents. You could buy a double handful of banana caramel squares for two cents. I know because I loved banana caramel squares, and every time I had any money I'd splurge a penny and buy a handful.

That was the year I buddied up with Jackie, a boy who lived across the river south of town. He rode a bus to school. He was the first friend I ever had who I hadn't known all my life.

Jackie was a talker. He could talk himself out of anything in class. I'd watch in awe and admiration at the way he could not only tell our teacher he didn't know the answer to the question she'd asked him, but convince her he was totally justified in *not* knowing it.

You could tell by the look on the teacher's face she loved Jackie's suave charm. She had that peculiar, forgiving smile teachers always have for cut-ups, and you'd shake your head in wonder about the complexities of life.

Jackie was the one who started us drawing aerial dog fights. He was good. All his planes looked real, especially the German planes going down in flames. And he was the one who kept teasing about showing our art to Mr. Z.

I was proud of my new, out-of-town friend who could draw good airplanes. I'd watch for his bus every morning. He always had a big smile on his face and acted glad to see me. We slouched around the school grounds together. He did all the talking. He wasn't even afraid of the girls.

"Let's go down to the candy store," he said to me one morning the minute he got off the bus.

I hesitated. It was almost time to go in for classes. Besides, I had no money and doubted if he did.

"Aw come on," he ordered, gesturing impatiently. "Dad give me a dime this morning. I'll buy you a candy bar. It'll only take a minute."

A whole candy bar! Well, all right, I conceded.

On the way there, he outlined a plan for us to get the candy bars without paying for them. He would distract the old man and I would sneak a couple of candy bars from the open box displays on top of the counter and slip them in my pocket.

I stopped in my tracks. "Uh-uh," I grunted, shaking my head vigorously.

He was talking stealing here. Even if my family never found out, God would, and he would toss me into the devil's fiery pit faster'n you could say spit. Although I was at the age when I began having suspicions about the existence of God and the Devil and religion in general, common sense told me that taking something from someone else without their permission was wrong, as wrong as wrong can be.

Jackie tugged on my jacket sleeve. "Aw, come on. I've done it lots of time. That old man got rich taking money off us school kids. He ain't even American."

Visions of our Spads shooting down German Fokkers popped in my mind. I yielded to his pull, thinking that maybe he'd just talk the old man into giving us some candy. I knew he could do it. I'd seen him operate.

He kept a tight grip on my elbow as we continued on our way toward the candy store. He ran over his plan again. I was a nervous wreck by the time we got there.

The first thing I smelled when we stepped inside was banana caramels. The old man had set a freshly opened box of them on top of his glass show case.

My caution evaporated. He wouldn't miss just two, would he? One for me and one for my best friend?

Jackie went into action immediately. He began pricing the candy bars, skillfully leading the old man down to the far end of the counter where he kept his attention by pretending not to understand the two-for-a-nickel bargains.

Mr. Z acted exasperated as he reared his head back and stared at Jackie through his grimy bifocals and patiently explained his two-for-a-nickel sale over and over again.

I edged closer to the open candy boxes. The smell of the banana caramels grew stronger. My mouth began to water. But my hands would not come out of my pockets. They remained jammed deep, my palms sweating so much I could feel the moisture seeping through onto my thighs.

Jackie kept glancing in my direction with a slight frown. I knew what he was thinking: Grab something, you dope. He even maneuvered so the candy store man's back was to me.

I dragged a hand out of my pocket. It felt like it weighed a ton. I managed to lift my arm high enough so my fingers played along the edge of the banana caramel box. I touched the waxy wrapper on one.

It would be so easy to curl my finger over a couple and slip them into my pocket. The powerful thought of the crime added even more thrill to my deep desire to unwrap a piece of banana caramel and pop it in my mouth.

Rat-a-tat-tat. Down went a three-winged Fokker in flames. I deserved a medal—or something.

Instead, I let my hand drop to hang empty by my side. I took a step back from the candy case. In that instant, it seemed as if I'd grown a little taller, aged another year or two, and I'd found a part of me I wasn't aware of that had pride in myself and who I was.

Jackie cut short his conversation with Mr. Z. He stalked toward the door, jerking his head for me to follow. Outside as we hurried back to school, he said, "I don't even want you walking with me. You're not my friend anymore."

"That suits me just fine," I said, suddenly full of anger—more at myself than at him for letting him talk me into something I didn't want to do. "I'd rather have Mr. Z for a friend than a thief."

He slunk away. We never spoke to one another again.

And I was glad, for I nearly failed arithmetic and would have if I'd kept drawing airplane dog fights instead of getting my lessons like I was supposed to.

The Hair Cut

A bar mitzvah for Jewish boys signifies they have reached the age of religious responsibility, of passing from boyhood into manhood.

I was raised a Baptist. My "bar mitzvah" was a hair cut.

Dad cut our hair when we four boys were kids. I was afraid of him on hair cutting days. He wasn't the same man. He seemed like a mysterious stranger to me. Maybe it was because he worked twelve-hour days in the oil fields—when he could get work at all, and had to come home and do choirs—the most trying one was to cut hair.

During the times he was unable to find a paying job, he'd work from daylight to dark plowing and planting every inch of our little acreage, trying to coax enough food out of it to feed his family. Once he even had to swap his prized model T for a cow and a calf and five gallons of molasses to get us through the winter.

When we saw Dad setting up his barber shop in the kitchen, we boys would huddle in the next room, fussing over who had to go first.

His clippers pulled more than they cut. If his razor was too sharp, he'd nick you with it on the hard spot behind your ears. If it was not sharp enough, it'd feel like he was pulling your hair out by the roots when he dragged it down the back of your neck. You could even hear it dragging and your imagination ran away with you. What was he doing? Skinning you alive?

If you cringed, he'd growl, "Hold still!" And you had to will yourself into immobility.

We all knew Dad didn't like cutting our hair any more than we did. But a quarter was a quarter and cutting four boys' hair saved a whole dollar. A dollar went a long way buying the groceries at the country store to feed us.

But all that lay below the surface of our daily living. When it was that time of the month, it was Dad against us.

First he'd drag a straight-backed chair over by the kitchen window where the most light was. Then he'd take down his cigar box where he kept his hair cutting tools, put on the dime-store glasses he'd bought to read the paper with, and start stropping his razor.

"Okay, who wants to be first?" he'd call out, glaring at us over his glasses.

None of us did. But since I was the youngest, my big brothers would shove me forward first. Why me first, I don't know. Perhaps they thought the world might come to an end before he got to them.

Dad looked nine feet tall standing there by the window stropping his razor and feeling its sharp edge with his calloused thumb.

Oh, Lord, I'd pray. May his razor be not too sharp and not too dull today. Amen.

As I got a little older, moving up the classes in school, I begged Mom for egg money so I could go get a store-bought hair cut. She refused to talk about it.

And it got worse. By the time my brothers left home, and each earned enough money to buy their own hair cuts, I was at the age when I thought the whole world was against me. One of the worst fights I ever got into was when one of the sissyfied uptown boys made fun of my "sugar bowl" hair cut. What made it worse, he said it in front of a bunch of girls who giggled.

To make matters worse, the teacher who stopped the fight blamed me for starting it and gave me a good paddling. The sissyfied boy got off by begging his way out of it with tears in his eyes.

It wasn't two days later that Dad got down his cigar box with his hair cutting tools in it and set the straight-backed chair in front of the window.

I gritted my teeth, straddled the chair, and clinched it until my knuckles were white as he flapped out his barber's apron and pinned it around my neck.

I managed to last through the clipping and pulling, clipping and pulling, but when he started dragging that dull razor down my neck, I snapped.

"For crying out loud!" I shouted and jumped up, knocking the chair over.

Angry tears welling up in my eyes, I ran out the back door. Dad came after me, waving the razor.

"You come back here!" he commanded. "I'm not through yet!"

"Yes, you are," I yelled back at him as I ran around the corner of the house, my barber's apron flapping.

I thought he'd give up the chase by then. He didn't. I headed for the opening to the crawl space under the house. Our dog, Boscoe, got into the act. He thought we were playing a game and came chasing after me, barking and jumping around in circles.

When I dropped to my knees and hit the crawl space opening, Boscoe grabbed the trailing edge of the apron and pulled me back, growling playfully.

"Git!" I yelled and kicked at him.

I saw Dad coming, still waving the razor. I backed into the hole, dragging Boscoe with me. I figured if I could get far enough under the house, Dad wouldn't come after me.

Boscoe was having the time of his life, shaking the apron and growling. When I kicked him loose from the apron, he started barking, still thinking it was a game.

I felt like a treed possum.

"You come out of there," Dad ordered, shading his eyes so he could see better into the darkness. The sunlight glinted off his razor. It reminded me of the huge swords the pirates used in the last sea movie I'd seen.

There was no way out. I couldn't hide here forever and I couldn't go back. I buried my head in my arms and began sobbing like a baby.

Dad called softly to Boscoe. The dog quit barking and went to him.

Things got quiet. I peeked. There was no one at the opening. I could hear footsteps walking across the floor over my head.

Now you've done it, I told myself. I can't stay under the house forever. What are you going to say when you have to crawl out and run away?

There wasn't but one answer.

I wiped away my tears with the now torn and dirty barber's apron and scooted out from under the house. I dusted myself off and marched back into the kitchen. Dad was putting his hair cutting tools back into his cigar box.

"I'm sorry," I said. I searched for words to apologize better, tell him somehow that I loved him and appreciated all he'd sacrificed raising me. But I couldn't find the right words.

In stony silence, I straddled the chair, my back to him. I heard the cigar box pop shut, then his work-callused hand appeared from over my shoulder. A well-worn quarter lay in his palm.

"It's time you start going to the barber shop uptown and get a real haircut."

I stared at the coin. It said it all. I wasn't just a little boy anymore. There was a world out there; I had to go live in it. He'd done the best he could to prepare me for it. Take my inheritance and go.

A little perplexed and totally surprised, I glanced up at him, then back at the quarter. I took it.

"Thanks, Dad," I said.

I got up from my straddle position on the chair, removed the barber's apron and said, "I'll get a job and pay you back."

His back was to me as he began putting away his barber tools. Then his shoulders started shaking.

Was he crying? Stunned, I asked, "Dad? Are you all right?"

He turned, laughing as he took off his dime-store glasses, wiped the tears from his eyes and said, "I wouldn't have missed it for anything—you running to get under the house—old Boscoe barking and having the time of his life—me chasing you with a razor. Suppose any of the neighbors saw us?"

We both laughed so hard, we got weak and had to sit down.

Mom came in and asked us what was so funny.

"Nothing," Dad said. "Nothing at all—just our little baby boy growing up, is all."

"Oh, you two——" Mom said, making a motion with her hand and turning away in a show of disgust.

We became close friends after that, Dad and I. In fact, he was the best friend I ever had.

The Cave

Delaware and other counties in northeastern Oklahoma are blessed with having natural caves, from nothing but deep washouts under a limestone ledge to those that lead you deep into the ground and open into caverns as big as a two-story building.

I've explored only one. While it didn't come close to the only other cave I've ever been in—Carlsbad Caverns in New Mexico—it was impressive.

But none, not even Carlsbad Caverns, compares to the most important cave in my life, the one we dug on a high bank on the shores of Salt Creek in the sandy hills of Creek County.

My big brothers and their friends decided to dig it late one summer when they ran out of anything else to do. I was allowed to tag along because my oldest brother, J.B., thought of the idea, and was the self-appointed chief engineer.

I tramped along behind bigger guys searching for a good spot to dig a cave. We explored Salt Creek from its source in the sand rock hills south of town to where it emptied a mile away into the Cimarron River.

One of the prime considerations I heard them talking about was to keep our cave a secret. I never could figure out who it was we were keeping it a secret from, but I did know that keeping projects a secret made it more exciting.

We—they—decided to dig our cave on a high bank where the creek made a sharp turn to the right. By having the entrance up high like that, our chief engineer said, nobody could get to it and get in it while we weren't there.

"How are we going to get in it ourselves?" argued his friend Neil. I liked to see Neil talk. He had a long neck and his Adam's apple bobbed up and down a lot.

"We'll dig us a secret passage to the woods and cover it with a trap door," brother J.B. said.

So we went back to the house and gathered up the tools we needed to dig a cave—shovels, a mattock, even a five-gallon bucket.

We trekked back to our cave-to-be site and the big guys began digging. My job was to carry the buckets of dirt off somewhere and dump it out were nobody'd see it and lead them to our cave.

Since I couldn't think of anybody who'd give a nickel for going in our cave even if they found it, I didn't go very far into the woods before I simply tossed the dirt out like you'd empty a bucket of water.

They got tired waiting for me to make my round trip, so they commenced tossing the dirt down the high bank and into the creek.

"We'll just damn up the creek and make a moat," chief engineer J.B. said.

A moat on our Salt Creek, everybody agreed, would keep everybody from wading the creek to get to our cave.

When the oil companies cleaned their storage tanks, they would flush the sludge into the creek. As the sludge floated down the creek on its way to the river, it would back up behind obstructions—such as a log or a dirt dam—and stay there until a heavy rain came and the creek would rise and flush itself clean.

You couldn't have a better moat than one covered with two or three inches of thick oil sludge.

Since they didn't need me to carry away dirt anymore, the big guys sent me to find some sheets of corrugated tin. Oil companies used a lot of it around oil wells, building engine houses, belt houses, and the like. If I couldn't find any discarded pieces laying around, I'd pull loose ones off the side of an engine house.

By the time I got back to the cave site, it had begun to look like a cave. Well, not a cave cave—more like an eight-foot hole in the ground about ten feet square.

By then all the big guys had blisters on their hands and our chief engineer decided there was no need to dig a secret tunnel to the woods. Instead, they cut a narrow stairway down the side of the dirt bank from ground level down to the mouth of the cave.

It would at least keep girls from getting into our cave because, our chief engineer pointed out, they would be afraid of missing a step and go sliding down the bank and into the sludge-covered moat.

To support our tin roof, we had to scatter out and find pieces of discarded 2-inch pipe, long enough to span the 10-ft. hole. We came up short and had to take a couple of joints from a pile of new pipe the oil companies had stacked up.

We laid the pipe across our hole in the ground, one every couple feet or so to support the pieces of tin. Then we shoveled a layer of dirt on top of the tin.

Our chief engineer suggested we cut some limbs, gather some leaves and things, and pile them on top.

"It helps hide our cave," he said. More secrecy stuff.

Now we were ready to occupy our cave.

Having to negotiate your way down the side of the bank (which we had started calling a cliff by now) along a narrow stairway made me wish I hadn't come at all.

With one eye on the accumulated sludge on the pond below and one eye on the steps, I made it.

We all agreed our cave was neat. It smelled of fresh clean dirt. The only light came from the entrance. And there was plenty of room for everybody.

To make it more livable, we furnished it with a crude table and chairs. Well, not real chairs—a log for a bench on one side and nail kegs and boxes on the other.

When winter came, our chief engineer figured out a way to put a door over the entrance. He also came up with the idea of setting up an empty oil drum and using it as a fireplace. We cut an opening in the bottom to put wood in and stole some more pipe to use as a chimney.

We had a place to go on cold nights now.

I was assigned the job of going out into the woods and gathering up dead branches and things that had fallen off the trees and breaking them up to use as firewood in our new fireplace.

I was always afraid of being attacked by bears or lions or tigers, or all three, in the woods by myself after dark. I got to where I could scamper down the narrow stairway on the face of the cliff carrying an armload of wood with no trouble at all.

To get the fire going, we used fresh crude we bailed from an abandoned oil well nearby. We'd slosh the firewood with the oil and toss in a lighted match. We even got a big kick out of the way it made a big *swoosh* and we laughed at whoever tried to light it and got the hair on his arm and eyebrows singed by not jumping back out of the way soon enough.

Neil filched a pack of cards from home and the big boys played poker, using matches for money.

I sat in the corner with my knees pulled up watching the fire burn, the jick, jack, joker sounds of poker playing, though loud and raucous, far away in my sleepy mind.

The sexuality in the jokes the big guys told between hands helped me understand what grownups did to have babies because I already knew about bulls making cows have calves, and how cats would have kittens after fighting with a wandering tomcat all night around the house. And everybody knew you had to have a rooster in the barnyard or the hen's eggs wouldn't hatch.

I also learned the meaning of death as I watched the fire feeding on the wood, turning form into nothing ash.

Like when somebody dies—one day you are form, the next day, nothing.

Ours was a good cave...a part of me the same as my arms and legs are. All real now, with form and function, but with the fire of life feeding on them they, too, will one day be turned into nothing but ash.

The Big Tree

The Indian boy lagged behind. He knew he was going to grow big and strong like his father. But until then, there were many things to do.

Like playing with acorns he had found under a blackjack tree.

He had a pouch full of them. He planned to trade them for something one of his little friends had that he might want.

As he followed along behind his family's *travois* across a treeless sea of grass, he opened his acorn pouch and shook its contents out into the palm of his hand.

One, his biggest acorn, slipped through his fingers and disappeared into the tall grass below. He dropped to his knees to look for it. He couldn't find it.

His mother called. He had to run to catch up before they reached the stand of timber. They camped that night beside a clear stream winding its way through the forest.

The boy wept over his lost acorn. His father told him not to cry, to be proud instead because his little acorn would someday grow into a big tree, the biggest tree in all the land.

The boy loved the story and dreamed that night of the day he would return to this place and find his Big Tree out in the field standing tall and strong.

That night a deer stepped on the acorn nestled in the tall grass and pushed it into the ground, softened by a recent rain.

The acorn soaked up the moisture. One side split. A fragile root pushed into the soft earth, a tender shoot struggled upward through the smothering grass in search of sunlight for its shiny new leaves.

As it grew, it felt the thunder from the skies and drank hungrily from the rain.

But there was another thunder that rolled across the land, an intermittent booming that left behind the acrid smell of smoke.

It was the sound of an artillery barrage laid down by Confederate soldiers, trying to prevent the Creek Nation's leader, Opothleyohola, and his band of loyalist from crossing the Cimarron River to escape into Kansas to join up with the Union army.

After that, the blackjack sapling grew undisturbed in peace and solitude for forty years, standing tall—reaching for the sky, basking in its own greatness now.

Creek Indian farmers brought their cows to the field where the lone blackjack grew. They called it the place of the Big Tree. When the sun was high the cows would stand in the shade of the Big Tree and chew on their cuds. Later they would make their way to the creek that snaked through the nearby timber and drink the cool water.

People often wondered aloud why the Big Tree grew where it did, alone like that out in the open.

After the Indians joined with the white man to create a new state called Oklahoma, the Big Tree became a part of that state.

Not long after, a white man drilled an oil well a few miles from the Big Tree and black crude came gushing out.

People rushed in from all over the world to make a claim on the riches. They built a town not far from the Big Tree. The wealth from the oil from that field alone, some said, financed America's Expeditionary Forces in France during the Great War.

One of the oil pioneers, folks called him old M.P., bought the land where the Big Tree stood. In addition to his oil rights, old M.P. farmed the land and raised stock.

To keep his cows from drinking from the creek, polluted now with wasted oil and salt water, he fenced them in with barbed wire. He stapled the strands to the trunk of the Big Tree, saving the need for one fence post.

Old M.P. loved baseball and got up a town team to play other town teams for miles around. They graded off a baseball diamond in the field by the Big Tree.

Cars beat out a road through the grass to the baseball field out by the Big Tree as people came to watch their husbands, brothers, and fathers play ball on Sunday afternoons.

My best friend, Basil, and I used the ball field too. During the lazy days of summer when there were no ball games and we got tired of looking for arrow heads along the creek, we would sometimes lie on our backs under the canopy of the Big Tree and watch Gods of War forming in the puffy white clouds, or a good likeness of John Wayne riding on his chestnut horse with a white mane.

We saw an Easter Bunny, a bear, a noble Indian.

I saw a beautiful girl's face with long flowing hair, but I did not tell Basil that. I just watched in yearning silence as the beautiful face grew old and wavered away.

We spotted a bird's nest on one of the limbs of the Big Tree. We climbed the rough barked trunk and peeked in the nest.

It had four naked birds in it, their necks stretched upward, their yellow-framed beaks wide open. We scurried to the ground, got a shovel, and dug up some earth worms.

With a fist-full of earth worms, we climbed back up in the Big Tree and dropped the wiggling worms into the gaping beaks and laughed the way the tiny birds swallowed them hungrily until their beaks didn't open any more and the naked bodies relaxed into balls, their big eyes blinking sleepily.

One Sunday after the baseball crowd went home, I saw the corner of a green piece of paper sticking up out of the dust where the cars went in and out.

I picked it up. It was a $5 dollar bill. I ran home as fast as I could and busted into the kitchen yelling, "Mom! Mom! Look what I found! A five dollar bill!"

She was not happy having to tell me it did not belong to me. And she made me take it to town and give it to old M.P.

I hoped against hope he would let me keep it. Or even give me a dollar for bringing it to him.

Instead, he took the $5 bill and patted me on the head and said I did the right thing.

Next day when Basil and I met under the Big Tree he asked what I was going to buy with my $5 bill. Nothing. Mom said it belonged to old M.P. and she made me give it to him.

Basil laughed. Your Mom's crazy, he said.

I flew mad. I beat him up there under the Big Tree.

At least in my mind, I beat him up. The fact that I got a bloody nose and a black eye and a split lip had nothing to do with winning or losing. I just whipped him, and that's the truth.

That night it came up a storm, a big one. I happened to be looking in the direction of the Big Tree when a bolt of lightning stabbed out of the clouds and cracked down on the Big Tree.

It's a goner, I thought, blinded by the flash. But the next morning, there it was standing tall, a fresh scar running from top to bottom down one side.

Way to go, I told myself, admiring the Big Tree's toughness. It struggled to cover its ugly scar before dry rot got in.

Down low, unnoticed by anybody, the trunk swelled and swelled each year, pulling the strands of barbed wire deeper and deeper into its heart.

I went away, married, and had a family of my own. Whenever we visited the folks over the years, I always noticed the Big Tree was still there, but now showing its age.

Squirrels ran in and out of its hollow center. Over half its limbs were dead.

And then one day, I returned to the old home place with my grandchild to show her where I grew up, and tell her the stories she loved to hear.

The Big Tree was gone, blown down, the neighbors said, by a wind not strong at all. It was the barbed wire in its heart that had weakened it, they said. And the cruel lightning scar.

Even the bustling oil field itself had dwindled down to one or two wells. And the creek had washed itself clean, as clean as the day when Indians camped there, a family with a little boy and his pouch full of blackjack acorns.

I told my grandchild the story of the Big Tree, and she wanted to do what the Indian boy did—find an acorn so she could grow her own Big Tree.

The Snipe Hunt

Elzie and Alfred, the Montrose brothers, were always pulling tricks on people. How they found the time to pull jokes on people while all the time sharecropping with their Dad to keep their large family fed I don't know.

Elzie was the oldest, a tall, reasonably good-looking young man with uncombed dirty red hair. He had slate-colored, mystic-looking eyes. I was fascinated by the methodical manner with which he chewed tobacco.

Alfred was short, red-headed, and freckled-face. He was chubby and laughed a lot.

Both brothers were older than me, Alfred a year or two, Elzie three or four.

"You ever go snipe hunting?" Elzie asked late one fall afternoon when we were lazying around with nothing to do.

"No," I answered, wary. I could almost tell by the looks on their faces they were up to something. "What's snipes?"

I noticed the way they exchanged knowing glances. Made me feel dumb.

"They're pretty birds," Alfred said, trying to suppress a giggle.

I didn't want them to think I was *totally* ignorant, so I said quickly, "There aren't any around here."

"I bet there is," Elzie said, mystic eyes narrowing. "They're real shy. Not many people ever see one."

"Really?" I asked, my interest rising.

"This is good country for them," Elzie said looking around. "They like river bottom country. Tall trees."

"Especially cottonwoods," Alfred said.

Elzie nodded. "Yeah. They like to catch that cottonwood fuzz that comes off the trees. They use it to line their nests."

My imagination kicked into high gear. A bird so shy that hardly anybody has ever seen one and catching cottonwood fuzz for their nests. I always wondered why God would make cottonwood trees. Its wood wasn't good for burning or

anything else, and they shed fuzz all over everything. Now I had the answer—
He did it for snipes so they would have soft fuzz for their baby birds to sleep in.

"I wouldn't shoot one if I saw one," I bragged.

"Oh, me neither," Elzie said quickly, eyes widening in horror. "What I'm talking about is catching them alive."

"How do you do that if you can't see them?" I asked, my curiosity growing.

You take a gunny sack, he explained, and go out into the woods just before sundown. It has to be someplace where nobody is likely to be around. Then you hold the gunny sack open in front of you and stand real still.

"Standing still is the most important part," he emphasized. "If you make any moves atall, they won't come around."

"Then what happens?" I asked.

"Snipes like to roost in gunny sacks because they're soft—like cottonwood fuzz," he said. "They'll come out of the sky and fly right down into your sack."

"Really?"

"Then when you get a goodly number in the sack, you clap it shut."

I shook my head in wonder and disbelief.

He added, "You can sell live snipes. Anybody'll give you a dollar for one with purple feathers on it."

"Honest!"

He nodded. "The hens—that's the she-birds—have lots of purple feathers. They're the ones that like soft things. Catch a few of those and you got it made."

"Wow!"

He and Alfred sat silent for a long moment. My mind raced.

"I know a good spot," I said.

"Well now, Alfred, run out to the barn and get this kid a gunny sack—and make sure it don't have no holes in it. I'd hate it if we gave him a sack with a hole in it and all the birds would get away."

Alfred took off for the barn. Elzie asked, "Now just where is this place at you was thinking about?"

"Down by the river," I said, breathless. "I bet there's a million snipes down there. We can—"

"You have to be alone."

That sounded all right with me. No use splitting the money. So I just described the place while we waited for Alfred to return with the gunny sack.

When he did, I examined it to make sure it didn't have any holes in it and rolled it up and put it under my arm.

"I bet I can catch a whole sack full," I boasted

"You won't if you move around any," Alfred warned.

I headed for the woods. The spot I chose was on a low bluff with a grand view across the river valley. I had in mind that if I had to stand real still holding the sack for very long, I could at least enjoy the view and make up stories I would write someday.

I tip-toed into position, shook out the sack quietly, and held it open in front of me. With one last wary look around, I stiffened to attention.

Even if I caught just two snipes with purple feathers and sold them, I would have enough dimes to see all fifteen chapters of the new Buck Rogers serial starting this coming Saturday and I'd have lots of money left over for other things.

I could get one of those new gliders made out of balsa wood which you could throw and it'd make a high loop and glide to a smooth landing. I would buy one for my brother and we'd have lots of fun looping them at one another pretending they were in an aerial dog fight in the war with German planes.

Or if I got enough snipes, I might ask Mom to order me that pocket watch out of the catalog—the one "just like all conductors use to keep the nation's trains running on time."

I would save some of the money so I could buy everybody in the family a nice Christmas present and I would enjoy seeing the happy look on their faces when they unwrapped the gifts Christmas morning.

I thought of so many wonderful things I could do with the money as I stood like a statue holding the opened sack in front of me.

I could hear birds singing as they searched for their roosting spots and tried to identify each. I didn't think a snipe would be able to see my eyeballs move, so I enjoyed the fall colors—all golds and browns and reds and yellow—lying like a beautiful multi-colored blanket over the hills.

The setting sun added its own golden hue, ever-changing as it sank lower and lower in the sky. Soon its restless rays left the hill tops and leaped into the sky to burnish the edges of the wispy clouds.

A flock of high-flying geese, struggling to keep its V formation in perfect shape, made a lazy circle and swooped down to land somewhere in the backwaters of the river to eat and rest. Tomorrow, they would take off early and continue their wandering journey southward.

Where do they come from? Where do they go? More importantly, how do they *know* where to go—and *when* to go?

I promised myself to look it up in the library.

Someday, I might even have my own book in the library. I would write a western. My opening lines would be: *Tom Morgan rode his white horse down the fence line, looking for a place where the rustlers had cut the wire and spliced it back—*

A squirrel in my line of sight started down a nearby tree trunk head first. He spotted me and froze, head out, big brown eyes glistening and tail jerking. Then when I didn't move, he began scolding me as if to try and make me do *something*.

I refused to move. Suddenly he went quiet. He looked to my right. Something must have gotten his attention. Then he scampered back up among the tree limbs and bounded away through the branches.

He must have heard something. Then I heard it!

My scalp tightened. I tingled all over. Was it the soft song of a snipe with purple feathers? Then I heard it again. It sounded like a smothered giggle.

I shifted my eyes just in time to see Alfred's red hair as he jerked his head back behind a tree.

My first reaction was anger. How could I catch any snipes with him and Elzie out here making all kinds of noise?

Slowly it came to me that I'd been made a fool of.

"Aw-w-w, you guys," I called out as I folded up the gunny sack. "There's no such thing as a snipe."

They came out from behind the tree doubled over laughing.

My anger dissipated and I laughed with them. They were such lovable cons—the kind it's impossible to be angry with.

Besides, my hour of solitude with nature was far more precious than a whole sack full of snipes with purple feathers.

A Gift for Arnold

Old Doc Phillips came out of the room in that pigeon-toed walk of his and grunted in a low voice to Mom and Dad, "It's pneumonia."

Mom's gasp was quick and sharp. A deep hurt spread across Dad's face. They moved away from us kids, their voices muted and hard to make out.

I knew what pneumonia meant. You die. They all did. Arnold couldn't. I was older than he was, a little over a year. I forced myself to smile when I slipped into the room where Arnold was. His face was as pale as the starched pillowcase under his head.

"What do you want for Christmas?" I asked, pretending indifference.

His already bright eyes glistened even more. "That airplane. The one with the yellow wings."

I nodded. We'd looked at it one day, pressing our noses against the plate glass window at the store. The picture on the side of the box showed that it was a World War I fighter biplane. It had a red body and yellow wings. It cost a dime. I didn't have one, and he knew it.

"I can make one," I suggested.

"Can you? Really?"

The excitement started him coughing.

"Sure." I was confident.

It was cold, even for December. I hunkered down in the sun on the south side of the house and went to work. Whittling out a propeller was the hardest part. I didn't have much time, but I wanted it to be just right.

I heard a distant drone from the sky. Airplane! I ran around the house to find it, heart pounding. It was what we always did when we heard an airplane—even getting up from the dinner table to run outside and look.

There it was—a biplane, just like the model Arnold and I looked at in the store.

But instead of going on over, the plane circled. Its motor quit. It began gliding toward Lauener's wheat field across from our house.

I could see the pilot peering over the rim of the cockpit, his aviator cap pulled tight over his ears, his goggles glinting in the sun, his white scarf whipping in the wind.

He's going to land!

The plane's wheels cleared the fence by inches, then hit the rough ground, bounced, hit again, and the plane rolled to a stop.

I tore through our front gate and climbed over the screeching barbed wire fence and raced toward the plane.

The pilot struggled from the cockpit, lifting his goggles. I skidded to a halt, panting heavily, now embarrassed.

There, with one leg over the cowling and a big smile on his face, the pilot seemed suddenly bigger than life…unapproachable. I wanted to turn and run the other way when he jumped to the ground, his aviator boots shiny against the green of the winter wheat.

"How about that, kid? I made it!" he said and laughed. I trembled, still clutching my half-finished propeller in my tight fist. He glanced down, saw it.

"You making an airplane?" he asked.

My face felt hot. I nodded, swallowing heavily. My hand was shaking when I held it up to show him. He took it and examined it carefully.

"Hey, not bad, kid," he said and handed it back.

By then others were coming, kids running, cars coming up our road from town.

The pilot held up his hands, announced, "No cause for alarm, folks. My radiator froze. Engine overheated and conked out. You got a mechanic here?"

Several sang out John Hull's name. He could fix anything.

The pilot placed a strong hand on my shoulder, leaned down. "Do me a favor, will you, kid? Watch my plane for me. Don't let anyone bother it while I go get help."

"Yes, sir," I said, my voice coming out in two squeaks.

Somebody offered to drive him. The curious remained, walking around the plane. None of us had ever seen a real airplane up close like that.

I took up my position as trusted guard, still clutching my propellor, defiant but uneasy with my awesome responsibility.

Jack Doolin ignored me and stepped up on the lower wing to peer into the cockpit.

He was two years older than me, which made him a grownup in my mind.

"Hey," I shouted, yanking on his pant leg. "He said for me not to let anybody touch it!"

"On your way, pip-squeak," he said, kicking my hand away.

Anger flooded through me. I bear-hugged his legs, and yanked. He came tumbling down on top of me.

Before I knew it, he was straddling me on his knees and pounding me in the face. Some of the grownups rushed in and pulled him off. He stomped away, cursing at everybody.

I didn't realize my nose was bleeding until I got to my feet and felt the hot liquid running down my upper lip. I kept trying to swipe it away with the back of my hand. A man handed me a handkerchief.

The same man told the pilot when he returned what a good guard I was, and about the fight.

The pilot said, "Thanks, kid." Then he and Mr. Hull went to work. It was almost dark before they had it fixed. Most of the crowd had gone home. The pilot told the rest of us to come back in the morning and watch him take off.

That night, Mom was more angry with me for having green stains on my clothes from wrestling in the winter wheat than she was over my bloody nose. I promised not to anymore.

I went in to tell Arnold all about the airplane. His eyes shone. He giggled when we talked about what-ifs—what if he'd take us up in his plane when he got it fixed? What if he never came back and Mr. Lauener would give the plane to us? What if we could grow up and fly it ourselves?

Arnold's eyes drooped, then closed. He coughed lightly in his sleep.

The next day half the town came back to watch the take off. The pilot enjoyed having an audience. He strutted, snapping the ear flaps under his chin as he prepared to climb into the cockpit. He paused and waggled a finger at me. I crept forward. He looked like he was a mile high standing over me tucking his white scarf into his leather jacket.

"Thanks for guarding my plane, kid," he said. He dug in his pocket. "Here's a little something to pay for the fight."

He pressed a dime into my outstretched hand.

"Merry Christmas," he said, laughing.

Stunned, I didn't even have time to say thanks before he turned away and climbed into the cockpit. He waved.

"Merry Christmas everybody!" he sang out.

"Merry Christmas!" all the people shouted, including me.

Mr. Hull spun the propellor. The sudden roar of the engine shook my insides.

The prop blast blew loose wheat-grass in our faces as he began moving down the field.

I squinted into the wind blast, rising to my toes as the plane's tail lifted, mentally helping the pilot get the thing off the ground.

The wheels lifted, just barely clearing the barbed wire fence.

We all cheered and clapped our hands. He circled the field and gave us one final wave before sailing away, disappearing into the distant blue.

I ran to the store. I gave the man my dime and hurried home with the cellophane-wrapped box.

I put it together in my secret working place. I tried to hurry, yet I wanted it to be just right. I was extra careful cutting the balsa wood with a single-edge razor blade, making sure every piece was glued in place just right. I stretched the tissue paper taut over the frame, careful not to let too much paste show.

At last I was finished. It was the best model airplane I ever put together. Grinning sheepishly, I held it behind me when I went in to see Arnold.

"Guess," I said.

"The airplane!"

I nodded, wondering how he knew, and handed it to him.

"Merry Christmas," I said. I tried to make it sound as joyous as the way the pilot's greeting had sounded.

His eyes grew wide as he reached for it, and his touch fiery hot when he took it from my hands. Making a weak motor sound with his mouth, he flew the plane back and forth, back and forth, back and forth, his arm getting weaker and weaker.

Then he flew away in his red airplane with its yellow wings, disappearing into the distant blue.

A Painless Death

The news story told how many dogs and cats the animal shelter had befriended within the last six months, how many had been adopted out, how many had been given a "painless death."

Painless?

Well, perhaps. Death itself is painless. But only where there is no love.

Sitting alone at the table reading the early morning newspaper and sipping my coffee, I fought back a tear and reached for a napkin to wipe away a sniffle.

The death of Boscoe still hurts, after all these years.

He was my first dog. The thought that he would die someday was the furthermost thing from my mind when I carried him home.

I hugged him to my chest, his overgrown paws flopping. He had a very distinct markings, black all over except for a snow white cross on his chest, and white paws. I hadn't yet decided what to name him. Then it came out of nowhere.

"Boscoe," I blurted aloud.

I cooed down into his blinking eyes, "How'd you like to be called Boscoe?"

He looked up at me out of those big puppy eyes as if to say, "Oh, pul-leese!"

It was so real that I busted out laughing. He cocked an eyebrow.

Then I ran through all the other names people use for dogs as I walked along. Boscoe grew limp. He wasn't interested. Nor was I.

"All right," I grunted, shifting him about in my arms. "Then Boscoe it is."

He cocked that eyebrow again.

Dad was waiting when I got home. We'd argued over me getting the pup. I was at that age when you suddenly discover how stupid your parents are.

Our neighbor living down in the Cimarron River bottoms stopped by one day and told us their old bitch had a bunch of mongrel pups and they were trying to get rid of them and asked did I want one. I clapped my hands and looked up at Dad and asked, "Can I?"

"I thought you said you wanted a bird dog?"

That set me off. Of course, I'd said that, but that didn't mean I meant it did it? If I wasn't old enough to go hunting by myself yet—according to him—why hold me to something I didn't mean?

Dad seemed nine foot tall when I saw him standing at the front gate waiting for me to come up with my mongrel pup.

Although secretly intimidated, I boldly held the pup up so Dad could see him.

"I'm going to call him Boscoe."

He shook his head.

"Now that you got him, you make sure you take care of him," Dad said, his words more of a threat than a caution.

"I will."

I put Boscoe down, laughing at the way he wobbled when he tried to walk. But when he sniffed at the toe of one of Dad's boots and lifted a leg, I panicked.

"Here, Boscoe!" I scolded, leaping to grab him.

Too late, his tiny squirt made dark spots on the leather. I glanced up, full of fear and ready to apologize all over the place. I thought I caught a slight smile somewhere behind that perpetual scowl before Dad turned away, saying nothing.

Boscoe grew fast. He romped and played with me, chasing sticks, leaping, barking, until he wore me out. Then he'd back away, his big eyes begging, his long red tongue lolling out, drooling. He'd bark happily as he waited anxiously for me to play with him a while longer.

His huge body never got enough food. I'd carry all the table scraps to him on a platter. He'd catch bits of the food in mid-air as I raked the scraps from the platter into his large aluminum pan.

He'd devour his meal in big gulps, scoot his pan across the concrete porch by licking it clean with his tongue. Then he'd race to block me from going back inside as if to say, "Come on, buddy. You've got more in that plate. Don't hold out on me."

And Mom often slipped him pieces of leftover pie when she thought nobody was looking.

Boscoe loved to go hunting, barking wildly and turning in circles whenever Dad and I stepped out of the house with the shotgun. But too often, just when Dad or I had a good bead on a rabbit bounding away, Boscoe would suddenly pop into sight, running like the wind to catch the rabbit and, of course, blocking the shot.

One day Dad said, with a trace of disgust in his voice, "That dog likes to chase rabbits more than he likes to hunt. You two go on without me. I've got better things to do."

After that, I didn't care how Boscoe hunted. He was responsible for ratcheting me up one more notch toward manhood—earning the right to hunt alone—and I was grateful.

I missed hunting with Dad. Boscoe did too. I saw him move quietly to where Dad was sitting one day in the shade of the huge elm in our backyard and nudge his hand with his nose. Dad smiled, reached out, and began scratching him behind the ears. You could tell Boscoe enjoyed that more than anything in the world—even chasing rabbits.

I figured Dad couldn't be all that bad if Boscoe thought he was such a great guy. It's funny how within a couple of years your parents can change from being so utterly stupid to so divinely wise.

Boscoe followed me everywhere, trotting at my heels. Only he didn't like going to town. Town dogs bothered him. They'd come yapping from out of people's yards, snarling, hackle hair erect, and sniff at his behind. Boscoe would tuck his tail and try to hide behind me. I was ashamed of his actions and I let him know it.

One day he tagged along when I went to the grocery store for Mom. Jake was at the store sitting in the shade of the store's covered porch talking with friends. His dog, King, lay at his feet, head on fore paws, relaxed but alert. He was a tough brute, half bulldog and half you knew not what—wolf, some folks claimed.

Alarmed, I stopped in the middle of the road. Boscoe, on my heels, bumped into my legs. Jake always bragged that King could whip any dog in the county, and liked to tell stories of challengers left dead after a furious dog fight.

The men stopped talking and looked my direction. I decided there was nothing to be afraid of. We weren't provoking a fight. I moved on.

King's ears came up as we approached. The hair on his back stood and a muffled, menacing growl rumbled from deep inside him as I stepped upon the porch. Boscoe stumbled on my heels, trying to hide from the belligerent King.

The men laughed at Boscoe's timidity. I was ashamed.

"Get on home," I commanded, pointing.

Boscoe looked perplexed. Just then Jake stomped his feet on the planked flooring. Boscoe yiped, turned tail, and scooted away. He stopped in the middle of the dusty road, peering back to see if anybody was chasing him.

The men laughed.

"Get on home." I yelled at him.

He lowered his head and gave me that begging, sideways look and refused to go back home. I left the porch and stomped angrily toward him, yelling, "Get! I said!"

Suddenly, Jake made a hand motion to King and said, "Sic 'im!"

King boiled off the porch and bounced past me stiff-legged toward Boscoe. Boscoe stood his ground, a slight snarl curling one lip. I panicked. I ran to the dogs, now circling warily. I kicked King and screamed, "Get! Get out of here!"

King whirled on me, those sharp teeth snapping at me. I backed away, stumbled, and went down. King pounced on me. I threw up both arms to protect my throat, and screamed for help.

Suddenly, a bundle of black fury came out of nowhere, tangling with King and sending him rolling in the dust. I scrambled to my feet and ran for safety on the porch as the two dogs began fighting furiously.

King got a death grip on Boscoe's throat, threw him down and began shaking him for the kill. I could hear Boscoe gasping for air. His frantic struggles grew weaker.

"Get!" I screamed.

I ran to get back in the fight, kicking at King. But a strong hand grabbed my arm and pulled me away.

"Better stay out of this, kid," Jake said, a grim look on his face. "It was your dog that jumped on mine."

Jake's killer dog had my Boscoe on his back, his jaws in a death grip on Bosoce's throat.

I knew Jake's old King would kill my Boscoe if someone didn't stop it. Jake, an older boy than me, was holding me back.

I yanked to get free of Jake's grip, couldn't. Then I saw Boscoe's big hind paws come up, catch King's underbelly and send him rolling.

Boscoe scrambled to his feet, weak, blood streaking the white cross on his chest. He braced, snarling. King found footing and returned to the attack, but hesitated when he saw Boscoe's angry stance.

Hypnotized, I quit struggling to get loose from Jake's grip and watched as the dogs circled.

King was more respectful now. He strutted, his blood-tinged teeth bared, his snarls rolling from deep inside. Boscoe waited, his head low.

Prickly tingles raced up my spine. My hair felt as if it were standing on end.

This was it, I knew. I tried to yank free again to go save my dog. Jake hung on, laughing uproariously. It was futile. He was too strong for me. Helpless, I watched in horror as the two dogs circled for the kill—King snarling, arrogant, with his head held high, Boscoe wary and bleeding badly now from the gashes King had already made in his neck and chest.

King lunged, a sharp fang ripping another long gash in Boscoe's shoulder before Boscoe could dodge. Boscoe's jaws came up from underneath, clamped on King's throat. King gave a little surprised yelp just before Boscoe lifted him high in the air and slammed him to the ground, shaking him like a rag doll.

Jake's let go of me and ran toward the dogs yelling, "Get! Get!"

He kicked Boscoe again and again with his heavy shoe. But Boscoe would not let go.

"Call him off! He's killing my dog!" Jake yelled at me.

I didn't know what to do and stood frozen like a statue. Then Boscoe lifted King high into the air and threw him into the roadside ditch. He turned on Jake, his red teeth bared, his deep growl meant business.

Jake eyes widened in fear. He backpedaled rapidly to get away from the advancing Boscoe. I jumped between them.

"No, Boscoe," I scolded.

Boscoe halted, a surprised look on his face. Then he gave all of us a disdainful look, turned and limped toward home, leaving a trail of blood.

He didn't understand. I ran after him.

"Here, Boscoe!" I kept calling.

He trotted faster, keeping his distance from me, ignoring my pleas. His big paws kicked up little puffs of dust tinged red.

He loped through our gate and crawled under our house. I hunkered down, looking under. I begged him to come out. I pleaded for him to forgive me. All I could see were those sorrowful eyes, eyes that accused me—and all the others—for creating a situation he wanted no part of.

Dad came from the barn.

"What're you doing?" he asked.

Swiping away a tear that I didn't realize was there, I told him about Boscoe's fight with King. Dad laid a sympathetic arm across my shoulders.

"Is King all right?" he asked.

"I don't know," I snapped angrily. "I hope he's dead!"

"Here, now," Dad said. "Don't talk like that. Jake loves his dog as much as you do yours."

"It wasn't Boscoe's fault. Jake sicced King on him."

"Oh, he did, did he?"

I wasn't in on the conversation the next day when Jake came and demanded that Dad pay for Boscoe killing his valuable fighting dog, but I could guess. Jake got a tongue-lashing he'd never forget. He acted meek as a lamb when he turned and walked away.

With Dad's help, we finally coaxed Boscoe from under the house. He could hardly stand, his infected wounds ugly and draining. Heartbroken, I tried to hug him. He growled me away, his unusual reaction telling me my touch hurt in a hundred places.

He refused to eat and made only a few attempts to lap some water. He grew weaker and weaker, spending more and more time sprawled on the porch, still as death. After Dad made his examination one morning before going to the fields. He backed away, his face grim.

"He's breathing hard. His fever is up. I don't think he's going to make it."

My eyes misted. I swallowed hard. I knew what Dad was going to say before he said it.

"You know what you have to do."

Yes, I knew. The terrible responsibility crushed my heart. I nodded. Dad patted me on the shoulder.

"Death is part of life. You can't have one without the other," he said and headed for the barn.

I went into the house, dug the family's sixteen-gauge from behind the cupboard, pocketed a couple of heavy shells and went back outside.

Instead of Boscoe coming running, leaping for joy when he saw the gun like he always did before, he lay there, his eyes shifting from the gun to my face.

"Let's go, boy," I called to him softly.

His tail thumped the porch feebly a couple of times, but he refused to get up. His tired eyes shifted to Dad coming from the barn. Dad had a shovel.

"Be sure and bury him," he said, handing me the shovel. "Most people don't bother. It's a hard thing to do. But you'll feel better afterwards."

"Yes, sir," I said, attempting to make my voice sound strong and grownup. I shouldered the shovel and started to call Boscoe again. But there was no need. I could see it in his eyes. He knew. He rose painfully to his feet and waited, as if to say, "I'm ready when you are."

He limped after me, as I went down the road heading for the river, the shovel over one shoulder and the shotgun in my other hand.

When I talked to him, he'd roll his eyes up toward me obediently, before shifting his gaze to the shovel, then the gun, then back to the road ahead.

At the river, I halted twenty paces from the four-foot sandy bank and stabbed the shovel blade into the soft earth so it would stand alone.

Strangely, Boscoe did not stop. He limped on to the bank's rim. He paused, stared for a long time across the muddy Cimarron River at something high on the hill on the other side, then turned to face me, his head up proudly. The breeze ruffled his long hair, making the heavily scarred white cross on his chest shimmer.

I clamped my teeth, set the gun stock against my shoulder and sighted down the blue-black barrel. Boscoe's image beyond my sighting bead melted in my blurred vision. My hand was trembling so much when I thumbed the hammer back that I could barely get it locked into a cocked position.

I felt the narrow toggle of steel resisting pressure from my trigger finger. I filled my lungs, held my breath, and squeezed harder. The gun exploded, kicked hard against my shoulder. I heard a distinct grunt before Boscoe leaped high in the air, did a backward somersault and disappeared over the edge of the sandy bank.

It seemed an eternity before the sudden stillness was shattered by a booming echo of the shot from the hill beyond the river. I prayed I would wake from this horrible dream and see Boscoe come bounding over the bank, leaping and loving. The echo was gone now, and the stillness returned.

Now would be the hardest part—dragging the lifeless body and tumbling it into a hole in the ground.

Clenching my teeth and trying hard to be a man, I broke the gun open and ejected the smoking shell. I inserted another load into the gun's gaping maw—just in case. Resolutely, I snapped the gun shut and moved forward, hoping with all my heart that he was dead and not just wounded. I peered over the bank's edge.

Nothing. A sandy clod, disturbed, slid down the slope and was immediately swallowed by the muddy waters of the Cimarron.

Both stunned and apprehensive, I looked downstream, my gaze following the sluggish current. Nothing, not even any tell-tale signs of blood showing in the naturally rusty water of the Cimarron. It was as if Boscoe had simply vanished from this earth. How could it be? One instant you're here, the next…gone?

I turned away, thankful tears flowing. I wouldn't have to bury him.

And to this day I still think Boscoe knew…

There's no such thing as a painless death.

Section II

You Learn a Lot in High School

The day after Labor Day I approached the high school building filled with an excitement edged with trepidation.

Now it was my turn to attend the big school, to be one of *them*, where football players swaggered up and down the hall, where pretty girls with red lipstick on and painted fingernails laughed all the time.

I'd always loved school, from the first grade. I had no trouble with my lessons, but in high school I knew you had to learn things not found in books.

A cool breeze swept over me as I walked into the spacious entrance for the first time as a pupil.

It was scary. So many new faces crowding around. It was like going into first grade all over again. I could have used an old friend. I searched frantically for Carrie.

She had always been my friend from that day in the second grade when the school bully caught us, Carrie and me, making mud pies.

When he started teasing me for playing with a girl, Carrie helped me whip him. He ran away crying and told the teacher.

All three of us were sent to the principal's office. I got whipped with a big board paddle for fighting and Carrie had to apologize to the bully.

Mud pies, hop skotch, birthday parties, hide and seek. We had fun together, Carrie and me, going through grade school. We even got into a fight once when I pulled too hard on one of her long golden ringlets.

But we made up before the year was over and chose one another to be partners at the maypole dance. She was beautiful in her yellow dress with its big bow on the back. And red shoes on.

I gripped her hand tight to keep from doing anything wrong as we skipped around the pole in time with the music, going inside and out of other partners, holding our streamers of crepe paper and weaving a colorful pattern down the big iron post.

The crowd clapped when we stopped and Carrie smiled at me. Somehow, the perspiration on her face made her even more beautiful.

Best of all was the feeling of her warm, moist hand in mine. She gave me a special squeeze. I never forgot.

But things changed in Junior High. Carrie got older faster than me, even grew taller. I felt awkward when we'd meet accidentally on the school grounds and found myself looking up at her.

Besides that, she began acting silly, she and her friends. They huddled in groups, giggling, falling strangely quiet when an older boy walked by.

It was a mystery.

We boys ignored them and played touch football and tore the knees out of our overalls and were sweaty and dirty when it came time to go in for classes.

That first day in high school, I couldn't find her in the strange faces floating all around... maybe her folks had moved away.

Well, forget it. You like books better anyway, I thought, trying to console myself.

And I did find my classes exciting. Literature, biology, wood working, engineering drawing, music, typing, social sciences, history. I loved writing themes, making book reports.

The first time I saw Carrie, we passed in the hall. I hardly recognized her. Her blond hair was cut short and she wore lipstick, but not much.

She was looking up at the football player she was with and laughing.

She didn't see me. I couldn't hold that against her. I worshiped football players myself, always dreaming I could be one.

But I was way too little to play. When classes were over and the football boys went out to practice, I would go to the town library and browse the shelves trying to find an interesting book to check out.

Sometimes I would wander into the back room where they kept pulp magazines stacked so high they'd be falling over. I liked to read the westerns and the World War I stories about fighter pilots shooting down German planes that had three wings.

And sometimes I would skim hurriedly, feeling guilty, through one of the Romance magazines, reading the parts where the man kissed the girl and I would sigh and say to myself, "So that's how you feel."

Carrie saw me one day. She smiled and I smiled back. I didn't bother to speak because I wasn't always sure how my voice would come out, squeaky or down low.

We passed on by. That was okay. By then, I was used to girls in my classes treating me that way because I was so small for my age. There were no lingering looks, no thrilling exchange of locked glances, no special smiles.

Even the boys who carried little nickle pornographic books depicting explicit sexual activities of comic strip characters teased me about being too young to look at them.

So I quit paying any particular attention to Carrie as one year rolled into another. I couldn't help but notice, however, that she went out with different guys from time to time.

In our senior year, Carrie and I had an English class together. I sat in the back of the room where boys always sat, and she sat towards the front. I stared at the back of her head a lot, feeling a stirring inside I couldn't understand.

I thought of her more and more for some reason, especially at nights in bed and alone in the dark. But she was different in my dreams. Friendly. A lot of fun—like when we made mud pies.

She must have felt me staring at her, for she turned quickly and caught me doing it.

I was so embarrassed that I felt my face getting hot and knew I was blushing. She smiled—laughing at me, I knew—and I ducked my head, ashamed.

When the bell rang, I scooped up my books and hurried out the door, wanting to get lost in the crowded hallway.

"Dale?" I heard her soft call.

I stopped and turned to face her as she came up to me. I expected her to be angry because she'd caught me staring like some idiot. But there was a pleasant smile on her face. I was shocked to be looking down at her now. I tried to stretch myself even taller.

I noticed, too, that my voice sounded low and stayed there.

She asked if I had my book report yet for our English class. I said no, but I'd planned on getting it before long. She said she hated to write book reports. I told her I liked doing things like that.

We talked easily and freely as we walked down the hall together, her hugging her books to her chest and me trying to keep mine balanced in one hand. I couldn't keep from staring down at her.

It was the same face I remembered seeing beside me making mud pies, the same blue eyes, the same smooth complexion. But now there were no ringlets to pull. Instead, the blond tresses looked so soft it made you want to reach up and stroke them.

There was a certain glow in her face. It didn't take a genius to figure that out. She was a woman now. Her body was different, all rounded out in places that made it hard to breathe when you looked at them.

"This is my next class," she said, stopping by a door. "It's biology. I hate it."

I stopped to commiserate with her, shuffling my books about awkwardly. We still had a few precious minutes before the next class took up and we spent it talking hurriedly, saying nothing in particular. When the final bell rang, I turned to leave and she reached out and caught my arm.

"I miss you," she said simply.

I stared down at her for an hour it seemed, trying to find something to say, like:

Why don't we go have a Coke after school?

Or just a plain old, *I miss you, too.*

The blood pounded in my ears. My lips worked, but nothing came out.

Then she whirled away and was gone.

I didn't hear a word the teacher said in my next class. When the bell rang, I snatched up my books and hurriedly pushed my way through the hall crowd to the door of the biology room.

I made it in time and was waiting when she came out, hugging her books. She smiled up at me.

There's a lot of things to learn in high school not found in books.

A New Year

"Be sure," Miss George cautioned in our one o'clock English class, "to date the themes I've assigned you to write over Christmas holidays nineteen hundred and forty."

Nineteen hundred and FORTY!

I gasped. The mere thought stunned me. It had been nineteen hundred and thirty-something all my life, ever since I could remember.

As she continued with her instructions, the groans coming from the back of the room where most of the macho guys sat swelled louder and louder. We were, after all, seniors. Seniors—especially boys—shouldn't have to write themes.

I groaned too and rolled my eyes toward the ceiling. I didn't want any of the guys to know I loved Miss George and her theme assignments.

She was a frail woman with graying brown hair. Her sparkling blue eyes behind her gold rimmed glasses always seemed to be laughing, even when she'd get angry at one of us.

Most of the guys called her Old Miss George, but you could tell they all liked her and were only trying to live up to their image as the rough and tough bunch who wasn't suppose to like school at all.

How could you not like a teacher who spent the first fifteen minutes each day reading passages from some classic novel like *The Count of Monty Christo* or *A Tale of Two Cities*?

The only trouble was that after lunch like that with her voice droning on and on, it would make your eyelids heavy and your neck would go limber and you'd be forever jerking your head erect and forcing your eyelids to open.

One way she had of waking us up would be to jump up from her desk and break out singing "Boomer Sooner." She would even wave her hands like a choral leader to get us to join in.

That very night at home, I dragged the small writing desk I had made the year before in manual training over to the window where there would be plenty of light, dug out some notebook paper, and began writing.

"1940 marks the end of an era," I wrote. "The thirties are gone forever—"

I paused and chewed on my pencil eraser, thinking. And the more I thought, the more scary it became.

I would graduate from high school next spring. I would truly begin a new life. What would I do with the rest of my life?

I knew what I wanted to be—a writer. But I had no idea how to be one.

Ever since I could remember being a being at all, I tried to describe things as I saw them, wanting others to share in the joy I felt at that particular moment, like looking at a beautiful sunset. There are no two alike. So you better describe it just right because it'll soon be gone forever.

How could I explain my feeling about this new era—the forties? Would the world be any different? It certainly would be a good time to change things— correct our faults, if you had a mind to. I didn't have a mind to. I thought I was all right just like I was.

My brain kept spinning out of control.

After the forties, there would be the *fifties*, then the *sixties* and on and on. It was then I realized there is no way to stop the years going by.

How about New Year's Eve nineteen and ninety nine? Oh, wow! When the clock struck twelve at midnight, it would be *two thousand!*

Impossible. What would the world do without having the nineteen somethings around?

Would I live to see the year 2000? Doubtful. I figured it up. I would be 77. Oh, Lordy! *Seventy-seven!* I doubted if my own Grandpa was that old, tottering along on his daily morning walks to town to pick up the mail.

Now I am there. I don't chew erasers on pencils anymore, thinking. Instead I stare blankly at a computer screen which is just daring me to put words on it.

While I might be like Grandpa was in 1940, I don't feel like it inside. I have the same wonder and awe about the years two-thousand-and-something that I did about the year 1940.

I just don't have Miss George around anymore to keep assigning me themes to write—and leading us in spontaneously singing "Boomer Sooner."

Odd how things never seem to change as each New Years Day carries us into a different year.

It never dawned on me in 1940 that a little man with a little moustache called Hitler on the other side of the world would affect my life.

Hitler's armies were breaking out of Germany and overrunning Europe. His fiery speeches to his goose-stepping army was scaring the world to death.

Every time he made a speech—they'd carry portions of it live sometimes on the radio—you could almost visualize a wild man frothing at the mouth. And each time he paused, you could hear the giant crowd thundering, "*Seig Heil! Seig Heil!*"

And today, on New Year's Day 2003, there is a big man with a big moustache called Saddam Hussein sneaking around from palace to palace in Iraq not saying anything but is still scaring the world to death.

On New Years Day 1940, Hitler meant nothing to me. Why be concerned? Hey, he was over in Europe and I was in Oklahoma. No way would what he said or did affect my life.

There were lots more important things in my life then than the rantings and ravings of a little man in Germany with a funny looking moustache.

But as it turned out, that little man with a moustache affected my life big time—and the lives of millions of others like me.

I read the results of a survey once about individuals in the history of mankind who had more influence on the greatest number of people. I was shocked to learn that Hitler ranked higher even than a carpenter named Jesus.

The survey was careful to point out that "influence" didn't necessarily mean for the good. "Influence" can go both ways. It works to the negative side as well as the plus side. In that respect, I suppose Hitler did affect a greater number of lives than anyone, at least in his own lifetime.

Some people estimate that he set in motion the events that killed 20 million people, most of them young men in their 20s.

What amazed me was how popular he was. All the Germans loved him. Even people in other countries thought he was doing a good job for his people.

And he was able to increase his popularity by promoting racism. We all know now by his example that once racism is set in motion, there isn't but one ending. He called it the "final solution." Which was, we know now, the gas chamber for a certain blood line.

The strange thing was that Hitler was able to hold onto his power until he relinquished it himself by committing suicide. His ministers and generals carried out his orders even when they secretly disagreed with them.

You can't disagree with a popular leader in your own country. Popularity has a way of rolling over you like a two-ton tank and squashing you into the ground.

This New Year's Day 2003 I am reading newspapers and watching television reports of the world playing cat and mouse with a man named Saddam who likes to fire a rifle from the balcony of one of his palaces to excite his people.

How is it possible, I think, that this can happen—one man affecting the lives of everybody else in the world?

It seems that although the years keep rolling over one another, there are always weird little men with weird moustaches somewhere in the world who think of themselves as the saviors of their people—and those who don't think so are eliminated.

I had fun writing that theme for the new era—1940. And Miss George gave me an A—but I didn't tell anybody. I just groaned and rolled my eyes toward the ceiling like all the other boys did when they got their graded papers back.

I hope you enjoy this little theme I wrote during the Christmas holidays of 2002—even though we're all watching yet another "savior" on the other side of the world and wondering how he's going to affect the lives of each of us.

Seems some things never change, do they?

The Barter System

You go to the store. You select an item, make your purchase, and go home. You take your item out of the plastic bag and notice it has a flaw. You check to see if your ticket is still in the bottom of the bag. It is. Good. You take your item back. You exchange it or get a refund.

It's a good system.

We used another system of exchange once—bartering. It worked, but reversing the process sometimes got to be a problem, as Happy James learned the hard way.

He was a teenage buddy of mine who lived with his family on a farm down the road farther from town than where we lived.

I was sitting on the couch in the living room reading a book one warm summer day when I heard Happy's shrill whistle.

I knew who it was. We all had our own distinctive way of whistling to call out our friends. It was more convenient than knocking on doors. None of us could whistle like Happy did. He could pucker up and curl his tongue behind those big buck teeth of his and let out a whistle you could hear for half a mile.

The story I was reading was Stevenson's *Treasure Island.* I wanted to finish it and tried to ignore Happy's whistle. But he kept it up.

With a sigh, I laid down my book, looked out, and was mildly surprised to see Happy with his family's team and wagon.

Now what?

I sauntered out. When he saw my puzzled look, his wide, toothy grin spread all over his thin face which was covered liberally with freckles, a distinguishing physical characteristic of his family. They were all tough, stringy farm folks. The men wore wide straw hats and neck bandanas to keep the sun from burning the tops of their big ears and the backs of their slender necks.

"Come go to town with me," he said, jiggling the leather reins nervously, impatient. "Daddy wants me to peddle some fresh roastin' ears and green beans."

It sounded like a legitimate errand. Still, I hesitated.

"I'll let you drive," he said, offering the reins and grinning mischievously. Oh, wow!

I scrambled up, settling in beside him on the seat. I reached for the reins. He jerked them away.

"The mules are a bit skittish in traffic," he said. "You gotta know how to handle them. I'll let you drive coming home."

He snapped the reins to get his team of mules in motion.

He'd tricked me. I considered jumping off. But that was Happy—always pulling a fast one, just for the heck of it. Maybe he would let me drive on the way home. I stayed put.

"Daddy gave me a bushel of beets for myself," he said, a tinge of excitement in his voice.

"A whole bushel?" I asked in disbelief.

He nodded proudly. "They look nice, too. But they're pithy. Daddy was going to throw them to the hogs. I said I'd like to have them to trade for something in town."

Happy's enthusiasm was infectious. I felt as if I were sharing in his wealth. I forgot about his little trick to get me to come along.

Bartering was an art, I knew, because I'd tried it. But my experiences had been small time—trading up or trading down to get the sack of marbles you wanted, a better pocket knife, even a straw hat, if you were lucky, for a kite you'd built but didn't fly very good.

But taking on the merchants in town… that was big time stuff for a teenager.

"What do you hope to get for a bushel of beets?" I asked.

"Two bushels," he corrected.

"You said —"

"Yep. I said it was a bushel." He thumbed over his shoulder. "I divided it into two sacks. Them city folks won't know the difference."

You had to hand it to Happy. This was going to be interesting! Fun, too.

In town, we drove the alleys. Each time Happy took a sampling of his corn and beans and disappeared into the rear doors of the businesses, he'd let me hold the reins.

I waited, proudly holding the team, imagining myself the stagecoach driver in one of John Wayne's movies.

Sometimes Happy let me drive if we were only going to move forward a few feet to the next business. I couldn't wait until we headed home and I'd get to drive.

It didn't take him long to get rid of the corn and beans. If he couldn't get cash, he'd swap a peck sack full for something—a jar of honey, a poke of flour, a box of crackers.

When he had taken care of his family's business, he was free to dispose of his beets.

We retraced our route. Happy ran in and out of business places with renewed enthusiasm. He was working for himself now. Even though he couldn't make a deal, he wasn't discouraged. In fact, he seemed to be getting a delight out of matching wits with hard-hearted men who kept their cash registers closed unless they were putting money in.

Then we came to the rear entrance to Mr. Guidio's shoe repair shop. Happy pulled up.

"I need a new pair of shoes," he said. "Here, hold the team. I'll only be a minute."

This time he wanted me to go in with him to change his luck, he said.

He whip-tied the reins on the wagon's brake arm and hopped down. I followed.

Inside, Mr. Guidio told Happy he didn't want to spend any of his hard-earned money on beets. Happy told him he would swap him a whole bushel of beets for a pair of shoes. They were fresh-dug beets at that.

Mr. Guidio thought a minute.

"Tell you what, young man," he said. "I have a couple of shoes a man left to have new soles put on them. He never came back to pick them up. I'll swap them for the beets."

"Let me try one on," Happy said. "If they fit, we've got a deal."

He pulled a shoe off the shelf and let Happy try it on. It fit. He grinned at me and said, "See? I told you that you'd change my luck."

Then to Mr. Guidio, he said, "Give me the other one. I'll wear them home. You can wrap up my old ones."

"Let me see the bushel of beets first," Mr. Guidio said.

Happy slipped the shoe off, put his old one back on and led the way, grinning broadly, out the back door. He dragged one sack of beets out of the wagon and handed it to Mr. Guidio.

Mr. Guidio hefted it. "Is this here a full bushel?" he asked, peering over his grimy reading glasses at the other sack.

"Sure is," Happy said. Then he looked at me sharply to not let on that each sack contained less than a bushel.

I got the message and kept my mouth shut as Mr. Guidio, a suspicious look on his face, shook his head then said, "Well, all right. A deal's a deal. Let's go in and get your shoes. I'll wrap them up for you."

They both disappeared into the shop.

Good, I thought, climbing back upon the wagon seat. Now we can go home and I'll get to drive.

I unknotted the reins and sat waiting.

Soon, Happy came out the back door in a bit of a hurry. He had his shoes, wrapped in brown paper, tucked tightly under one arm. He scrambled upon the seat and snatched the reins from me. He slapped the mules' rumps and down the alley we went. I grabbed the edge of the seat and hung on.

"Hey," I warned. "Don't you think this is a bit too fast for city driving?"

He kept slapping the mules, urging them to go faster.

"I got to get out of town before that old man finds out I beat him out of half a bushel of pithy beets."

I was disappointed that I didn't get to drive home.

When he pulled to a stop in front of our house, he said, "I think I'll put on my new shoes here. My Daddy'll be surprised when I come walking in with new shoes on."

His smile kept getting wider and wider as he eagerly unwrapped his new shoes.

They were beautiful...both for the left foot only.

Gun Control

My Mom and Dad, George and Lula Denney, had followed work in the oil fields but finally settled down for good in Oklahoma on a little acreage in Creek County to raise and educate their growing family. Whenever Dad found work drilling a well for an oil company, they'd have extra money to spend.

Dad had always wanted a good small game gun. So he bought one—a little double barrel .410 with a full choke. Brand new—light, well balanced, and accurate. Only a few of these were ever manufactured and sold.

Mom was shocked when he brought it home.

"George, are you out of your mind?" she snapped. "With all these young boys in the house—"

It was frightening to see Mom, a diminutive woman with her long hair tied up in a bun behind her neck, standing up to Dad, who was a big, balding, barrel-chested man with a red face.

He stubbornly insisted that he was entitled to at least one foolishness in his life and promised her faithfully that he'd teach us boys how to handle a gun, so that no harm would come of it.

Whenever I got to go hunting with Dad, he'd let me shoot squirrels with his new gun, carefully coached, of course. He assured me that when I got older he would let me hunt on my own.

Always when we returned home, Dad would clean the gun and oil it well before he put it back in the corner behind the buffet.

To placate Mom's feelings over having the gun in the house, Dad would always caution, "Don't any of you boys ever ask me if you can use it."

We honored his request because—well, because he was Dad and if you didn't do what he said, he had a way of punishing you without ever laying a hand on you that was worse than a good beating.

And we all knew how Mom felt about having a gun in the house. Touch that gun and you might cause a divorce in an otherwise very strong marriage.

But one day Jake, one of my best friends, came by with his rusty single-shot twenty-gauge and his rabbit-hunting dogs. He wanted me to go rabbit hunting with him.

Somehow, I got the feeling he was rubbing it in—he had a gun and I didn't.

"I don't know," I said. "Dad's working. Mom's gone to the Ladies Missionary Circle at church. They gave me a bunch of stuff to do while they were gone."

"Aw, come on. We won't go far. We'll get back before they do."

Still, I hesitated. Jake added, "I'll let you shoot my gun. We'll take turns."

"I won't have to shoot yours," I bragged proudly. "I'll just take Dad's gun."

Surprised, Jake watched as I boldly dragged the little .410 from behind the buffet.

"Let's go," I said, and headed down the road with Jake toward the oil lease.

This was my first hunt with my "own" gun. I tried to keep from acting too excited to keep Jake from hoorawing me.

Soon, Jake's dogs jumped a rabbit and chased it under the derrick floor of an oil well. Jake and I raced to the well, yelling at one another, both too excited to pay any attention to the well's pumping jack, its large concrete block counterweight on the backside going up and down with each slow stroke.

Jake got on one side and I got on the other. I dropped to my knees to peer under the derrick floor. I was holding Dad's .410 in my left hand, butt on the ground, barrel pointing up.

While looking for the rabbit I inadvertently tilted the .410, moving its muzzle just enough to slip it into the downward path of the concrete counterweight. Down came the heavy block, slow and easy, settling onto the end of the gun barrel and gently but firmly bending it into a smooth arc to a near perfect ninety degree angle without kinking either barrel.

That same instant, the dogs flushed the rabbit. It took off toward the creek. I whipped Dad's .410 to my shoulder, only to discover the muzzle was pointing at my feet!

The rabbit got away. Jake turned to ask me why I didn't shoot. There I was, stunned, staring at the barrel of my gun, now bent like a wet noodle.

Jake roared with laughter.

We finally puzzled out how it happened. Jake thought it was extremely funny. I sure as the heck didn't. I had to face Dad. On the way home I kept toying with the thought of running away—to China or somewhere.

But that was out. I had no money and I didn't know how long it would take to get to China. I might get hungry before I got there.

There wasn't but one way out—tell the truth. Jake, still laughing, suggested I tell Dad I fired both barrels at once and it got so hot it just melted down.

I tried to get Jake to stay with me until Dad came home, thinking there'd be safety in numbers.

"Not on your life," he said. "I'm getting out of here."

It took a while after Dad came home for me to tell him. I went over a thousand apologies in my mind. None fit the occasion. But I knew the longer I put it off, the worse it was going to get. I finally pulled the gun from behind the buffet and held it up.

Mom gasped. Dad stared, mouth open. But before I could say a word, Dad asked critically, "Where did you get that old thing?"

All my manly apologies evaporated into thin air. By acting like the gun was not even his, and refusing to even discuss the matter, Dad's mental punishment was worse than a flogging.

He was also suffering mental anguish, I knew, because of the severe I-told-you-so look on Mom's face.

Crushed, I put the gun back behind the buffet, vowing never, ever to lie, cheat, or shade the truth, ever again.

Miraculously, I thought, the family held together. Nobody ever said another word about the gun. But when squirrel season rolled around again, Dad dragged the bent shotgun from behind the buffet and tried to straighten it.

Mom kept telling him to just, "throw that old thing away."

Dad stubbornly kept at his blacksmithing. He did a commendable job, but simply couldn't get all of the hump out of the gun's barrel. So he sawed it off in the middle of the hump. That gave the barrel a slight curve upward at the end, but it would shoot.

He kept hunting squirrels with it. All he had to do was remember to aim a little low. And Mom, without saying a word, would dutifully cook all that he brought home.

But she nearly went berserk the day Dad shot our old milk cow.

The cow was forever poking her head through the rear barnyard fence to nibble on the grass on the other side. She would keep stretching her neck farther and farther, pushing more and more of her weight on the strands until she damaged the fence.

Dad tried everything he could think of to break her of this bad habit. Nothing worked—until the day we were sitting at the table eating dinner when Dad glanced out the window and saw our cow poking her head through the fence, her rear facing the house.

"That dad-gummed cow—!" he growled as he jumped up, stomped into the living room, and grabbed up his sawed-off shotgun.

Mom panicked, yelling, "George! George! What do you think you're doing!"

She tried to stand in his way. He pushed her gently to one side, stepped out onto the back porch, took aim—low, of course, to allow for the upturn at the end of the gun barrel—and cut loose with both barrels.

Following the ear-shattering "boom" from the porch just outside the kitchen door, there was a loud screeching of the fence as our cow, stung by the pellets all up and down her rear end, fought to get her head back on our side of the fence where it belonged.

Dad knew the distance was too great for the scattered squirrel shot to break the skin.

But Mom didn't know that. It was days before she'd even speak to him again.

I think what brought her around was the fact that our cow never stuck her head through the fence again. And we all settled back into a peaceful routine around the house.

Gun control is a good thing—me and our old milk cow both learned a lot about that.

Thanksgiving Love Story

I simply couldn't help it. I was in love with cousin Faye—one of those long-range affairs. Her folks lived in Kentucky, mine in Oklahoma.

She came every Thanksgiving with her family, all the way from Kentucky. They'd stay several days. Faye was a couple years older than me, but we would have lots of fun playing together.

It was all right to fall in love with her, I kept telling myself, over and over, because you had to go a long way back to connect our families. She wasn't really my cousin. Fourth, maybe. Something like that.

I thought she was the cutest girl in the whole wide world, and got prettier every year.

She had long dark hair, dark eyes, and lips that I couldn't keep from staring at. She had a habit of repeatedly parting and closing them—like she was nibbling on my very soul. If I didn't make myself look away, I'd get so worked up inside that I couldn't breathe.

Faye and I exchanged letters—silly stuff. But as time passed, they got less silly. Then her letters stopped altogether. So did their visits. It had been three years.

So it was sort of a surprise when they sent a postal card and said they were coming. They had a new car, Aunt Louise wrote, and they were wanting to take a trip.

I read Aunt Louise's hurried scribbling on the way home. I was walking on air when I handed the card to Mom. She read it aloud to the rest of the family. I tried not to show too much joy because I didn't want anybody to know I was still in love with Faye.

Everybody was delighted they were coming, and we all started doing things to get ready—cooking, fixing up, making plans.

The closer it got to Thanksgiving, the more nervous I became. I knew Faye would be more filled out now. I hadn't done bad myself, growing up, I mean.

Funny how one year you are an awkward, pimply-faced string bean and a couple or three years later you could pitch hay right along with the rest of them.

Then a horrible thought hit me. Would she even come this year?

I prayed over and over: Oh, Faye, please come.

Now that we are grown up—almost, I said to myself—we can talk about grown-up things instead of doing kid things like sailing homemade boats in the creek down below the house and wading after them, me with my overalls rolled up and you with your dress tail tucked up under the elastic edge of your panties.

On the day they were supposed to arrive I pretended to be tightening wires on the front gate so I could keep an eye out for the tell-tale sign of a dust cloud coming down the road. I tightened every wire on that gate twice before I saw the dust cloud coming.

I was so excited I accidentally cut my finger on a barb. I was trying desperately to stop the bleeding when the brand new '40 chevy sedan stopped in a swirl of dust in front of our house.

I didn't have time to get a bandage. I snatched a leaf off a nearby lilac bush and wrapped it around my finger.

Aunt Louise slid out from under the steering wheel, smiling and waving. She came hurrying toward me, arms outstretched.

I was shocked when I saw it was Faye instead of Aunt Louise.

She'd bobbed her hair and was wearing a silly little hat. She had on a gingham dress with a wide starched white collar.

And she was wearing high heels!

I back-pedaled.

"I'm bleeding," I warned, holding up my stuck finger with the lilac leaf wrapped around it. "It's liable to get on your dress."

"Oh, you poor dear," she said, edging close. "Let me see."

By then all of my family had spilled out of the house and all of her family had climbed out of the car and there was all kinds of back-slapping, hugging, and cheek kissing going on.

Faye took my hand, her soft fingers caressing my skin.

"It's nothing," I boasted. "I just cut it, is all."

I tried to pull my hand back, but she held on. She unwrapped the lilac leaf and examined the cut. It had already stopped bleeding. Her perfume set my senses spinning.

"What happened to your hair?" I asked.

She glanced up, her dark eyes teasing me from under her long lashes.

"I cut it off. Do you like it?"

"Uh. Yeah," I stammered. "Yeah. I guess so. I—I was kinda used to it the other way. Long."

She laughed and then, without warning, threw her arms around my neck.

"It's so good to see you," she said.

Her warm body against mine was a feeling I'd never felt before, a real scary feeling.

"Yeah, you too," I said after gulping twice.

I wanted to hug her back, but I was afraid I'd get blood on her pretty dress.

She backed away, laughing, holding my hands. She looked so beautiful all dressed up, and there I was in overalls with a lilac leaf wrapped around a bloody finger. I nervously tried to brush down the hair that was always sticking up in my cowlick.

After our monstrous Thanksgiving dinner and everybody was sitting around talking to one another in a sleepy monotone, Faye and I walked outside. She'd traded her high heels for some loafers.

"Let's go for a walk down by the creek," she said, hooking her arm in mine.

"All right," I said.

It was a beautiful fall day, warm and sunny. It was one of those rare autumns when the foliage color was simply perfect.

"So, what have you been doing lately?" she asked.

I liked the feel of our arms linked, her body against mine. I tried to keep my emotions under control.

"Nothing much. Just helping Dad on the farm. Graduated from high school this year."

"How about a girl? You have a girl yet?"

My face suddenly felt hot. I scowled, looking down at her upturned face. "Naw."

"Really? Don't kid me now." Then she laughed and said, "You're blushing!"

I looked away. "No, I'm not. I—I'm just so full of turkey and dressing I can't see straight, is all."

By then we were at the creek. "Is that where we used to sail boats?" she asked, pointing.

"Yeah."

"That was so much fun."

She led me to a spot where the grass was still green. She sat down and pulled me down with her. She broke a wand from a nearby fern and tickled my face with it.

"Cut that out," I said, seizing her hand. She made no effort to pull away. I held on. Even when I relaxed my grip, she let her fingers lay in mine.

She didn't say anything for a long time. I didn't either. Then we talked about how red the leaves were on a sumac bush, about the minnows wiggling in the water. She told me about enrolling in college but not yet knowing for sure what she wanted to be.

All at once I had this feeling we were strangers coming together for the first time. I looked at her and I knew without doubt that I was in love with her, and wondered if she was with me.

After several hours, we headed for the house, holding hands. They would be leaving soon. I just had to tell her how I felt. I stopped.

She turned to look up at me, a question on her face.

"I love you, Faye," I blurted.

She smiled, patted my arm, and said, "You're sweet." Then she stood on tip toe and kissed my cheek.

"I love you, too," she said. "You've been my favorite cousin ever since I can remember. Some day, I hope you can come to Kentucky and meet Howard."

My breath caught.

"Howard?" I gasped.

"He's the boy I've been going with all through high school." She laughed. "He says he wants to marry me. But I don't know if I want to or not."

We walked on and she told me all about Howard. I was too crestfallen to hear anything she said. The next day when they all climbed in their new chevy sedan, Faye called out the window to me, "Write me. Okay?"

"Okay," I said, nodding.

I never did. I don't know what ever happened to cousin Faye.

Or Howard—damn his soul to hell.

The Romancing of Lizzie

I fell in love with her instantly. She was a single-seater, standing tall on her skinny wheels, daringly exposing her rear end.

I stroked her wing-like fenders, walking around, enjoying the intimacy of her touch. Her tires were sound, thumping true when I kicked them.

The little engine under the hood was no bigger than Mom's sewing machine.

Richard was asking ten dollars for her. Eddard and I had pooled our money—six dollars. We pretended reluctance to buy.

I wanted her badly. She would be perfect for Eddard and me to go to school in. We were big boys now—seniors. He lived on a farm down in the Cimarron River bottoms.

We'd talked. He would keep it at his place and would come by and pick me up every morning.

"Want to try her out?" Richard asked. He grabbed the crank and went to the front.

Eddard nodded and slid into place under the heavy wooden steering wheel. I scooted quickly onto the seat beside him.

"You crazy?" I whispered. "Neither of us know how to drive."

"I can do it," he muttered. "I've watched others."

Richard inserted the crank through a hole in the radiator. He gave it such a hard spin that it bounced the front end.

She coughed, as if she had a bad cold, and started shaking all over.

"Adjust the spark," Richard called, running around to help Eddard reset the spark and gas levers on the steering column until they had the engine chuck-chucking just right—like Mom's sewing machine.

"Take her for a spin," Richard said. "But watch out for highway patrols. I didn't tag her this year."

Both joy and fear romped through me as Eddard began manipulating the pedals with his feet.

Somehow, he managed to press the correct pedal and soon we were going lickety-split down one of the many dusty roads that laced the oil fields in Creek County, doing fifteen miles an hour easy, dust boiling up behind.

We talked on the way back. Where could we get another four bucks to buy her?

Richard was waiting, grinning. Eddard leaned out.

"We'll give you six," he said. "Cash money."

His bold offer took my breath away. Even more surprising, Richard said, "I'll take it."

I counted out the money with trembling hands and we left, proud new owners of a real Model T. We were calling her our Lizzie before the day was out.

The minimum on license tags was twelve dollars—twice what we paid for her. Forget the tag. We'd stay off the highway.

Our gasoline was free. We ran drips at night. These were drain traps in pipe lines carrying raw gas from wells. Cool night air condensed fumes inside the pipe. The liquid dripped into a reservoir. Workers collected the unrefined gasoline every so often and hauled it away.

It was against the law to tap drips, but we did it anyway.

You never knew what quality of gas you were getting. But Lizzie's little engine, we learned, would burn anything, from liquid as clear as coal oil to thick stuff as dark as molasses.

And, we found out by accident, she really didn't need any engine oil. When she developed a knock, we drained her oil into a rusty syrup bucket and dropped her pan so we could tighten her rod bolts.

Working underneath, Eddard inadvertently kicked the bucket over, spilling the oil.

Undaunted, we filled the crankcase with water. Lizzie ran just fine until we found enough used oil to replace the water.

Eddard taught me how to drive. What a thrill it was feeling Lizzie respond beautifully to my every desire. My love for her deepened.

And she was a big hit at school. Guys would pile on, sitting on the fenders and standing on the running boards so jammed up it made you wonder how Lizzie could carry all of us, chugging around town.

She became an even bigger hit when we wired onto the high voltage side of the coil and grounded it to Lizzie's frame. When you were sitting in the car, you didn't feel a thing. But if you were standing on the ground and touched the car, it gave you one hell of a jolt.

The guys had fun bringing their girl friends and having them grab the door handle. The girls squealed from the electric shock and everybody laughed.

Even our superintendent's arrogant dog got into the act. He came sniffing around and lifted a leg to wet on one of Lizzie's skinny wheels.

The instant the stream of water hit the hub, the dog let out a yelp and took off running, yapping wildly, his tail tucked between his legs.

Everybody doubled over laughing. It carried over into classes. Someone would make a little yelping sound and set off a new round of snickering. Frustrated teachers tried to stamp it out but failed miserably.

The superintendent was furious. Eddard and I barely escaped suspension. But Lizzie didn't. She got barred from the school grounds—permanently.

It was sad having to leave Lizzie all alone parked on a side street somewhere while we walked to school.

To make her feel good, we rounded up a gang that Saturday to go fishing.

"Let's see how fast she'll go down the highway," Eddard boasted.

I held onto my hat as Lizzie gathered speed. I yelled out the window for everybody to keep a lookout for highway patrols.

The guys hanging on whooped and hollered. Eddard grinned and pushed the gas lever higher. I was exhilarated. I sensed that Lizzie felt it too, like a wild stallion turned loose.

Then one guy whistled and pointed. There it was—a black and white patrol up ahead.

Eddard whipped onto a side road without slowing down. Lizzie dug in her skinny wheels, kicking up plumes of sand as she made the turn.

The excessive weight of guys hanging on almost turned us over. Eddard fought to bring her under control.

The next thing I knew we were sliding sideways toward a deep ditch, a high bank on the far side.

Kids started leaping off, tumbling and rolling in the dirt. Lizzie's right wheels skidded into the ditch and her top plowed into the high bank. Shattered glass sprayed all over me. Then it was quiet.

Eddard managed to get his door open. Those of us still inside the cab climbed out.

We were lucky. The kids standing on the running board on that side would have been crushed if they hadn't jumped.

We all pushed and tugged until we got Lizzie out of the ditch.

My heart was broken. Lizzie looked a sight. Her top was pushed to one side, her windshield broken, her side glass in splinters.

"Let's see if she'll run," Eddard said, voice full of doubt.

He set the spark and gas. I cranked her. To my surprise, the motor started, but sounded funny—like she was sobbing.

We dropped the gang off in town and Lizzie made it on her own to Eddard's place down by the river.

After surveying the damage, Eddard said, "Why don't we just get a hacksaw and cut her top off? It won't hurt the running of it none. Make a sport coupe out of her."

Might as well. We worked all day, laughing some, crying inside mostly. Lizzie just sat there, patient, rocking from side to side on her high wheels as we sawed and hammered.

We had a coupe, all right, after the amputation.

"Let's take a spin uptown in our new car," Eddard said.

I could tell he wasn't happy. I know I wasn't. He set the spark and gas. I cranked and cranked until I gave out. Not even one single sputter. I leaned on the radiator, gasping.

I knew it was useless. Eddard did too. Lizzie wasn't the same. We'd done her wrong.

We talked. We could store her in the barn. But her tires would go flat. She'd be covered with bird droppings in no time at all.

Neither of us wanted that for her. So we hitched a plow horse to her and towed her across the pasture to the edge of the ten-foot-high, sandy river bank. We unhitched the horse.

Grim-faced, Eddard said, "Okay. Let's do it."

We pushed. Lizzie resisted, finally yielding to our determined, grunting pressure, gathering speed.

She went over easily, then disappeared beneath a swirl of muddy water. A few drops of oil surfaced, spreading rainbows.

Neither of us spoke as we turned away.

We didn't want the other to hear words that we knew would catch in our throats.

Our romance with Lizzie had ended.

The Power of Prayer

I knew something strange was happening in our neighborhood when I let Mary Boston walk home with me after church and all the guys teased me about it.

There was no need of that. We'd all been playing the same games together all our lives, hadn't we? The only difference was we were growing up—sort of. We'd developed into a gang of boys with gangly arms whose hair wouldn't stay combed and girls with long legs and bony knees who always got mad every time you touched one of them.

Mary's family lived on a farm farther from town than we did. She'd always seemed more quiet, more serious than the rest of us. She had straight black hair, cropped below her ears. Her eyes were so dark, you felt like she could look right through you and her skin always stayed a soft brown, summer and winter.

All I did was give her permission to walk home with me when we left the church. I was getting old enough that Mom didn't gripe at me too much when I didn't stay for the regular services after morning Sunday school or evening BYPU (Baptist Young People's Union) class.

"Sure," I told Mary when she asked. "We're both going down the same road, aren't we?"

I left her at my house and let her go on home alone.

I always felt comfortable with Mary. She wasn't silly like the other girls, giggling over nothing. But just the same, getting teased over a girl was a terrible burden to bear.

I began dodging her. I'd either wait until she'd already passed our house going to church before I went, or I'd go early and be playing with the other guys in the church yard by the time she got there.

She tricked me one evening by going early then waiting for me at the big tree halfway to town. There I was, hurrying so I wouldn't be late for my BYPU class, when she stepped out from behind the tree.

"Why are you mad at me?" she asked. She was like that. No beating around the bush. Just come right out and say it.

"Who, me?" I was always coming up with something brilliant.

"What have I done?"

"What are you talking about?" I said, trying to act surprised.

"You know very well what I'm talking about," she accused as we continued on our way to church.

I denied anything was wrong. How in the world could you confess to a perfectly good friend, especially if she was a girl, that you were afraid of her because the guys would tease you about being with her?

We just barely made it to church before the final bell for BYPU class rang. I broke away from her and mingled with the guys tromping up the stairs to our classroom. The boys always scrambled for the seats in the rear, as far away from the teacher as we could get.

I made up my mind to skip regular services that evening for two reasons: One, I knew Mary always stayed for the preaching, and, Two, in summer time like this, you'd always have time to play mumbly peg or some other game with some of the guys before it got too dark.

Of course, there was a third reason—a secret I'd never told anybody.

My imagination ran wild when I walked home by myself after dark. I'd see all kinds of threatening beings behind the trees and fence posts.

There were times when I'd hear sounds that made my hair stand on end and could actually make out the shapes of gorillas hiding in the bushes.

When I was younger, I'd run. But not anymore. I was too old to be running from gorillas in the dark. I'd walk bravely on, scalp tingling with fear of being attacked from behind.

The BYPU teacher kept talking. Darn her! Couldn't she see the night shadows outside creeping up on us?

Finally, she wound down. There was still some light outside. I was ecstatic—until she said, "I'm going to ask Dale Denney to dismiss us with prayer tonight."

What? Me? You can't mean...! I couldn't breathe as everybody in the room bowed their heads. I'd never done that—prayed out loud with other people listening. I'd prayed lots of times to myself.

The hardest prayer I ever prayed was at the end of service one morning when I bowed my head like the preacher asked us. I closed my eyes real tight and asked God to bring me a .22 rifle for Christmas. I even mentally described it to him, the one on page 425 in the Sears & Roebuck catalog—an inexpensive single shot.

Of course, he didn't, just like I expected him not to.

The room was so quiet, I knew every kid in the class could hear what I heard, the blood rushing and roaring and pounding in my ears. In desperation, I glanced quickly about, seeking help. Even my buddies near me had their heads bowed and their eyes closed. They all had smirks on their faces.

I could run. I shot a glance toward the door to see how far away it was. That would be a disaster.

Then say something, you idiot. Anything. My mouth began working, but no words came out. I searched frantically through my memory, trying to find the usual phrases you always hear in dismissal prayers.

Watch over and guide us. 'Til we meet again. Thank you, Lord. I couldn't get them arranged in proper order.

Perspiration trickled from under my arms and ran down my ribs. Yet my mouth was so dry, I couldn't have said anything even if I could think of anything to say.

It was so quiet, I could hear the guy next to me breathing. Or was that a snicker?

"Please, God. Help me!" I begged silently, fervently.

Suddenly, Mary Boston began praying. Her voice was strong. She was saying all the proper things.

Relief surged through me. I was able to breath again. I vowed to stay until the evening church services were over and walk Mary home—all the way down to her house by the river. And if a giant gorilla tried to get us, I'd tear him apart with my bare hands. Then when we got to her house I would tell her how much I appreciated the way she stepped in and rescued me. Maybe even kiss her goodnight.

I didn't give a hoot what the other guys would say about Mary and me.

Instead, the second I heard her "Amen," I bolted for the door, so embarrassed that I could die. I ran down the steps two at a time. I scurried out the front door and headed for home without looking back.

Tears stung my nostrils, made my vision blurry. I could hear other kids behind me yelling for me to wait up. I broke into a dead run.

When I got to the big tree, I stopped to catch my breath and try to straighten out all the crazy thoughts whirling around in my head.

It was hopeless. I leaned against the tree, hiding my head in my arms, fighting tears. I swore I'd never go near a church ever again, hating God for doing this to me.

"Dale?"

I jumped out of my skin, thinking it was God until I whirled and saw Mary.

"I'm sorry," she said.

I quickly tried to swipe away the dampness on my cheeks with the heel of my hand before she could see any wetness in the deepening gloom.

"What for?" I said, trying my best to make it sound like a bear growling.

She just stood there, a slight smile on her lips. I'd never noticed how red they were before.

I reached out and took her hand. "Want to walk home with me?"

She didn't say anything. She didn't have a chance to. I began jabbering about the stars, the moon—everything except what had happened back there.

I didn't even slow down at our house. I kept right on walking with her all the way to her home, secretly wishing a gorilla would jump out of the bushes so I would be able to tear it apart with my bare hands—for her.

We stopped at her front gate. I faced her, still holding her hand. I'd run out of anything to say. Fact was, I didn't want to say anything.

She stood on tiptoe and kissed my cheek.

"Please don't be mad at me," she said softly.

I promised not to.

I didn't see a single gorilla on the way home. Not one.

Oklahoma Boy from Texas

Everybody in the little town of Turkey in the Texas panhandle knew Bob the barber loved playing his fiddle at local dances, but they couldn't understand when he hung up his barber apron, put on his white cowboy hat, tucked his fiddle under his arm and headed for the big time in Fort Worth.

The great depression had set in during the 30s and anybody who could earn fifteen cents for a haircut had better hang on to a sure thing, his home town folks warned.

"You gotta do what you have to do," Bob the barber said on his way out of town.

Nowadays, the people of Turkey have set aside a special day in March every year to honor their barber who went out into the world to "do what you have to do."

For Bob the barber, playing his fiddle at an occasional Saturday night dance wasn't enough. He found more fiddle-playing time in the big city, eventually forming his own string band. He was invited to fill in a fifteen-minute spot on a local radio station and was billed as Bob Wills and his Texas Playboys.

He created a unique style of western music which he called Western Swing. When he was offered a thirty-minute spot with a stronger sponsor over KVOO radio in Tulsa, he took it, bringing his "Texas Playboys" name with him.

Bob's western swing music became a part of the culture of northeastern Oklahoma.

I grew up in the town where Bob Wills played his first out-of-town dance—a dying oil community in Creek County. The dance was held on the second floor of the town's only two-story building, the meeting room for the local Masonic lodge.

Those of us who were too young to go to the dance sat on the curb across the street and listened to the Bob Wills music floating out the raised windows. We could see the shadows of the dancers keeping time with that fascinating western music.

No one called Bob Wills' music Western Swing then. It was too new. But we all knew it was special.

Farmers would hurry to the house at noon to sit with their families during the Bob Wills broadcast, enjoying a full half-hour of the toe-tapping music coming from their battery-powered radios.

In town, folks gathered around static-prone radios at the local hardware store during noon hour, or in the pool hall. You could walk down main street in any small town within a fifty-mile radius of Tulsa's KVOO radio station and never miss a beat of one of Bob Wills' tunes during his broadcast.

In our town, the local appliance dealer, Catfish Eubanks, took advantage of Bob Wills' popularity by trucking his most expensive floor model radio out on the sidewalk in front of his store to attract a crowd.

Catfish would keep up a running monolog between tunes on how you could enjoy Bob Wills each and every day "right in your own homes" with one of his radios. Catfish sold a lot of radios.

As strange as it may sound, we would listen closely when Bob's announcer, O.W. Mayo, would read the long list of people who sent in a "card or letter" making song requests. One of them might be somebody you know, and getting your name read "on the radio" made you famous.

Mayo would also run through the schedule of the towns and their Legion halls where Bob Wills and his band would be appearing during the next few weeks. If he was scheduled to be at a town anywhere near, that's all you'd talk about until the day of the dance, then you'd get up a gang of guys and gals and go.

One of the moments when I felt more homesick than at any time in my life was after I had enrolled at Oklahoma University in Norman in 1942.

I was over 100 miles from Tulsa—out of KVOO range. I felt lost from 12:30 to 1:00 every day. People there didn't know Bob Wills—other than he played "country" music, which was beneath the music tastes of any "cultured" college student.

Campus radios stayed tuned to big band music—Artie Shaw, Vaughn Monroe, Glenn Miller—others.

When some enterprising promoter scheduled Bob Wills and his Texas Playboys to play for a dance in the Oklahoma University gymnasium, my college friends scoffed. Anyone even caught listening to country music on the radio was made fun of, much less going to one of his "boot-stompin'" shindigs.

I didn't plan to attend. I'd left my true love back in Jay and wouldn't even think about going to a dance without her.

However, my English teacher, a very pretty young thing, told us she was going. She apologized, explaining that her boy friend was from Tulsa.

I couldn't wait to get to her class the next day to hear what she had to say about Bob Wills.

"Frankly, I was surprised," she told us. "Bob Wills played all the popular tunes, songs like *I Don't Want a Walk Without You, Somebody Else Is Taking My Place, Moonlight Cocktail, There'll Be Blue Birds Over The White Cliffs of Dover.*"

She said she even had fun dancing to his western tunes.

I knew she was hooked. Bob Wills might have been a barber from Turkey, Texas, but he was no fool. He knew what music to play at a dance on the University of Oklahoma campus. But he also knew he was born to play Western Swing, and play it he did.

As his popularity grew beyond the broadcast range of station KVOO, so did his critics. Many called him corny. They poked fun at the way he carried on during a tune, singing out with things like "Take it away, Leon," to his steel guitar player; or calling, "Ah-Haa. Come on in, Big Al!" to his piano player.

Bob's enthusiasm added even more life to his swing arrangements of ordinary western and country music. Then when Bob himself would tuck his fiddle under his chin and start his bow dancing on the strings, you couldn't help but feel lively inside as the stirring notes flowed out all around you and pulled you right into the song emotionally.

Bob Wills' Western Swing music kept spreading across the land, building its own momentum. It was inevitable that Hollywood would call, and it did.

"Our Bob Wills has made the big time," we said here in Oklahoma, and joined the lines to buy tickets to his first movie. We sat proudly in the dark and watched Bob and his boys on the big screen playing square dance music at a ranch house.

The plot called for the sheriff to rush in and ask for volunteers. He needed a posse to chase the bad guy. Bob and his boys ran outside, mounted their horses, and joined the chase.

Bob's only speaking part—other than "Ah-haa, take it away, Leon"—was when the sheriff met up with him and his boys at a fork in the road. Bob pointed to the left and shouted, "They went that-a-way!" And off the posse rode in a cloud of southern California dust.

All of us Bob Wills fans here in eastern Oklahoma left the theater unable to shake the feeling that somehow, some way, Hollywood had been making fun of us by having Bob recite such a corny line. But then, we were used to people in

California ridiculing us through John Steinbeck's derogatory "Okie" label, and let it go at that.

This barber from Turkey, Texas, single-handedly lifted western music from the beer halls and road houses to a new plateau of appreciation.

But nothing changed Bob Wills. He led his band by waving his fiddle bow and keeping time by stomping his cowboy boots with the same enthusiasm in movie specials before world-wide audiences as he did at many Legion dances in Oklahoma.

He paved the way for super stars like Gene Autry and Roy Rogers. His *San Antonio Rose* pushed its way into the so-called pop charts, challenging the supremacy of tunes named in the Lucky Strike Hit Parade and sung by a skinny, virtually unknown kid named Frank Sinatra.

The man loved his music. His band played *Faded Love* with as much sincerity and respect for the listener as Glenn Miller did playing his nostalgic and popular *Miss You.*

Bob died in 1975. But his legacy lives on. So-called country music is at the top of all charts now, not only here, but around the world.

Not bad for a barber from Turkey, Texas—

Just doing what he had to do.

Creation vs. Evolution

Our town got into a big fight once over Cornelius Brigham and Thomas Elwood, two nice guys who everybody loved.

Mr. Brigham was our high school science teacher. He was a tall man and sort of puffy fat. Fact was, his face always looked as if it had been freshly ironed—there wasn't a wrinkle anywhere. He had pleasant brown eyes which seemed to have a touch of humor in them. His voice was—well, sort of like a girl's.

Mr. Brigham taught all kinds of science, from biology to physics. He demonstrated what he taught. That's why I liked him. I'm not very bright at abstracts and I like having things demonstrated to me.

Like electricity. Mr. Brigham told us you can't see it, but we know it's there.

"I'll show you," he said.

He dragged the workings from an old style telephone out of his desk drawer, the kind you had to crank to get the operator, wired two wires to it, and asked for a volunteer.

I jumped up, always eager to please my teachers. He handed me the two wires.

"Hold one in each hand," he said.

I did—like holding the reins to a horse.

"Now by turning this crank, I'm going to make electricity," he said. "You'll be able to see it by watching Dale's reactions."

He grabbed the crank and gave it a quick turn. A jolt hit me. It felt like the bones in both my arms were going to jump out. I yelped, threw the wires away, staggered backward, and fell over my seat.

The class roared with laughter. Mr. Brigham smiled. I crept back into my seat, my arm bones still aching.

Mr. Brigham made a point of the fact that while we couldn't see electricity, we knew it was there.

We studied about dinosaurs the same way—even though nobody had seen them, their bones told us that they had been here.

I used Mr. Brigham's philosophy when it was so hot in the summer that we slept outside a lot of times and I looked up at the stars before I went to sleep.

You couldn't touch them, but I knew they were there. I could see them. I tried counting them one night to see how many there were. I must have been whispering too loud as I counted because my older brother asked sleepily, "What're you doing?"

"Counting the stars."

"Don't you know if you count all the stars you'll die?"

"No. I didn't know that."

"You will. So quit counting and go to sleep."

I was glad he had warned me. I surely didn't want to die. So I quit counting the stars. I decided I could just ask Mr. Brigham how many stars there were.

He laughed when I asked him if you'd die if you counted all the stars. Then said, "If fact, you probably would be dead before you counted all of them because there's so many you wouldn't be able to count all of them in a dozen lifetimes."

He told me the earth and our sun and moon that made up what we called our solar system was nothing but a speck in the Milky Way where we were located, and that the Milky Way with its billions of stars was nothing but a speck in a universe that contained billions of galaxies like our own Milky Way.

Wow! I left his room in a daze and was really glad my brother stopped me from trying to count all the stars or I'd have been a goner, for sure.

It so happened along about that same time in my life that Mr. Elwood, our Sunday school teacher, was teaching us about God creating Adam and Eve.

He was a short, wiry man with a heavy shock of black hair. You hardly ever saw him when he wasn't smiling. He promised us boys he'd take all of us to Tulsa some Saturday night to see a wrestling match. He never did, but I liked him anyway.

Scotty, our preacher, even bore down on Adam and Eve pretty good in his sermon after Sunday School.

I liked the story—especially the part where the Bible said, "in His own image."

I took that to mean, like electricity, I couldn't see God, but I knew he was there because I looked like him.

I'd study myself in the mirror and I could see God—also the thing that was me.

Would I still be me in God's image without first ever seeing electricity demonstrated or seeing fossils and being able to count stars?

I didn't know which to ask—Mr. Brigham or Mr. Elwood.

Then I decided that it wouldn't be right to ask either one of them who I was. I liked being me like I was.

I enjoyed reading the science book in Mr. Brigham's class. I studied the drawings of a man who looked like a hairless ape progressing through four or five other drawings into a fine upright human being with no clothes on but with his right leg forward far enough so you couldn't see his you-know-what.

I wondered which one of the figures in the drawings first noticed the stars and tried to count them. Obviously, if he didn't know enough to wear clothes, he didn't know about electricity yet.

I also enjoyed reading the Bible in Mr. Elwood's class. I noticed that it said Adam didn't have any clothes on either. So it stood to reason he wouldn't have known about electricity either. Suppose he knew about the stars?

I did notice the dimensions of Noah's ark and assumed it didn't have any room for dinosaurs. So it was obvious to me that dinosaurs must have been older than when God started telling His story—unless, of course, God played around with dinosaurs and decided he didn't like them because he couldn't've made one of them special in his image.

We only stayed on the subject of Adam and Eve one or two Sundays in Mr. Elwood's class. I soon realized the Bible didn't bother itself too much about the apes and the stars and electricity. It was more interested in me. I liked that.

On the other hand, the book we used in Mr. Brigham's class wasn't interested in me at all. But I found it fascinating learning about things, and I was a thing, wasn't I?

I had no problem at all with what I was learning. But a real row developed when a vacancy came up on the School Board. A lot of people talked our preacher, Scotty, into running. He did, and was elected by a landslide.

He wasn't there long before he made a big to-do over some of the things Mr. Brigham was teaching.

That caused people to choose up sides.

And you know when that happens, people say things they hadn't ought to say and it hurts somebody's feelings and then these people start saying things they hadn't ought to say.

Fortunately, Scotty left town to accept a pastorate at a bigger church in Dallas.

Things quieted down for a while until this lady moved to town with three kids and no husband. One of her boys was called down one morning for shuffling his feet too much when the teacher was opening her class with a prayer.

She got mad at the teacher. She claimed her boy shouldn't have to listen to teachers thanking God for trying to help themselves be themselves. So she got in the race for filling the vacancy on the School Board that was created when Scotty left.

She got elected. She tried to banish the Adam and Eve story from school activities and tried to stop people for thanking God for helping themselves be themselves.

And the community row started all over again.

It didn't take long for people to figure it out—there's no problem with letting Mr. Brigham teach what he loved best, which was all about things, and letting Mr. Elwood teach what he loved best, which was the way God tries to help us be ourselves.

They're both one and the same, because each of us are both objects of science and subjects of something inside our brains that makes us who we are.

Our problems develop when we try to legalize our personal beliefs.

An Insignificant Decision

You never know when a little decision can lead to big changes in who you are, where you go, careers you follow.

Especially early in life. I faced such a decision about walking Laura home that Saturday night.

And she wanted me to, I could tell. Her dark eyes, a slightly upturned nose, and close-cropped black hair around a creamy complexion all combined to give her striking beauty without her even half trying.

I was with the guys from my end of town doing what we always did on Saturday nights, sitting on the fenders of cars parked in the bright lights in front of the drug store and carrying on sidewalk flirtations with girls going by.

Laura came out of the drug store, alone. She saw me and smiled, paused, then came straight toward me.

I wasn't sure she even remembered my name. It'd been over a year and I'd grown a lot.

"What have you been doing?" she asked, ignoring the others.

"Nothing much," I managed to say, then added with a sense of pride, "Just working, is all."

As we made small talk, I was aware of the sudden, deafening silence of my friends. I could hear their thoughts clicking like mad: What's going on between Dale and Laura?

I fought down a rising sense of panic, all the while getting angry at myself for feeling that way. Laura and I had gone all the way through school together, for heaven's sake!

But I'd always thought of girls in my class, especially when we reached high school, as being older than me because I was small for my age.

And, I suspected, they all thought I must have spent all my time studying because of the good grades I made. I did study a lot, but I was very much aware of the girls. It was just that —you know. Like Laura and me.

Her father was a doctor, mine an oil well driller whose skills went begging in a dying oil field.

Guys in my end of the town called Laura one of those "uptown" girls.

She wore make up. I did good if I remembered to comb my hair that morning. She wore expensive clothes. I wore overalls. She was one of the first girls in my class who started wearing an expensive wrist watch.

Laura and the girls she ran around with seemed to have a lot of money. Me and my gang of guys had to scrounge hard to earn enough change to go to the show on.

It wasn't until we were seniors in high school that Laura and I became what you'd call friends.

It began the day we both approached the same corner a block away from school at the same time. I didn't know whether to speed up or lag back to avoid the embarrassment for either of us of having to walk the final block with somebody not in our social class.

"Good morning," she said. Her warm smile brushed away my fears.

"Good morning, yourself," I said, swinging brazenly into step beside her. "Going my way?" I quipped, feeling real proud to have thought of something so dashingly bold.

"You might say that," she laughed. "We've been going the same direction since the first grade, haven't we?

My palms began to sweat. I didn't understand why.

"I'm dreading our English test today," she said.

"Yeah. Me, too," I said, lying. I loved all my English courses.

I couldn't help noticing the stares of the other kids when we walked across the school grounds together. I tried to stretch myself so I would at least be as tall as she was.

The next morning, I timed it so I'd meet her at the corner, feeling a little foolish doing so, but was surprised to find her there waiting for me.

It thrilled me. Then we began seeking one another out in the hallways between classes, stopping to chat a little about this and that, laughing at nothing, whispering gossip.

I loved being close; the smell of her was intoxicating.

It hurt when I saw her one night going to the show with one of our football players, and later riding around in cars with her other uptown friends and their dates.

Even so, when she asked me if I would write an English theme for her, to help bring her grades up, I said sure, jumping at the chance to show her I was as good as any football player.

I knew it was cheating, but I didn't care. That's what friends do—support one another, I reasoned. Perhaps she could do me a favor sometime.

But when I handed her the finished theme, I was unable to shake the feeling I'd sacrificed my integrity. And for what? What was even worse was the feeling that she had deliberately bought me with her beauty, her social status, and charm.

So I began going a different direction to school, avoiding the corner where we'd been meeting. It was easy to dodge her in the crowded hallways between classes.

Our improbable friendship faded away. Just as well, I thought. It had been a princess and pauper thing. It would have never worked.

But things changed rapidly for me during the year after we graduated. I shot up like a fast-growing mule weed—and looked like one, tall and skinny.

I had a job in a lumber yard. It didn't pay much, but I'd earned enough to buy a sharp-looking khaki outfit and a new pair of shoes.

Now here I was, almost a head taller, and dressed halfway decent, standing with her on the street in public on Saturday night. And she was acting as if things between us were like they used to be, meeting at the corner, in the hallways, talking, laughing.

"Are you going to the late show?" she asked casually.

"Plan to," I said. "Are you?"

"It's supposed to be a good show," she said. Then after a quick peek at her sparkling gold watch, added, "I have a couple more things to do before time to go."

When she glanced up, the way her look lingered caused my heart to pound. My face felt hot.

Was she asking me to take her? Social status didn't count now. We were adults—almost. Our graduating class had scattered. There were no football players anymore. No friends riding around in cars having fun.

It would be perfectly normal for us to go into the drug store and have a Coke together while we waited for the late show to start. I'd be proud sitting beside her in the movie. And I could walk her home.

The thought of us dating tonight and in the future took my breath away.

She appeared to be waiting for me to ask. How could I, here in front of my gang? What if she said no?

After a long, somewhat awkward pause, she said, "Well, I'd better hurry and get my errands done before the show starts."

"Yeah," I said. "See you."

She walked away. None of my friends said a word to me about her. But I could tell by their muted conversational tones they were mystified. When it came time to go to the show, we purchased our tickets and went in.

Before the house lights dimmed, I saw Laura come in, alone. She settled herself in a seat on the far side of the theater. She caught me looking at her. We exchanged smiles.

During the show I stared at the screen, not seeing. Was it possible that an uptown girl really and truly saw me as I was, really and truly enjoyed being with me more than a popular football player?

After the movie, I lagged behind when my group moved away into the darkness toward our end of town. I was alone under the brightly lit marquee when Laura came out.

"It was a good show, wasn't it?" she commented.

"Yeah—"

The word hung between us. She hesitated, then walked on, ever so slowly. At the corner half a block away, she paused under the street light and looked back—obviously waiting.

I remembered the theme. I turned away and followed my disappearing buddies.

When I glanced over my shoulder. She was gone, vanished into the night—and I never saw her again.

Not long after, I left home seeking a better job and built a new life with new friends in a new world.

Would I have remained in the lumber business and be living in another town today if I'd walked Laura home that Saturday night?

How to Get a Job

Just thinking about it was both exciting and scary.

No more school—ever.

I kept my eyes fixed on the girl in front of me as we marched down the aisle in slow time with the procession music which Miss Willoughby was playing on the piano.

"Stay in step," Miss Willoughby insisted during our practice sessions.

The idea was, she said over and over, that by staying in step as we marched single file down the aisle, our long graduation gowns and hat tassels would be swaying in unison.

She'd even appoint someone—usually one of our cheer leaders—to stand on the stage, her arms up and swaying back and forth to keep our gowns and tassels swinging just right.

I didn't want to be the one to mess up, even though Miss Willoughby would have no more say over what we did or did not do after tonight.

This was it. It was all over.

That was the scary part. My entire life had been centered around this school, from my earliest memories to now. I'd been in class with most of these kids since the first grade, and most of whom I would never see again after we received our diplomas tonight. So staying in step down the aisle to keep my gown and hat tassels swaying in unison with my classmates would be my very last test.

Since I had always scored well on all my tests, I sure didn't want to mess up now.

I thought I did a good job. We filed into our seats and sat down together as Miss Willoughby hit the final note.

Now what? I didn't hear any of the long, supposedly inspiring speeches. My thoughts were on the future.

Going to a university was the farthest thing from my mind. That cost money. Nobody had any money that I knew of.

Schools prepared you for jobs, but they don't tell you how to go out and ask for one.

I got lucky last summer. The owner of the lumber yard saw me passing by and called me over. Said he'd pay me to help him unload some lumber. He gave me eighty cents. I was delighted. It was the most money I'd had at one time in my life.

Everybody expected boys to find work after they graduated as roustabouts in the oil fields, or helping their dads work their farms hauling hay, plowing, or raising livestock.

Some of the boys in my class talked about going to California or Washington. That sounded exotic, but I knew they were boasting. They were just as lost as I was.

Nobody ever asked me what I was going to do when we graduated. I was glad they didn't, because I planned to be a writer and write books. It was an impossible dream, I knew, and because reading and writing was sissy stuff, I was ashamed to tell anybody, not even Mom.

The only writing job in town was with the local newspaper. Only I didn't know how to ask.

I'd tried one day after school when I was on my way to the post office to get the family mail.

I saw the local editor coming down the street. He was an elderly gentleman named Eli who was never seen without a cigar protruding from the center of his mouth, his lips wrapped around it, giving his dirty white moustache a bristly look.

He wore his grimy felt hat pulled low over his shaggy brows as he shuffled back and forth between his print shop and Pete's Domino Parlor. Everybody knew he depended on his printer, a skinny man called Claude with a big Adam's apple, to get the paper out.

Although Dad subscribed to the local weekly, I seldom read it because there was nothing in it, it seemed, except Mr. and Mrs. So-and-so was here visiting their daughter for the weekend.

I could think of a million stories people would be interested in. For instance: How it feels pitching hay with sand burs in it in ninety-degree heat and sweat running down your arms.

And how about Charlie Mason, the farmer out across the river? He loved turkeys and spent most of his time raising them. Who ever heard of a farmer who raised turkeys?

I could see stories everywhere I looked in our little town. No telling what kind of stories you could find out there in the whole wide world.

The only trouble was I didn't know how to sell my ideas to a grungy-looking old man.

Now's the time, I told myself that day when I saw him coming down the street. Full of resolve, I tried to catch his eye as the distance between us decreased.

My resolve began to melt when I realized that he represented unknown years of education and experience in the newspaper business. I knew nothing. My palms began to sweat and I almost dropped the books I was carrying. All I had left in me as we passed was to utter a squeaky, "Hello."

He nodded, removed his cigar, grunted something, replaced the cigar and went on by.

However, the more I thought about it, the more I became convinced that the local newspaper was my destiny. Why not, I finally asked myself, offer to "help"? Sweep out. Clean up. Burn trash—anything.

It would be a start, at least. The idea excited me. I let my ego feed on the exciting thought for a few days after graduation. Then one day I talked my way out of going to the Cassidy farm with Dad to pitch hay and put on a clean change of clothes.

"What are you—?" Mom asked, her question hanging. It wasn't Sunday, and she knew I was up to something, and since I was out of school now she was hesitant about prying into my life.

"I'm going to run uptown a minute," was all I told her.

Unconsciously, I knew by not committing myself to anyone about my plan, it would lessen the embarrassment when I failed in my mission.

I headed straight for the newspaper office. The building that housed the printing plant was one of the first brick-fronted structures built during the oil boom years. It was located on a side street, near where the railroad tracks used to be.

I tried to see who was inside before going in. But the plate glass windows were so grimy, all I could see was my own image squinting back at me. The front door, with its once beautiful oval glass, dragged so heavily on the floor I had trouble pushing it open. The only clear floor space was an area just inside the door.

I could see the tops of the heavy printing machinery protruding above piles of debris, mostly cardboard boxes and discarded papers.

What a horrible fire trap! Apparently, Eli and Claude moved from place to place along trails leading from the front counter to the linotype, to the makeup stones, to the type cases, to the press, to the folder.

Beyond, the entire back wall of the building had rotted away and the roof sagged so low its dangling boards were kissing the tops of the tall weeds growing in the alley.

Claude's hatchet-face bobbed up from behind the linotype.

"Yessir?" he asked in that deep voice of his.

I was so fascinated by the prominence of his bobbing Adam's apple that I found it difficult to organize my words.

"Is Mr. Eli in?" I finally squeaked.

"Nope. He ain't never in. Can I he'p?"

I panicked. Mumbling some sort of weird apology, I turned and bolted out the door, vowing silently never to go near another weekly newspaper office again if I lived to be a hundred.

School learning is good for you—finding jobs is lots better. They should teach you how to ask for jobs.

The Graduate

The commencement speaker droned on and on, telling us our graduation from high school was not the end, but the beginning.

What if you didn't want to go?

I felt as if I was being pushed out the door. I always loved school, a feeling I'd kept strictly to myself because no self-respecting boy was supposed to even "like" school, let alone "love" it.

There was nothing more thrilling to me than learning something new—from how to diagram a sentence in English classes to studying the hypotenuse in geometry.

But half way through my senior year, I suddenly realized that knowing about hypotenuses didn't do you a whit of good when it came to talking to girls.

All I knew about girls was from listening to jokes older boys told, like Bill Childs. He was the best. I missed him when he graduated a couple years before I did.

Now I was graduating myself. I felt lost.

"What do you want to be when you grow up?" asked a visiting cousin of mine one day when I was in grade school. She was already grown up, had two kids, and a husband who had a good job with an oil company.

The question shocked me. Did you have to "be" something when you grew up? I never wanted to "be" anything except what I already was.

"An engineer," I said out of desperation.

"That's nice," she said. But when she kept on talking I realized she thought I meant going to college and studying engineering when what I really meant was a guy who drives a train and toots his whistle.

But the question started me thinking. I began looking around at men who were already "being" somebody.

Old man Tippin owned a grocery store. I didn't want to own a grocery store. I didn't like the smell back at the butcher's counter. And Old Man Tippin was fat. I didn't want to be fat.

My best friend's Dad worked for an oil company. That would be nice, I considered. He chewed tobacco and bought a new car every year or so and drove around the oil lease, stopping at the oil wells and twisting on throttles and things and spitting tobacco juice.

That didn't appeal to me at all. I did, however, like to climb to the top of the oil rigs—you weren't supposed to—and pretend I was an airplane pilot. I could fly across an ocean or something and get famous like Lindberg did.

I once considered owning a theater. That way I could see every show that was ever made and it wouldn't cost me a cent.

But the theater owner in our town was a sissy-looking guy who wore a starched white shirt all the time. I didn't like wearing starched white shirts. I'd rather pay a dime to see a show than wear a starched white shirt.

After the ceremony was over and we were checking in our caps and gowns, all my classmates were chatting happily to one another about what they were going to do that summer, of going to the big city and finding a job, of going to college that fall.

College was out. Dad had done all right with just an eighth grade education, he preached over and over, and he thought it was too uppity for kids in families like ours to go to college.

In a way, he was right. Only football stars and girls whose parents wanted them to marry somebody rich went to college from our town.

Besides, I didn't have the slightest idea what I'd study if I went to college. None that I ever heard of taught courses on how to be yourself.

The thought did occur to me, however, that at college the girls there wouldn't know who I was and maybe I could learn to talk to them without blushing and making a fool of myself.

After dutifully turning in my cap and gown with all the other kids—most of whom I'd gone to school with all my life—I took my diploma and went home.

At first it was sort of like when school was out at the end of any other year. I felt free. The summer was before me. No home work to do. No themes to write. No more algebra problems to work out.

I even gave college some real serious thought—not to learn how to "be" something, but to continue the excitement of learning something new from books.

They might even have books there that told you all about girls and things.

But every time I mentioned going to college, Dad would argue that you couldn't have a more decent life than being a farmer.

And to help me get started, he said, I could help him take care of Chris

Cassidy's farm that summer.

Chris had asthma and couldn't work. His own boys had all grown up and left home. His wife was doing poorly.

But he did have a good-looking daughter. Oleta. She had graduated a year or so ahead of me. I could make up excuses to go to the house and see her—get a drink of water or something. She might teach me something about girls I didn't know.

So I told Dad okay.

I learned real quick that I certainly didn't want to be a farmer. The hay we had to put up in the barn loft was full of sand burs that stuck to your pants legs and fell in your face every time you forked up a load.

And Dad always took a jug of water when we went out in the fields. I could never find an excuse to go to the house and see Oleta.

Until the day he hitched a mule to a weed plow and sent me down to cut weeds out of the corn rows. He said he'd be on down later.

It was hotter'n a pistol and the corn was higher than my head. The mule was not only stubborn, he was smart. He knew right away that I didn't know how to handle a weed plow or guide a mule and he started wandering around wherever he wanted to go.

I cut down more corn stalks with my plow than I did weeds.

Dad hadn't showed up by noon and I made a bee line for Chris' house.

I knocked on the screen door.

"Who is it?" a cheery voice called out.

My whole body tingled. It was Oleta. And alone, I hoped.

"Just me," I answered. "I came for a drink of water. You got one in there?"

She appeared on the other side of the screen. She was wearing a house dress and had her hair bundled up in a red bandana.

That shocked me. I'd never seen her like that. All the time at school, she would be dressed in something clean-looking and fresh, and her hair would be brushed and hanging loose.

"Oleta?" I asked without thinking.

She laughed. "Yes, it's me. Don't I look a mess?" She opened the screen door. "Come on in."

I knew I was getting in way over my head, this being the first time being alone with a girl and all—and without one bit of learning how to do it from books.

But I went in anyway. After all, I did have a high school diploma, didn't I? And I'd learned all there was about girls from Bill Childs' jokes, hadn't I?

Oleta gestured toward the pail of well water sitting on a wood bench by the window. It had a dipper in it.

I scooped up a big dipper full of water and took a few swallows.

"How do you like farming?" Oleta asked.

I grinned and shook my head. "It's not for me."

"Me neither," she said. "Bill Childs and I are getting married next week. He's got a job in Tulsa. I hope I never see a farm again."

Bill Childs was the best joke-teller ever. I reckoned he knew enough to get married.

"Thanks," I said, dropping the dipper back in the bucket.

I sure didn't want to get mixed up with a girl who was marrying a guy who knew as many jokes as Bill Childs did.

I went on back to the corn field. Dad was standing in the shade of a tree trying to figure out what I'd done to the corn field.

Then he turned to me and said, "I think you'd better go on to college. You sure can't plow."

Wally the Pig

When Dad started talking about butchering the hog that morning, I didn't pay much attention at first. Then it dawned on me that the "we" he was talking about was me and him, because all my older brothers had left home.

This was the first fall since I could remember that I didn't have to go to school. I was enjoying being the kid brother all alone at home and old enough to do what I pleased.

Doing the dirty work that goes with farming didn't figure in my plans. I was more the bookworm type. The family accepted that, assigning me the more mundane jobs like feeding the animals.

While we didn't really live on a farm—just three acres at the edge of town—we raised a big garden, had a milk cow, kept chickens, had dogs and cats for pets, and butchered a hog every fall.

Besides all that, I simply couldn't stand the thought of butchering Wally. He was—well, Wally, my friend.

Dad bought him cheap that spring from a neighbor because he was the runt of the litter. He was a real cutie—a lovely white, with delicate-looking pink ears. I had to start off feeding him with a baby bottle.

I tried to teach him proper table manners, scolding him playfully—that's when I started calling him Wally—when he'd get greedy and sling milk all over me and him both. But it's useless to try to teach a pig table manners.

We let him have the run of the barnyard when he got older. He'd meet me at the gate when I went to feed the chickens and followed me around like a dog, talking to me happily in that pig language of his.

He was jealous of me feeding the chickens. Every time I tossed out a handful of feed and the chickens came running, Wally would try to chase them away. They'd flutter around, cackling and raising all kinds of heck.

Mom would get onto me for letting Wally chase the chickens. It made them stop laying, she said.

I'd scold Wally about it, but not very hard because he was having so much fun. I really thought the chickens were enjoying it too.

But Wally's freedom ended when he got strong enough to root under the garden fence. He ate up one whole row of carrots before we could stop him.

Time to pen him up, Dad said, and did.

Our little pig pen behind the barn had a strong board fence around it. I hated to see Wally in prison like that. When I went feed him, we'd still communicate by me scratching behind his ears and him grunting his contentment as he chomped hungrily on the table scraps.

Before breakfast was over that morning, I had my mind going in high gear trying to find a way out of actually participating in the butchering process. Always before, I might have to build a fire under a drum of water used to scald the pig, then I'd get to go play with my friend who lived down the lane when I was younger, or go browse the book shelves in the city library when I got older.

"Can't we do it tomorrow?" I finally asked.

Dad scowled. "It might rain. We better do it while the doing's good."

I knew that he knew what I was trying to do—get enough time to dream up some excuse for not helping.

All right, I told myself. It's time you grew up. People kill hogs every day. It's routine on a farm.

But I felt like I was going to my own hanging when I followed Dad to the barnyard. I built the fire to heat the water while Dad laid some planks on a couple of sawhorses to make a butchering table.

Dad had his own way of killing hogs. My tension mounted when I saw him get his sledgehammer and head for the hog pen.

"Fetch me an ear of corn," he said.

I hurried to the corn crib. I notice my hand was trembling when I grabbed up an ear of corn.

Dad was already standing in the pen when I got back, holding the sledge hammer down by his leg. Wally was eyeing him warily, nostrils working, ears forward; the perfect picture of a very suspicious hog.

"Toss him the corn," Dad said.

I did. I was filled with guilt because tossing the ear of corn to Wally made me a party to the killing.

I thought Wally might be smart enough not to fall for the trap, but his greed overrode his sense of reason. He went for the corn. When he got real busy crunching on the unexpected between-meal treat and grunting his happiness, Dad eased up beside him and lifted the sledge high in the air.

I looked away to keep from seeing the dastardly deed done. But I couldn't close my ears from the sound of the sledge hammer hitting the hog between the eyes.

I was somewhat relieved when Wally suddenly quit grunting. That meant he was unconscious. When I looked back, he was laying on his side, kicking a little.

Before I could look away again, Dad whipped out his sharpened butcher knife and slit Wally's throat. Blood spurted out all over his hand and turned the pigpen mud red all around Wally.

I wanted to run away. Instead, I gritted my teeth and stood my ground.

Even before the blood was all drained from the once live and lovely hog, we dragged him to the scalding barrel. It took both of us to wrestle him as we doused him up and down in the steaming water to loosen the bristles. Then we stretched him out on some boards and started scraping with butcher knives to get the hair off.

The stink of wet hog hair made me want to upchuck.

Dad used a single tree to hook into the elbow ligaments of the hog's hind legs and hauled him up with a block and pulley roped to the limb of a cottonwood tree.

Then he scooted a washtub beneath the dangling head, sliced his belly open from top to bottom and dragged out all the entrails. They fell into the tub with a loud, splashing plop.

"Dig out the eatables," Dad told me as he dragged the tub aside.

As far as I was concerned, there wasn't anything eatable inside a hog—not by me anyway.

While he busied himself washing the still steaming carcass by tossing buckets of water all over it, I plunged my hands into the tub full of hog innards.

Somehow I expected the mass in the tub to be cold—probably because all the meat I ever handled came from the grocery store and was cold. So the shock of finding it still pleasantly warm was almost more than I could stand.

Could it be possible that this part of Wally was still alive? came the repugnant thought.

I found the liver and laid it out and went back in for the heart. When my hands closed over it, my imagination ran wild. I could swear it was still beating.

But the sight and feel of hog innards wasn't near as revolting to me as the smell.

They say hot dogs are made from stuff like that. However, you can smear a lot of mustard on a hot dog, sprinkle on a liberal amount of chopped onion, pretend it's something else, and go on enjoying the ball game you're watching, or whatever we all do when we eat hot dogs.

I helped Dad lay the hog carcass on his makeshift table. He sharpened his butcher knife again and went to work cutting it up for salting down and hanging up in the smokehouse to cure.

Dad tossed the odds and ends into a dish pan which I knew Mom would grind up to make sausage, adding sage and other stuff to make it taste like something besides cast-off bits of hog meat.

I had to take the hog innards to the woods and bury them deep so they wouldn't be dug up by stray dogs.

Don't tell anybody this, but I must confess I wept just a little and said a silent prayer at the burying, consigning Wally's remains to a beautiful afterlife in hog heaven.

I never wanted to go through a thing like that again. So the slaying of Wally was one of the prime reasons I left home—that very next spring.

I just wasn't cut out to be a farmer.

The Alien Seed

You remember the classic science fiction movie *The Body Snatchers*? It was made in the early fifties. Aliens from outer space had a plan to take over the world. They simply planted a seed somewhere close by you and the pod which the vine produced grew into your likeness. When the pod—your image—matured, it slipped into your body while you were asleep.

You weren't you anymore. You became an alien that looked like you. But you were one of them.

That's what happened to me. The seed was planted when I was fresh out of high school and reporting for my first salaried job—$5 a week. My new boss asked if I had a social security number.

"If it costs anything, I don't want one," I said. I already had plans for my five dollars.

It didn't cost anything, he explained. It was a new law. You just applied for it. Everybody on a payroll had to have one because your employer had to withhold two percent from your wages so you'd have something to retire on when you reached sixty-five.

I scoffed at the idea. Any fool could see that two percent of $5 wouldn't be near enough to retire on when I reached sixty-five.

But what the heck. If it didn't cost anything, I might as well apply for one. When it came in the mail, I put the card in my billfold and forgot it. Life was too exciting to be worrying about what things would be like in half a century away.

As I worked through the years, the percentages deducted from my paycheck continued to rise. The years I was in business for myself, not only did I have to match the social security amounts I deducted from my employees' payroll checks, I had to pay social security on myself.

I still didn't believe in it, but it was the law. You pay, or else.

After Congress turned anti-business in the seventies, it made self-employed people pay every quarter, then later you had to deposit ahead of time what you *estimated* your income was going to be. That way, the government could use your money instead of you using it yourself.

The only time I didn't pay social security taxes was during the years I was with the US Army Corps of Engineers. Government employees have their own retirement system. This includes members of Congress.

My card in my billfold turned yellow, got dog-eared. Somebody said you could always get another one if you lost yours. I never had to.

Then, suddenly it seemed, the half-a-century was gone. I debated long and hard about drawing my social security. Over the years Congress had converted it from a retirement fund into a managed welfare system. Politicians call it compassion.

I was full of shame when I applied for my social security benefits. I still didn't believe it was right. Besides, I didn't feel that old.

I sat down on the back row in the reception area, isolating myself from any of the people around me for fear they might somehow contaminate me with their old age. Then I saw the hand-lettered sign over one of the windows up front. "First Time Applications Here," it read.

Embarrassed, I got out of my seat and stepped quietly forward. There was no one at the window. Beyond, I could see people working at their gray metal desks. They acted as if I didn't exist. The thought occurred to me that I was already dead and I was there in spirit only and that, of course, they couldn't see me because I was invisible.

But I knew they weren't *that* busy. I had sat at one of those gray metal desks when I was a government employee. You don't work. You just pile things on them because if you do all your work today you might not have any work to do tomorrow and that would be bad.

I cleared my throat.

A woman, who had been out of line of sight to one side, appeared suddenly. "Yes?"

"I'm one of them," I said, pointing up at the sign, keeping my voice low so as not to disturb either the old folks behind me or the lackadaisical-looking people at their gray desks beyond the window.

The lady snapped a card from a Rolodex and handed it to me, saying crisply, "Wait until your number is called."

Of course, of course, of course. I should have known. Get a number.

I glanced down at the slightly soiled Rolodex card. The number was twenty-seven. I turned away and crept back to my seat at the rear of the room.

Soon, an emaciated-looking young man with his black hair falling down on each side of his face stuck his head out a door and called out in a surprisingly strong bass voice, "Number twenty-seven?"

I jumped to my feet, holding my card high, jubilant, feeling that somehow I had leapfrogged all the others sitting in the waiting room. I hurried forward and handed the young man my card.

He motioned with his head and led me to another row of chairs where people were waiting.

A lady behind the gray metal desk called out, "Next."

She worked her way down to me.

"Next?" she called, smiling.

That was me. I forced a tight, frightened smile as I stepped forward to take the chair beside the nice lady's gray metal desk.

"Your social security number, please," she said. Not, "How are you today?" or, "Your name, please," or, "How's the weather outside this morning?" I pulled out my billfold and dug out the yellowing card I'd carried for over fifty years. I handed it to her.

Like the seeds in *The Body Snatchers*, my social security card was the seed the government had planted near my person in 1941. Now it had matured and, because I had fallen asleep figuratively and let my government get away with this assault on individual integrity, it was taking over my body. I wasn't me anymore. I just looked like me. Now I was a number and would remain a number until the day I died.

The lady, working on one of those new-fangled computers, scanned my record of earnings and said something like this: We take your best quarter of your highest salary within the last five years and multiply it by a factor of five.

She lost me after the first two phrases. The amount I had paid into the system had nothing whatsoever to do with what my monthly check would be.

She had me sign a piece of paper. Happy that it was over, I smiled at her when I got up to leave. She smiled too. That's the way it works, giving away government money. Both the people who get it and the people who give it are happy. The only persons not happy are the taxpayers, and they are not there, so they have no say in the matter.

To make things worse, my mother called us boys by our middle names, for whatever reason. Mom had named me Clyde Dale. I had been Dale all my life—except when I was in the army. But that was only temporary, and you didn't mind being someone else when you were in the army, for you knew you were going to get out, one way or the other.

I didn't realize it, but when I signed up for my social security and had to write underneath the instructions "Last name first, first name, and middle initial," I was finished as Dale.

Even my doctor back home, whom I had known for years, came into the examining room one day reading my chart, looked up, and asked briskly, "How are you feeling today, Clyde?"

But the checks keep on coming, regular as clockwork. The compassionate politicians keep adding any number of liberalized benefits and generous cost of living raises which were not a part of the original law when it was enacted in the thirties.

And now I am one of them. I will do everything in my power to keep getting the free money. What do I care if future generations will have to pay for what I'm drawing? Or won't have any funds in the kitty for their own retirement? I'll be dead by then. When you die, they stop your social security check and that's it.

For all of you who worry about your social security check—don't. Congress is powerless to take it away. There will always be a nice lady in a social security office somewhere sitting behind a gray metal desk who will simply say, "Next?"

And you will be one of us.

A Long Way from Home

This is gigging season. I'd never heard of gigging until I came to Delaware County sixty years ago about this time of year.

That first Sunday afternoon, bored with nothing to do, I'd flopped my rear down on the flat-topped stone fence in front of the courthouse, hoping some girls would come by so I could flirt with them.

Delaware County had nothing, absolutely nothing, I thought, and was beginning to regret I'd left home to come here, when about sundown this little '35 Ford nosed into the curb.

A guy poked his head out the window and called, "Hey. You want to go gigging?"

I was cautious. The last time somebody had asked me to do something and I didn't know what it was, I wound up on the butt end of the snipe hunting joke.

That's where the guys give you a gunny sack and tell you if you go in the woods at dusk, hold the sack open and make chirping sounds like a bird, the snipes will come flying in from all directions right down into your sack. You could get as much as fifty cents for a sack full of snipes, they told me.

It wasn't until way after dark that I heard the stifled laughter and looked over my shoulder and spotted the other guys behind a tree laughing at me.

Even a snipe hunt, I thought, would be better than sitting here on the fence doing nothing.

"Why not?" I said, sliding my rear off the fence. I crawled into the car.

"Washbourne. Wayne Washbourne," he said as we shook hands.

I could tell he was Indian. I'd been here less than a week and most everybody I'd met was Indian, or part.

He was a short man—not exactly a man, just an older boy. He had a round face, a ready smile, and large, dark eyes. He wore his straight black hair parted low, with most of the hair combed to the right.

His father, he informed me, had given the land to the county for its county seat. The town had been named after him. Jay Washbourne.

Wayne convinced me gigging for fish was no joke. It was, he said, a Cherokee tradition. And Delaware County is the only county in the state where gigging fish is permitted.

The snipe hunting episode kept hanging around in my mind.

On our way down to Spavinaw creek, Wayne told me story after story of guys falling out of their boats and dunking their lanterns.

"It gets scary swimming in the dark," he said. "Especially if you don't know which way is closest to shore."

The gathering place for the giggers was at the low water bridge crossing the head waters of Spavinaw Lake

Wayne parked on the gravel bar by the communal campfire and we got out. You could see the gigging boats up and down the creek, their Coleman gasoline lanterns little suns in the night.

Then I knew this was no snipe hunt. I began to get excited. I was fascinated by the way the fishermen gigged from a standing position in their flat-bottomed boats, their legs only shadows in the shielded lantern light and their upper bodies lost in the darkness above.

"Would you like to give it a try?" Wayne asked.

Before I could say no, Wayne called to a passing boat.

"Hey, Ray. Come here."

The gigging boat moved close.

"This here's that new boy in town." Wayne explained. "He's never seen gigging before. He said he'd like to try it. Take him out for a round. Show him how it's done."

"Sure. Why not? Hop in, young feller."

The snipe hunt popped back in my mind. But, wary, I went ahead and climbed into the boat. Somebody handed me a long-handled gig. I clutched it in the middle, standing in the center of the boat, balancing myself like circus performers do doing their high-wire act.

The boat floated silently away from the gravel bar, seemingly suspended in space with darkness above and the rocky creek bottom below dancing beneath the ripples. The only sounds were the lantern's hiss and an occasional thump of a gig handle against the side of the boat.

The man up front made a quick move, his gig prongs striking the gravel below.

"Missed," he muttered.

The gigger behind laughed softly. I stared over the side. I saw shadows darting. But by the time I positioned myself to spear with the gig, the shadows would be gone.

The other two kept jabbing their gigs downward with swift sudden moves. When they speared a fish, they'd swing it around, the fish twisting and thrashing to get free.

They'd shake the speared fish off into the boat. It would flop mightily for a minute or two, then lay still, sliding to the lowest point in the bottom of the boat, which was where I was standing.

In no time at all, I was ankle deep in dead, dying, bloody fish.

The depth of the water was deceiving. What appeared to be only two feet deep often turned out to be ten. Spearing and expecting to hit bottom at two feet when it's ten throws you off balance. I would have tumbled in several times if one of my companions hadn't reached out to grab a handful of my shirt or hook a finger in my belt.

In a circle of light floating eerily on the water and staring into the depths below, you lose all sense of time and space. There is no horizon on which to orient yourself. You are floating noiselessly inside a ball of light.

I remembered the story in Greek mythology where a faceless, hooded boatman poles souls of the dead across the river Styx to the underworld.

Was I dead? No, but a part of me was. My previous life in another part of Oklahoma.

We worked our way up one side of the creek and down the other. I lost track of where we were until I looked up and saw the camp fire drifting toward us out of the darkness. The boat's prow crunched into the gravel bar, and my companions helped me stumble out of the boat onto the shore. Wayne was there.

"You get any?" he asked, grinning in anticipation.

"You crazy," I said, steadying myself on solid footing. "There's no way in the world a man can stand in a boat and gig a fish."

The giggers standing around laughed. They enjoyed the back-handed compliment I'd handed them. I edged to the fire. I wanted to dry out the bottoms of my trouser legs, which I did as the men worked cleaning a batch of fish and dropping them into an iron pot of boiling grease.

Wayne turned his back to the giggers and, facing me, said in undertone meant only for my ears, "They don't take just anybody out like that. They like you."

"They don't know me," I said.

"They know you," he said and turned away.

How could they know me? Maybe it was Wayne. Yeah, that was it. I was with

Wayne. He was Indian, not a white man like me.

Suddenly, the shadows standing around became people. This was their world. I had entered it. A stranger among strangers. When they invited me to eat, I accepted eagerly. I picked a morsel from the pile mounded on a newspaper in the bottom of a cardboard box.

The fish, coated with a mixture of salt and corn meal, had been cooked fast, which made the pieces crisp and crunchy on the outside and steamy smooth on the inside. I wolfed them down, filling in occasionally with pieces of white bread and an occasional crunch on a quarter of sweet onion.

As we ate, I listened to these "aliens" tell of their women, their drunk times, their women, their bosses at work, their women, their crops, their old ladies, and the time old man Dick fell in the "crik," turned his boat over, doused his lantern, and started swimming the wrong way to get to the bank.

Laughter.

"Liked to have drownded."

More laughter.

I stared into the glowing coals, realizing that I was a long, long way from the world I'd grown up in...my mind was drifting farther and farther into space—like floating through the night in a circle of light on a gigging boat, not knowing how to spear a fish, but willing to give it a try.

This was truly a new world.

And I was glad I came to Delaware County.

When Smoking Was Cool

I learned to smoke because it was part of growing up. Actors in all the movies smoked. Some had a neat way of taking a cigarette from a package and tapping one end on their thumbnail to pack the tobacco down before placing it gently between their lips.

Cigarette lighters varied from the dainty piece decorated with inlaid gold which elegant ladies carried in their tiny jeweled purses to the macho clacker that defied even the wind when you spun the wheel over the flint to spark a flame. It was called a Zippo.

Lucky Strike sponsored the most popular musical radio show on the air—the Hit Parade, starring up-and-comers like Frank Sinatra.

Tough guys smoked Camels. The manufacturer of Camels had a secret they bragged openly about to promote their brand—President Roosevelt smoked Camels. But they'd never use that to sell their cigarettes, boasted their salesmen as they traveled across the land delivering their cartons to every crossroads store in America.

Every newsreel shot in New York's Times Square showed the ten-story billboard of a man smoking a Camel. His mouth was a dark circle and puffs of real smoke came out, making rolling smoke rings that floated gracefully over the scurrying crowds on the streets below.

Smoking was as much a part of the social graces as not spitting on a public sidewalk, not cursing in a mixed crowd, and being man enough to accept the responsibility of raising a child you created out of wedlock.

I had to learn to smoke.

My first experiment was smoking cornsilk. I'd steal matches from the match holder Mom kept hanging on the wall near the kitchen stove. Then I'd stuff half a sheet of newspaper into my pocket and stroll nonchalantly across the garden to the corn patch. As soon as I got out of sight of the house, I'd select beards of dried cornsilk and roll them in a piece of newspaper. When I stuck a lighted match to them, sometimes they'd flare up so much that the flame would burn the end of my nose.

It's a wonder I didn't burn up the whole corn crop.

I graduated to tobacco when Junior Mattix and I picked up cigarette butts under the grandstand at the baseball field where the town team played on Sundays. We'd tear the butts apart and shake the tobacco into an empty Prince Albert can.

We went to our secret hiding place in Mattix's abandoned chicken house. We'd roll cigarettes out of our Duke's Mixture blend and smoke them one after another until all of the tobacco was gone and we were both too sick to walk when we headed for the house, but were too ashamed to admit it.

A friend of ours who had a job sacking groceries stole a package of Lucky Strikes one week. We helped him smoke them all up before he got caught. We thought it was neat smoking "taylor-mades" and blowing smoke out our nostrils like they did in the movies. Before the pack was gone that afternoon, we even made some serious attempts at inhaling real tobacco smoke.

After graduating from high school and getting my first job, I felt the only thing lacking to reach full manhood was learning to smoke on a regular basis. This meant an investment in a cigarette lighter and enough money on hand to keep a package of cigarettes—Luckies, of course, since they sponsored the Hit Parade—in my shirt pocket.

In the meantime, I got by bumming—mostly from a friend I worked with. That came to a crisis one Sunday when we were in the drug store looking for some girls to flirt with and he pulled a fresh pack of Luckies out of his tee shirt pocket.

The deep green packages weren't covered with cellophane then. The cigarettes were packed in foil, which was folded over neatly on top and sealed with a federal stamp across the center.

I watched in fascinated awe as he slipped a fingernail under the edge of one of the folds on one end and ripped it open with a neat, deft movement without destroying the federal stamp, which you were supposed to do according to federal law. Such surgical boldness took my breath away.

Then he held the pack upside down in his right hand and tapped the opened pack gently on the index finger of his left hand. Two or three fresh, firm cigarettes scooted out far enough for him to make a selection, which he did by nipping one with his lips. Then he gently tapped the others back in place and dropped the package back into his shirt pocket.

God, he looked so cool doing it.

With a sinking heart, I watched him clack open his Zippo, light up, and blow a couple of smoke rings my direction. They were beauties. I stared at them in open-mouthed wonder as the smoke rings floated gently through the air, getting larger and larger until they simply disappeared.

But I was determined to hang onto my dignity and not bum a cigarette from him since he didn't offer me one. However, the smoke rings broke me down.

"How about me bumming one?" I asked. "I bet I can do that."

He blew a smoke ring in my face and sneered, "Why don't you buy your own, cheapskate?"

That made me mad. I headed straight for the tobacco counter, dug out seventeen cents and tossed the coins on the glass-topped counter.

"Gimme a pack of Luckies," I said, trying to act as if I'd been buying cigarettes all my life.

I pulled in a deep breath to steady my nerves before beginning my own very first surgery to open a pack of cigarettes. Rip, rip, rip, I went.

I botched it. Tore half the federal stamp in the process. When I tipped the package and tapped it on my finger, several cigarettes spilled out and went rolling across the floor.

I grabbed for them and began stuffing them back into my package. I figured if smoking cornsilk wrapped in a newspaper didn't hurt me, what harm could a little floor grit sticking to the paper do?

Since I didn't have a Zippo yet, I used book matches to fire one up.

This was my first big investment in cigarettes. And to prove I was more of a man than my friend, I inhaled furiously, again and again and again.

By the time I was finished with it, I was sick. Sicker'n I ever got smoking Duke's Mixture with Junior in our clubhouse. I was more than sick. I was drunk. The drug store went into a lazy spin, like a merry-go-round in slow motion. I swore that if I lived I would never, ever smoke another cigarette. I even debated about throwing away the new pack I'd just bought, but the loss of seventeen cents was just too great of an economic factor to simply throw away.

Well… I finished that pack. Then another. And yet another.

I eventually learned the art of ripping open a new pack of Luckies with dexterity without disturbing the stamp. I bought me a Zippo, and could snap it open with a flick of my wrist. I could inhale as good as Humphrey Bogart and hold it in my lungs and let the smoke drift out of my nose and mouth as I talked without getting sick.

Now I was a man-of-the-world. I had learned to smoke! But, by damn, I never, ever learned how to blow smoke rings—even though I kept trying for twenty-five years.

I'm proud to say I quit before smoking became a social disgrace. I simply didn't like being eternally tied to a package of cigarettes, a Zippo lighter, and an ash tray.

Giving up smoking was tough. I tried every way I could think of to quit. I finally decided the only way to overcome the addiction was to erase smoking from my mind—not even think about it one way or the other. It worked for me. I still feel that way. Smoking is not a part of my life. Let those who smoke smoke. Let those who don't don't.

My personal experience makes me want to laugh at this national hysteria we are going through over smoking. When I began smoking, you thought smoking was cool and getting pregnant out of wedlock was a disgrace. Now getting pregnant out of wedlock is cool and smoking is a disgrace.

It makes absolutely no sense to me for society to ostracize one of its own for enjoying a cigarette while forgiving one of its own couples for yielding to the joys of sex and participating in creating a life which they do not want, which you do not want, and which nobody wants.

Stan's World

I was born in, raised in, and graduated from public school in Oklahoma.

I was never out of the state until after I got my first steady job racking balls for $5 week in a small town in northeast Oklahoma. One of the first things I did was to hitchhike a ride to Southwest City in Missouri just to see how it felt to cross a state line.

I didn't see anything there that made me want to ever leave my native state. Nothing, not even the derogatory epithet "Okie" developed by John Steinbeck in his novel *The Grapes of Wrath*, failed to diminish my pride in being a true Oklahoma native.

Until I met Stan.

Every morning when I opened the pool hall, I'd look across the courthouse square and see old Stan coming down the street, bow-legged, wearing overalls and a black cowboy hat.

He always got there before I finished sweeping out. He'd take his favorite seat, fourth one from the end next to the first cuspidor.

He'd finger his plug of Brown Mule from his bib pocket, gnaw a chunk off, and settle back to spend his day watching the boys play pool.

Someone said he was a hundred years old. He looked it. His dark, leathery face, laced with wrinkles, still retained a firmness that gave it life. His nose, though large, was straight, a characteristic of the Cherokees. The bags under his slow-moving, dark eyes sagged and exposed too much red of his lower lids. His lips were set in a perpetual downturn at each corner.

Every morning I'd have to bump his shoes with my broom to let him know I had to sweep under his feet. It looked like he'd learn. So one morning, aggravated, I said, "Move your feet, will you?"

He shuffled his feet aside and said something in Cherokee which I interpreted as cussing.

To cover for my ignorance, I retorted, "To hell with you, too. You ought to be paying rent on that seat. Ever think of that?"

My sophomoric anger welled from a hurt. I'd never heard anybody speak anything but English. And the way Steinbeck wrote it, Oklahomans didn't do a very good job of that.

But before I'd finished sweeping, I was sorry I'd said what I did and consoled myself with the thought that he probably never learned to speak English.

I purposefully opened up early the next morning and hurried to sweep out from under Stan's seat before he arrived. I watched him out of the corner of my eye when he came in. Before he sat down, he stooped to look under his seat. I thought I detected a smile as he turned to sit down.

I felt better, and, watching him surreptitiously, I wondered what was his life was really like? Not many men began their lives as rambunctious Indian warriors fighting to stop the relentless flow of whites moving westward and ended them sitting in a white man's pool hall watching white men play pool.

I found myself wishing I could speak Cherokee so I could talk to him.

One day when we were alone, Stan in his favorite seat, and me staring out the front window, I felt those bleary eyes fixed on me.

It was a message. But what? I decided to play a game of pool solitaire on the table in front of Stan. I selected a stick, placed the cue ball, and broke the racked balls with a hard shot. The colored spheres scattered, thumped wildly around the table and came to a silent stop.

I began to run the table. After each shot, I studied the position of the balls carefully before choosing the next. I pretended Stan wasn't there, watching my every move. I came up against a difficult choice. I was standing with my back to Stan, slowly chalking my cue tip, trying to make up my mind.

"Eight ball in the side pocket," came the strong voice from behind. It startled me, but I was just as quick to smother my reaction. I calmly leaned across the table without saying a word, taking careful aim, and sliced the eight ball into the side pocket.

"Thanks," I said and gave him an acknowledging nod. His down turned lips straightened into a half smile. I offered him the cue stick. "I bet you're a pool hustler. Take this and show me what you can do."

He shook his head. "Too old."

"Awwww. How old? Sixty? Seventy?"

His smile deepened every wrinkle in his face. "That too long ago. I forget."

"Someone told me a hundred. Are you a hundred?"

"I carry gun in Watie's army."

"You're putting me on," I said.

He shook his head, grin widening.

To prove him wrong, I turned to the scoreboard. I jotted down the dates of the Civil War and said, "You had to be at least fifteen to fight with the Confederacy in General Stand Watie's Cherokee Brigade."

I deducted fifteen from 1861. "That puts you being born in 1846, give or take a few years."

I faced him, juggling the piece of chalk in the palm of my hand. "According to those numbers, Stan, you're a hundred, or right up there somewhere."

He nodded.

Now that we were friends, I tossed the piece of chalk in the chalk tray and I sat down beside him.

"Tell me how it was back then, after the war. Did you young bucks burn out settlers and fight with the U.S. Calvary all the time? Like in the movies and stuff?"

He laughed softly. I guess it was a laugh. It didn't show in his face much, just a few more wrinkles appearing at the corners of his eyes, but he shook all over.

"I chop cotton. Plant garden. Milk cows. Raise chickens. Butcher hog to have meat in winter."

"You mean you were just a farmer? You didn't ride around the country killing people?"

"It wrong to kill people."

"Yeah, I know. But—"

"Cherokee write out government on paper like white men do in Washington. It say it wrong to kill people."

"I read about that. Your people came out here. It was called the Trail of Tears, wasn't it?"

"Many Cherokee come before that. My father come with them. I born here."

"Here? You were born here in Oklahoma?"

"Not Oklahoma then. Cherokee Nation."

"You make it sound like it wasn't much different than it is today."

"Not. My father help build new Cherokee Nation here in Indian Territory. He farmer. He say we no longer people of our ancestors. White man come. Take all."

Same old story, I thought, a trifle irritated. White man evil; Indian good. I chided, "What's wrong with that?"

"Not wrong...Not want."

"Why not? It's a great country, isn't it? Aren't you glad to be a citizen of such a great country?"

"I not citizen of your country. I Cherokee. Your country come to me. I did not go to your country. I citizen of Oklahoma because I born here. I live in house my father built. I come now every morning to sit here and watch young men play pool. One day I will not come. My world will no longer be."

During that summer on hot afternoons when nobody came in to play pool, I entertained Stan making difficult shots—with his advice and consent, of course. But when anybody was there, he acted as if he didn't know me. Our secret friendship seemed to pull us together even closer.

Then on a cold, misty day the following March—the kind of day that makes you wonder if winter will ever get gone and let spring come in, I opened the pool hall a little early to build a fire in the coal stove so the place would be warm for Stan when he got there.

It wasn't until I began sweeping trash from under the fourth seat from the end near the cuspidor before I realized it was empty. I paused, frowning and glanced across the square.

The street was bare. The mist collected on the front panes, blurring my vision. I felt a chill and shivered involuntarily.

Stan's world had ended—like he said it would. I cleared my throat and resumed sweeping, the truth weighing heavily on my shoulders.

Stan was a true native of Oklahoma. Born here, lived here, died here. He didn't come to our country...we came to his. I suppose by rights all of us in this part of Oklahoma should be Cherokee citizens, not the other way around.

The Bootlegging Business

Folks here in northeastern Oklahoma were never bothered much by our state's prohibition laws, which existed from statehood until they were repealed in the fifties.

You could pick up a bottle every time you went to Missouri, which almost everyone did at least once a week to buy groceries, a new pair of shoes, or a new strap for a harness.

You'd just lay the bottle on the seat beside you and come on back home. No one would bother you.

Or you might even get two bottles—one for you and one for your neighbor, if he'd of asked you to.

Sometimes guys would by a peck sack full of pints and half pints and have them handy if someone were to ask, "You don't happen to have an extra bottle you'd sell a feller, do you?"

Of course, you'd have to charge him fifty cents or a buck more than what you paid for it—just good business sense, was all.

And most of us went to church on Sundays. If we didn't go, we felt guilty about it and had respect for those who went and took their kids.

Hypocrisy? Well…

Those of us who lived several counties away from any of our state's borders had a little tougher time.

Bootlegging was big business—and dangerous.

Some were freelancers. They'd make "runs" for anybody who needed a supply. If they had regular routes, they'd contribute to the campaign funds of the sheriffs in all the counties they had to go through on their way to the border and back. This type were, in effect, wholesalers.

Others were more daring. To increase their profits, they'd drive the back roads. They were easy to spot. A trunk load of whiskey was so heavy, the rear springs would bottom out and the rear bumper would drag on the high spots.

If you got caught by the sheriff doing this, it'd cost you plenty for not playing the game according to the unwritten rules.

One of my high school classmates, our class queen in fact, married a boy whose older brother was just getting started as a supplier. It was tough breaking into the business. The old hands would run you off the road, even shoot your tires. You knew, too, the local sheriff had orders from the other bootleggers to make it tough on you.

My classmate said her older brother-in-law helped her buy a car so she could get a license registered in her own named and paid her to make trips to Missouri for him. The sheriffs didn't stop nice-looking young girls sailing down the highway.

At our last class reunion, she laughed about it and said, "It was the only job I could find back then and the pay was good. It sure beat twenty-five cents an hour working in a doctor's office."

Every few years, we'd have a vote to repeal prohibition. But our bootleggers would finance the church workers' anti-liquor campaign and we'd vote to keep prohibition in.

Hypocrisy? Well...

Beer joints, like Pete's Place where I lived, only sold beer to make their business legitimate. Their real money was in the little room behind the bar where they kept their whiskey and where they mixed drinks for you.

Pete planned on getting raided every so often, especially when it came close to elections.

The sheriff would call ahead and tell Pete what time he'd be there. Pete would put all the whiskey in the trunk of his car and take it to his house—except for a bottle or two which he'd leave setting on the cabinet near the sink in the back room for the sheriff to find and have his picture taken with.

Then Pete would slip the sheriff a sawbuck or two for his time and trouble—and to help with his campaign expenses.

Our sheriff made a mistake once. He was so busy he sent a green recruit to raid Pete's place in our town. The young man was proud to be a deputy. He polished his badge everyday until the sun was so bright glinting off it that it nearly put your eyes out.

The young man with the bright badge didn't call Pete ahead of time. He just stepped inside the front door, fumbled for his pistol, and yelled, "This is a raid. Don't anybody move!"

After it was over and everybody had settled back down to normal and was talking about it, Pete moaned, "I don't hold it against the kid for doing me the way he did. I didn't even mind him carrying out several bottles for his own use. But there was no reason for him to pour all the rest of it down the sink. No reason atall!"

Many bootleggers built roadhouses where you could go and enjoy a night of dancing and fun.

Some of the places would tolerate you bringing your own bottle and charge you for the ice and 7-Up or Coke or whatever you liked to mix it with.

Other places had a big guy at the door who patted you down to make sure you weren't bringing any booze in with you. You had to buy it there. And the ice. And the soft drinks.

Some places featured live bands. But most had juke boxes with some lively Bob Wills tunes on them. But who cared? After a couple of drinks, anybody'd dance with you if you asked.

Classy bootleggers printed calling cards. They'd deliver your order to your door. I had a bootlegger's card when I went into the army. One of the guys saw it one day when I was digging for some bills and asked, "What's that?"

I told him. He thought it was hilarious. Being born in Oklahoma and raised here, I naturally thought bootlegging was a way of life everywhere.

Hypocritical? No, not really. We're just human beings. As long as your culture keeps your little wrongs little, then you turn out okay—most of the time.

After the state highway patrol was formed, bootleggers had to start contributing to the campaign expenses of legislators and governors. This raised the cost of doing business. To offset this increase in overhead, they began bringing their booze in by the truck load.

Unfortunately for them, they backed the wrong man for governor in the fifties. In retaliation, the new governor-who-wasn't-supposed-to-be ordered his men to start stopping the trucks coming in. Then he used this publicity to convince church people we'd be better off legalizing liquor so we could tax it and have more tax money to spend on our kids' education.

Sounds familiar, doesn't it? You want to win elections, you say it's for our kids. Works every time.

The laws were repealed. Our bootleggers became legitimate. The tax money was used to hire more educators to find out why our kids weren't getting educated and the educators formed a union that began contributing to the campaign expenses of our legislators and governors so they can get more money for themselves. Our kids got nothing.

Now, I know some folks might find this amusing, if you're in the mood to be amused.

But I have written it with a sense of sadness. Beer was our generation's marijuana, whiskey our cocaine. Our roadhouses could be compared to where the young today go to "hang out."

The difference, as I have lived it, is that our crude culture kept our failings from becoming big faults.

Without a restraining culture, we revert to survival of the fittest. Our "little" failings become dominant characteristics. Road rage, school shootings, random drive-by murders are not wrongs. They are simply "happenings" which are exciting and makes you famous. And you can converted fame into wealth.

Were we hypocritical believing one thing and doing another? Well, yes...

But hypocrisy is a definition. You can be just as hypocritical saying there is no God, then calling on him when you're in trouble as believing in God and asking him to forgive you when you make mistakes.

We have to choose. There is no in between.

A Dog's Tail

It was one of those typical large family gatherings during the 4th of July weekend. Linda, a niece who lives in an affluent area of Tulsa, was telling me a very interesting story about an activity that I knew absolutely nothing about.

It was a fox hunt—a real bona fide English-style fox hunt, complete with the traditional riding regalia and a large pack of baying hounds controlled by a MFH (Master of Fox Hounds, who sends signals to the dogs with loud notes from his shiny brass bugle.)

Only they are not called dogs, Linda scolded me good-naturedly when I used the term. They are "hounds." To emphasize just how traditionally English their hunts were, she went on to explain that even the dogs' tails weren't called "tails." They were called "sterns."

Nor do the sterns start wagging when the hound gets a scent—it feathers, as in "the stern went up and began feathering."

"The only thing different from the way they do it in England and the way we do it here in Oklahoma is that since foxes are rare, our hounds are trained to chase coyotes," she explained. "But coyotes are just as smart and elusive as foxes are."

I was fascinated. She promised to call me sometime when the group came to this area to enjoy a fox (coyote) hunt.

I can't wait. All my life I've seen English fox hunts in movies and on TV and thought how exciting it would be to hear the bugle call and "ride to the hounds."

Of course, I'll be a passenger in the observer trailer. I wouldn't know how to ride a horse if my life depended on it. I tried it once and the animal I was on knew darned well I didn't know what I was doing and headed straight for the barn. When he got in his stall and wouldn't budge, I gave up trying to make him "go" and climbed down.

But as Linda talked enthusiastically about her fox (coyote) hunting passion, I couldn't help contrast it with another "hunt" I went on in the spring of '41.

"You want to go with Pop to find his coon dog?" my new friend Bill Powell asked.

You bet. As a new boy in town, I was willing to do anything at anytime to please anybody. "Pop" was Jeff Lindly, his step father.

Jeff was a tall, thin, but very tough man, both physically and mentally. He had to be, as the county's sheriff several terms during the thirties. When he was sheriff, they wore guns because they had to, not as symbol of authority.

I didn't have the slightest idea how you go about finding a lost coon dog. The only dog I ever tried to find was old Boscoe, who'd wandered away from our house one day, not touching his food or water for days. I was too young to understand why a male dog would do that.

I thought he'd gone out into the woods to chase a rabbit and got lost. I would walk through the timber yelling, "Here, Boscoe! Here, Boscoe!"

But when he came home, he didn't come from the woods. He came from the direction of town and he was chewed up so bad I thought he'd been in a terrible fight. It wasn't until later that I realized what those "fights" were all about.

So I was mildly surprised when we crawled into Jeff's pickup one evening after dark and headed out of town.

How in the world would you go about finding a coon dog after dark?

Surely he wasn't going to steal one somewhere, was he? Not Jeff. There wasn't a more honest man alive. But I could relate to his feelings because of the way I felt when I "lost" Boscoe.

As we headed north, Jeff told us about the hunt they'd had the night before. The county coon hunters had gathered up on the flats, placed their token bets, and turned their dogs loose.

When the dogs picked up a scent, they'd let loose with a chorus of baying that you could heard for miles. The men would pile in their pickups and drive the backroads to keep as close to the chase as possible. Every so often they would stop, kill their engines, and just listen, the collective sounds of the baying animals music to their ears.

"That's my little Midge," one would exclaim jubilantly. "Listen to her go!"

Each hunter could distinguish his own hound's baying. And each hunter could "read" the sound, whether his dog was leading the pack or whether his animal's cry was one of frustration as it was trying to pick up the scent.

"My Old Blue was out in the lead most of the night," Jeff said proudly as we turned off the main highway and headed toward the flats. "I think the other dogs gave up. They all came back to camp... except Old Blue."

After a long moment, Jeff added, somewhat sadly, "No telling where he is by now. He might have chased that coon clear over into the next county."

"Suppose he's took up with somebody else?" Bill asked.

"That or somebody's chained him up so he can't come back."

If a coon dog doesn't come home on his own initiative, I learned, he will return to the spot where he was let out to begin the hunt.

Jeff pulled off onto a logging road, wound down into the timber, and stopped at the place where they'd camped the night before. We got out. Jeff sent Bill and me out into the darkness to find wood while he built a fire.

We sat around the fire for a long time. Jeff told us more coon hunting stories, mostly about the unbelievable accomplishments of Old Blue.

I could feel his sense of loss.

Soon he went to the pickup and came back to the fire carrying what appeared to be a cow's horn. Which is what it was, only it wasn't a cow's horn. It was a steer's horn, hollowed out with its sharp tip cut off.

Jeff raised it to his lips and blew it as loud as he could. It made the darndest sound I ever heard, reverberating through the night. I just knew they probably heard it all the way into Jay, ten miles away.

I glanced at Bill. He just sat there and grinned. Evidently, Bill had gone through this before.

But I felt sorry for Jeff as he hooked the horn to his belt and returned his attention to the fire.

He told us more about the hunt the night before. I could tell the way he paused between his slow moving sentences that he was listening to every sound coming out of the night even as he talked, listening for any sound that would tell him Old Blue was coming back.

Every few minutes, Jeff would stand, turn his back to the fire and blow a blast through his horn. He'd always face in a different direction.

Bill and I kept the fire going as we waited into the wee hours of the morning for Old Blue to come back.

He never did. I could see the deep sadness in Jeff's face as he finally had to admit to himself that Old Blue was gone, done in by his own devotion to his duty to run down the coon no matter what.

We put out the fire, scattered the smoldering sticks, climbed into the pickup, and came home.

As we pulled into the Lindly driveway, the truck's headlights raked the porch.

There was Old Blue, his head lifted and ears cocked as he recognized the sound of his master's pickup.

"Well, I'll be doggoned," Jeff said.

You could feel the extreme joy in his otherwise laconic remark.

He shut off the engine, switched off the lights, and we climbed out. You could hear Old Blue's tail thumping the porch, as if to ask, "Where've you guys been?"

I've never seen Jeff's face happier—and I had the pleasure of knowing him for years.

I am eagerly looking forward to going on the English-type fox hunt this fall. I intend to write a story about it. I surely hope Linda will forgive me if I slip up and call one of the hounds a dog and refer to its "stern" as a tail...

Because there's nothing that makes a man feel as wonderful as the sound of his lost dog's tail thumping a welcome on the pine flooring of his front porch.

Finding Love

I woke up and glanced out the window that overlooked the town square. It was a beautiful spring day.

My heart began pounding when I saw Jane Ann and Nita sitting on the courthouse lawn in the shade of the oak tree. They appeared to be looking for something in the grass.

"I'll do it!" I said aloud and rolled quickly out of bed. First, I'll buy her a Coke. Then I'll ask her to go to the show with me.

I noticed my hands trembling as I punched my feet through the legs of a freshly washed and heavily starched pair of khakis.

I slipped on a white T shirt that I'd worn only one time. The chest pocket where I carried my cigarettes didn't sag too much.

I pulled a snaggle-toothed comb through my hair and ran down the steep steps to the entry leading out onto the sidewalk.

I took a quick look around. The town square was vacant. It buoyed my spirits. Although I was the new boy in town, I had every right to speak to the girls. Besides that, I'd been introduced to them a few days ago.

Jane Ann was beautiful, ebullient, and forward. However, it was Nita who intrigued me. She seemed shy. There was a natural curl in her blonde hair. She had the loveliest blue eyes I'd ever seen, emphasized by a faint band of freckles across the bridge of her nose.

I tried to act casual as I strolled up the sidewalk. Jane Ann saw me.

"Hi, there," she said. "Where are you going?"

I paused, not feeling a bit nervous—until Nita glanced up, a slight smile on her lips. I choked. I gestured helplessly toward the café.

"Going to get something to geek, I guess," I said, only vaguely aware I'd said something terribly stupid. I tried to cover it up quickly by asking, "What're you guys doing anyhow?"

"Trying to find a four-leaf clover," Jane Ann said. "Want to help?"

"Sure," I said, surprised at my own boldness. I strode toward them, John Wayne style. I was afraid to look at Nita because every time I did I got all queasy inside. I plopped down on the grass with them and, like they were doing, began fingering through the patch of clover.

"I'll bet a Coke I find one before you do," I said, glancing up at Jane Ann.

"It's a bet," Nita said, blind siding me.

Then I had to look at her. I had a feeling she could see into my very soul. It made me all up tight again. I couldn't say anything—just stared.

Jane Ann jumped to her feet and said, "There's none here. Let's go look in that patch over there."

Was she asking me, or Nita? My bewilderment must have shown.

"No. You go on. We'll stay here," Nita said.

WE! She said We!

My heart began thumping again. I was afraid they would hear it. I dropped my attention quickly to the clover beneath my fingers, my ears burning and my throat so constricted I couldn't have said anything if I wanted to.

"You'll be sorry when I find one first," Jane Ann said, hurrying away.

I kept my head down, my awareness of Nita's presence so strong that I imagined I could hear the whisper of her fingers moving through the soft clover fronds.

My inner self screamed: Now was the time to ask her.

But how do you ask a girl for a date? I argued back.

All through high school, I didn't think I was worthy of any girl. Now, here in a new town, holding down a good job, a stranger to everybody, I could start over, couldn't I?

But what if she said no? I heard the soft pluck of her pulling a sprig of clover.

"You owe me a Coke," she said softly, holding out the green four-leaf frond.

"Awww," I tried to make my groan sound sincere. "You cheated. Let me see it. I want to make sure."

When I took it from her, our fingers touched. The shock was overwhelming. I could hardly see the sprig of clover as my thoughts churned. I pretended to be still suspicious as I examined the four green, heart-shaped leaves.

"You win," I said handing it back.

Instead, she pushed against my fingers, her soft, cool palm a nerve shattering caress.

"No. You keep it," she said.

My spirits soared! She was giving me something to remember her by, I thought, until she added, "You might need it for good luck with Jane Ann."

My mouth fell open. My lips felt suddenly dry and hot. "What do you mean?" I stammered.

Her smile was both cryptic and accusing.

"I thought you knew. It was her idea to come up here and look for four leaf clovers this early in the morning. I wondered what she was up to until I saw the way she kept looking up at the window of your room."

Frustrated, I jammed the clover into the pocket of my T shirt and rose grandly to my feet.

"I owe you a Coke," I said in the manliest voice I could muster. "You want it now—?"

Nita had an amused look on her face. She leaned back, propping herself up with her hands. She shook her head.

"No. I want you to owe me."

Filled with helpless anger, I spun on my heel to stalk away and ran smack-dab into the trunk of the tall oak tree. Embarrassed, I scooted quickly around it and headed for the café.

"Where are you going?" Jane Ann called.

"I'm hungry. I haven't eaten yet." I flung over my shoulder.

She had a puzzled look on her face when she glanced at Nita. Let them fight it out, I grumped to myself as I went on my way.

When I finished my meal, I lifted my pack of cigarettes from my T-shirt pocket. The four-leaf clover dropped to the table. I made a quick move to brush it off onto the floor before anybody saw it.

But my hand froze in mid air. Staring down at it, I remembered the touch of her hand against mine. She said she wanted me to owe her, didn't she?

I gently picked it up and returned it to my shirt pocket. Back in my room, I placed the wilting clover carefully between the pages in my journal.

And there it stayed, so green and beautiful, reminding me how our hands touched.

Perhaps someday ...

An American Tragedy

Time to pick up the mail. I crossed the street to the small wooden building on the east side of the square.

I witnessed an American tragedy there. I'd gone to pick up my laundry, which I'd sent home for Mom to wash. I was standing in line behind a chunky young man who kept glancing back at me as if he wished I would go away. We'd met. The kids called him Dutch.

I was the new boy in town, fresh out of high school, and wanted to be as friendly as possible.

"Hi, Dutch," I said.

He mumbled something that sounded like, "I wish they'd hurry up."

Meaning the talkative lady at the window, I guessed.

"Yeah. Me too," I agreed.

"I'm in a hurry," he whispered over his shoulder. "My old man ordered some parts. He's waiting on me to get back."

His family owned and operated a local sawmill. They seemed to have plenty of money. The kids threw around fives, tens, and twenties while the rest of us counted change carefully paying for our Cokes and things whenever we congregated in drug stores.

Lumbering was big business then. Their huge saws would whine from daylight to dark, shaping 2 x 4s and planks out of trees harvested from the forests of Delaware County.

Dutch always had a car to drive. Some of the kids told me he'd been driving since he was seven. They described how he would slide to the front edge of the seat and hang onto the steering wheel so he could reach the foot pedals. Apparently, the parents made no attempt to control their children.

The talkative lady first in line at the window finally took her bundle of mail and stepped aside. We all moved up one notch. Dutch was now second, me third.

"I forgot something in my car," Dutch said abruptly.

"I'll hold your place," I said. I wanted to be friendly. I knew I was still on probation, being new in town.

"No need of that," he said and hurried out the door.

Mystified, I closed the gap in the line. The holdup this time was the postmaster himself, who turned talkative, asking the man about his coon dog that disappeared.

"Disappeared, hell," the man grumbled. "He got stole. And I know who done it."

He began listing the clues one by one which confirmed the theft—at least in his mind.

I shifted my weight impatiently from foot to foot, trying to send a message to the postmaster. It didn't do any good.

Before the man finished his story, Dutch returned. He got in line behind me. When the man who'd lost his dog finished by threatening to get the law on the alleged thief, the postmaster looked around him to ask, "Next?"

I stepped aside and motioned for Dutch to take his place in front of me.

"You were here first," I said.

"No," he said, shaking his head vigorously. "I'm not in no hurry."

The post master fixed his gaze on Dutch. "Did you come to pick up that package for your dad?"

Dutch nodded meekly. When the postmaster disappeared from the window to get the package, Dutch moved reluctantly to the window ahead of me.

The post master returned, ripping a tag from the package.

"You'll have to sign for it," he told Dutch, sliding tag toward him. I could tell Dutch was trying to see where I was the way he kept glancing sideways, just enough to see me out of the corners of his eyes. He kept shifting to block my view to what was going on.

I didn't understand, so I tried to keep a respectful distance away, since there was no one else behind me. But at the same time, his nervous actions aroused my curiosity. I simply had to see—without him seeing me seeing.

He gripped the pencil awkwardly in his fist, poised above the line where he was supposed to sign. He started making little circles in the air, then glanced up at the post master.

"I forgot how to make an X," he confessed softly, obviously for the postmaster's ears only.

That shocked me, but it didn't seem to faze the postmaster. He made an X with his finger on the counter, explaining patiently, "Don't you remember? Just start up here, draw a line down this way. Then jump over here and draw another line down. Make them cross in the middle."

Stunned, I thought, how, in modern-day America, could there be *any* healthy young man *anywhere* unable to sign his own name, or even know how to make an X?

Following the postmaster's instructions carefully, Dutch made a shaky X on the signature line, then, hiding his embarrassment, grabbed the package and hurried out the door without even looking my direction.

I hated myself for not doing what he had wanted me to do—go ahead of him. He had been trying to hide from me the embarrassing fact that he couldn't read or write.

I was still staring after Dutch when the postmaster asked, "Yes?"

I hadn't lived here long enough for him to remember my name. I told him and asked if I had a package. He went to search.

I glanced out the window again, saw Dutch toss his package in his car, climb in, and back away, spinning his rear tires.

I tried to imagine what it would be like not being able to read or write. I couldn't even imagine it, because I'd been reading ever since I could remember. And enjoying every page I ever read.

I could, however, remember learning to write—just barely. But I probably wouldn't have remembered it at all if the school I attended hadn't made us take penmanship drills every year up through the eighth grade to improve our writing skills.

I hated the push and pulls, but I enjoyed doing the ovals strung together, like trying to draw a coiled spring. I labored over trying to make my letters match the ones in the pictures across the top of the blackboards.

All the teachers, regardless of what subject they taught, would grade you on your penmanship as well as on the quality of your answers.

The ability to write down your thoughts, to me, was a way of contributing to the vast storehouse of man's knowledge on the bookshelves in our nation's libraries. I had always dreamed of having my name on some of those books myself.

I knew I would surely die if I couldn't read. Or write. No matter how freely I could throw around fives, tens, and twenties.

I always felt awkward around Dutch after that because he knew I knew. I kept trying to find some way I could tell him that I never told any of the other kids, especially after he narrowly avoided a wreck one day when I and some other kids were in the car with him.

It crossed my mind that he was trying to get rid of me for knowing he couldn't read or write. Which wasn't true, of course—just a vain thought on my part.

Dutch and I became good friends. When I told him a year later I was going to leave Jay and enroll at Oklahoma University, he acted impressed, asking serious questions about what it would be like going to college. His inquiries became more of a longing than curiosity.

He even offered to drive me to Norman. He had no idea where Norman was, or how far, but he said it didn't matter. He would take me—if I would show him the way, because he was unable to read road maps.

That was the American tragedy—a lost mind.

So today we are building our fifth post office in seventy years. Construction has commenced. Within a few months we will all be making our way to our new post office south and west of the square.

And if I happen to get in line behind someone acting nervous, I'll give them plenty of space.

I don't want to ever again see a fine young man in America who doesn't know how to make an X.

The National Youth Administration

President Roosevelt called it the National Youth Administration. We called it the NYA. You worked part-time going to school and the government paid you $6.00 a month.

Dad was a Republican and dead-set against any of us boys signing up "for any kind of a government hand-out."

"Any time you take government money, you do what the government says," he argued. "That man—(meaning president Roosevelt)—is going to ruin this country, giving away tax money like that."

Mom was a Democrat. It beat using egg money to buy books, she said. I signed up. Dad quit speaking to me.

Perhaps it was the subtle shift of allegiance from family to "that man in Washington" that caused the rift. I couldn't put my finger on it, but I felt it, and I didn't like the feeling.

Or perhaps it was slipping from boyhood into manhood that strained our father-son relationship.

No matter. I was determined to get through school. I had my heart set on being a writer. I couldn't tell Dad that. We worked the field of hay in silence, me forking the shocks up onto the wagon, him distributing the load.

Forking hay did help me with my first NYA job. The janitor handed me a broom and lectured me on how to use it.

"Don't even try to sweep up a flat sheet of paper," he warned. "You're wasting your energy. Just bend over and wad it up with your left hand—" he demonstrated—"like this. Now see how easy it is to push it along with your broom?"

He taught me everything he knew about janitoring, and by the end of the year I, too, became an expert at handling a push broom.

"They going to put that down on your diploma?" Dad asked.

I bit my lip to keep from snapping back. Seniors do that sometimes. And I loved my Dad. It was that "man in Washington" that caused it all, I confessed bitterly to myself.

My senior year, I was given a more responsible job—patrol officer at the highway crossing. I had to wear a white belt and shoulder strap. I mentioned my promotion to Dad. "Humph," was all he said.

I did feel like a fool standing out there in the middle of the street. All the kids had enough sense to know when to cross the street, or not to, if a car was coming. Dad, I finally concluded, had a point—this was a waste of taxpayers' money.

However, one day when a group of girls in my class, including one who I was secretly in love with, approached the crossing, I bravely faced the oncoming car and held up my hand. The car slowed and then, to my astonishment, came to a complete stop. I puffed up importantly as the girls crossed the highway under my stalwart protection.

"Oh, thank you," said the girl I was secretly in love with.

Her sweet "thank you" turned me into a tough cop.

When the girls were safely across, I scowled at the driver of the car and waved him on. Maybe I could be a detective. Nothing wrong with being a detective and writing true detective stories, was there?

Shortly before graduation, the NYA people told us about their college program. You arranged your schedule so you could work four hours a day. They furnished you room and board and enough cash to buy books with.

Since our state universities didn't charge tuition for state residents, I figured I could make it—with Mom slipping me a little egg money on the side now and then.

Only trouble was, boys enrolled in engineering school. How could I learn to be a writer studying engineering?

It helped when the Japanese bombed Pearl Harber. Dad thought it would be a good idea, being an engineer with a war going on. He even promised to help, and grudgingly admitted that signing up for the NYA would be a good thing.

He gave me all the money he had, which was $18. And cautioned, "Don't spend it foolishly."

I promised not to. I picked up my high school transcript and, with high hopes, I hitch-hiked to Norman. I found the NYA dormitory and made my application for government assistance. The kindly man wearing glasses which kept falling down on his nose surveyed my transcript.

"Well, well," he said. "With grades like these, you shouldn't have any trouble passing the entrance exams."

"What're those?" I asked, perplexed.

"Everyone has to take entrance exams," he explained. "They want to know if you have the basics you need to learn on the university level."

"I thought that was what the transcript was for," I said.

"It's the rule. Some high schools are better than others. They give their own exams here… just to make sure."

I wasn't afraid of tests. I'd always scored high, hadn't I? On everything except algebra. But who needed algebra writing novels? Let somebody else count the words.

I was just barely listening when he briefed me. Entrance exams would be Thursday. They would have the results Friday. Classes would start Monday. In the meantime, I would begin work immediately as a laborer, helping the university build a new dormitory for football players.

He gave me my room assignment. My roommate spent all his time standing in front of a mirror combing his hair and whistling "Blues in the Night."

I never did like that song and certainly not now hearing it sung over and over by a boy standing in front of a mirror combing his hair when I was trying to brush up for my entrance exams.

At work I was given a wheelbarrow and thrown into a line of guys who shoved their wheelbarrow under a cement mixer, pushed it over to an elevator, rode up the elevator to the second floor, staggered with their load across the floor of the new building, and dumped it into forms.

Wait until I tell Dad about this, I thought. You really earn your money here. This wasn't "make- work." He might even vote for Roosevelt.

The entrance exams were tougher than I thought. I had an uneasy feeling when I handed in my test paper and returned to the dormitory.

The next day when I came in from work, the kindly NYA man whose glasses kept slipping down on his nose called me in. I was dead tired from pushing wheelbarrows full of concrete all afternoon. He told me I had failed two of my entrance exams—algebra and English.

English! Stunned, I stared at him in total disbelief. Algebra I could understand. I never did like fooling around with all those xs and ys and stuff.

But English! I'd made straight As in English! My love for books was one of the factors that made me want to be a writer. I tried to fight back the tears welling up in my eyes. I didn't know whether to be angry or embarrassed.

"That can't be right," I blustered. "English was my favorite subject because I—I—"

I simply could not tell him I wanted to be a writer, especially since I flunked the English entrance exam. At that moment I was glad I had never told *anybody* because obviously I could never be one since I wasn't intelligent enough to pass a test in a subject so basic to the needs of a writer.

"Does this mean I can't go to college?" I asked, begging really. I couldn't go home. What would I tell Dad?

His hesitation told me what he was going to say before he said it.

"I'm afraid so. The government will not finance a student taking remedial courses."

I could hear Dad saying, "I told you so."

To heck with the NYA—and the hair-combing boy whistling "Blues in the Night" all the time.

I checked out of the NYA dorm and found a room in a private home. I eventually found a job washing dishes for my meals and another job as a janitor (which I'd learned in my first NYA job) in a machine shop for cash money to take care of my other needs.

I took the two remedial courses and made good enough grades to enroll as a full freshman the following semester—in the college of liberal arts to learn how to be a writer.

Dad had been right all along—when you take their money, you let them tell you what you are, even if you aren't, and what you aren't, even if you are.

The Letter

We celebrate New Year's Day because we all hope it will be a watershed day in our lives.

Out with the old, in with the new. Starting over. We've made our resolutions and are full of determination to really and truly change our lives.

For the better, of course.

My most miserable New Year's Day turned out to be a day that changed my life—because I sat down and wrote a letter to a girl I barely knew.

The year 1941, just passed, had been a wonderful new experience for me. I'd made it through high school. I'd left home. I had a job. I was paying my own way.

But far above and beyond that, I had met an entirely new set of friends in my new home in northeastern Oklahoma. And my being the new boy in town seemed to be exciting for them too.

The guys accepted me for who I was, not as just one of those little Denney kids whose parents lived on the outskirts of town and eked out a bare living on their little acreage.

Fortunately for me, growing up I had failed to recognize I had a "place" in the local society. There were the rich uptown kids whose parents had benefitted from the local oil boom. Then there were the rest of us.

And I was just me—mostly quiet and sort of bashful, especially around girls. Oh, I had a few very close friends who happened to be girls.

But girls who are friends are just that—not prospective dates.

Here in my new environment, there seemed to me more families like mine back home—just barely getting by—than there were any so-called rich kids.

Every day was fun. We could go swimming in streams of nice clear water. Have fun at the local skating rink. Going to the Saturday night "Preview" was a big social event, with the preliminary being gathering in town and on the courtyard to flirt and pair off, if you didn't already have a date.

Nor was there "that smell" in the air, a combination of sulfur, salt water, and spilled oil that I'd grown up with.

Even so, it was several weeks before I had the courage to actually ask a girl to go to the show with me. And I was shocked when she said yes. I sat stiff as a board next to her in the theater and kept a respectful distance from her walking her home afterward.

Nevertheless, it was a thrilling new adventure for me. Before the year was over, us "older" guys started making the rounds of the area dance halls, especially if the band was Bob Wills.

I had my first experience of drinking too much liquor—and didn't like it, especially the after-effects.

The only thing that bothered me all year was that I'd been formally introduced to a girl shortly after I arrived.

Her name was Juanita Graham.

That was it. Just an introduction. We never dated, hardly ever spoke to one another the entire year. But there was something about her that made me want to know her better. When she came to town with friends, I was always aware of where she was. I'd try to work my way into her group just so I could be near her, hear her talk, feel the thrill whenever she looked at me.

I found out where she lived. I also learned that she was from a large family, that her mother was a widow. All the guys said she was real strict about who her daughters went with. I didn't want to be rejected, to go back to being just another one of those Denney kids.

I kept my misery a secret. But I kept hoping.

Then came the Pearl Harbor bombing. Watching the smoke billowing from our overturned battleships, I knew my life would never be the same.

I gave up my job and returned home for the holidays prior to enrolling at Oklahoma University in late January for the second semester.

I'd have to wash dishes, probably, for my meals—find other work to pay for books and a place to sleep. A daunting future.

That's why my 1942 New Year's Day was so miserable. Not only was I giving up the best year of my life, but also a chance to get better acquainted with Juanita.

On impulse, I sat down at Mom's kitchen table with some notebook paper and penciled this letter:

Miss Graham,

Doubtless you will be in a measure beyond that of surprise when you receive this letter from me. To write to a bare acquaintance is something I have never done before. But, as they say, "There is a first time for everything."

I miss being with all you guys. Remember the night we ganged up in the courtyard waiting for the preview to begin? Four or five of us kept trying to get in Charlie's jacket all at the same time.

I tried to get up enough courage to ask you to go to the preview with me that night but—I just didn't. I wound up going to the show with another girl.

I'm sitting at the kitchen table writing this. This is New Year's Day and there's not anything to do around here. I guess I'll try to get in a few semesters of college before I have to go into service.

I saw you the night before I left. I was in Jones Drug Store with my brother when you and Sue Hampton came in and got some Cokes. I kept pretending to listen to my brother talking, but I didn't hear a word he said. I was listening to you, hoping you would look my way, just once. If you had, I might have—who knows?

If this letter offends you, please forgive me. If and when I get enough time to come back for a visit, I'd like to apologize, if an apology is necessary. Or if not, I'd like get to know you better.

I signed it with a great flourish, trying to impress. I did not know her address. Desperate, I simply put her name and the town and dropped it in the mail box.

Then I wished I hadn't. What a stupid thing to do. What if her mother got the letter first and read it?

What I'd done, I cursed to myself, was fix it so I could never go back again. And I swore I wouldn't.

And then I got her reply. I stared at the strange feminine handwriting on the envelope. Hands trembling, I ripped it open.

It was from her. She said she was surprised that I had written. She had heard I had left town and was curious as to my future plans. Was I ever coming back?

Yes! Yes! Yes! That very weekend.

I even spent money buying a bus ticket instead of hitch-hiking so I could get there faster. But when I got there, I didn't know how to get in touch with her.

Call? I'd never used a telephone in my life. Besides, it was doubtful her family had a phone—few people did. Only the wealthy.

Walk out to her house? What if her mother ran me off? I'd wasted precious money on a bus ticket to get here, and for what?

Miserable over my foolishness, I walked the streets, in and out of the drug stores hoping to "accidentally" run into her.

Just as I was about to give up, there she was, standing at the curb with several of her friends, waiting for the preview to start.

I smiled and walked up to her. She appeared shocked when she saw me. Even asked, "What are you doing here?"

"I came back to ask you to go to the show with me," I said, feeling strangely more at ease than frightened.

She accepted. I was floating on cloud nine when we went in.

Walking her home, it seemed so natural that we held hands. She was proud of me when I told her I was going away to college. I didn't even try to give her a good night kiss. It wouldn't have been proper—on our first date.

So the letter I wrote sitting at Mom's kitchen table on a New Year's Day did change my life dramatically, making it truly, truly the beginning of a "Happy New Year."

Because we continued writing to one another, our friendship kept growing.

Chocolate Malts

My heart was broken. I barely heard what Frankie was saying as we walked down the dusty road carrying our bathing suits rolled up tight.

Nita had turned me down again when I asked her to go to the preview with me the night before. That was it, I kept telling myself over and over. Forget her.

I couldn't. But I forced myself to at least be civil chit-chatting with Frankie.

And it would be nice going swimming. The creeks here were not like back home, where I learned to swim in muddy farm ponds. My first summer out of high school when I came here and went to the creek with Frankie and some of the guys, I could see bottom and was afraid to dive in. They said it was ten feet deep. I didn't believe them.

We stripped and jumped in, naked as jaybirds. It was so cold, I gasped under water and almost drowned. I'd never had so much fun swimming laughing, playing tag, or just laying on the gravel bar in the sun.

I'd even written about loving to swim in the creek in one of my letters to Nita, suggesting we make going swimming our first date when I came home.

She was working in the drug store when I come home on Spring Break. I started drinking chocolate malts. Thick, I insisted. She said she'd get fired if she put too much ice cream in them.

To make up for that, I'd drink three or four, just for an excuse to talk with her. I finally got so full of malts one night and was so malted out of my senses that I asked her to go to the show with me.

She surprised me and said yes. Well, it was more than just a yes. She said, "I've been wondering when you'd ask."

I even tried to kiss her good-night on our second date, but she turned her cheek.

Her deft movement to deny me her lips thrilled me because it told me she was somebody special, somebody who wouldn't show love until she was sure. I vowed I'd never try again unless I was sure that that was what she wanted.

Exchanging letters caused me to hate school because I knew I was in love —
with Nita. And she didn't know.

I boldly signed off one night with, "Love, Dale." After all, it was only a
formality. Surely she wouldn't be offended, would she?

And she signed her answering letter the same way. I was on cloud nine,
wherever that was.

Then total misery set in when she wrote me about Lloyd. It wasn't a real date,
she'd written. He plays on the men's basketball team. I play on the girls team. We
travel together.

Why did she tell me? I wrote angrily. To make me miserable? If you want me
to quit writing you letters, just say so.

But the next morning I ripped that angry letter to shreds. I wrote another
one. I ignored the subject of basketball game dating.

When I came home at the end of the semester, I asked her twice for a date.
She had excuses. I accepted them at face-value— until I saw Lloyd taking her to
the Saturday night late show.

Walking to the creek that day, Frankie mentioned Nita, trying, I knew, to get
me to tell him, man to man, what was going on. Then I knew all the kids were
talking about me and Nita and Lloyd. Probably laughing at me. It made the hurt
go deeper.

Before I could say anything, we heard a car coming, and moved to the edge
of the road to let it pass, dreading the dust it would swirl up. But instead of going
by, it slowed to a stop.

"You want a ride?" someone called.

It was Lloyd, his handsome head hanging out the window of his dad's
pickup. I could make out a girl's hair behind the sun's glare on the windshield.
Nita?

I was shaking my head no, but Frankie yelled out, "You bet. It's hotter'n a
pistol."

He hurried around to the passenger side. I had no choice but to follow. Sure
enough, it was Nita. She had to scoot over against Lloyd to make room for us.

Frankie kept right on talking. I stared straight ahead, mute, thinking about
what an idiot I'd been signing my letters "Love, Dale."

And she wouldn't even let me kiss her good night. Had she let Lloyd?

I peeked around Frankie at her. *Didn't our letters mean anything to you?* She
flashed me a quick, nervous smile. I jerked my gaze back ahead. She was teasing
me.

The boys and girls at the swimming hole were yelling and having a big time.

When they saw us, they pointed out the bushes the boys changed behind and the ones the girls used.

I didn't even want to go in. But there was no way out—except to start walking back to town. I dawdled, changing. But Lloyd and Frankie jumped into their bathing trunks quickly and ran to dive in. I was standing alone when Nita came out from behind her bush.

She was so stunningly beautiful in her red bathing suit and hair piled up on top of her head that my whole thinking apparatus went haywire. I tried to say something, but all I could do was grin foolishly.

She smiled and came to stand beside me, still working on her hair to make sure the loose ends wouldn't get wet when she went in for a swim.

"Aren't you going in?" she asked.

I nodded, afraid to speak because my throat felt so tight.

She stuck her toe in the water and jerked it back.

"Br-r-r," she said hugging herself.

I wanted to put my arm around her and pull her to me and make her warm again—like the night I walked her home and it was so cold she snuggled under my jacket.

"I have to get used to the cold water before I go in," she said.

She sat down on a rock overhang and eased her feet into the water, splashing gently.

Was she inviting me?

Hopes rising, I sat down on the rock beside her, my big feet plopping in the water so hard I splashed some on her.

She gasped, cringing away.

"I'm sorry—"

"That's all right," she laughed, then looked down into the water and grew quiet. Our reflections danced together on the ripples. The sound the others were making seemed far away, echoing off the limestone bluff.

I decided to ask her one more time to go out with me, to a show or something.

"Nita, I..." I paused, struggling for the right words.

"Yes?"

I glanced up and saw Lloyd swimming toward us. He looked like Tarzan trying to catch a crocodile.

I felt like picking up rocks and throwing them at him. He pulled himself upon the rock, tall, handsome, with a beautiful athletic build, water dripping from his wavy black hair.

I knew I didn't have a chance.

"I'll be seeing you," I blurted and dove into the water and swam to join the others in a game of tag.

As I was pretending to be having fun that day, I made up my mind to wash Nita out of my life forever.

But before the week was out, I had to have a chocolate malt. I went into the drug store and settled into my favorite chair at a back table. Just another customer, was all.

I tried to make it strictly business, and hardly looked at Nita when she came to take my order for a chocolate malt.

She made it, delivered it, then sat down at the table with me.

I sucked furiously on the straw, finally complaining, "You made this so dad-blamed thick, I can't drink it."

"I know—you like them thick. I made this one—special."

It was the look in her beautiful blue eyes that told me what she really meant.

So I asked her if she would go to the show with me that night.

And she said yes.

Well, it was more than just a yes. She said, "I was wondering if you'd ask—again."

I still love chocolate malts. Thick.

Getting Drafted

I watched the people on my TV scramble over the debris looking for bodies.

Some idiot had driven up beside the hotel with a bomb in his car. He set it off, blowing himself to kingdom-come and taking fifty people with him.

After that got your attention, the TV people slipped in a two-minute commercial. Nexium, I believe it was. The purple pill. Or maybe it was Viagra.

When the TV people got back to the war, the camera zeroed in on a widow somewhere here in the United States, weeping about her husband getting killed.

A bunch of civilians had been killed, too. But they didn't count. The one soldier and weeping widow, in our TV producer's opinion, meant more than 600 dead civilians any day.

Well, I thought, what do you expect when you sign up to be in the army?

When there's a war on, somebody somewhere is going to try and kill you.

When I was drafted into the army from civilian life, Nita wept a little that last night on her doorstep before I left. I doubt she'd have done it, though, if there had been a TV camera focused on her. Fact was, she didn't even come to the bus station to see me off the next morning because she said she didn't want people to see her cry.

Like a lot of young men, the farthest thing from my mind when I was drafted was getting killed. That's something that happens to other guys.

I had a bigger problem. I knew I'd flunk my physical. The only thing lower than being 4-F was being a draft-dodger. And if people thought you were normal and didn't pass the physical, you had to be a draft-dodger.

While I was healthy as a horse, I was near-sighted. I could see up close just fine. Things farther away turned fuzzy. Nobody knew this but me and I wanted to keep it that way. I'd bluffed my way through life up to now. I'd given it my best playing ball, taking mighty swings with the bat and getting teased for "missing it a mile."

Out hunting, I'd pretend I saw the squirrel up in a tree and point my gun in the direction the other guys were aiming theirs and fire away at any clump I could see.

In school I always scramble to get a seat up front so I could see the blackboard without having to squint too hard.

Same thing in college. I enrolled in engineering because that was what all men were supposed to do, only to learn later the reason they did was so they could get deferments from the draft.

Getting a deferment in my mind was the same as dodging the draft. I didn't want the guys at home calling me a draft-dodger. I dropped out of school.

Sure enough, within a month I got the letter. As soon as I pulled it from the box, I read: Clyde Dale Denney.

Yep. This was it. Nobody but my family and my draft board knew my first name. My heart began to pound. My hands were shaking as I ripped it open.

"Greetings," I read. "You have been selected by your friends and neighbors to..."

I didn't read the rest. There was no need. So excited I could hardly breathe, I couldn't help thinking: What would it be like? Over there?

You knew in your own heart war wasn't all fun and games. When you shoot at people, they shoot back. Big shells and bombs blow people apart. But they didn't show things like that in the newsreels and movies. Everybody in a uniform was a hero.

Even if you did get killed, it would be better than staying home and being called a draft-dodger.

Now all I had to do was pass my physical. If I did, I would be able to walk down the street in my new army uniform, shoulders back, proud.

Patriotic? Love of country? Not exactly. There's another meaning for patriotism—a love of the people you live with, the "friends and neighbors" the president referred to in his letter.

I asked a lot of questions of those who had passed their physical.

"They just herd all of you in this big room. They made us take our clothes off."

"Everything?"

"Everything. You could put your shoes back on after the doctor checked to see if you were flat-footed."

Then they shuffled you from room to room, naked as jay birds. Different doctors punched and gouged and thumped you all over, listened to your heart, checked your teeth, made you bend over and checked you for hemorrhoids.

The first thing you know, they said, you're raising your right hand and

217

swearing to uphold the constitution and all that.

"How about the eye test?" I asked, still not satisfied.

"They make you look at this chart, is all."

"What does the chart say?"

"It don't say anything. It's just got a bunch of letters on it. The letters get littler and littler on each line. You couldn't read the bottom line with a telescope," they said.

I could fix that, I thought. I faked an ankle sprain and went to see old Doc Cowan. He had an eye chart on the wall. When he had his back turned trying to find me some pills, I sidled over to the eye chart and tried to memorize it.

I kept going back with a different ailment, sneaking looks at Doc's eye chart until I had it down pat—even the hard-to-read bottom line.

When I went for my physical, it was just like the guys said. They put us in this big room and, stripped down to our birth suits, we were shuffled from doctor to doctor, shoes flapping and laces dragging.

When the sergeant gave me the eye test, I rattled it off line by line, including the bottom line the guys said you couldn't read with a telescope. I wanted to be sure I passed.

I didn't know it, but it was different than the one Doc Cowan had in his office.

"What was that bottom line again?" the sergeant growled. I rattled it off again.

He yanked me out of line.

"Follow me," he ordered and led me into a little office. A fully dressed officer with all his brass shining was sitting at his desk with his back to me.

I tried my best to stand at attention. It's hard to do that when you're naked as a jay bird with your shoe laces dragging.

The sergeant handed him my papers.

"He didn't get a single letter right," the sergeant explained. "I think he's faking it because he even read the bottom line that nobody can read."

The sergeant left. The officer looked me up and down. I was sure wishing I had some clothes on.

"How come you don't wear glasses?" he asked.

"I never needed them," I lied. "I was just nervous, is all. I never had any problems seeing the blackboard in school. I made good grades all the time."

He studied my papers. I saw him fingering a rubber stamp that said "Rejected" on it.

I sensed this was a crucial moment in my life. This man covered with shiny brass could send me home where I'd live out the war in shame, or send me into the army where I could join all the guys whipping the Japanese and Germans.

"I went to college," I blurted. "I ought to be good for something."

"Oh?"

He flipped a page and took a second look.

"Engineering school, I see."

"Yes, sir."

He studied thoughtfully a minute, finally mumbling, "We need engineers bad."

Then he dropped the "Rejected" rubber stamp and picked up one that read "Accepted." He whammed it down hard on my stack of papers.

"We can fit you with glasses and send you to Engineering school," he said, handing the papers to me. "You're in the army now, soldier. Go get in line."

I grabbed my papers joyously and hurried to fall in line with the others, naked as a jay bird, shoes flapping, shoe laces dragging.

Soon I'd be wearing a uniform. I was so proud.

The thought of getting killed never entered my mind.

Maybe it was because they told us in the movies and newsreels that armies fought armies, and ships sank ships, and airplanes shot down were just numbers.

Wives and sweethearts who lost loved ones didn't cry. They stood tall. Proud.

Because their patriotism, too, was the kind where you love the people you live with.

The Bus Stop

1941: In our town, the bus stopped on Main Street in front of Kessler's RX Drug Store.

I waited inside, sitting at an elegant marble-topped table supported by legs made of twisted steel rods. I was so excited about my new job a long way off that I couldn't concentrate enough to read the *Tulsa World*, its pages scattered about the table top.

There wasn't any news anyway. None that I cared about. Hitler had overrun Europe and pushed the Russians back to Moscow. London being bombed to rubble. So what? That had nothing to do with me.

I did see one item of interest, however. Congress was debating about lowering the draft age from twenty-one to twenty. I still had a couple years. I could save up some money from my new job and maybe get in a few hours of college credit before the army got me.

My older brother J.B. had sent for me to help him build a new room on his house. His wife was pregnant again. He lived in Jay, Delaware County, a far away place.

Besides that, he wrote on his postal card, he needed extra help managing his two businesses—the county's only movie theater and a pool hall nearby.

I knew I could help with the carpentry work. Dad had taught all of us boys how to hammer nails and use a saw.

I didn't know didly-squat about pool halls. I'd never been in one. But I loved movies and I would be able to see all I wanted for free. His offer of $5 a week sounded like gobs of money.

Overhead a ceiling fan chuck-chucked away, stirring the air. Mr. Kessler, always dressed in a stiffly starched white shirt, puttered around in back among his prescription stuff.

I debated about walking over to the soda fountain and striking up a conversation with Rex who was lazily washing dishes and putting them away.

I knew him well, but he didn't know me. He'd graduated from high school in '38—two years before me. He was a football star. I'd spent my school activity in the libraries searching for a good book to read.

Rex wouldn't be drafted either, the news story said. He was married now. Had a kid. Working as a soda jerk to support his family.

His days of glory were over and he knew it. Mine, I dreamed, were yet to come. We had nothing in common. I moved my hand-me-down suitcase aside so I could stretch out my legs and lean back.

There were others waiting for the bus, too. Two black women, one older, one younger. They stood in the vestibule just outside the front door, pretending that's where they preferred to wait.

The younger woman was trying to keep a feisty little girl in check. She appeared to be about five or so. She acted proud to be wearing what was obviously her new dress—a red one with a wide starched collar.

The little girl got away from her harassed mother and pressed her forehead against the glass door, shading her eyes from the sunlight with her small brown hands, and stared at me with her big brown eyes.

I smiled at her. She grinned bashfully, turned away, then came back—just to make sure, I guessed, I had really smiled at her. I had, and did again. She acted so proud.

She didn't understand, I knew, why she and her mother and grandmother couldn't come inside and sit at one of the empty marble-topped tables to wait for the bus like I was doing.

It was the rule, not of my making nor of theirs, that they waited, standing, outside, and I waited, sitting, inside.

It was the rule.

The bus slipped into view, stopped, its air brakes hissing. The doors opened. The driver stepped down and stood by the door with his paper punch in his hand waiting to take our tickets.

The two black women stood aside to let me get on first. They pretended not to see me, nor I them.

The driver offered to put my suitcase in the baggage compartment. I thanked him, but told him no. It was light and I would put it in the overhead rack.

I selected a seat up front. I liked riding there so I could see out the windshield and watch the road come sliding beneath us as we rolled down the highway. There were many empty seats there. I tried one, then another, until I found one that gave me the best view.

The two black women and the little girl passed in the aisle, heading for the seats in the back.

The little girl's big brown eyes fixed on me as she was towed by. She gave me another bashful smile, as if we were old acquaintances by now.

"Hi," I whispered, hoping no one else would hear, but not caring if they did.

She ducked her head and hurried on by, clinging to her mother's hand as they headed for the seats in the back.

It had been love at first sight, the little dark girl and me.

1943: Okie cursed as the tire tool slipped from his hand and hit the concrete driveway, the clang sounded unusually loud in the stillness of the morning air.

If I had been in the mood to laugh, I would have laughed at Okie's frustration. He was one of my many new friends I'd made in this town far from home.

But I was in no mood to laugh. I waited in the Texaco Station doorway, gripping the handle of my battered suitcase.

Okie, perhaps glancing shamefully around to make sure there were no ladies or children who might have heard his muted curse, saw me. He grinned sheepishly and came toward me wiping his hands on a shop towel he'd pulled from a rear pocket of his blue overalls.

He spat a stream of tobacco juice to one side.

"Where to? Tulsa?"

I nodded. I didn't want to talk, afraid I'd cry.

"One way?"

He knew. I tried to sound grown up, brave. Soldiers are, you know. Now I was one—or soon would be.

"Yeah."

I followed him inside the station, feeling the grit beneath my shoes. He stepped behind the glass counter, pushed aside some of the clutter and began writing the ticket, gripping the dull pencil in his oil stained hand.

Finished, he handed me the ticket and leaned aside and spit in a can on the floor behind the counter.

I paid him, avoiding eye contact. But he did not return to his work fixing the tire.

He knew. There was no need for small talk. Yet we made it anyhow. He leaned on the counter and we both kept looking down the street for the bus to come.

"They say the war'll be over by Christmas," he said.

"Hope so."

I'd wanted to go—at first. It would be a big adventure going to Europe. Or the South Pacific. Or Africa. You could get killed tomorrow, run over by a bus or something. So the fear of death was not a factor.

But love was. She had cried last night when I told her good bye. That made the difference. Did Okie know about her and me?

I glanced at him, his stubble covered jaw working slowly on the chew of tobacco.

Yes. Of course, he knew. Everybody in small town America knew what everybody else was doing all the time. It was the way it was. A lovely way to live—all one family.

My brother drove up, stopped at one of the gas pumps.

Oh no! He'd said he wouldn't come. Said he had too many other things to do. We both thought Nita would be here. Now he would wonder why. That she didn't love me? I couldn't tell him why.

Okie went out to fill his gas tank. It didn't take much. I knew then he'd come to see me off, pretending not to.

The bus came around the corner a block away and growled its way up the street. It stopped in front of Okie's station, brakes hissing. I picked up my suitcase and went out to get on.

The bus doors flopped open. My brother didn't ask about Nita. I loved him for not asking. He extended a hand, forcing a smile. His grip was tight, a holding on. I let go. I climbed up the steps, hefting my suitcase in front of me.

"Don't take any wooden nickles." His voice carried a false cheerfulness.

"Yeah. Right."

The doors flapped shut behind me. There were plenty of seats up front where I liked to sit and watch the highway come rolling beneath us. I chose one, then changed my mind.

I made my way to the back of the bus and settled into a seat there.

The little black girl with dark eyes and a bashful smile was part of America too.

I would be fighting for her. And Rex, the faded football star. And Mr. Kessler in his stiff white shirt; Okie, my brother — and especially the one who cried when we said goodbye last night.

Off to War

It all began with the letter I received from President Roosevelt that began: Greetings, Your friends and neighbors have selected you...

First the physical, then the goodbyes.

My last night with Nita was March 8, 1943. I walked her home from a movie. There were no street lights. I stood with her on her doorstep, only a pale lantern glow framed the door's window behind her.

I hated to leave, but at the same time, I was excited about going into the army. It would be a new adventure. I would be going to new places, get a chance to travel to other states, perhaps even to another part of the world.

Finally, it was time to go. I felt the dampness from a tear on her lips with that last kiss.

"Goodbye," she whispered.

"Goodbye? Aren't you coming up to the bus station in the morning to see me off?"

She shook her head. "I don't want people to see me cry."

I caught the morning bus to Tulsa, transferred to the afternoon bus to Oilton, my home and where my parents still lived. That very night I sat down and wrote her a letter.

Tuesday
3-9-43

Dear Nita,

Surprise?

> *I know I told you I probably would not write you before getting located, probably on Sunday, when I learned what my address would be in the army.*

As I write, I'm looking at your picture sitting on the little table in Mom's living room and am feeling so lonesome for you that I can hardly stand it. And it hasn't even been twenty-four hours since I kissed you goodbye.

I seem sorta empty right now. I feel as if I have lost something that I treasured so highly. Never before has anyone, under any circumstance, showed such feeling for me as you.

I have said again and again that I would be happy to go to the army if it were not for having to leave you. If you had not become such an important part of my life, I could leave Jay in a happy mood; but there would be in my heart the longing, the secret longing, that all young people have for a relationship with the opposite sex. You have fulfilled that longing.

These are some of the things I wanted to say to you, but never seemed to have the courage to do so. I am able to do it easier on paper. I hope it is just as good this way.

I want you to adapt yourself the best you can to life without me, Nita. I don't guess I need to tell you this, but I just want you to know that I want so much for you to be happy. I have found no greater satisfaction than when you told me that no one could ever take my place.

I seem to be in a dark mood right now that I must get out of. I feel dazed. I have a feeling that I don't care what happens to me. But this can't be true, for I do care, and care a great deal. I hope this mood is only temporary, and before long I can find a certain degree of happiness being without you.

I don't know whether or not you saw me getting on the bus this morning at Okie's Texaco Station. I know I wanted to see you so bad that I came close to running down the street to the drug store where I knew you were working and probably looking out the window, watching me get on the bus.

J.B. came (it's hard for me to get used to calling my older brother simply Denney like everybody in your town does). He pretended to be coming to get gas for his car, but I could tell he wanted to say goodbye. He has said over and over he would go if he got drafted, but he won't. He has a wife and two kids, not to mention his left arm and its stiff elbow. He waited with me until the bus came. He shook my hand and said, "Be a mean boy," and turned away quickly.

I had to stand up on the bus from Tulsa to Oilton. I guess it was as good a time as any to get used to standing at attention, the way they say you have to do a lot in the army.

I played two games of pool uptown before I came on out to the house. My heart wasn't in the games. I stopped at the Sylvesters, even though Bob is still there in Jay. I left Bob's picture of him and his girlfriend with his mother. She was tickled to get it. However, she said Bob's girlfriend was not as pretty as mine. A nice compliment.

There is no need for you to answer this letter, for I will be gone from here by the time you receive it. I'll send you my new address as soon as I find out what it will be. In the meantime, I'll write as often as possible, and I sincerely hope you will answer them all.

Love,

Dale

Fort Sill, Oklahoma

March 12, 1943

Nita,

Well, here I am at Fort Sill. You ought to see me in my new uniform: nothing fits. I even have a new name. Clyde. Bet you didn't know that, did you?

All my life I've been known by my middle name, Dale. But the army uses first names. I've always hated my first name "Clyde." That's why I've kept it a secret, like it was a bad disease or something.

But now the secret's out, because I won't get your letters unless they're addressed to: Pvt. Clyde D. Denney, 38467226, Company B, Reception Center, Fort Sill, Okla.

I hate the name "Clyde." I have never used it. And when they called us out for our first formation, the sergeant called the roll. When he sang out, "Clyde D. Denney," I didn't answer. I thought, hey there's another Denney in this outfit. I better look him up. He might be one of my cousins.

But when the sergeant bellowed again, "CLYDE D.

DENNEY!!!" I realized it was me and I squeaked a weak, "Here," and he went on to the next name.

I'm sorry now, Nita, that I didn't spend at least one more day with you. But I felt I owed Mom and Dad some time before going off to war.

When I told Mom I'd come home because I'd been drafted, I could tell she wasn't happy. Brother Don went in last winter and now they were taking her baby boy. She tried to be cheerful about it. I caught her sniffling as she was fixing supper. She blamed it on the onions she'd cut up to put in the fried potatoes. But I knew better.

My orders instructed me to report to Sapulpa, our county seat, at 8:00 Friday morning. So I spent my final day paying my respects to long-time friends of the family.

When I stopped in to say goodbye to Mr. and Mrs. Sylvester, they asked me how I planned to get to Sapulpa. It was only thirty miles. There wasn't but one way to go, I said: hitch hike.

They offered to drive me that very afternoon. Delighted, I accepted, for I could get there early enough to find a hotel room before dark. I had never stayed all night in a hotel before, and wasn't sure how to go about registering and everything.

I hurried home and started packing. Mom and Dad acted pleased that I had a ride. Mom tried to help, but she was only getting in the way. Dad stood by, watching silently.

I closed my flimsy suitcase and hefted it. They followed me out onto the front porch. I didn't know what to do. The last time I had kissed my mother was when I was in the sixth grade.

As far as I knew, Dad had never hugged one of us kids in his life. But we knew the love was there. I finally turned to leave and gave them an awkward wave and said, "Well, I gotta go now. I'll be seeing you."

Mom made a motion as if she were reaching for me to pull me back.

"You'll write, won't you?"

Me? Write? Of course. Writing was my life. If I couldn't write, I'd die.

"Yeah," I said. "I'll write."

I hurried away, not daring to look back. I didn't want to see them standing there, hearts breaking, I knew, watching yet another one of their sons going off to war.

227

In Sapulpa, the Sylvesters dropped me off in front of a large hotel. I crawled out with my suitcase and started to walk away from the car.

"You come back here and give me a goodbye kiss." Mrs. *Sylvester commanded.*

Even though I knew they were the emotional type, I hesitated. She poked her head out of the car window and puckered up. Embarrassed, I took a deep breath and kissed her hard on her lips. She laughed and said, "Now I feel better letting you go."

I wished then I had kissed my own mother goodbye. Dampness in my eyes made their car blur as they drove away.

I fingered away the moisture in the corners of my eyes, walked boldly into the hotel, crossed the white tiled flooring to the registration desk, and told the balding clerk I wanted a single for one night. He eyed me suspiciously.

"You one of those draftees leaving in the morning?"

I nodded.

"You'll want a wake-up call then. That'll be two dollars for the room and fifty cents for the wake-up call."

Wake-up call? What was a wake-up call? I didn't have to report to the train station until eight. Nobody I knew ever slept that late. But I said nothing. I paid him and he handed me a key.

I certainly didn't need a wake-up call. Being in the army was such a great adventure that I didn't sleep a wink that night. I wondered if I would make a good soldier. How would you know when to salute?

I already knew how to shoot a gun. We guys had rabbit-hunted all our lives. Squirrels, too. Quail. Heck fire, we'd throw a tin can in the river and see who'd be the first one to sink it with a well-aimed shot from a .22 rifle.

The possibility of getting killed has flitted through my mind in short bursts, but only as a scene of glory.

Then I'd be filled with a sense of emptiness, as if I'd lost something that I treasured so highly. And I had, because never before has anyone, under any circumstance, showed such feeling for me as you have.

I do want to say this, however. Since there's no way of knowing how long I'll be gone, or where I'll be sent, I think you should try to adapt to a way of life without me. All I want is for you to be happy, with or without me.

Naturally, I want you to wait for me. But at the same time, I'm telling myself that I have no right to expect you to. We are both so very young, me just turning twenty yesterday and you only seventeen next month.

How long will I be gone? A year? Two? Maybe forever. You'll meet other guys. They'll ask you to go out with them. Dancing, perhaps. The thought of somebody else kissing you is more than I can stand.

Or what if I run into another girl somewhere? Someone who would just want to be friends to start with. Then before I knew it, she would be in love with me. What would I do? Especially not knowing what was going on at home. Really knowing.

When the first light showed in the window at the hotel, I climbed wearily out of bed and dressed. The last time in civilian clothes, I told myself. Downstairs, the balding man gave me my fifty cents back since I hadn't needed a wake-up call.

I thanked him and took the money. I planned on buying breakfast with it at the train station café, but a man insisted on paying for my meal himself.

He said he'd been in the last war. He said he was sorry they hadn't finished the job and we had to go back. There'll always be wars, he said, until the American idea of government is spread around the world.

I didn't rightly know what he was talking about. So I just thanked him for my breakfast and joined the other draftees gathering up behind a roped-off area.

A man who said he was on the draft board came in and briefed us about our day's trip on the train to Fort Sill. He brought a local minister along to pray for us and hand out small editions of the New Testament.

Then the train came chugging in. We were herded into a special coach. It was neat. I'd never been on a train before. It was like sitting in your living room and the whole house moving.

We arrived here at Fort Sill by mid-afternoon. They lined us up and marched us to the reception center.

Soldiers in their brand new uniforms lined the street and yelled, "Cannon fodder! Cannon fodder!"

We knew it was a tease. We were in the army, and I am proud to be a part of it.

They gave us our uniforms today; and it is just as I feared, it looks sloppy on me. I really wish you could see me. I'm a scream.

They have a full length mirror at one end of the barracks with instructions tacked to the wall on how to wear your uniform. None of us wanted to be seen posing in front of the mirror, but I along with all the other guys keep sneaking a look at ourselves when we get a chance. You at least want to look like a soldier, whether you feel like one or not. I don't look like me anymore.

According to the scales here, I have gained twenty pounds, clothes and all. At six feet one inch, and 165 pounds, I am satisfied with my physique.

I just now looked down at my army shoes lined up just so-so under my bunk. They look about sixteen or seventeen inches long! I knew I had big feet, but oh, lordy! How will I ever make it on a long hike swinging those things all day long?

The barracks is a long building with upper and lower bunks on either side of a wide aisle. There's a latrine at one end where we shave and shower, only I don't have to worry about shaving every day like most of the guys do. At first, it was hard to get used to, being in the open like that, but you get used to it.

Our personal living area is about five feet by eight feet. This is not walled in, of course, but we are responsible for this much of the barracks. In this small space, we keep all our clothing, toilet articles, and other personal effects. Most of the small stuff is either in a foot locker or barracks bags. If you want something, you have to dig and dig until you find it. Besides living in this area, we are supposed to keep our bunks, which occupy most of the space, made up so tight that when an inspecting officer flips a coin onto your blanket it will bounce.

Boy, they sure have a system here: when they do anything to you, they do it in a hurry, but you always have to wait in a long line before it happens.

Every little whipstitch somebody's always yelling, "Fall out!"

And we all rush out to line up for some sort of instructions.

I heard they usually keep new recruits here in the reception center about three days.

Tomorrow is the day they usually give shots to recruits. All the old-timers—anyone who has been in the reception center more than three days is called an old-timer—talk about the doctors and medics using dull, square-pointed needles when they give you shots. I feel sorry for one poor guy. He told me he's never had a shot in his life and wanted to know if it hurt. The thought of people sticking needles in him scares him to death.

They put you on KP—kitchen police—the next day after you get shots. They said it keeps your arms from getting sore waiting on tables, doing dishes, scrubbing down tables and floors, and swabbing out garbage cans.

I am looking forward to receiving a letter or two from you before I ship out.

I used to wish I would be sent away off somewhere, but not now. I don't want to be sent so far from you. In other words, I still love you.

Fort Sill sure is a busy place: soldiers everywhere, big green army trucks racing this way and that pulling big guns on wheels. This is where they train for the artillery. The big guns out on the firing range make it sound like thunder. When I first heard it, I kept looking for storm clouds in the sky until someone told me what it was. I can't even imagine what it would be like hunkering down in a foxhole somewhere and having big guns like that throwing big shells at you.

I have only twenty or thirty minutes before lights-out and must hurry to finish this letter. I doubt you can read this. I am writing this under the most trying circumstances. There is such commotion going on all around me, and I have to write sitting on my bunk with a stationery box for a desk.

I bought a toilet kit today, but forgot to get any paper to write on. I borrowed some paper, an envelope and pencil, and am using my knee for a desk while sitting on my bunk. There are excited new soldiers standing all around my bunk gabbing, all talking at once, it seems. A friend is sitting on the other side of my bunk teasing me about writing to my girl so soon. I just gave him a smile and continued writing.

Gee! Here 'tis Saturday night, and I sure wish I were back in Jay with you waiting for you to get off work at the drug store so we could go to the preview.

I don't feel so bad about being in the army—in a way. I am not as enthusiastic about it as I was. I guess I didn't realize how hard it is to be away from you—especially when they tell us we are in for the duration of the war, plus six months.

I am almost out of paper to write on and must stop here. I plan on going to the show with the guys in a few minutes, so I guess this is all I'll write today.

Don't send any of the pictures we took on our last Sunday together when we went walking down along Brush Creek, that is, if you have them back by now. Wait until I get stationed more permanent.

With Love—even though my uniform doesn't fit.

Nor my name.

Write soon.

Love,

"Clyde"

Mail Call

"Mail call!"

The sound reverberated through the barracks, picked up by others who parroted it on to those who might have been too far away to hear.

I dropped the huge army shoe I'd been buffing so I could pass tomorrow's inspection and joined the stampede to the barrack's entry.

It'd been a week since I'd heard from Nita. Maybe it would be today. Maybe five or six letters at once, forwarded from my old outfit at Fort Sill in Oklahoma. Wouldn't that be great?

I was more anxious, however, to get her reply to the letter I wrote telling her I was shipping out. In it, I had actually proposed to her. Not in so many words, but the same as. That had been a week ago. If she had answered, I should be getting her reply in today's mail.

I watched eagerly as the scrawny redhead wearing a private first class stripe took advantage of his important mission by climbing up on bench and ordering everyone to be quiet.

He got a lot of razzing, which only delayed him sorting through the letters, and start calling off names. I was impatient.

Aw, come on, you guys. Quiet down, will you?

The PFC finally began calling the names.

"Butler?"

"Here!"

"Stepnowski?"

"He's on guard duty. I'll take it."

The PFC tossed him Stepnowski's letter and kept calling out names. The packed group kept dwindling. Still none for Denney. I craned my neck to see if the orderly had another stack of mail laying at his feet. There was none.

Soon he was finished. He got more razzing from those of us who didn't get any mail.

All except me. I turned away in quiet disappointment.

"Promise me you'll write every day," she'd said.

I promised, then made her promise she'd answer every letter I wrote.

So much for promises. I sat down on my bunk and began polishing on my shoe again, trying to forget the disappointment. Being a soldier, you had to be macho, no matter what. A lot of guys handled a situation like this by going out and getting drunk, perhaps picking up a girl in a bar somewhere.

Somewhere in the barracks a radio was on, turned so low that I could just barely hear it.

It was Frances Langford singing. *You'll never know how much I miss you. Daytime, night time, nothing I do can make me forget how much I miss you.*

Oh, golly. I miss her so much.

Hurt, and feeling all alone in the world, I dropped the shoe I was shining and stretched out on my bunk, my hands under my head, staring at the ceiling.

"We haven't talked about it," I wrote in that last letter, "but I want you to know that I intend to ask you to marry me. Writing this in a letter is not right, I know, but there's no telling how long it will be before I see you again…"

Maybe never, if I have to go overseas.

The words blurred on the paper. It was several minutes before I could continue.

"I intend to do it proper the next time I see you, face to face, the way it should be done…"

That was such a stupid thing to write in a letter. A proposal that wasn't a proposal. How could she answer a thing like that? That was probably the reason I'm not getting any letters from her. Maybe she decided to put a stop to our courtship right now. Neither of us were old enough to get married, legally. She no doubt had more sense than me.

I began reviewing all my moments with her, trying to find any clue which might give any indication that she would not want to marry me.

The way we met—the hours we spent just walking and holding hands—the times we sat in a movie with my arm over her shoulders and her leaning against me—the letters we wrote when I went back to the university—the sad moments the night before I was to catch the bus the next morning to go to the army induction center.

Now I could hear Jo Stafford singing "Long Ago and Far Away" on the radio.

It *did* seem so long ago, even though it had been only four months. But it *was* far away—far, far away. She was in Los Angeles and I was in Baltimore. About as far as you can get and both of you still being in the states.

When Glenn Miller's "Moonlight Becomes You" came on, I began chewing on my underlip to keep the tears from welling up. One of the guys might come by and see me, and I'd never live it down.

How many times had we stood close with the moonlight on her face? She had the most beautiful eyes in the world. Her lips—just waiting to be kissed.

"Hey, Denney!"

I lifted my head. "Yeah?"

It was the redheaded PFC coming toward me—carrying a letter. He tossed it on my stomach.

"This must of dropped out when I was sorting the mail. I found it under the first sergeant's desk."

I snatched it and whipped my feet off the bunk, trying to read her handwriting. My hand was trembling so much it was hard to do.

"Sorry," the PFC said.

"That's okay," I nodded. I was wanting him to leave, for him to get the hell out of my sight before I opened it. He turned away, mumbling once again that he was sorry.

Then I was afraid to open it. What if she said I had the wrong idea? What if she said she had met someone else there in Los Angeles? A nice soldier or sailor whose parents were wealthy. What if —

I ripped the envelope open.

And enjoyed every letter of her beautiful handwriting.

The Proposal

For its special Valentine edition, the *Tulsa World* asked people to send in their love stories, telling how we met, how we proposed and things like that.

There sure were some screwball situations—all the way from a guy dressing himself in a suit of armor (get it?—a knight in shining armor), to a guy who wrote a book about how much he loved his girl and gave it to her instead of asking the usual, "Will you marry me?"

The guy in the suit of armor made it just fine until he got down on one knee to ask the question and couldn't get up.

And the girl who got the book from the guy threw it across the room when he asked, but accepted anyway.

I wish I'd sent in mine, about Nita and me. The big trouble I had was that it was so obvious that Nita and I were going to get married, there was no reason to ask. But it had to be done.

I may not have ever, if the rear axle on our car hadn't broken late one night in Fayettville, Arkansas.

To make it even more weird, the same girl who created the situation for Nita and me first getting acquainted also created the situation when I proposed.

Her name was Jane. She and Nita were best friends. They were together one evening and Jane arranged to have a boy introduce me to them. (At least Nita says it was Jane's idea, and she's stuck to it all these years.)

Jane did all the talking, but I was more interested in Nita. I thought she was the prettiest one. On top of that, she had cute freckles.

But Nita didn't seem to be paying any attention. (At least that's Nita's story, and she's stuck to it all these years.) Maybe that was another reason I was intrigued by her.

I suffered all that summer and into the fall wanting to go with Nita, but was too bashful to ask.

When I went away to college, I got lonesome and wrote to everybody I could think of, which included several girls.

Then I got the idea to write Nita. She was a friend, wasn't she? Hadn't we been formally introduced?

I wrote teasingly, saying I was writing to all my friends and reminded her she was one because we had been introduced.

She answered, teasingly, accusing me of putting her on my mailing list of all the other girls in town.

But what she didn't know was that as soon as I received her letter, I was so happy that I quit writing to all the other girls.

At least, I thought she didn't know. The truth is that in a small town everybody knows what everybody else is doing all the time—including the mail they get, because everybody in a small town likes to keep up with the latest developing love story.

By the time the semester had ended and I returned home, it was easy to ask Nita for a date.

Shows were the only place you could go on a date, unless you had a car. While some guys got to drive the family car, most of us just walked.

Nita and I went together the months I was home from school, and wrote to one another when I was away. We kept writing when I went into the army. By then, we were writing one another almost daily, our letters often passing in the mail.

With the war on and everything, any futures we might have planned were gone.

But you can't walk away from love. So when I got my first furlough—only one week—I figured it was time to get things settled between us—were we, or weren't we?

But why ask? It was so wonderful being together again, holding hands, looking longingly into one another's eyes, and sneaking a kiss when we could.

It wasn't proper to kiss in front of anybody then. Not that you didn't want to. Oh, gosh, did you ever want to!

It was so obvious that we were going to get married, why ask? You could even tell by the way everybody smiled at us when they saw us that it was all over town that we were going to get married.

Then I began to fret. Wasn't there some other way to propose other than by asking, "Will you marry me?"

That sounded so stupid. I kept racking my brains for a more romantic way to ask.

My furlough was so short, I didn't have time to think. We rushed from here to there to see my folks, my friends, her folks, her friends.

By bedtime, we were both so pooped that the usual good-night kiss became only a formality as we parted company for the night, her to her own bed with her family and me to a spare bedroom in my brother's house.

This was my last day home, I reminded myself when I woke up that morning. It had to be tonight or never.

I began rehearsing lines again. I thought of a hundred ways to let Nita know we were going to get married without using the stupid, "Will you marry me?"

But before the day was half gone, Jane came joyously tripping along and suggested we go on a double date that night. She said Cotton, who was home on leave from the navy, asked her for a date, and could get his Dad's car. He volunteered to drive us over to Fayetteville and pay a surprise visit on another young couple.

You don't throw away a chance to double date, especially when you get to go big time riding around in a car. So we went.

On the other hand, you don't "arrange" to get married with your girl when you're out running around on a double date and can't even kiss in public.

I was miserable and getting miserabler by the minute, especially when we left Fayettville so late I knew it'd be midnight before we got home.

I probably wouldn't even have time for the perfunctory good-night kiss, let alone launch myself into a grand and eloquent speech about us arranging things to spend the rest of our lives together.

My misery increased.

Then it happened. We were sailing down a street through Rogers, Arkansas, when the car quit. The engine would race, but the car wouldn't pull. Cotton coasted to a curb and stopped.

Cotton and I made a quick inspection and agreed it had to be a broken rear axle.

We had to get home. If two young couples stayed out all night, our lives would be ruined, not to mention the disgrace it would bring on four families.

We talked it over and decided the best thing to do would be call home and at least let our families know the car broke down.

Jane and Cotton went to find a telephone. Nita and I remained with the car.

It was cold. We snuggled together to keep warm. We were in a heck of a pickle. I found myself praying that Cotton and Jane would get hold of somebody and they'd get word to our families, especially Nita's mother.

The farthest thing from my mind was proposing.

After a long, long moment of silence, Nita finally asked softly, "Dale, what's going to happen to us?"

What did she mean by "us?" Marriage?

My heart pounded. Now was the time. I searched for my best speech to arrange our marriage. Then I panicked.

Did she mean us, me and her? Or us—me, her, Jane, and Cotton bringing disgrace to our families?

Or she could be thinking of global politics with "us" being the Americans and British against the Germans and the Japanese. We were getting whipped pretty bad.

I blurted, "Will you marry me?"

As soon as the words were out, I realized they weren't stupid at all. They were the most beautiful words I have ever spoken in my life.

I didn't need a yes. I sensed it, her body close to mine relaxed completely.

"Oh—I don't know," she whispered, worried, I knew about our future.

But I felt we were already married during the remainder of that night. Cotton's dad roused my brother out of bed and they drove over to tow us home.

No, Nita didn't say yes. Her answer, "I don't know," was enough for me.

Even so, after fifty-eight years, I'm still afraid to ask what she really meant by "us."

She might say she was honestly worried about the outcome of the war, and hadn't planned to marry me.

Suppose?

A Soldier's Marriage

CBS ran a series during its nightly news honoring the death of a soldier killed in the war in Iraq. And the guy they choose is usually one who has just married, the beautiful bride smiling happily in their wedding photo. The implication that his love has been destroyed by the war in Iraq. Why do they do this?

You know and I know why. They want to demonstrate how terrible the war in Iraq is by glamorizing the death of a single soldier and his lost love.

How strange this philosophy is. Never before in the history of mankind has a soldier been anything but a soldier. When they get killed they are casualties: just a number among thousands. War, in whatever form, is one of the craziest things man has ever invented. It makes absolutely no sense whatsoever. But when your way of life is attacked, you have but one choice: fight back.

That's when the personal life of a soldier ends. However, there is no holding back love. The possibility of you getting killed in all this madness is very real. So real, in fact, that you come to accept it as a part of living.

This possibility was running through my mind as I stared at my reflection in the darkened window of a transcontinental train racing westward through the wintry night across Indiana. What should we do? I kept asking myself over and over. Get married? Or wait? The engineering school the army sent me to at Johns Hopkins University in Baltimore would be over in nine months. After that I'd probably be sent overseas. If we got married now, it'd have to be a quickie. We had only one week between semesters, plus the weekends, and with four days of that time used up in traveling to and from Oklahoma, that left only five days at home. Would we even be able to get a marriage license at the courthouse, this being the Christmas-New Year holiday season? Would our preacher be available? We'd have to call our family and friends. How long would we be married? Three days? Four?

Not a pretty arrangement for a beautiful young girl from a nice family who deserved all the pageantry that goes with a normal, well-planned wedding.

Our love story had been one of sweet innocence. We'd met so young. I fell in love instantly, too young. She did too, she confessed later, shyly, for she was a proper girl, raised in a proper family.

Then came Pearl Harbor. We both knew the separation would come, either temporarily or permanently. We tried not to talk about it for a year, just enjoyed being together, making every lingering good night kiss count.

The movement of my buddy John Cahill sitting beside me told me he was waking up, even before he asked, "You decided yet?" I glanced at him, shook my head.

He stretched, yawned, then added, "Don't do it."

I turned back to stare out the window. He knew. You don't live in the same room with a man for six months and not know everything there is to know about him. He had seen me writing Nita a letter every day. He knew we planned to get married. We made good roommates, both from Oklahoma, neither dating, him married and me faithful to my girlfriend back home. Which complicated my problem. One of the requirements when we signed up for the army's special engineering program was not to get married, because we would be restricted to the campus except on weekends. Those who were already married were not to allow their wives to come live nearby. Distractions, they told us, would not be tolerated because, they emphasized, we were at war, and our nation could not afford wasting its resources on young men who would not, or could not, for any reason fulfill their assignments.

Besides not being able to sleep, I was exhausted from fighting our way through the crowds, standing in line, always standing in line—even to get a stale sandwich. We had gone through a hectic week. And it had been right in the middle of the tough finals that our unit commander, Colonel Helms, had issued strict orders that because of the travel delays during the holidays, any cadet who lived more than twenty-four hours of travel time away from Baltimore would not be permitted to go home. Every cadet, he stressed, who did go had to be signed in the following Monday at eight o'clock sharp. No excuses.

Since there'd be no bed check, Cahill and I decided to chance it. After our last exam on Friday, we packed our things, sneaked off campus, and caught the city bus for downtown Baltimore. The crowd at the station was so pressing that the best we could do was find hard wooden seats in the conductor's car behind the engine.

Coal smoke seeped in. Sleep was impossible for me as the train barreled its way westward. Cahill tried to be helpful. "Look at the spot I'm in. Our baby's due in a couple of months. If they don't give me an emergency furlough, I'm going to go home anyway."

Going AWOL would be the end of his chance to be given an officer's commission by the army. That was another requirement they'd laid on us: no furloughs in mid semester, except emergencies. Even then, if you had to be gone more than a week, you'd be sent back to your regular outfit.

There was more to it than that, I knew. Regardless of rank, now or in the future, we were at the army's mercy, which, in turn, was at the mercy of world events. Leaving an unattached girl behind if you had to go overseas and, possibly, to the front lines, would be a world of difference than leaving a wife with child who might wind up waiting for a husband who would never return.

"You don't have a chance," I told him. "If Colonel Helms restricts us to twenty-four-hour travel time in between semesters, you think he'd going to let you go to Oklahoma in mid term?"

He shrugged, his mind made up. AWOL. My good friend would wind up serving time in prison. I hated the thought, and returned my gaze to the window. The rising sun's weak rays slanting from behind us turned the snow dust stirred up by the train into billowing clouds of tiny yellow jewels, reminding me how the set of rings I'd sent her sparkled. I apologized in my letter, vowing to buy her more expensive ones after the war.

She wrote back how thrilled she was. She'd tried them both on. She couldn't wait to be wearing the wedding ring all the time.

Even when daylight came and I could no longer see my reflection, I still stared out the window at the snow-covered fields sliding by. The transcontinental mainliner didn't go through Oklahoma. We transferred to a bus in St. Louis, an overnighter to Tulsa. Cahill got off in Miami. I made it to Tulsa just at daybreak on Sunday.

I took a taxi to the rooming house where Nita was staying. I kept ringing the doorbell until somebody opened the door. It was Nita, in a robe covering her night gown. I grabbed her up in a happy bear hug and swung her around until she ordered, gasping, "Put me down. People will see us."

She forced me to sit in the front room of the boarding house alone, fidgeting, while she dressed and made herself, as she said, "decent and presentable." When she reappeared, she showed me the rings, sparkling like yellow jewels in the snow dust of a morning sun.

All the consequences which might come because of the world situation, and what effect it might have on our lives, did not even come close to dampening the way we felt about each other. We did get married. And nature handed us a bonus: a heavy snow stopped all bus travel out of Tulsa, giving me another twenty-four hours with Nita. I'd be a day late getting back to Baltimore.

I called Cahill. The buses were still running out of Miami. He said he'd sign in for me. I got away with it. But when I showed my marriage license to get my wife's allowance started, Colonel Helms knew I'd violated his restricted travel order. He called me in. I tried to explain about being late. "…Then I got snowed in—"

He held up a hand, stopping me. "You're getting yourself in deeper and deeper, Denney." He let me off by taking away only two of my free weekends.

Best of all, when Cahill applied for an emergency furlough a month later, Colonel Helms okayed it. "If Denney can get to Oklahoma, get married, honeymoon, and get back within a week, I guess you can make it," he said.

Like I said, sometimes love rearranges the world situation, instead of the other way around.

The Lipstick Express

It seems so strange that World War II veterans have never expected any type of monument to commemorate how they saved the world from being overrun by madmen and now, when one has been planned for our nation's capital, protesters are stalling its construction with every court shenanigan they can think of.

The World War II memorial is for our nation, not just for those who happened to be in service at the time of the conflict.

It is for the mothers who said, "Here is my son. Take him. Train him to shoot, to kill." Many of these mothers only received a telegram in return, expressing regrets that her son was killed in action in some foreign land, on some remote jungle island nobody ever heard of, somewhere in a sea of sand in an African desert.

It is also for members of the news media who willingly suspended their right to freedom of speech to help keep our military secrets secret.

And for their young loves left behind, many with a child forming in their wombs.

Such a monument would destroy the beauty of the mall, critics are claiming.

They do not know how awfully, awfully close it came to having jack-booted German soldiers goose-stepping their way down that mall.

Tom Brokaw's now famous book, *The Greatest Generation*, has spotlighted many of our national heroes who still say, "Hey, I'm no hero."

So very, very many hero stories never made it into Brokaw's book.

There was Oklahoma's own Lieutenant Colonel Leon R. Vance from Enid. He was cited for heroism and given the Medal of Honor for bringing a crippled bomber back to an English beach with part of a lower leg hanging on only by a bit of skin.

The saddest part of his story is that the hospital plane bringing him back home went down over the Atlantic. There were no survivors.

244

The Enid Army Air Field was renamed in his honor as Vance Air Force Base.

Would there be any Leon Vances in our culture today? On the other hand, I sincerely hope there will never be another situation where our young people would be put to the test.

For every Leon Vance—a true hero—there were millions and millions of non-heroes like me.

I wouldn't want a monument built on the mall in Washington DC to memorialize my time in service. I served because it was expected of me.

But I do think the millions of young girls like my wife Nita deserve recognition. They were a part of the conflict too. So very many of them went through hell to be with their new husbands when it should have been a time of romantic bliss in their young lives.

Nita came to Roswell NM to be with me. We'd been married nine months and had been separated six of those nine. Roswell was one of thousands of sleepy little rural towns which were suddenly overwhelmed by military bases springing up around them.

Besides the large Air Force base just outside of town, Roswell's meager population, which also supported a German prisoner of war base, was reduced to almost zero.

Because of my educational background, the army decided to send me to X-ray school. While awaiting reassignment, I was put on general duty in the local hospital, working twelve-hour shifts.

Even so, Nita wanted to come be with me, and I wanted very much for her to do so. But first I had to find a place in town for her to stay.

I did the usual things we all did when we tried to find a place to live off base—go to the USO, check the bulletin board, buy a local paper. Then we'd start looking.

Luckily, Roswell was small enough that you could walk from one end to the other in thirty minutes. I began walking the streets, checking addresses.

The sun went down and I got desperate. The best I could find was a bedroom in a private home. The owners had obviously converted an interior storage closet into a bedroom to rent to kids like us.

I took it. It didn't even have any outside windows. It was a miserable place and I still get the shivers today just thinking about it.

Nita didn't complain. Since I'd be leaving soon, she didn't bother to find a job. She went shopping and entertained herself each day, waiting patiently for me to get home at night. We'd usually go see a movie after eating out.

Sure enough, within a week after Nita got there, those of us shipping out were told to pack our things. We were leaving immediately after work that night.

I asked for permission to call my landlady so I could get word to Nita that I wouldn't be home. Asking was a mistake. The young lieutenant in charge cited regulations: GIs were not supposed to talk about troop movements to anybody anywhere any time.

I argued that a group of lowly GIs traveling on a passenger train from Roswell, New Mexico, across the mesquite plains to San Antonio, Texas, wasn't a shipment of troops. That order was to stop soldiers for blabbing about being shipped overseas to keep U-boats from sinking troop ships.

No dice. The lieutenant in charge wouldn't budge from his orders.

They forced me onto the truck with the others and off we went into Roswell. I learned at the train station that I had thirty minutes before our train arrived.

There I was—within a ten-minute walk to our room. I knew Nita would be wondering what had happened, waiting in that miserable room of ours, when I didn't show up at my usual time. I had to at least see her before I left and tell her I was being shipped out.

I told the gung-ho lieutenant I had to use the restroom. As soon as I got out of his sight, I sneaked out a side door and lit out for our room across town.

I figured I could get there, tell Nita where I was going, kiss her goodbye, and run back to the station in time to catch the train.

In the meantime, when I didn't come home at my usual time, Nita called the base to inquire. They refused to tell her where I was going, only that I was on shipping orders.

But she demanded to talk to the base commander. How she got through to him, I'll never know. And he had more sense than his subordinates. He told her where I was going and on what train.

She just had a few minutes to get to the train station to see me before I left. She lit out for the station.

By sheer luck, we ran into one another on the street. Had one of us gone down another street, we'd have missed one another.

She didn't want to stay there without me. I wanted her to go. We didn't give it another thought. We grabbed a taxi and ordered him to hurry to our address. We made him wait. We ran inside, threw everything we had in suitcases and ran back out to the waiting taxi.

At the station, we bought Nita a ticket to San Antonio on the same train we were scheduled to travel on. The only seats available were coach.

Once on the train, I gave up my berth in the Pullman so I could ride with Nita. We managed to find a vacant bench seat. We sat up all night, grabbing what little sleep we could leaning on one another's shoulder.

And, of course, stealing kisses after the lights were turned low.

It was the same hectic scene when we arrived in San Antonio early the next morning. There was a truck waiting for me. Nita said she'd get a hotel room. We'd get together later.

When I reported to my commanding officer at Brooke General Hospital, I had no idea why he kept grinning every time he looked at me until I looked in the mirror later.

I had lipstick smears all over my face.

I was one of millions of service men and women who never set foot outside the United States during the greatest war in mankind's history. I know I don't deserve to be a part of a memorial in Washington DC.

On the other hand, why not? Nita and I were products of a national culture, the likes of which our nation had never experienced before and will never experience again.

What greater beauty could be preserved than the national culture that existed in the United States of America when its very existence was threatened in 1941?

Dedicated to all of us.

A Classic Car

Why do they call them classic? I wondered as I walked down the row of classic cars on display.

The age? The chrome? Gussied-up interiors?

Then I noticed the way one man was polishing an already shining hood with such loving care and I knew.

It was love.

That's when I began looking for a '36 straight-eight Chrysler coupe. I couldn't find one. It was a shame.

That was our first car. Nita and I were living in New Mexico. I was in the army. We'd dropped the atom bomb on Japan and the war was same as over. I put in for a furlough.

We wanted to go home in style. We'd saved a little money and decided to buy a used car. Neither of us knew how to drive. Oh, I knew how, I told myself. It was that I'd never actually done it.

We both liked Fords. But it was discouraging. Used cars still had new prices on them because of the war.

Then one evening when Nita was still at work, a salesman led me to a car in our price range, sitting in a back corner of the car lot.

"This baby is years ahead of her time," the salesman bubbled excitedly. "She's even got four-wheel hydraulic brakes!"

Not only was it not a Ford, it was a *Chrysler!* I tried to get away. The salesman hung on and kept talking.

The cab was low and dinky inside. A long gear shift lever curved up from a big hump in the floor.

"Just listen to this horn," the salesman said and pressed the button in the center of the steering wheel. It did have a classy sound. Loud, too.

"Hop in," he encouraged. "Take her for a spin. See how a *real* car rides."

I slid under the wheel, trying to act like I'd been driving all my life. I started it up, pressed down the clutch pedal, and shifted into low gear.

I stiffened and gripped the steering wheel. I began pushing down the accelerator as I eased up on the clutch. The car didn't move. The rpms wound higher and higher.

Suddenly, the clutch caught. The rear wheels threw up plumes of gravel. I shot out of the used car lot in a cloud of dust.

I slammed on the hydraulic brakes. The car screeched to a halt in the middle of the street. I froze with cars honking at me from two directions.

In my rear view mirror, I saw the salesman come running. His hat flew off. He grabbed the door handle, yanked open the door.

"Why didn't you tell me you didn't know how to drive, soldier," he said in a shaky voice. "Move over. I'll take you for a spin."

Embarrassed, I let him drive me around. I was impressed.

That night Nita and I talked it over. It would beat the heck out of riding the bus. We decided to go for it.

I went back the next day and made the deal. The salesman offered to drive me home. I told him she was mine now and I could handle her. I drove her all the way to our apartment in low gear.

Evenings we took her to the park and taught ourselves how to drive. It was exciting just owning a car. I would jangle my car keys everywhere I went.

When my furlough came through, Nita and I were so anxious to get going that we threw our clothes in a suitcase and headed for Oklahoma that night.

I was secretly glad the thirty-five-miles-per-hour speed limit during the war was still in effect because I had an excuse to creep along while I was learning to drive.

The speedometer said she could do 120. I wondered if it really would go that fast. But I sure didn't want to get stopped, not having a license. I held her under thirty just to be on the safe side.

It was near daylight by the time we reached Amarillo. We were both so sleepy we could hardly hold our eyes open. We pulled off on a side street to catch a bit of shut-eye.

We couldn't get comfortable in the cramped cab. We kept wiggling around stretching our legs this way and that behind and over and under the gear shift lever. I accidentally hit the horn button with my elbow two or three times.

I'd just dozed off with Nita's head in my lap when I became aware of this beam of light flashing around. I squirmed into a decent sitting position. Nita tried to sit up, straightening her hair and dress at the same time.

"Where you kids heading?" the gruff voice behind the light demanded.

I could just barely make out this policeman's cap beyond the beam of light. "Oklahoma," I squeaked.

He asked for my furlough papers. He glanced them over, reading by flashlight. I just knew he was going to take me to jail for not having a driver's license. Then he flipped his beam over the car.

"Nice car. Way ahead of its time," he said returning my papers. That made me feel better.

"She sure is," I bragged.

"Can I see your license?"

Thinking fast, I said, "I lost my driver's license in New Guinea. I just bought this car to get home in. I'm gonna get a new driver's license when I get there."

I could tell he knew I was lying. But I guess he was happy the war was over like everybody else. He backed away.

"Quit honking that dad-blamed horn," he grunted. "You're waking up the whole neighborhood."

The interruption ruined our dozing time. We started up our old straight-eight Chrysler coupe and eased back out on the highway.

The gallant old car seemed to say "to heck with it" after that. I let the old straight-eight take over. The speedometer needle kept climbing. Shoot fire, going eighty was nothing to her. She took us flying across the Texas panhandle in nothing flat.

I was proud of her. She performed like a dream. We made two more trips to Oklahoma in her and I ignored the speed limit all the way. She'd get us there and back in nothing flat.

But she had a tough time in the hills of Oklahoma the summer after I was discharged. She was built for the open road, not winding gravel roads that had gullies washed in them every time it rained. She'd bottom out and the swirling dust choked her carburetor.

By then, she was a Senior Citizen, in car years, gulping oil like medicine. Even so, she took us to the University of Oklahoma and it was because of her that I was able to get a part-time job delivering mail. She was always ready to go, rain or shine.

But her tires got so thin I winced every time I ran over a rock. The shoes on her fancy hydraulic brakes wore out. I had a hard time stopping her one day. I nosed into the rear bumper of another car and damaged her grill, giving her the look of an old woman who'd lost her teeth.

When she got to overheating, I decided to sell her. With one final sigh, she just barely made it to a used car lot in Oklahoma City.

The man offered me $250 and I took it.

I pocketed the money and left. It was like selling your own grandma.

Now, walking down the line of classic cars on display, I choked up thinking about our old straight-eight, '36 Chrysler coupe.

She had been a faithful old girl, come to think of it. And like the salesman had said, years ahead of her time. She taught me how to drive and got me out of trouble when I didn't have a driver's license. She helped me earn a living when I was going to school. She was a part of our life that would never go away.

Yes, she would fit in here, I thought as I got in my pickup and drove away.

If I could find her now, I'd put sixteen coats of shiny black paint on her and chrome everything under the hood. And I'd re-upholster the seat Nita and I squirmed around on trying to get comfortable so we could get some sleep that early dawn in Amarillo.

I'd make certain the horn worked, too. We'd travel all over together and be in parades and she'd be the grandest girl of all.

Suppose I could find her?

It would be such a sweet reunion.

The 40s Culture

Everyone seems to be arguing about patriotism these days—whether what you say and do proves you are, or what you say and do proves you're not.

And how strange it seems to watch the TV talking heads squirm when talking about patriotism. Their dilemma is they have elevated themselves above "taking sides," claiming objectivity as their domain even when their country is at war.

How different, I think, than during WW II.

For one thing, we loved our country, not because it was ours, but because our country was us—the Johnsons, the Peters, the Sixkillers, the Williamses. Some of us were the best, some of us not so good.

We depended upon the pastors of our local churches to establish the parameters of common decency. Our government made no attempts whatsoever to assume command of our daily lives. Nor did Hollywood try "to send us a message about religion or social mores." Quite the contrary, Hollywood respected all religions and social customs.

We hoped with all our hearts that our country would stay out of the war raging in Europe. There were more important things to do—like finding enough food to take care of our families, and seeing to it our kids got through school. And our parents controlled the schools, not the education establishment.

Every day the newspapers carried maps with black arrows showing how the Germans were spreading across Europe and into Africa.

The white arrows represented our friends. The black arrows pushed all the white arrows out of Europe. France gave up, almost without a fight. Russia was like a wounded bear—it first signed on with Germany, then begged for help when Germany turned the black arrows toward Moscow.

Our news people made no pretense of being objective. They knew that if those black arrows eventually swallowed up our country, they wouldn't have a constitution to guarantee their freedom of speech.

They had to be patriotic or lose everything.

The clincher was when Japan bombed Pearl Harbor. Newspapers and newsreels showed pictures of our burning battleships. And the next day they were praising the patriotism of our young men lining up to enlist in the armed services.

Even Hollywood turned its efforts to fighting the war. Every movie made pictured stiff-backed German soldiers and buck-toothed Japanese as unquestioned villains.

In the movies, when one of our soldiers got shot, you didn't see any blood. You saw him clutch his chest and fall to the ground. His buddy would hold his head up as he was dying, and the dying soldier would ask his buddy to be sure and mail the letter he wrote that morning to his girl back home. Then he would simply close his eyes and go limp. It was an honorable way to die.

Hollywood stars also left their comfortable homes in California and made tours to entertain the troops, exposing themselves to bombs and gunfire in many cases. None of them—nary a one—spoke out against the war. In fact, many of the top stars joined the services to help do the fighting.

It thrilled you to watch newsreels showing our planes zooming around in the sky and hear the machine guns on the battlefields go *rat-a-tat*, and your insides shook when the big guns on the battleships fired.

You never saw any dead Americans in the newsreels, just Japanese and Germans and Italians.

Everybody was involved in the war, everybody patriotic. Your mother saved grease to make explosives with. Your Dad made long trips in the family car only when absolutely necessary to save rationed tires and gasoline.

People came off the farms to catch one of the buses that ran day and night taking workers to defense plants which were open twenty-four hours a day, seven days a week to manufacture clothing, guns, tanks, ships, and airplanes.

Business leaders yielded to the military, turning over all their assets to fight the war on the home front. Farmers who stayed home worked harder to raise more crops to feed the nation.

Our news media led the forefront, preaching we would win, that it was only a question of how long it would take. They never, ever showed any good side of the enemy, nor would they ever allow the enemy use our own media to tell their side of the story.

Young men were proud to have been "selected" to serve. And very excited, because many of us had never even been out of the county where we were born.

Getting killed was the furthermost thing from our minds. Children of the

thirties, we were accustomed to living with frightening unknowns, such as the diphtheria epidemic, the crippling polio scare. Our parents well remembered when the common flu killed more American civilians and soldiers during the last war than bullets did on the battlefields of Europe.

Your uppermost thought, when you turned away from your girl and climbed on the bus that would take you to the army induction center, was that you hoped you wouldn't mess up learning how to be a soldier and disgrace your family and, by association, give your town a bad name.

We were proud, dressed in our uniforms for the first time. We'd practice saluting in front of a mirror until we developed just the right salute we wanted, smart and snappy.

The excitement begins to wear off at the end of the day. It would be about this same time of day when you used to go out to your girl's house back home and pick her up and go to the show. She seems so far, far away now—off in another world. You get some paper and sit on the edge of your bunk and write her a letter.

You try to be lighthearted and tell her about all the things that happened to you that day. But before you know it, you're crying inside, and telling her how much you miss her.

The worst part of writing to your girl back home is when you can't think of any words to express how you feel. You sit there staring into space, remembering that last kiss when you tasted the salty dampness on her cheek.

You bite your underlip to keep tears from coming, and you jot a quick, unabashed, "I love you." You sign your name and drop it in the mail box.

Over the next few weeks, you pay close attention when they teach you how to make up your bed, how to march in step with other guys, how to disassemble a rifle blindfolded and put it back together, how to pack, unpack, set up a pup tent, how to dig a foxhole.

You work hard to be a good soldier, hoping that you will be promoted soon so all the folks back home will be proud of you.

All the reporters write stories about how great you are. They show pictures of troop trains filled with soldiers leaning out the windows, smiling and waving.

Even advertisers use soldiers, sailors, and marines smoking their brand of cigarettes, drinking their brand of beer.

And you are the hero in every movie you see—you either die honorably, or you recover from your wounds and return home to find your girl waiting for you.

Even your own griping takes on a tone of amusement. All of our hatred has been directed toward the enemy.

Patriotism is not love of country. It's love of family and friends…which, of course, is what your country is.

So why be ashamed of it? Why argue over whether you are or are not?

Patriotism is not "supporting the troops."

It's the sharing of love with one another.

That's why, when asked to, you unhesitatingly climb down the ladder dangling over the side of the ship and hop into the landing boat. Scared? Of course. But somebody's got to stop those black arrows from spreading around the world. If it's up to you to do it, so be it.

You hit the beach…

Death, fright, dismemberment, and pain are part of it. Your job is to inflict more death, fright, dismemberment, and pain on them than they do on you. It's high time to stop all this senseless killing and willful waste. You cease being you and become somebody else—that anomaly of history, a soldier.

You have a job to do for the folks back home, and you try to do it well.

When it's all over and you're still alive, you find a spot off to the side of the road somewhere in a foreign country and write a long letter to the girl back home…

You are being patriotic, is all.

Amarillo Surprise

There's a move on to refurbish stretches of the famous Route 66, especially here in Oklahoma. America's main street, as it was called, stretched from downtown Chicago to downtown Los Angeles. It had bisected our state, giving us the distinction of owning more miles of America's first transcontinental motor highway than any other state.

After reading the news story, I thought: Oh, my! Can it be possible that this famous highway has gone from a dirt road, to being Main Street of America, to becoming nothing but a memory in my lifetime?

I was born within thirty miles of this highway, three years before it was even named Route 66, in 1926.

During the deep depression of the thirties, the partially paved road carried thousands of distraught families westward in search of the promised land.

During World War II, Route 66 was a primary east-west artery for the shipment of men and materials. Its traffic sustained thousands of roadside businesses through the sixties. Then it was obliterated during the construction of Interstate 40 in the seventies and eighties.

It seems as if I have spent my entire life traveling up and down this famous road. It entered our state at the northeast corner, dropped down through Tulsa, and on to Oklahoma City where it turned due west toward Amarillo.

Amarillo!!!

The very thought of that town made me shiver. Dawn was just breaking that cold February morning in 1945 when I stood beneath a Route 66 sign on the outskirts of Amarillo, trying to thumb a ride.

I stomped my feet to keep circulation going and blew on my hands to keep them warm. I couldn't stop shivering, no matter how hard I tried to relax. My teeth chattered like crickets in a cracker box.

My hope was to make it to Jay, hitch-hiking, by midnight—to room five in the Duffield Hotel to be exact. That's where Nita was staying until my

256

reassignment orders came through. The last two months had been the longest we'd been separated during the first year of our marriage.

Was she ever going to be surprised. I'd been promised a week furlough, but I'd had to write and tell her it had been canceled. Then our reassignment orders changed. I was given my furlough papers after all.

I grabbed my orders and ran. I didn't even take time trying to call Nita. Long distance phone lines were so clogged out of army bases, sometimes it would take hours to get your connection.

Plus having to call the hotel number. Mrs. Duffield would have to go find Nita. And if Nita happened to be out, that would be that.

It would take me thirty-six hours by bus. I knew I could beat that hitch-hiking, especially wearing my uniform.

And I'd be on Route 66, the Main Street of America.

My prewar hitch-hiking experience to Oklahoma University and back kept telling me to establish eye contact with the driver. People have a hard time passing when you are looking them in the eye.

It worked. A man in a late-model Ford stopped. I seized the door handle and climbed in, still shivering. The air from the car's heater washed over me, warming my chilled bones.

"Thank you, sir," I chattered, my cheeks and lips so numb I could hardly talk, "I was beginning to think nobody would stop."

"How far you going, sergeant?" he asked.

He was a well-dressed man—blue suit, red tie, felt hat with a snap-down brim, shiny black shoes.

His expensive looking wristwatch appeared new. A Christmas present?

"A place called Jay. That's about a hundred miles beyond Tulsa. I'm going to try and make it by midnight."

He whistled his doubt. "That's nearly five hundred miles. I don't see how you can do it. The war-time speed limit of thirty-five has slowed things down considerably."

"I figured it up," I bragged jokingly. "You can make five hundred miles in fourteen hours and twenty-eight minutes at thirty-five miles per hour."

He laughed. "Assuming you don't have to wait long between rides. Not many people drive long distances these days with tires and gasoline rationed. You might be spending more time thumbing than riding."

"Yes, sir. But I hope not."

Before I realized it, we were doing eighty. Hey, I thought. What's going on here? Was he some kind of nut?

Telephone poles flew by like fence posts. I forgot about being cold and looked for something to hang onto.

"You don't have to hurry on my account," I said. "I don't want you to get caught speeding or anything on account of me."

"Oh, I'm not hurrying on your account," he said. "I have an important meeting to attend at the Air Force Base in Clinton, Oklahoma, in—" he glanced at his expensive watch—"exactly two hours."

I hope he makes it, I prayed. Oh, lordy, I hope he makes it.

His name was Costilini, he said. Sounded foreign to me. We didn't have any foreigners in Oklahoma. It had been settled by so many outlaws who'd changed their names to something like Jones or Smith that you hardly ever heard a foreign-sounding name.

I was mentally debating about asking to be let out when I heard the siren. I glanced back and saw this Texas Ranger pulling up on us, his red dome light flashing.

Costilini glanced in his rear view mirror and let up on the gas.

"Looks like we have a minor delay," he said, unruffled.

Now I'm going to be arrested, I thought in misery. This guy's one of those Mafia gangsters you read about, sure as shooting.

We stopped and the Texas Ranger pulled in behind. Costilini already had his wallet out by the time the Ranger got to his window. He flipped it open. The Ranger took a quick look.

"Sorry, sir," he said, stepping back and saluting.

"Would you mind radioing ahead? Tell your people I'm coming through?"

"Yes, sir," the trooper said.

Costilini gave him a quick salute and pulled back upon the pavement.

I stared at him wide-eyed. "Are you a general, or something?"

He waggled a finger. "Now don't tell me you've forgotten your army rules, sergeant. You're not supposed to tell strangers about troop movements, remember? Same thing holds true for every one of us involved in war work."

My wild ride with Costilini came to mind when I read six months later about us exploding the first atomic bomb in the New Mexico desert. Could he have been one of them? The guys who built it?

But at the time I was relieved to know he was somebody important and fell asleep, head nodding.

He awoke me with a shake, saying, "Sorry, sergeant. This is Clinton. I have to drop you off here."

"Yes, sir," I said. "Just let me out at the next corner."

I checked the time. Almost nine. If I could keep getting good rides like that, I would be with Nita in room five at the Duffield Hotel in Jay tonight.

I hoofed it out to the edge of town, ducked into one of those thousands of roadside cafes on Route 66, slurped down a quick cup of coffee, and hurried back out to take up my stand beside the highway.

I thumbed desperately as car after car drove on by. Locals, I kept telling myself. People simply wouldn't pass up a soldier trying to thumb a ride.

After about thirty minutes, here came a car load of girls. I didn't bother to thumb, but they stopped anyway and asked if I wanted a ride.

They didn't appear to be the type of girls soldiers ran into in what was then labeled the red light district in big cities. Must be some high school girls on a lark.

Dubious, I asked, "How far you going?"

"Just how far do you want to go?" one asked.

"Oklahoma City?"

"Get in. We'll take you."

I hesitated, then finally decided what the heck. A ride was a ride.

The two girls in the back seat made a place for me between them. They were all still snickering—the kind of mirth that says I-know-something-you-don't-know.

Their actions made me uncomfortable. I mentally pulled myself into a tight, compact shell, admonishing myself not to say anything which could remotely be interpreted as sexual.

I'd made a terrible mistake.

What should I do? If I demanded they let me out, I'd be stranded out in the middle of nowhere.

If I stayed with them—what sort of mess would I get into?

I pulled myself into a tight ball between the two girls squeezed into the back seat with me.

What should I do? A ride was a ride, and I had two-hundred-plus miles to go. I wanted so desperately to surprise my wife.

Nita and I had rented a room in Jay's only hotel so she wouldn't have to stay with her family while I was waiting to be reassigned from the army base in Amarillo.

To get away from the girls, I told them I had to use a restroom.

They all laughed as if I'd made some kind of risque joke. They pulled into a service station. I bailed out.

I stayed in the restroom, peeking out through a crack, until they left.

I went inside to buy a pack of cigarettes. An elderly couple paying their gas bill was asking the attendant how far it was to Oklahoma City. They were tired and couldn't make up their minds whether to try and make it all the way before dark, or get a motel room and wait until morning.

"If you're tired, I'll drive for you," I suggested.

They acted delighted, not only for having a driver but also for "doing something for the war effort" by giving a service man a ride.

The woman kept cautioning me every time the speedometer needle edged beyond thirty-five.

"It's against the law," she warned.

"Yeah, and our tires are thin," the man said. "There's a war on, you know."

As if I didn't know, me in an army uniform.

"Yes, sir," I said, slowing down.

They both eased off to sleep. I eased down on the accelerator.

They were surprised when we pulled into Oklahoma City so soon.

"It's this Route 66," I told the lady. "These stretches out here in western Oklahoma are fairly new. You can really make time on them."

They let me out in front of the state capitol building. Route 66 made a ninety-degree turn there. The spot was always overcrowded with east-bound hitch-hikers. I squeezed in among them.

I fretted, checking my watch every fifteen minutes. I still had two hundred miles to go, and the sun was on its way down.

A car stopped in front of a sailor near me. I ran and jumped into the back seat before the guy could get moving.

The driver, a beetle-browed man, gave me an "uninvited guest" look. But I remained seated and slammed the door. He moved on, asking, "Where you boys headed?"

"Chicago," the sailor said.

"Hey, me too," the driver said.

They compared addresses in Chicago.

"How about you, sergeant?" the driver asked, eyeing me in the rear view mirror.

I started to say Tulsa because they both would know where Tulsa was. But if this guy was going to Chicago, that meant I would be able to ride with them on through Tulsa to Claremore. It was just sixty miles from there on to Jay—a lonely, winding, less traveled road, but closer all the same.

"Jay," I said.

The driver slammed on his brakes.

"Jail?" he questioned harshly. "You running from the police?"

"No, no, no!" I said, shocked. "Jay." I spelled it out. "It's a small town in the northeast corner of Oklahoma."

He kept glancing at me skeptically.

"If you don't mind," I said. "I'll ride with you to Claremore. I have to get off there and go sixty miles east."

"Say, ain't Claremore the town Will Rogers was from?" the sailor asked.

"Yeah," I said. Actually Will Rogers was from Oolagah, but I saw no need to complicate things, especially when he and our driver began swapping stories about the humorous things Will Rogers had said. They asked me a lot of questions.

I didn't know any more than they did about Will Rogers, but I did know I was sure proud to be an Oklahoman right then.

I was quite familiar with the road from Oklahoma City to Tulsa. I'd been over its turns and twists many times. The trip took three hours—if you didn't get behind too many slow-moving trucks you couldn't pass because of the curves and hills.

It was ten o'clock when we got to Claremore, and turning colder by the minute.

I got out, poked my hands into my pockets, hunched my shoulders, and hurried to the east side of town.

My hopes now centered on making it to Pryor. I knew about the buses the defense contractor sent out in all directions from Pryor, where they manufactured powder in a plant there for the war. They picked up and carried workers from as far away as fifty miles in all directions. One ran through Jay, picking up workers for all three shifts and taking them home.

I saw some very weak headlights coming. I began thumbing desperately, leaning as far as I dared into the path of the oncoming vehicle so they'd be sure and see me.

The vehicle slowed and stopped. It was a Model T truck. I didn't care. I opened the door and crawled in, shivering. It was a farmer and his wife.

"Our place is five mile this side of Pryor," he said. "You're welcome to ride that far."

I told them my story, that I'd left Amarillo that morning and was hoping to surprise my wife.

"I was hoping I could at least make it to Pryor in time to catch the swing shift powder plant bus to Jay," I said.

"Don't you think we could run him on into town?" the woman asked her husband. "It wouldn't be very patriotic to make him walk on a night like this."

"Well…I s'pose so."

And they did. I caught the bus to Jay. It was almost one o'clock when the bus rolled to a stop in front of the Delaware County courthouse to let me out.

I hurried down the street to Duffield's Hotel, ran up the stairs two at a time and, heart pounding, knocked gently on the door of room five.

No answer. Puzzled, I knocked again, louder this time, the echoes bouncing hollowly up and down the hall.

A scrawny man in baggy long-johns opened the door, scowling and angry.

"What the hell you want?" he said.

I was so shocked, I couldn't talk. What was this man doing in Nita's—our—room?

Then anger flowed through me. I reached out and grabbed a fistful of his underwear and drew a fist back.

"Dale!" a woman called, stopping me from hitting him.

It was Mrs. Duffield, standing in the door of her apartment across the hall, her dark hair awry.

"Nita's not there," she said.

"But—" I stammered. "I—"

I didn't know what to ask. Was afraid to ask anything. I let my fist fall to my side. The guy I had hold of backed into the safety of his room.

"Nita checked out this morning," Mrs. Duffield said. "She told me that if you couldn't come home, she was going to catch the bus so she could spend this week with you in Amarillo."

Amarillo!!!

The Great Escape

I thought of Wolfgang Swertzferger the other day when I was sitting in my easy chair watching the rabble-rousers on television swarm through the streets on the other side of the world, burning the American flag and shouting, "Death to America!"

Wolfgang worked for me in the German prisoner of war camp in Roswell, New Mexico. I taught him how to take X-rays.

He was a tall man with slightly stooped shoulders and a hatchet-like face. He combed his long blond hair back. Strands of it were always falling to one side. He was forever reaching up to finger them back in place.

He was well into his forties, maybe his fifties—I'm not sure. One thing I was sure of was that he was far too old to be a foot-soldier. But Hitler was desperate, drafting anybody between the ages of sixteen and sixty who could walk, and throwing them into the front lines.

Wolfgang was very polite and tried hard to please me. He knew working in the X-ray department in a nice clean hospital was a lot better than having to go out in the fields and chop cotton for the local farmers.

There wasn't enough work in the X-ray department to keep one man busy. But since I lived in town with Nita and went home every night, Captain Bellucci, our chief surgeon, thought it would be a good idea to have someone on the base at all times who could take x-rays in case of emergencies.

After working with Wolfgang a year—me trying to teach him English and him trying to teach me German—we couldn't help but become friends.

One day when we were talking politics, he said in that heavily-accented English of his, "Hitler say we'd march across America—but he didn't say we'd pick cotton all the way."

He enjoyed showing me photos of his wife and kids. She was beautiful, a typical middle-age mother. His kids, two girls and a boy, were posing playfully like normal teenagers. They had a nice home in Dresden.

Dresden was a beautiful city, he told me, a very ancient city with many historic cathedrals.

But after we fire-bombed Dresden near the end of the war, Wolfgang didn't talk much about his home and family. Nor did I mention it. It was a sad thing, but what did they expect after fire-bombing London for three years?

Governments fight—and it's the people who suffer.

They get hungry. They get sleepy. They try to find a warm place to live.

Some believe in God. Some do not. Some want to be free. Others want strong leaders to take care of them.

As I watched the rabble mob on my television demonstrating in the street on the other side of the world, it was like watching a bad movie you've seen before. The story line is about a wild man being able to take control of a country and its people.

Sooner or later, just strutting around and making threatening speeches is not enough to control his people—he's got to attack somebody somewhere.

Then all hell breaks loose. A lot of people die. A lot of people starve. A lot of property is destroyed. Too much damage is done to the world before the wild man is brought down.

Here in America, we thought it was hilarious when Mussolini was caught with his private whore by his own people and literally hung up by his heels in a public square and spit on.

In my mind, I think that's why Hitler shot himself, or took poison, whichever. He even ordered his own body to be cremated so his own people wouldn't spit on him—which they probably would have done.

The only reason Emperor Hirohito, who was considered by the Japanese people as divine, was spared was because General MacArthur wanted to use him to help convert Japan to a democracy, which he did quite successfully.

Unfortunately, Joseph Stalin survived. There were some who very much wanted to go ahead and turn on Russia after Germany and Japan fell and eliminate Stalin.

But we said no, enough is enough. Old Joe is our friend. Let's all go home. Maybe he'll turn out to be a good guy. He finally did—the day he died.

Russia is still trying to recover from the shambles Stalin made of his country.

Our government used the German prisoners in New Mexico to solve a manpower shortage for the farmers and ranchers. They contracted with the land owners to furnish labor for a price, then paid the prisoners a small salary for work performed.

You soon realized the Germans in the camp were just kids like the rest of us—they just happened to be wearing a different uniform.

The prisoners in the Roswell camp were congenial, for the most part, and most were more than happy to be chopping cotton in New Mexico rather than running from the Russians on the eastern front.

They had good food, good living quarters, and the best medical facilities, all according to the terms of the Geneva Convention, which dictated that prisoners of war be fed the same rations the capturing soldiers were fed, also clothed and sheltered in a similar fashion.

None even tried to escape. Even so, they were proud to be Germans, which was understandable. Without anyone telling us, we all realized there was a difference between a German and a fanatical Nazi.

Our hospital was seldom used, although well-equipped. Statistically speaking, German soldiers were healthy. But Captain Bellucci did like to take out appendices whenever a prisoner complained of a stomach ache—he said he needed the experience doing surgery—but otherwise, those of us working in the hospital had very little to do.

We'd gather around in the pharmacy and listen to the World Series baseball games, or play ping-pong in the library, or write letters to friends, which is what I did mostly.

When Germany surrendered, our rules became even more relaxed. German prisoners' spirits rose. They'd be going home soon.

And the clincher for "going home" for all of us happened early one morning that July.

I was riding the government bus to the army base before good daylight. We all settled down for the quiet fifteen-minute ride, some grabbing a little "shut-eye," others staring out the window at nothing and thinking of home. Soldiers always thought of home when they didn't have anything to do.

Suddenly, the pre-dawn gloom turned into a high-noon brilliance, everywhere. It was gone as quickly as it came.

We sat in stunned silence, not believing, questioning in our own minds, "Had the others seen what I just saw?"

"What the heck was that?" someone finally muttered, peering out his window, looking high and low.

"Lightning?" another suggested.

"You crazy?" another scoffed. "They ain't a cloud in the sky."

He was right. There weren't any clouds. Nor had there been any clouds for the last couple of months in this semi-desert part of New Mexico.

"Probably an ammo dump somewhere gone blooie," another offered.

Couldn't be. There had been no sound. Nothing. We all sat tense, wondering. At the base we told friends about it. They laughed, calling us nuts.

The prisoners had seen it, too. They began chattering and whispering among themselves. Then the talk died down.

Nobody mentioned it again—until we bought a newspaper a month later and read about Hiroshima. Then we knew the light we'd seen early that morning was light that came from the detonation of the world's first atom bomb at White Sands in the New Mexican desert.

And we'd been a hundred miles away with a mountain range between us and "it."

Good God!

Yet its ungodly power made us all happy and proud of our country for being able to build an atom bomb.

It meant we would all be going home soon—us, the prisoners, and all the other soldiers all over the world—on both sides.

We immediately began making preparations to close the base and send the prisoners home; there was a festive feeling hanging over the camp.

The prisoners were happy to be going home. We GIs were happy too—most of us had accumulated enough points to be going directly to the nearest separation center just as soon as we put the prisoners on a boat for home.

I wasn't a bit ashamed telling Wolfgang goodbye. We were friends, even more so now that the war was over.

I asked him to write as soon as he arrived back in Dresden, and gave him my home address.

He said he would. We parted with a handshake. He seemed sad, which puzzled me.

The next morning when I got to work, I was surprised by the hustle and bustle going on.

"Scrub up," Captain Bellucci ordered as soon as he saw me. "We have a gunshot wound. I need to use your fluoroscope. I have to operate on your X-ray table."

Gunshot!

There hadn't been a gun fired on our base in two years. "What happened?" I asked. But the real question was, Why? Who would try to escape when they were all going home?

One did, I was told as I got busy in the scrub room. Our guards found him hiding in a barn on a nearby farm. Instead of giving up, he made a run for it. A guard shot him, hitting him in the hip and bringing him down.

Scrubbed, gowned, and ready, I hurried into the semi-dark x-ray room. The patient lay stretched out on the X-ray table. Our surgical technician was working feverishly trying to staunch the flow of blood.

I paid no attention to the wounded patient. I worked to set up the fluoroscope, bitching about the patient's blood getting all over my X-ray table.

"I sorry," came a weak voice. It sounded familiar. I paused to look down. "Wolfgang?"

He tried to smile. I couldn't believe it.

"Why in the heck did you try to escape? Don't you know you're going home?"

He nodded. "Yes. That's why I ran away. I want to stay in America."

We fixed him up. But he didn't go home with the others. I had to take him in an ambulance to the General Hospital in El Paso. He would be sent home later.

That's when I learned why he didn't want to go home. He read me the letter. It was from his uncle. His wife and kids were killed in our fire-bombing raid on Dresden.

I never did hear from Wolfgang. I like to think he became an American.

"Death to America," the rabble rousers kept shouting on my TV set.

It was like watching a bad movie you've seen before—

The Discharge

The war was over. We'd whipped them. Nita had new clothes laid out for me when I walked into our tiny apartment with my army discharge rolled up in my hand. I handed her the piece of paper and began shucking my uniform.

It sure felt good to be a civilian again, to wear loose-fitting clothes. I felt naked with the top button of my shirt open and not wearing a tie. Nita sat on the bed, her face reflecting surprised shock.

"What's the matter?" I asked. "You act like you've never seen me before."

"I haven't. I mean—you look so different in—in those."

"You said you'd take me for better or worse. Is this better? Or Worse?"

She laughed. I took her hands and pulled her to her feet.

"Now what?" she asked.

Demobilization after WWII was a cultural shock that shook our nation—two ways.

One was social, the other was the way we governed ourselves.

Socially, we'd gone from using outdoor privies to wanting the comfort of beautiful bathrooms, from bathing once a week to bathing every day, from trying to find a house to rent which somebody'd built a hundred years ago to wanting a brand new one right now—one with an attached garage.

We went from wearing overalls to school—one pair had to last you all week—to dressing up every day, complete with tie, white shirt, and suit.

Where the big city used to be a worrisome place you had to go through to get somewhere else, and full of people nobody would want to neighbor with, it was now a place where we all wanted to live, and not even know who our neighbors were.

The new shopping centers were handy, with plenty of parking spaces around them, and you could go from store to store without getting wet if it was raining, or even hot, in the totally air-conditioned malls.

There were no far-away places any more—more than likely you'd been there on a three-day pass, or recovering from a shrapnel wound in your leg.

Before the war, when you wanted to go to California to look for work, you hitch-hiked to save money, or rode the bus. And you figured it might take a week to get there, or more if you got hung up somewhere in a little town in the desert.

Now if you wanted to go to Chicago to interview for a job, you'd have your wife drive you out to the airport and you got on an airplane and you'd be landing at O'Hare Field almost as soon as your wife got back home with the car.

Going to college wasn't a wild dream anymore—it was a must, and the government made it easy with the new GI Bill. They paid your tuition. The University built little houses out of plywood, just off campus, that were neat to live in.

Just as soon as you got your degree, you were going to get a good job with a big company and make a lot of money—not have to live like your parents all your life in a house out in the country.

Most men wore snap-brim hats and women dressed up even when they went to baseball games and football games. Or shopping downtown. Once in a while after work you might run to the grocery store at the nearest mall without a tie on and wearing slacks—just to grab a loaf of bread or something.

What we had saved and paid cash for before the war, we now bought on credit. Merchants like car manufacturers made it easy to buy one of their new cars—just promise to pay for it a little each month. It was so much fun; you'd get one every couple years and drive over to your friend's house to show it off.

"Man, I like that new smell," your buddy would say when he got into it and you took him for a ride.

You talked of chrome glistening and engine horsepower and of your plans for seat covers later and perhaps even getting air conditioning put in.

Driving around with windows rolled down was okay except for two or three months in the summer when you dressed up to go to church.

And the second thing that happened was how we saw our government.

Before the war, nobody had any use for the government. What good was it? It couldn't plant a garden like your family did to eat out of during the summer, or for canning things to put in the cellar for winter.

It couldn't raise a pig for butchering in the fall, like your family did every year.

It couldn't sell a calf to get enough money to buy your kids a pair of new shoes when school started.

The government couldn't plow a single furrow, or chop cotton, or get hay mowed and put up in the barn.

So who needed a government, anyway? Governments were necessary, probably, to dilly-dally around with the kings and queens and world leaders in countries on the other side of the world, but with the war over, what was the government good for?

Except to deliver the mail, of course. But that was a given. You had to have someone pick up your letter and take it to someone else somewhere, else how could you keep in touch?

Besides, the mailman who came down your road to bring you the mail was a lot of help. You could wait for him at your mail box and he'd give you a ride into town if you asked him to, or he'd take a box of food down the road a ways to the family who'd lost a loved one.

But the war changed all that. Our government had done such a fantastic job mobilizing the country for the war, and had done such a fantastic job shutting everything down after the war, that we realized we lived in the greatest nation in the world. We loved, admired, and respected our government.

And since it had done such a fantastic job building ships and planes and tanks and things, why couldn't it run electricity out into the country so people could have freezers to put meat in and refrigerators to keep milk in and electric lights—even out in the barn?

Naturally, our government had to make up new laws for things like that.

And who but the government could build highways for our new cars to run on, not only so you could get back and forth to work better, but also so you could drive lickety-split for hundreds of miles to go camping on weekends, or run up to see Uncle Bill and his family back in Tennessee whom you haven't seen in no telling how long.

After passing more new laws, that is.

And we needed new laws to collect the taxes we needed to do all these good things.

To make it easier for us to pay our taxes, our government designed a way for us to pay them without us knowing we were doing it.

It passed laws to make our employer collect the taxes by withholding them from our paychecks. That way, income taxes came to mean a check the government sent you at the end of the year.

Even neater, if the employer didn't pay your taxes for you, the government would go after him, not you.

And before the war, we all laughed at the social security thing, because when grandma and grandpa got too old to raise crops or milk the cow, we made a place for them to come live with us. They could help around the place, doing what they felt like doing, until they died.

It took a while after the war before we realized how valuable social security was. Now your parents could stay in their own home out in the country.

This was a good law, because it would have killed them if they'd had to come live in one of your bedrooms, in your house in town where they would no longer hear a rooster crow before daylight, only the sirens of police cars chasing other people, and ambulances hurrying people to hospitals and fire engines hurrying to a fire.

After "Now What?" we changed from being a nation of independent, self-sustaining individuals to a mass of people mired in a morass of laws.

No longer can we wait beside our mail box to ask our mail carrier to give us a lift into town.

For it's against the law—probably.

Section III

Me and Old Elmer

Good, I think, when I enter the laboratory and see a urine sample sitting on the cabinet near the sink. Now I have something to do.

I find a place to stack my school books, shed my jacket, and pull on a lab coat before I slip the work order from beneath the bottle.

A frog pregnancy test? Hey, this is away over my head. There wasn't even a patient's name on the order.

Dr. Rebo knew better than ask me to do a frog pregnancy test. I grab the phone and dial him.

"Doc, I've never done one of these. Shouldn't we wait until your regular lab technician is on duty?"

"No," he says quickly. "I don't want her to know. Nor anybody else, understand? You can do it. Just follow directions in the manual."

I had answered an ad to do part-time work as an X-ray technician. That's what I did in the army.

However, they wanted someone who could do basic lab work and fill in for the lab technician on her days off. Would I be willing to learn—at reduced pay, of course?

Dr. Rebo, who was doing the hiring, was a handsome, likable guy, and promised he'd help me learn how to handle a microscope—make blood counts, do simple urine tests. I said okay, let's give it a try.

The pay was disappointing. Nita and I had hoped my part-time income, plus what she was making at her job, would give us enough to rent one of the upscale apartments on campus, which was every veteran's dream at Oklahoma University in 1948 after the war.

I don't like this, I'm thinking as I replace the phone. Suppose my report says the woman is pregnant when she shouldn't be? Or suppose it says she isn't when she is—whoever she is?

The doctor's wife, perhaps? Maybe his daughter. She was old enough to be pregnant. Or it could be the woman in admissions. A blind person could see from the way she fluttered her eyelashes at Doc that something was going on between them.

Okay, I sigh. He's asking for it.

I reach for the manual and flip it open to the frog pregnancy test section.

I already knew where the frogs were—down in the basement in a dry fish aquarium with a board on top to keep them from jumping out.

It was part of my job to feed the frogs. We had two. I named them Elmer and Fudd. I liked Elmer best. He could jump farther than Fudd and would eat all of Fudd's hamburger meat if I'd let him.

The first instruction in the manual said: "Filter three cubic centimeters of the patient's early morning urine."

I glance at the bottle of amber fluid. Early morning? Wonder if the doctor knew that? Oh, well—I shrug and go on reading.

"Get frog."

That was simple enough. I go down in the basement, deciding on the way to give Elmer the honor. I scoop him out of his home, drop him in a gallon jar with a wide mouth, screw the lid on, and carry him back to the lab.

Hey. This is easy. Nothing to it. Just follow directions, is all. The next step was "Take up 3 ccs of patient's urine in syringe."

I rig up a syringe with a needle on it and pull 3 ccs of urine into it. Holding the syringe up in one hand and the manual in the other, I read the next step: "Take frog in left hand and place him (yes, it had to be a him—female frogs wouldn't work) on a towel. Pull towel over frog with its rear legs extended and exposed. Immobilize frog's right hind leg by placing left thumb on foot."

I lay the syringe aside, lift Elmer from the jar and stretch him out on a towel.

He fights back when I fold the towel over him. I squeeze on him as hard as I can without squashing him. I read next step.

"Insert needle in frog's extended leg just under the skin."

This was getting delicate. Gritting my teeth, I pick up the syringe and poke the needle in Elmer's hind leg. Elmer struggles to get away.

Hold still, Elmer, I mutter. The sooner we get this done, the less it'll hurt. I lean over to read the next step in the instructions.

"Run needle up the leg under the skin and into the frog's bladder, which is located on his back just above his pelvic area."

On his back? Wow! How convenient for pregnancy tests! I read on.

"Do not inject urine until you are sure you are in bladder. To do otherwise, frog'll die. If you are in doubt whether you are in bladder or not, start injection and watch. If you are in bladder, bladder will puff up. If there is no puffing up, abandon effort and go get another frog because you have killed this one."

Well! That's pretty blunt. Since I know I have old Fudd in reserve, I boldly work the needle up Elmer's leg just under the skin and, I hope, into the bladder. I start the injection.

Bladder puffs up! Success!

Strangely, Elmer gets quiet—like he's enjoying it.

I remove the needle and return Elmer to the jar. He hops about, happily, it seems to me. I'm happy, too. I read the next step in the instructions:

"After an hour and a half, catheterize frog."

Good Lord! How do you catheterize a frog? I consult one of our nurses. She's no help at all. She insists they don't make a catheter tube small enough for a frog. And when she starts getting nosy about what I'm doing, I have to clam up.

She softens and suggests I do the same thing I did to make the injection— in other words, use the needle to draw the urine from the frog's bladder.

Of course. Why didn't I think of that? I return to lab and stare at Elmer. He's acting so happy that I hate the thought of sticking him again. Waiting, I think things over.

It has to be done, Elmer. The doctor ordered it. I suppose the patient, whoever she is, would like to know herself whether or not she's pregnant. So? What if I do kill you, old friend? The patient has more rights than a frog.

I study Elmer. Poor guy. I could only hope that his sacrifice to humanity will be worthwhile.

I continue studying the instructions:

"Place drop of frog urine on microscope slide. View urine drop. Presence of spermatozoa in frog's urine indicates positive pregnancy."

Really? I read it again. Whose spermatozoa? The frog's? It has to be. How could it be a man's?

No wonder Elmer's acting so happy, hopping about like that in the jar.

Okay, buddy, I say to myself. You've had it. It's needle time again. I take him out of the jar. He's hard to handle, squirming and twitching.

Then he wets all over everything! My hands. My lab coat. The counter top. Luckily—some of the drops get on a slide.

Glory be! I don't have to catheterize him! I drop him back in the jar. I place the slide with a drop of his urine on it under the microscope. I take a peek.

Wonder of wonders! I see a mass of spermatozoa wiggling all over the place. Boy, are they ever excited.

Good old Elmer. He came through for me. I make out the lab report.

"Pregnancy test with frog is positive."

I send the report back to Dr. Rebo and start cleaning up the mess Elmer made. I notice he's settled down quietly in the bottom of the jar, breathing contentedly.

You naughty boy, I tell him. The phone rings. It's Dr. Rebo. He's angry. Am I sure the test is positive? I stammer yes, adding quickly, "I followed the instructions to the letter. Old Elmer —"

He doesn't believe me, he snaps—OR the frog. Then he slams his phone down.

I stare at Elmer in the jug. Could it be that since we were both amateurs, we could be wrong?

But I knew Elmer and me got it right when the woman in admissions quit her job. Her reason?

She was pregnant.

And the doctor gave me a big raise for doing such a fine job.

Or to keep my mouth shut.

Whichever. I didn't care because Nita and I were now able to move into that apartment we had our hearts set on.

Thanks to old Elmer.

Little Bo-Peep

Nita and I went to visit the folks after I'd graduated from Oklahoma University with a degree in literature. I knew I'd be rich and famous in a few weeks when I got my novel finished and published.

I was strolling down the street one day when Walt Martin stopped me. He owned the theater and invested a lot of money in other property around town.

"I hear you're a writer now," he said.

I proudly owned up that I was. Or would be someday—

"I need somebody to write the paper."

I didn't know what he meant. Turned out old man Eli, who owned our weekly, *The Oilton Gusher*, had died. His heirs wanted to sell it to the owners of publishers in a nearby town. Walt bought it to keep it a hometown paper.

He knew absolutely nothing about printing and publishing. Why didn't I buy it, he asked, since I could write?

The thought was staggering. I could turn the world upside down with my scintillating editorials.

"I don't have any money—"

"You don't need any. Just pay me twenty-five dollars a month."

Oh, wow! With your own newspaper, you can make politicians jump. You can clean up corruption in your county—state too, as soon as you get well known for your insightful editorials.

I tried to be rational by confessing I knew absolutely nothing about the printing business.

"Claude can do all that stuff," he said. "You know Claude, don't you?"

Who didn't? He had been Eli's printer. Had been ever since I could remember. He was a tall, skinny man with a limber neck and big Adam's apple that bobbed continually when he talked. He kept his long, dirty-blond hair combed back; strands of it were always falling down over his ears which he had to keep flipping back.

He lived in a tar-paper shack by himself on the south edge of town. We boys growing up would turn his privy over every Halloween. Then we'd go back the next day and help him set it up. He'd never get mad at us.

With Claude doing all the work, me doing all the writing, and Nita doing all the office work, I didn't see how I could lose.

My hand trembled as I signed the agreement. Lordy, lordy! I was proud.

Nita wasn't, however, when I told her.

"You what?" she said, shocked.

I explained the deal, which included Claude to do the work.

"People who work have to be paid every week. We don't have money for that."

Her level-headed wisdom always irritated me.

"I can learn how to run the press and stuff. Then we can let Claude go," I argued. "All our advertising from then on will be clear profit."

Nita resigned herself to my folly. I went from nothing and nobody to being town kingpin overnight.

I would be able to pontificate to my heart's desire. Just as soon as people started reading things I wrote, they'd see the light.

The world's religions would come together. Politicians would quit passing laws and leave people alone. Educators would quit trying to make sweet little social angels out of our kids and start teaching them how to read and write and do multiplication tables.

Our little newspaper would soon be the talk of the literary world.

I couldn't wait to get started.

First we had to move our stuff from the Oklahoma University campus to Oilton. We rented a three-room, second floor apartment in one of the oldest buildings in town. Above Pope's grocery store. Pope had a feed store in the back, which turned out to be a haven for mice. The pesky rodents dined in Pope's feed store at night, and had the run of the apartment upstairs during the day.

What's a few mice, when you're on a mission to change the world? Just set more traps. Sometimes the sound of mouse traps popping would keep you awake all night.

The bathroom was across the hall. We shared it with another family whose kids kept forgetting to unlock our access door.

But these are minor inconveniences when your head is full of great ideas on how to change the world.

The stairway leading to our floor was steep and dark. It opened on Main

Street. It was difficult carrying what few pieces of furniture we had—a bed, a couch, a stuffed chair, a dining room table and two chairs—up those stairs.

We had everything we needed to set up housekeeping except a refrigerator. No problem. I made a deal with the local appliance dealer: Let us have a refrigerator and I'll give you special advertising rates for a year.

Okay. So I made a poor business decision. Just wait until my reputation for correcting all the ills in the world spreads far and wide, then advertisers will stand in line to buy space in our little paper.

Since the appliance dealer would only deliver to my front door—which in my case was the sidewalk in front of Pope's Grocery—I had to find help to get our shiny new refrigerator up that long dark stairway.

I knew just the young man to ask.

Bo-Peep.

He was the youngest in a family of eight boys. People called him Bo-Peep because when he was growing up he had long curly hair which kept falling down in ringlets. He cried every time his parents threatened to cut them off. His older brothers teased him, called him Little Bo-Peep. The name stuck.

The high school coach couldn't wait until Bo-Peep got old enough to play football because all his brothers had been so big and strong that coaches for miles around didn't want us on their schedule unless they had to.

Our coach made a running back out of Bo-Peep because it took at least three boys to bring him down, and only then if they got a good hold on him—one on his back and one on each leg. Even then Bo-Peep could go another ten yards if two or three more didn't get there to help push him over.

The City Marshal attempted to arrest Bo-Peep one night for public drunkenness when he came out of the local bar on Main Street and was talking too loud. The Marshal tried to handcuff him. Bo-Peep laughed and held both arms out straight from his shoulders sideways and said, "If you want to handcuff me, go ahead."

The Marshal grabbed one arm and tried to pull it down. He couldn't, even when he swung on it like a child swinging on a tree limb. He finally had to find a couple of Bo-Peep's older brothers and talk them into taking Bo-Peep home before he got into trouble.

Bo-Peep acted proud when I asked him if he'd help me move my new refrigerator up the steep stairs.

"You going to put my name in your paper?" he asked, nodding so vigorously that his curly hair bounced.

Sure, I promised. I knew editors weren't supposed to "give publicity" for favors. On the other hand, I rationalized, editors always knew when they were doing something not quite ethical, so that made them ethical. Besides, they had a constitutional right to publish anything they wanted to publish. They weren't like politicians, and preachers, and educators, who needed us ethical editors to keep them in line.

I borrowed the dolly which Pope used in his feed store and had Bo-Peep ready when the merchant unloaded my new refrigerator onto the sidewalk. Bo-Peep bear-hugged it and headed for the stairs.

"No, wait," I called. "You'll break your back. Let's use this dolly."

Bo-Peep looked disappointed, as if I didn't trust him. He tilted the refrigerator with one hand so I could scoot the dolly in place.

To show my confidence in his ability to man-handle a little thing like a refrigerator, I didn't bother to strap the shiny new load to the dolly. We began working our way up the stairs, me guiding the dolly and Bo-Peep below, lifting it a step at a time.

Our team effort worked beautifully until we reached the top step. Bo-Peep, still wanting to prove his strength, lifted the refrigerator too high and it scooted off the dolly.

Its sudden downward slide caught Bo-Peep off balance, shoving him backwards. Down they went, Bo-Peep leaping backwards three or four steps at a time, trying to brace himself against the sliding refrigerator which kept coming at him like a freight train.

"Get out of the way!" I shouted, fearing for his safety.

Instead, he kept trying to stop it. When he hit the bottom landing and could get better footing, he was able to bring the refrigerator to a halt.

Still supporting the bottom end, he looked up at me, curly hair awry, with alarm in his face and said, "Do you think we hurt it any?"

Hurt IT? I was so relieved HE wasn't crushed that I sagged against the wall and stayed there until I could gather enough strength to go down and examine our new appliance. The only "hurt" was a few scratches on its side.

But if it hadn't been for Bo-Peep's determined effort to stop its long, downward slide, it probably would have been smashed beyond repair. When we finally got it in the apartment and plugged it in, it ran as good as new—which is what it was.

Sometimes you get lucky and bad things turn out right. I promptly forgot about the incident and plunged myself into the work of getting out my first newspaper.

I wrote what I thought was the most scintillating editorial ever to be published. Just wait until the governor and legislators read THIS, I kept telling myself as I labored to get the paper put together and on the press.

Bo-Peep came into the newspaper office early on publication day. He went straight to the press and picked up a paper that hadn't even been folded yet.

I watched him read it with a sinking heart. I was so full of guilt that I felt like a pile of ashes inside when he looked up at me and asked, "Whereabouts is my name?"

"It'll be in the insert," I lied. "I won't be printing that until tomorrow."

So I had to set more copy and give away enough free advertising space to come up with enough material for an insert. My lead story in the insert was how Bo-Peep saved my refrigerator.

Of course, getting the insert together, printed and folded into the regular paper caused me to be a day late getting the paper out. All my advertisers got mad.

But I learned real quick that people's names in a local newspaper mean a lot more to them than all the "world changing" editorials a man can write.

It doesn't make any difference how much constitutional right you have.

And another thing I learned: it is the Bo-Peeps of the world who do all the heavy work for people who have degrees from universities, and all they ever want is a little bit of recognition for the things they do.

They don't teach you things like that in colleges.

Firing Claude

My dream about revolutionizing the world turned into a nightmare real quick. I never had any idea that it took so much equipment to print a four-page weekly. I thought the big, black, hulking pieces of machinery in the back shop were pieces of junk that needed to be hauled away. Instead, I learned that you needed every one of them to get the paper out.

The king of the monsters was the linotype. This awkward-looking machine was a mechanical marvel. Compared to handset type, you could cast a line of type in hot lead on a linotype in a flash, ready to place in the page layouts.

At least, Claude could. He would scoot his chair up to the keyboard and keep the machine going full speed.

He tried to teach me. I was scared of it. Claude was patient. Soon I was going good enough that he left me to myself.

Just when I thought I had mastered the monster, it fought back. I let the pot of lead get too hot. It squirted hot metal every which way, most of it in my lap and down into my shoe.

I leaped backwards, tipping my chair over and banging my head on the wall behind me.

I jumped up and, hopping around on one foot, yanked my other shoe off and shook the pellets of hot lead out onto the floor. My sock was still smoldering in several places.

I glanced up and saw Claude laughing. When I scowled, he tried to straighten his face and quickly got busy working on an ad layout.

It didn't take me long to realize Claude was not the dummy I first thought he was.

Like all printers, he had a special intelligence all his own. His entire working life had been centered around putting words together letter by letter, then turning around and taking them apart letter by letter and dropping them into the appropriate cubicle of a font case.

My eyes ached and my head hurt after working all day doing that, because type fonts were a mirror image of what it looks like when printed on paper.

But Claude could read a page of type upside down and backward as fast and as easily as I could read the finished newspaper itself.

He would read my editorials upside down when he was making up the pages and make comments—always negative.

Sometimes I'd take his comments to heart and soften my phrases, or delete them entirely.

But when you're out of sorts, you can take only so much negativism before you have to fight back.

I exploded on him one night when we were having trouble with the press. I was tired, angry, and frustrated because we were already past our deadline. The drive belt kept jumping off, causing the newsprint to tear in little pieces and get all over the inking rollers.

Each time we'd have to shut down, clean up the mess, and reset the motor. And each time Claude would study our work and mumble, his Adam's apple bobbing, "I don't think we got it quite right."

Then it would happen again. We'd fix it, and Claude would say the same old thing.

About the fifth time when Claude backed off and said, "I don't think it's going to work," I threw my wrench down and said, "Can't you say anything positive once in a while?"

His eyes bulged and his Adam's apple bobbed nervously as he tried to bring up some words, finally muttering, "All right, then. I'm positive the dern thing won't work."

I broke down laughing. He joined in. It saved the day for us. Giggling, we reset the motor one more time—and the belt never jumped off again.

After a couple of months, I felt Nita and I could handle getting paper out by ourselves.

It was time to let Claude go. Our cash flow was terrible. I sure hated to do it. I'd come to like him. Besides, he was always there, always working.

That night, Nita and I had a long, agonizing talk about Claude. Neither of us wanted to do it. But it came down to Claude or food on our table.

I tried to be business-like, firing him. But every time I faced him, and that Adam's apple began bobbing happily, I simply couldn't do it.

I finally did it when his back was turned. He was bellied up to a stone, tearing down a page of type. As I passed behind him, I blurted, "I hate to say this, Claude. But we're just not making enough money to pay you."

He turned and stared at me a long time, his Adam's apple perfectly still. I would have given my right arm if I could have taken back those words. But I couldn't. It was done.

He turned away and continued breaking down the page and putting the type back in its proper bins.

"Claude—?"

"I heard," he said, still refusing to look at me. He kept working.

I returned to the linotype and pretended to set some type. But what I was really wanting was for Claude to get mad and leave so I could go to the restroom and bawl like a baby.

I sensed he was standing behind me. I glanced over my shoulder.

"Yes?" I asked.

"You and your Misses don't have to pay me when you don't have the money."

"No, Claude. That wouldn't be right."

"They ain't nothing in this town I can do," he said. "They ain't nothing around here I'd want to do if there was. I love it here. I wouldn't know what to do with myself if I couldn't work at the newspaper."

That night when Nita and I were eating supper, she asked, "Did you let Claude go?"

"Yes."

Then I saw the tears well up in her eyes.

"But he talked me out of it. He told me being a printer was all he knew how to do. He said he'd work for nothing."

So we always tried to find a little cash somewhere at the end of every week to give to Claude.

He was delighted.

So were we.

The Chicken Guy

The political fight for mayor was heating up. I was the new newspaper editor in town in '48 and didn't know whose side to be on.

Old Doc's or Walt's.

Doc was a holdover from the old days. Walt represented the progressive new element. I was for progress, of course. I was young and felt it was time for my generation to take over the world.

But Doc had delivered me. His fee? A bushel of peanuts, Dad said. So I felt I owed Doc *some* allegiance. He seemed to me like he'd been eighty years old forever. He always wore a gray suit, was bowlegged, and walked pigeon-toed. He'd converted an old home on main street to serve as his office.

Doc never had any interest in politics until things got so bad somebody had to do something. The oil boom had died out. Our once -fancy paved streets had deteriorated. Weeds were growing in the cracks. Our network of water lines leaked. The sewer system had long ago failed, and the city had no choice but to dump the untreated effluent into the Cimarron River.

Doc vowed to rid the town of its unkept reputation. He ran for mayor, won, and began ruling with an iron fist.

He had to sacrifice proper maintenance on the water supply system to do it. Once it was done, however, people blamed him for letting the water supply system go to pot. They hated him for banning car washing on days of high water usage.

People don't like dictators when things are going good.

Walt owned the picture show and bought old buildings and fixed them up and pushed to get renters in them. He always wore a clean white shirt, starched, and opened at the collar. He had a habit of doing a little side-to-side jig whenever he got excited.

Things came to a head when a man came to town and talked at our Chamber of Commerce meeting and proposed to put in a business of raising chickens on an assembly line basis.

Hey! He was talking *industry* here! It's the magic word to galvanize any town in the good old USA into salivating action.

Not only was the visitor wearing a suit, he had his blond hair slicked back and his smile showed so many gleaming white teeth it took your breath away. You soon became so fascinated by the aerial dance of his hands, you forgot to listen to what he was saying—really saying.

It sounded like a brilliant idea. He would bring baby chicks in the front door and put them in the first cage. A week later, he'd move them back to the second cage and re-supply his first cage. He'd keep moving the chicks back from cage to cage until they were fryer size. By then they would be in the back cage near the rear door. He'd take them out and truck them off to market.

The idea was so pure, it was exhilarating. We started calling him the Chicken Guy. Walt said he could let the Chicken Guy have one his vacant buildings rent-free. It was next door to the newspaper.

But when the Chicken Guy applied for water, Doc turned him down.

It was a stupid idea, Doc snorted, and didn't mind telling any of us who argued with him that we were all a bunch of nitwits to fall for a crackpot scheme like that.

Seems like there's always somebody standing in the way of progress.

It was time to use the power of the press. I came out against old Doc and for Walt. I'm not talking just editorially. I'm talking about using "objective journalism."

It starts with viewpoint. Instinctively using the campaign tactics honed to perfection by politicos in the nineties—character assassination—I cagily tip-toed around Walt's lack of qualifications to govern and bore down on how Doc had let the town run down. He was against bringing in new business. We needed a new man for the future.

If you spend time tearing down an individual just right, it's like a dog fight—the first dog that goes down, they all jump on him, friend and foe alike.

Walt won the election. We had a big celebration on Main Street—as if we'd been freed from years of oppressive dictatorship. Walt was jigging all over the place and slapping me on the back every chance he got, giving me credit for his victory.

I saw Doc watching us from the porch of his office. I wanted to go apologize. But I didn't know how.

As soon as Walt took over, he issued the Chicken Guy his permit to hook onto the city water supply.

We all waited in high anticipation for our new "industry" to get underway. When the Chicken Guy showed up one day wearing coveralls, backed his pickup to the front door of the building next door, and began unloading chicken wire, I grabbed my camera and hurried to take his picture. I splashed his coming across the front page.

The Chicken Guy made cages and lined them up from the front door to the rear of the building, setting them on stilts so they'd be about four feet off the floor.

I reported the Chicken Guy's progress regularly to my eager readers: how he rigged up a watering trough to run alongside the cages on one side, and a feeding trough on the other; how cute the little cheeping chicks were as they dashed from feeding trough to watering trough. You could almost see them growing. Our "industry" was coming to life.

Also coming to life was the smell of you-know-what that was dropping through the screen onto the floor below. I began to get an uneasy feeling that I knew what old Doc meant about this being stupid idea.

When I mentioned the smell, the Chicken Guy claimed he had a solution, his hands waving confidently as he explained.

He was going to install an automated conveyor belt running the length of the building underneath the cages. The conveyor belt would catch the droppings and carry them to a bin at the rear. When the bin was full, it would be sold to farmers in the area for fertilizer.

However, since he was "under-capitalized," he said, he would use a roll of grocery wrapping paper for a conveyor belt.

He put the roll on a broomstick in front of the building and pulled the paper to the rear of the building. He patiently explained to a growing number of doubters that he would truck away the droppings each night and pull out a fresh strip of paper daily. His scheme worked fine when there was only one batch of baby chicks in the first cage.

But as more and more chickens were brought in, and more and more droppings fell on the paper, the weighted paper would tear apart when he'd try to pull it and he'd have a mess to clean up. The odor became unbearable.

The weather turned blistering hot. None of our buildings in town were air-conditioned. Desperate, the Chicken Guy opened both front and back doors and installed an exhaust fan.

This spread the odor all over town. The only way any of us could conduct business was to keep both front and back doors shut tight. It was better smothering to death than putting up with the smell. Even then, it was so bad in the newspaper office, it seemed like the odor was coming through the brick wall.

Public pressure against the Chicken Guy got so bad he finally called it quits. Everyone heaved a sigh of relief when he carted off his final load of chickens and their droppings. The odor lingered on into the winter.

I found I could tolerate the diminishing smell and figured that by spring, I would be able to open the doors to my business again.

But what I wanted most was to apologize to old Doc. I made a stab at it when I developed a late spring cold and went to see him and ask him to give me something for it. When I began stammering around with my apology, he brushed aside my words and began bragging on the way Walt was running things.

"You backed a good man," he said. "He's a builder. That's what we need."

Humiliated, I said, "Yeah. Well, thanks, Doc. Thanks for the pills and...everything."

I turned to leave. Old Doc stopped me.

"Just a minute, young man. You owe me a bag of peanuts."

Old Ben

All we had between us and the killers was old Ben. I tried not to look at him sitting in the back row of the city council chamber.

Even at sixty or better, he was still a handsome man, tall and rangy, quiet. He wore a wide-brimmed white hat and carried his pistol strapped high on his waist.

He should have retired years ago. I'd already checked it out. The state had an excellent retirement plan. Maybe what we were doing would push him into it.

But I would have felt better if he hadn't showed up at the meeting. He knew what it was all about. My palms felt wet. I kept wiping them on my pants legs.

The mayor rapped for silence. The buzz in the room dissipated. All eyes fixed on me.

I pushed back my chair and stood, trying to appear calm. My initial thought was: You asked for it.

And I guess I had. When I came home with a college degree and bought the local newspaper, my idealistic goal was to change the world with my fearless editorials.

I couldn't hide behind my words in a paper now. I, along with others, was clamoring for protection, something we thought Ben was incapable of providing.

A couple of Bonnie and Clyde characters and their friends had gone on a bank-robbing spree across the state. They gunned down a bank guard and two lawmen before dropping out of sight. Police reports said they were armed to the teeth and dangerous.

We all knew one of the gang owned a farm north of town. And when someone said they had seen a strange car at the killer's farm, we panicked.

I, for one, never really thought about Old Ben as police protection—at least not until now.

"No offense to anyone here," I finally said, my voice shaking a little. After all, Ben was wearing a gun. But I met his glare head-on and blurted it right out. "I propose we form a committee to contact county and state law enforcement officers. In short, we need help."

Silence.

Old Ben's chin lifted, his face hardened.

The mayor cleared his throat. "You want to make that in the form of a motion?"

I nodded. "Yes. I'll make that in the form of a motion."

It seemed ages before Mrs. Coltrane jumped to her feet and said, "I second it—or whatever you're supposed to do."

There was a strained laugh.

The motion passed and, of course, the mayor named me chairman of the committee.

Ben got up quietly and left the room.

I hoped he didn't remember. If he did, he might think what I was doing was spiteful revenge.

It was on a Halloween night. Some of us boys "borrowed" a luggage wagon from the railroad platform, loaded an outhouse on it, and went racing down the highway with it.

We thought it would be a great joke to set the outhouse on the school steps and paint "Principal's Office" on the door.

Then a car came roaring out of the night, its headlights blinding. Brakes squealed. Ben came boiling out of the car. We scattered. Ben whipped out his pistol and fired two shots in the air.

"Halt!" he yelled.

I ran like a scared rabbit into the night across a vacant lot. I tripped over a barbed wire fence, ripped my britches, and fell into a ditch. I lay there panting, shaking like a leaf, worried sick because I knew he'd tell my parents.

"You boys come back here," he called. "Get this thing off the highway before somebody gets killed crashing into it."

We crept out of the darkness, ashamed. I kept my head down, hoping he wouldn't pay any attention to me.

We took the outhouse back and returned the baggage wagon to the railroad depot.

Ben never told my parents anything. But I did get a good switching from Mom for ripping my britches.

We boys always sniggered around after that, calling Ben old Two-Shot Dunham. Kid stuff.

This wasn't.

We called state officials and told them about the rumors. The state informed us they'd have someone check it out.

Unknown to us, they called Ben and asked him to go out to the farm and see if there was anything to the rumor.

Ben promised he would. Without a second thought, he took his Winchester from the pegs on his office wall, checked his pistol to see if he'd forgotten to load it, climbed into his little '34 Ford, and drove out the dusty road toward the farm.

Halfway there, he saw a strange vehicle coming to meet him. He had a feeling. He turned his car sideways, blocking the road. He got out, cradling his Winchester and waved the approaching vehicle to a stop.

The car slowed. Somebody inside poked a double-barreled shotgun out a window.

Ben never heard the blast, felt only the giant fist that hit him in the chest and face. It slammed him backward into the ditch. He felt his strength pouring out with his blood.

The car began turning around in the narrow road. Ben forced himself to a sitting position, his left arm useless, the world turning a deep red.

"No you don't," he mumbled as the car careened away in a cloud of dust.

With a great effort, he lifted the now-heavy Winchester with his one good arm, propped it over a raised knee, and sighted through the film of blood. He squeezed the trigger. The gun's recoil against his strength was ten times normal.

The car kept going away, the dust boiling. He fired again, and again, and again. The car swerved, bounded over the ditch, and smashed to a sudden stop against a tree. A man fell out, limp.

Another man carrying a shotgun jumped out and ran. Ben swiveled his rifle on him, fired. The man went down. A woman inside the car screamed. Two men scrambled out with their hands in the air.

"Don't shoot! Don't shoot!" they begged.

Holding the Winchester on the bank robbers, Ben staggered to his car and radioed for help.

How he managed to keep his consciousness until help arrived, no one ever knew.

The two men Ben killed were the gang's ringleaders. The others, including the woman, got life in the pen.

Ben was laid up in the hospital six months. Doctors had to remove one eye. They had to do so much cutting and stitching on his face, the ugly scars ruined his rugged good looks. His left arm hung limp. He coughed a lot, trying to keep his lungs free of the phlegm which kept accumulating around the buckshot still lodged there.

When I gathered up enough courage to go see him—to get the story, of course—Ben answered my questions coolly and deliberately.

He had that right. But he softened somewhat when I commented on the large number of flowers about the room.

When he was able to get up and around, he strapped on his pistol and came to the Council meeting his first night back on the job. The place was packed.

"I couldn't have made it without you all taking the time to come see me," Ben said at the tail end of his little speech. "But I'm back. Ready to go to work."

I kept my head down, ashamed to look him in the eye.

Nobody objected—including me. And I happened to be working late that first night Ben was on the job. I heard him cough before he opened the door and poked his head in.

"You all right?" he asked.

I gave him a friendly wave. "Yeah. Just polishing up my weekly editorial. I don't think anybody'd bother to get me."

He gave me a two-fingered salute and grinned. "If I remember right, you could always run faster'n any kid in town. Anybody'd have a devil of a time catching you, even if they did come in to rob you."

Then he did remember. I laughed. It was my turn to return his two-fingered salute.

I sat staring with unseeing eyes at the door, humbled and full of deep appreciation. An ending for my editorial floated through my mind:

All the words of idealism ever written and all the laws of justice ever recorded would be useless against the crazies in our society without the Old Bens of the world backing them up with their guns, and having courage to use those guns for our protection when the time comes.

I went home to my family, content, knowing that out there somewhere in the night was Old Ben—dutifully making his nightly rounds.

The X Factor

I was already aggravated over being late getting our weekly paper put together, printed, and in the mail that week when I glanced up and saw this well-dressed man standing in our front office.

Nita was out running errands. So I heaved a disgusted sigh, told my printer to keep working to get the forms on the press, and I'd be right back.

"Soon's I get rid of that salesman," I said, snatching up a shop towel and trying to get most of the printer's ink off my hands as I trudged to the front office.

"Yes, sir?" I said.

He had "salesman" written all over him. I had no time for listening to a sales pitch—especially right then.

He offered to shake. I declined graciously, showing him my ink stained hands.

He didn't back down, keeping his hand held out. It embarrassed me. So with one hard swipe of the shop towel and a quick rub on my pant leg, I let him grasp my hand.

I thought his grip would break my knuckles. He commenced talking before I could say, "Get lost," or any other form of a sweet goodbye.

He had a little moustache that twitched fascinatingly when he talked. His dark blue eyes hypnotized me. I even stopped wiping my hands on the shop towel to listen—especially when he asked, "Would you be interested in doubling your money in twenty years?"

"You bet," I laughed, and thought: if I had any.

He spread his shiny colored brochures on the glass counter and explained the plan to me. For a few dollars a month, my account would keep building and building and building. My eyes got bigger and bigger as I followed the course of his well-manicured finger as it climbed up the chart.

I forgot all about getting the paper out.

Unbelievable! And there was a bonus: As long as I "made my little investment" every month, I'd be insured. Any time I wanted to quit, I'd get all my money back, plus interest. In case I died, Nita would get the entire face amount of the policy.

If I'd had any money in the bank, I'd have written him a check then and there for my first month's "savings."

I had to tell him no.

"Tell you what," he said without skipping a beat. "I'll enlist you as a trainee."

His company, he said, which was one of the soundest financially in the United States (and he had the brochures to prove it) needed a representative in that area.

Part of the deal was that I, as the local newspaper editor of "prominence in the community," who knew everybody in town, would need to call people and set up appointments for us—in the evenings—at their home.

All I had to do was accompany him on a few evening calls until I learned how to make a presentation on my own.

Not only that, he would share his commissions with me.

How would I like getting four or five hundred dollars in checks out of the post office every month and taking them to the bank?

Hey. I could do that. Every week I talked to each merchant up and down Main Street trying to sell ads, didn't I? They'd all probably be tickled to death to have me give them a chance to make some real money.

Nita was skeptical. It'd be better'n wasting my time trying to sell them ads, I argued.

I started with Gail Kessler. He owned one of our drug stores. He was such a hard sell, I figured if my new friend could sell Gail, we had it made.

Gail had always been nice to me, as nice as puddin' pie. He was a plump man who wore a fresh, starched white shirt. His sharply creased trousers, held up with a neat black belt at the top, sloped from his barrel-like waist to his glistening shoe tops.

His hired help worked the fountain. Gail liked to spend his day behind the counter near the front door where he kept his glistening sets of Fostoria glassware. Every month or so, Gail would give me a dinky ad with so much copy to set; it wasn't worth it—but business was business.

And it was Gail who had advised me early in my journalism career when I showed up in his store, grungy and grimy from a hard day setting type, trying to sell him an ad which I so desperately needed, "When you're trying to sell, Denney, dress like you're prosperous. When you're collecting money, it's okay to dress like you're down and out."

From then on, I made the Kessler Drug my first call every Monday morning, before I had time to get grungy working in the print shop to get the paper out that week.

I figured Gail would buy anything from this well-dressed stranger with a plan to make money.

I even spiffed up a bit myself. Gail and his wife greeted us pleasantly and invited us in. We settled into his plush overstuffed chairs. I settled back to watch my new friend go to work.

He spread out his literature and began his pitch. Gail was polite and friendly, exactly the way he was with me every week when I went in to try and sell him a two-bit ad.

Pretty soon, Gail had diverted my new friend from his sure-fire savings plans and had him engaged in a deep conversation about economics in general.

It was all over my head. I didn't know but one economic: you either had enough money to pay all your monthly bills, or you didn't. If you didn't, you carried the ones left over to the next month. That gave you a thirty-day relief from economics.

I was down emotionally when we left Gail's home without even getting close to selling a savings plan which could have brought me checks to my post office box from now into eternity.

But my new friend patiently explained how it worked: You had to make X number of calls before you made a sale.

Well, if it was that simple…Even if you didn't make a sale, you gained ground by lowering the odds on the X factor. And soon the checks would be rolling in.

As we worked through my list of business acquaintances and failed to make a sale, I had to admit the obvious, which Nita kept pointing out—I was being used to help my friend get in the door. I hated the feeling.

To get back at the stranger for using me to open doors for him, I scheduled a meeting with Tom Sheffield, who had never worked a day in his life, that I knew of.

Tom and his wife were delighted to see us. They shooed their three kids out of the living room. Tom's wife picked up the scattered newspapers and pulled up straight backed chairs for my friend and me.

My friend didn't change his presentation one bit. He laid out his glossy colored brochures and went into his smooth pitch.

It was the same with Tom who had nothing, as it was with Gail who had plenty.

Almost before I realized what was going on, my friend was leaning forward like a jungle cat stalking an unsuspecting prey. Tom and his wife acted hypnotized.

"Now don't you think this is a good chance to provide a solid financial future for those youngsters of yours in the other room?" my friend asked.

(Those youngsters fighting in the other room right then, I thought, would probably never get old enough to have a future.)

Oh, yes, Tom and his wife nodded in unison.

I simply couldn't believe what I was witnessing. The only couple in town who couldn't afford one of these insurance policies were putting their signatures on the contract.

They managed to scrape together enough change for the first month's premium. I doubted they would ever make another.

I was sick when we left their unpainted home.

"See," my friend boasted, "It's simply a matter of mathematics. All you have to do is make X number of calls and you make a sale. Works every time."

I declined to make any more appointments for my new friend and he left town the next day.

I didn't like using the X factor when I went out selling ads. If they said "no," I went on to the next guy.

But I always tried to "look prosperous" when I went to pick up Gail's two-bit ad the first thing every Monday morning before I got to grungy-looking. And we got along just fine.

The Truth, The Whole Truth...

You would think that Mrs. Fisher would be the last person in the world to run away with a bread salesman.

But she did.

And that's the truth, Mr. Fisher told me when I went into the Fisher grocery store to try and sell the Fishers an ad. He was dumpy, too, just like Mrs. Fisher was. Only he didn't have any hair and his wife had coal black hair with one strand always falling down across one of her puffy cheeks.

Mr. Fisher didn't seem overly angry or embarrassed about it.

"We got along just fine," he said me, coming out from behind the meat counter and wiping his chubby hands on his already soiled apron. "I had no idea..."

"I'm sorry —" I tried to sympathize, but didn't know how to do it.

Truth was, however, I was glad, because Mr. Fisher was easier to sell an ad to than she was. I was so proud of myself, being the new owner of the newspaper in town, when I sold my first big grocery ad to the Fishers.

I talked Mr. Fisher into running some specials on his meat, promising with all my heart and soul that he'd be surprised at how much meat our little paper could sell for him. It would pay for his ad, ten times over.

He said okay, over Mrs. Fisher's objections.

I worked hard that week making up a big Meat Special ad for Fisher Grocery. Great savings, I ballyhooed in print. Save dollars here, dollars there, dollars everywhere. It turned out to be a darn good grocery ad, even if I do say so myself.

Then after the ad came out in our paper, I was all puffed up importantly when I went to ask Mr. Fisher if he had any meat left.

Mr. Fisher was at home taking a nap, Mrs. Fisher said. So I asked her how their meat sale went.

"It didn't make no difference," she said, her scorn showing. "I still rang up the full price at the register and no one complained. That proves you waste your money advertising."

I never forgot her sarcasm. So I was glad now that she'd run off with a bread salesman. I mentally shifted from ad salesman to news reporter. Here was my chance to get even—do a juicy, gossipy-type news story about her "unfaithfulness."

"She say goodbye, or anything?" I asked.

I was going to be more than happy to do the story. Would be expected to. In a small town, everybody wants you to put in print what everybody already knows.

He laughed.

"Goodbye? She was always telling me goodbye. Every time she got mad at me...which was a lot more than once or twice."

"She really meant it this time?"

"Seems so."

First things first. Sell the ad and do the story later. Besides, with Mrs. Fisher gone, this was going to be an easy sell.

"We're putting out a special edition this week, Mr. Fisher. We want to fill our paper with Easter ads. We have three sizes already made up you can choose from."

I unfolded the sheet of newsprint displaying the three sizes.

"This one is ten dollars—" I tried to make it sound cheap. "This one is twenty-five. This one's—"

"Gimme the ten-dollar one. You want your money now?"

"No. That's not necessary. I'll bill you at the end of the month like always."

"I better pay you now. If Mrs. Fisher comes back and finds I spent ten dollars on an Easter ad, she'd be mad as all get out."

Come back? Maybe I'd better hold off on the news story for now.

"Well, okay —"

He went to the cash register and opened it.

"Well, I'll be darned. She took all our money too."

Now I was involved, dad-gum her. Just wait'll she sees the news story I was going to write about her—the little, fat, two-timing so-and-so.

"That's okay," I said. "I'll just bill you —"

"No. No. Don't do that. She might come back."

He closed the cash register drawer.

Well, if I wasn't going to get my ten dollars for running their Easter ad, at least I'd get a good gossipy news story.

"Did you suspect anything going on between her and the salesman?"

He shook his head, thought a minute, then said, "Come to think of it, it did cross my mind. The way he talked low to her when he came in with an armload of bread. I guess she thought he was a real dandy in his white uniform and red bow tie." Mr. Fisher focused his eyes on me. "And you know what?"

"What?"

"Even that bow tie was fake. It was made out of celluloid."

"Why don't you call the bakery in Tulsa and get him fired?"

Mr. Fisher thought about that, then shook his head.

"No. She'll be back. I don't want her to come back and be mad at me for getting her...her—"

"Lover?"

"Yeah. Him. Getting him fired."

"You really think she'll be back, huh?"

"Oh, yes."

"She's done this before?"

"No—"

It was a real puzzle, especially for me. How was I to write a story about Mrs. Fisher, co-owner of the town's respectable Fisher Grocery Store, running off with a salesman who wore a celluloid bow tie?

Just print the truth, our journalism professor always insisted. The truth, the whole truth, and nothing but the truth. That's what journalism is all about.

I stared blankly at Mr. Fisher's round face. What was the truth here?

I even questioned at that moment if there was such a thing as the truth. Facts are one thing, the truth is another.

Why do a story at all? If she did come back, like Mr. Fisher seemed to think, then a story about it in the paper would just make things worse.

People would be talking about her from now on, even making up stories about Mrs. Fisher that wasn't true at all.

Corroborate, the journalism professor admonished in his lectures.

I didn't have time for corroborating. It was Easter and I had lots more Easter ads to sell.

But I knew I had to have something in the paper about Mrs. Fisher's absence.

I considered putting a few lines in the Personals column, say Mrs. Fisher made a business trip to Tulsa this week.

However, if somebody saw her getting in the delivery truck with the bread salesman, they'd know it was no business trip, wouldn't they?

And they'd laugh at my paper for printing such foolishness.

I could ignore the whole thing. Why print things that'll wind up hurting people, or worse, making other people laugh at you?

I lucked out. Mrs. Fisher came back before I got the paper ready to print that week. I didn't have to write a story about her running off with the bread salesman.

All I had to worry about now was catching Mr. Fisher alone so I could collect my ten bucks for the Fisher Grocery Easter ad.

But my luck ran out. Mrs. Fisher was in the store by her by herself when I dropped in a few days later to collect. I pretended to be picking up some groceries.

"Where's Mr. Fisher?" I asked, casual.

"Haven't you heard? He ran off with a little hussy that comes in here selling sewing machine thread."

"Oh——?"

"That's a good story for you to print. They didn't fool me a bit. I saw her making eyes at him every time she came in. They way they leaned over the meat counter talking and her laughing, I knew Mr. Fisher was telling her dirty jokes."

"You want me to print a story like that?"

"It's the truth."

"Well...I was in here a couple of weeks ago to sell you all an Easter ad, and he told me you'd run off with a bread salesman."

She laughed.

"Buster? He's my cousin. More like a brother. His wife and I are good friends. She's been sick. He was behind on his bills. I took some money and went with him to get his electric turned back on."

Truth?

Depends on who's telling it. And truth just doesn't exist on its own. You've got to create it. And the creator controls what it says.

Mr. Fisher never came back, so I assumed that Mrs. Fisher was telling the truth.

And I had to do a story about him running away with a sewing thread sales hussy because Mrs. Fisher said she wouldn't give me my ten bucks for the Easter ad unless I did.

The Con Game

When Nita and I bought this little weekly newspaper right after we were fresh out of college, we inherited Catfish Eubanks.

He was an energetic little man with one brown eye and one blue eye. He joked about it, adding, "And they call me Catfish because they say I'm all mouth."

And when he got you laughing, he'd sell you a refrigerator or a stove or washing machine. He sold us a combination radio and record player, which we needed like a hole in the head.

"Don't worry about it," he said. "I'll take it out in advertising."

He loved to advertise, about as much as he enjoyed face-to-face selling, always "buying" a quarter page, sometimes half a page, even a double page spread on occasion.

Nor was there any work involved on my part making up the ad for the newspaper. They came from national advertising agencies already set up. All you had to do was plop them in place and print.

I say we inherited Catfish because he had worked out a system with the former owner of the newspaper. The system bothered me, and I tried to get up enough courage to do away with it. But I hesitated because Catfish was a major source of my revenue.

It was called double billing. Rural newspapers, I learned, had two ad rates— one for local merchants and another for out-of-town businesses and politicians.

Our "local" rate was twenty-five cents a column inch. Our foreign rate was fifty cents.

Everybody knew this, even national manufacturers and their ad agencies. Manufacturers tried to get the local rate by offering to rebate dealers one half the cost of any ads they ran which promoted their products.

We'd give Catfish two invoices—one reflecting the twenty-five cent rate, another at the fifty cent rate. Catfish would pay me the twenty-five cent rate and send the bill for the fifty cent rate to his manufacturer. They'd dutifully rebate him one-half, which meant Catfish got his ad free.

This double billing situation bothered me. It was cheating, pure and simple. I kept trying to screw up enough courage to tell Catfish I wasn't going to do that anymore, but I simply couldn't turn down $20 or $40 every week.

But then I learned a great lesson.

This stranger walked in one day. He was a well-dressed, likable young man— curly dark hair with a ready smile that showed a gleaming set of teeth.

"How much are your ad rates?" he asked.

The first thought I had was that he was an FBI man who'd come to arrest me for helping Catfish cheat his appliance manufacturer.

I caught Nita's warning look.

Well, he was a "foreigner," wasn't he?

"Fifty cents a column inch," I quoted our foreign rates without batting an eye.

"How many pages?"

"Four. Maybe six. Depends on how big an ad Catfish wants to run this week."

"Who?"

"Catfish. Our largest advertiser. He owns—"

"Could you run eight pages?" the young man asked, uninterested, I could tell, in Catfish.

"Sure, if I could sell enough ads."

"If you run eight pages, I'll buy the whole paper, other than what display ads you already have."

Eight pages! Solid! My blood pounded. My brain turned into a calculator and began chunking up figures. Lordy... oh, lordy, lordy, lordy!

I eyed him sternly. "I'll not sell my front page."

Dedicated journalists don't sell their front pages, the professor at journalism school told us.

"Okay. Could you run an insert?"

This guy knew what he was talking about. An insert was a single page, printed both sides and inserted into the paper, usually in the center. They were a headache, primarily because you had to have two people working the folder.

"That would mean two more whole pages," I pointed out, trying to be real business like.

"I know. I'll buy them too."

"Well, ah—" I said, dubious.

I saw Nita frowning her suspicions. I hesitated, trying to build up enough resolve to at least ask him a question or two but when he said, "Cash. In advance," all my resolve crumbled.

He slipped a fat billfold from his jacket pocket and began tossing bills onto the counter. I started punching the adding machine. The amount kept climbing, higher and higher. I got so excited that I had a hard time breathing. By the time I had the total on the adding machine, he had the correct number of bills laying there for me.

"I'll have to use your phone," he said. "All of the calls will be long distance."

"Now wait a minute—"

He dropped another twenty on the pile.

"Only to Drumright. They won't amount to much."

Drumright was only seven miles away, a town twice as big as ours. The pile of bills was just too much.

"Well, okay then," I said, snatching up the money.

Frowning her disapproval, Nita got up and let him have her chair. He sat down went to work. He had a Drumright telephone directory. He began calling businesses in Drumright and telling the owner that he was working for our paper that we were putting out a special edition boosting Drumright merchants.

He had a looseleaf notebook filled with blurbs about different types of businesses. Each blurb was about two hundred words or so. When this was set in columnar reading matter, it came to only three or four inches of type, which would only be $1.50 or $2.00 at my "foreign rate."

"We've written up an advertisement for you. Would you like to hear what it says?" he'd ask.

Of course, they all wanted to hear what the little dinky paper in the little dinky town to the north had to say about them. They always said yes. Then he'd read the ad to them.

When you listen to a couple hundred words of puff about your business being read to you over the phone, long distance, it sounds as if the guy is talking for forever. You visualize the ad must be a quarter page size, at least.

"How does that sound?" he'd say, finishing.

You could see the person on the other end of the line being very pleased. They would ask, "How much will all that cost me?"

"Only ten dollars," the con man said.

I could imagine the surprised look on the face of the merchant on the other end of the line. Their paper charged $1.00 an inch. He would be quick to jump on this "big" ad for "only ten dollars."

I felt sick. He paid me a buck fifty, maybe two whole dollars, for the space, and was selling it for *ten dollars!*

On top of that, he'd hand the copy to me and I had to set the type on the linotype.

You stupid idiot, I told myself. I get a buck-fifty. The con gets $8.50. Besides that, I had to set all the type on my linotype.

Usually you can make up a quarter-page ad in ten or fifteen minutes, using large type with plenty of white space. But a typeset ad was solid print, time consuming.

I worked all night and half the next night to get all the copy set and the paper printed.

The con man grabbed the first few issues off the press, jumped in his car, and headed for Drumright. I heard later how he took our paper into a place of business and showed the owners their ad—exactly as he had read it to them on the phone.

The merchant had no argument. He'd thought he had been taking advantage of a dumb editor in the dinky town to the north. He meekly paid. The con man got his cash money and left town—fleecing all of us.

Nita measured the number of column inches he had sold. "You want to know how much he made off you?" she asked.

"No," I told her.

She laughed. "I'm going to tell you anyway."

I put my hands over my ears and ran to hide out in the print shop.

It was the oldest con game in the world—taken in by your own greed—and I'd fallen for it.

From then on it didn't bother me a bit participating in Catfish's double-billing practice.

It was a good deal all the way around—I was cheating the manufacturer by double-billing Catfish, the manufacturer thought he was cheating me by buying space at the local rate through his local distributor, and Catfish got his ads free.

And so, I learned, a con is legitimate when each side thinks he's conning the other.

The Law in IT

A Christmas in the sixties was one of the best for Nita and me. Willard showed up at our front door. He was a big man, obviously Indian with his olive colored skin, high cheek bones, dark eyes, and straight black hair, trimmed neatly.

He had his hands stuffed deep into his khaki pant pockets, trying to hide something, the grin on his face a mile wide.

"Remember me?" he asked.

Of course. I invited him in and introduced him to Nita. He pulled the object from his pocket. It was wrapped in a newspaper.

"I brought you a Christmas present," he said bashfully. "I made it special for you—for helping me get started. I had to wait a long time to get the right piece of wood."

I took the clumsily wrapped gift, too surprised to speak. I peeled away the newsprint.

It was a wooden letter opener.

I was so overwhelmed I was unable to speak...

I first met Willard when he walked into my office. At the time, I was editing the *Tulsa Magazine* for the Tulsa Chamber of Commerce.

He carried something that day also—a long slender bundle about three feet long wrapped in a piece of muslin.

Oh, my gosh! I thought. I've written something about Indians that made him mad. He's come to blow me away with a sawed-off shotgun!

"You the editor?" he asked, his voice soft and friendly as he began unwrapping the bundle.

I was tempted to say, "No. He's out right now."

But I didn't. Relief flooded through me when I saw it was a wood carving. He placed the tall, slender object on my desk and said, "I need your help."

It was a wood sculpture of an old lawman, complete with up-tilted cowboy hat, handlebar moustache, a heavy star hanging on a loose shirt, low-hanging pistol, bow legs, and boots.

"The Law In IT." was the carving's title, nicked into its base. Every Oklahoman knew we were Indian Territory—IT— before we became a state.

"It's an old marshal," he explained.

There was no need for him to tell me that. The carving explained itself, especially if you knew and loved Oklahoma history as I did, being born and raised here.

"He's Indian, doing a white man's job, enforcing the white man's law in Indian Territory. Both races respect him. He is able to keep the peace because he's who he is."

The philosophy aside, I examined the piece in more detail.

When I commented on the way the wood's grain appeared to be whisker stubble, his grin broadened. "That's intentional. I don't just grab a piece of wood and start cutting. I study the grain, the knots; sometimes the shape of the piece of wood itself tells me where and how to cut."

Both amazed and full of wonder, I said, "You're obviously a professional. Who are you?"

"My name's Willard Stone," he said, offering a hand.

I'd never heard of him. I couldn't help noticing two fingers missing on his extended hand, his index finger and the long finger next to it, not even stubs left. I took the crippled hand in my own, mumbled my own name. I asked what it was I could do to help him.

He said he had a regular eight-hour day job, that he did his wood sculpting at night.

He wanted to quit his job and go into wood sculpting full time. But he couldn't quit his job because he had a family to feed.

He needed publicity.

"Go on," I encouraged, already fashioning the story in my mind. I'd build it around a wood-carver who'd lost two of his most important fingers handling a knife.

He hardly knew what I was talking about when I mentioned this fact. He'd lost them playing with a blasting cap when he was thirteen.

He shrugged it off. "If you want to do something bad enough," he said, "handicaps don't stop you."

He explained that he used a hand saw to make a rough cutting, then sculpted the rest with his pocket knife…held in his crippled hand.

He invited me to hold the Old Marshal carving, to feel it. He explained how he put a natural finish on all his work by rubbing them with his hands, letting the natural oil from his skin work its way into the wood.

He was a Cherokee, he said. Not full blood, he confessed. About half, as near as he could figure it.

"Sometimes I feel I'm a Cherokee, and sometimes I feel I'm a white man," he said, laughing. "I guess when you get right down to it, I'm a little bit of both."

He explained it was the division of cultures that he was trying to overcome in his art. The Old Marshal was an example. He was undeniably Indian, yet he was keeping the peace in a white man's world.

When Willard showed me photos of his other pieces of work, I could easily see that not only were his carvings good *as carvings*, each depicted this strong philosophical theme of different cultures blending to create a better world.

I ask him if the Old Marshal was for sale, hoping against hope that, somehow, I would have enough money to buy it; knowing at the same time that I didn't.

"I wish I could sell it to you," he said. "I promised it to our governor. But it'd be perfect here in your office. I can tell how much you love Oklahoma by the things you write."

He offered to pay me if I'd do a story on him and his work.

I waved his offer aside, told him a good subject like him and his work was perfect for the Tulsa Chamber of Commerce publication. Our magazine was mailed to prospective industrialists all over the country, and would make a strong, favorable impression on people who didn't know our state and her people.

"In my opinion, Willard, for whatever it is worth, you should quit your job and work full time at wood sculpting."

He gave me that soft Indian smile, thanked me, took the Old Marshal, and left.

I did the story, even managed to get some photos of his work to go along with it.

A short time later, Willard was invited to display some of his carvings in a New York art show. He sold every piece for what he felt were fabulous sums. He received enough commissions, he said, to keep him busy for a year.

I felt good about whatever small part I had helping Willard get started. However, I felt bad that I had not arranged to buy one of his pieces before his fame spread and his art brought more than I could ever afford.

Now he was giving me a piece for Christmas. It was a replica of the Old

Marshal's head, carved from a thin piece of mahogany, the up-tilted hat brim was the blade for the letter opener. The details in the face, handlebar moustache and all, had been so expertly crafted with the flow of the grain that, true to form, he appeared to need a shave.

As usual, Willard had spent no telling how many hours rubbing the piece with his hands to work the oil from his skin into the carving's silky finish. I swallowed hard to keep from showing too much emotion.

"No way will I ever use this for a letter opener," I told him. "It means more to me than that."

"I try to make all my pieces fit the personality of the person I do them for," he said. "I knew when a friend sent me that piece of wood, it was for you, since you love Oklahoma so much."

It was the facing from a cabinet drawer, he said, salvaged from the battleship Oklahoma after it was sunk by the Japanese at Pearl Harbor.

That made it even more precious.

Willard's fame as one of the world's foremost Indian wood sculptors spread around the globe before he died at his home in Locust Grove—doing what he loved to do most, creating beauty from pieces of ugly wood, trying his best to bridge the culture gap between the Indian and the white man.

Now his son Jason is carrying on his father's work in his Locust Grove studio.

Nita and I keep Willard's carving on our mantle—just above our TV set which carries stories daily of bitter racism going on in our country.

Often I glance up at the Old Marshal and remember how Willard Stone tried to create, through his art, a world of living together, at harmony with one another.

It would be so easy to do…

Sally the Christmas Tree

How does a person "just know"?

We meet hundreds of young ladies before we are married, or, if you are a lady, young men. We always "know" when we meet the one we will spend the rest of our life with. Especially when we don't let our reasoning process get in the way of "just knowing."

I have bought several automobiles in my life. The ones I reasoned my way into buying always turned out to be a headache. But the ones I found sitting on a car lot just waiting for me were the ones I enjoyed most. They ran well, lasted longer, and I didn't mind it so much when I was forced to spend money on them when they got older.

They simply looked like my car or pickup the second I laid eyes on them.

Same way with finding a Christmas tree. You look and look and look, and drive to every lot in town before finding the one you've been looking for. And sometimes the one you select isn't nearly as perfectly shaped or filled out as well as many others you've seen during the search.

However, you can complicate the process, like I did when our son Scott was at the age when he knew there was no Santa Claus but pretended there was so we could keep on playing the game with him, at least for another year.

He liked for me to tell him stories. I made one up about our Christmas tree. I even gave it a name—Sally.

I described how proud Sally was to come to our house and have us decorate her so beautifully. She was so grateful that she promised to bring us a lot of presents Christmas night.

Even before the tree had any presents under it, Scott would spend hours lying on the floor on his stomach, chin propped up by his hands, just staring at the tree.

Sure enough, Sally did what she promised. She brought us a lot of presents Christmas night.

But a week or so after Christmas, when Nita and I began removing the tree's decorations, Scott went running through the room, on his way to his new bike with training wheels outside. He slid to a halt and asked, alarmed, "What are you doing?"

"Taking down the tree," I told him. "We need to get it out of here. It's dried out and the needles are falling all over the place."

"What're you going to do with her?" he said.

As soon as he said "her" I knew I was in trouble. It wasn't a tree. It was Sally, an aged, decrepit, falling-apart Sally.

"The trash man comes tomorrow. I have to get it out to the curb so he can pick it up," I explained, trying hard to make the tree an "it."

His under lip trembled and his eyes welled up.

"What's the matter?" I asked.

"I don't want Sally to leave," he said, and broke out crying.

I looked at Nita and she looked at me, her look asking, "Now what do we do?"

I shrugged, and hung an ornament back in its place.

We backed off from taking it down. Then the next day when Scott was at school, we took down the tree and I carried it away to the trash bin, thinking Scott wouldn't even miss it when he got home. He'd be more interested in trying to learn how to ride his new bike. He wanted to get those training wheels off. Made him look like a girl, he said.

I was wrong. When he came home and saw the tree was gone, he began crying again. Except this time it was a mad cry. Not only was the tree gone, I'd tricked him. So, in effect, he lost both a Christmas tree and a father all in the same day.

"Now settle down, son," I said in my best man-to-man tone of voice. When I saw it had no effect, I lied by saying, "I didn't throw Sally away."

"What'd you do with her?" he demanded.

I told him I put her in our car, that I drove out to the river hill, and that I found perfect spot to plant her.

I could see his mind start working, visualizing where the tree was. I kept right on talking.

"I found a spot high on the hill," I said. "It had a beautiful view. You could see for miles and miles. I figured Sally would like that. So that's where I planted her."

Scott seemed somewhat satisfied. I plunged on.

"She'll invite the birds to come and build their nests on her limbs. And she'll help the young birds learn to fly by catching them when they fall out of their nests.

Scott's face brightened, his eyes widened.

"When winter comes and it rains, icicles will hang from her limbs and she'll be the prettiest tree in the forest."

"Can I go see her?" he asked, breathless.

"You don't have to do that. We'll find her on one of the Christmas tree lots next year."

He frowned skeptically. "How will we know it's her?"

"Oh, we don't need to worry about that. When we get close, she'll start calling out softly so no one else will hear. She'll say, 'Here I am.' And she'll keep calling until we find her."

A big satisfied grin spread across his face. I knew he knew I was making up another story. But he was satisfied and ran on out to learn how to ride his bike so he could get those sissy training wheels off.

Every year after that until he got too "old" to go with me to find our Christmas tree, we made a game of it—both of us going together from lot to lot, stalking up and down the walkways, both of us listening for Sally's soft call, "Here I am."

And we always found her.

Somehow, we always "just know."

We are better at "just knowing" when we don't let scientific reasoning get in the way. The human mind reaches beyond reality. It is us. We are animals, yes, but the mind is not animal. It separates us from the animal world.

"Just knowing" brings us happiness.

Vince and Me

I hung up the phone, starry-eyed.

Oh, wow! A federal appointment. Security plus. The man on the phone had said: Since you are so well qualified, I know you'll be able to take over our Public Relations department from day one without any difficulty.

But he didn't tell me about Vince. I would have to find out the hard way.

The position was with the US Army Corps of Engineers, Louisville, Kentucky District. It had navigable jurisdiction over the entire length of the Ohio River, one of the Corps oldest and most prestigious Districts.

It was tough for Nita and me to leave Tulsa, where we had a nice home near a good school for our son, Scott. But this was too good a deal to pass up. We were excited, making the move.

When I reported in, the personnel officer took me straight to the top man's office, Brigadier General Wessels. The General was a small, feisty type of officer, quick to scowl, quick smile.

He told me I would be assistant to the Vince, Chief of the Public Relations department.

"But I was told I'd be head of the department," I argued.

He waved aside my objections, explaining that Vince had thirty-five years in government service. He'd said he was going to retire. Until he did, I would work under him.

It was a big let-down. But there was no backing out now.

The personnel man took me to the Public Relations office and introduced me to Vince.

He was writing something on one of those yellow note pads, holding up the top sheet as he worked on the second page.

He quickly dropped the top sheet as if he were hiding something. He stood, his back ramrod straight as he leaned over to grasp my hand.

He was a tall, skinny man with a hatchet face, a small moustache, and eyes that continually blinked behind his gold rimmed spectacles.

The personnel man left. Vince waved a hand at a nearby desk. "Make yourself at home," he said affably.

Then he settled back into his chair, lifted the top page of his yellow pad, and resumed writing.

I was right. I found out that Vince was, indeed, hiding something—a crossword puzzle. He'd clip it out of his morning newspaper and bring it to work with him every day. He kept it hidden in his yellow note pad. Everybody knew it.

Since he never did any work, I had to do everything. I was on the road a lot, setting up our public hearings.

I would contact the local papers and business leaders. I'd rent a hall or get permission to use the school gymnasium. I'd set up the loud-speaker system.

Then I would brief General Wessels on what to expect from the local people, whether they were hostile or friendly to the proposed flood control project in their area.

General Wessels liked the way I handled things. He asked me to write it up. He wanted to circulate it through channels to other Corps Districts and Divisions around the world as a guide for other PR people.

Proud, I did as he asked. As a courtesy to Vince, I routed my first report across his desk. He read it, turned white, and handed it back, lecturing me on how to write bureaucratese.

It is the art of using a lot of words to say nothing about nobody no where no how—especially when it comes to what you yourself have done.

Frustrated, I began sending my reports straight to the General, bypassing Vince. I think Vince knew what I was doing, but didn't care—if I goofed up, he could always say it was my fault. And he would be rid of me.

Then the unthinkable happened. The river was up and rising. When this happens, the Corps shuts down all locking operations. They open gates on the dams to control the flooding and keep the river from overflowing the levees which protected the towns.

Tows are forced to tie up to a shore anchorage to wait out the flooding. (Tow boats push long trains of steel barges lashed together, but they are still called "tows".)

One of these shore-anchored tows above the Markam dam between Louisville and Cincinnati came apart during the night. The coal-filled barges drifted downstream, lodging against the dam. Some were able to be retrieved without incident, some even washed on through the open gates.

One, however, got broadside against a pier between two opened gates. The strength of the water current crumpled it around the pier like it was a limp bread wrapper.

Word flashed all up and down the river. They would not be able to close the gates. The navigation pool (lake) above the dam would be drained.

Alarmed shipping interests called Washington. Recreational marina owners panicked—and there were scores of these because this particular pool stretched along the highly industrialized and heavily populated city of Cincinnati.

Our telephones were ringing madly when we got to our office that morning. This was big news, not only locally but nationally.

Washington brass called General Wessels and told him to get our PR people to work, and fast. Didn't he realize this jeopardized the Corps' 100 years of solid work controlling the nation's navigable waterways?

General Wessels passed the order on to us. Vince panicked. He said he was sick and went home.

General Wessels called me to his office.

"What can you do to get us out of this idiotic public relations nightmare?" he asked.

I considered doing what Vince tried to teach me—do nothing. They can't do anything to you if you don't do anything.

Besides that, Vince was Chief. He'd get the blame. He might stay gone for good.

But I simply couldn't do it Vince's way. I heaved a sigh and said, "Nothing to it. Just tell the truth."

General Wessels was hesitant at first, arguing that telling the truth might cause unnecessary panic. He felt our engineers would be able to clear the gates and close them before we lost the pool.

"And if they can't?" I questioned.

He grinned. "Okay, Denney. You win. What's our first step?"

I suggested that we set up an information center at the dam. I insisted the General spend as much time as possible at the site.

That way, I explained, the news people would be able to get direct comments from him. When photographers and TV cameramen came, we'd escort them along the top of the dam so they could get dramatic photos of the crumpled barge clogging the gates.

After several aborted efforts to dislodge the collapsed barge, our engineers finally decided the only solution was to use explosives.

They calculated that since the concrete pier was stronger than the steel barge, the explosive force would be away from the pier, thus ripping the steel barge in two. The freed pieces would then be washed through the gate openings.

But despite me explaining this decision in detail to the press, the headlines came out, "Corps To Dynamite Markham Dam."

This did cause panic. Corps engineers were called everything from stupid on down. Washington brass was irate.

I was in hot water for sure now. But General Wessels stood behind me. I did everything I could to reassure the public through the news media that the Corps engineers knew what they were doing—just trust them.

The world watched and waited as the tow boat carrying the explosives eased up to the crumpled barge, lowered the charges between it and the dam's pier, and backed away.

There was a loud WHOMP when the charge went off. The crumpled barge was ripped in two and the pieces were swept through the dam's gates, exactly as the engineers predicted.

Then the words of praise started coming in. Vince was so delighted, he announced that since he had me, there was no need for him to retire.

I'd worked myself into a miserable situation.

But when a higher position opened up in the Chicago Division which had jurisdiction was over all five of the Great Lakes, General Wessels recommended me for the post—against his personnel wishes, he said, but felt I deserved it.

Best of all, I got away from Vince. When I reported to the two-star General in the Chicago office, he smiled and asked, "Tell me, does old Vince still work on his crossword puzzles all day long?"

I knew then and there that no matter how hard I worked as Public Relations Officer for the US Army Corps of Engineers, my reputation would never spread as far and wide as Vince's crossword working expertise did.

The Camping Trip

"Dad, can we go camping?"

You bet. Sounds like a reasonable request from an eight-year-old, energetic boy, doesn't it?

Nita and I didn't do much camping. We lived in Oklahoma City at the time. Nita was born and raised in northeast Oklahoma. What few times we'd gone camping, it was more of a family gathering on a lake or stream near where her family lived.

Some of us more macho types would actually sleep out, pretending the rocks under our sleeping quilts didn't bother us. Every mosquito within a hundred miles, it seemed, came swarming at sundown to suck your blood and make the little kids cry.

But we had fun, teasing one another, kids swimming, guys actually catching fish.

Still, who can turn down a son's plea to go camping?

"I'll start making plans with mother—"

"No," he interrupted. "Just you and me."

That caught me by surprise. But after thoughtful consideration, I decided it was time we got out in the wilderness alone, just the two of us, father and son, have man-to-man talks.

I broke the news gently to Nita. I didn't want her to think she was being left out.

"We'll go this weekend. Spend the night on Beattie's Creek," I told her. "I'll rent a tent and a couple of cots."

She thought it was a good idea, agreeing that I should have some time alone with Scott.

"Besides, I've been wanting to go see Mother," she said.

Hey, this was going to be just dandy—nobody getting upset or angry or anything.

Scott and I got busy. We rented a tent—a dandy. It even had a canvas floor and flaps to raise to let the cool night air in with netting to keep mosquitoes out.

Nita suggested we also rent a Coleman stove to cook on.

"No," I said. "I intend to stick as close to nature as possible. We'll cook over an open fire."

She had her doubts, but I pointed out that I knew all about cooking over open fires. I did it lots of times when I was a boy scout.

I didn't explain what I meant by "lots of times." Actually it was only twice.

No matter. It was time to teach my son the real art of camping.

"Can I take Mike?" Scott asked as we were loading the car.

Mike was his buddy, an Irish Setter.

Well, a boy needs his dog on a real camping trip, doesn't he?

"Sure," I said.

I failed to consult with Nita on that. I should have, because it was obvious she didn't enjoy sitting in the back seat as we sailed up the turnpike towards Delaware County with an Irish Setter in the front seat between Scott and me.

Despite the car's air-conditioner, it got hotter and hotter in the car.

I never knew an Irish Setter had such long tongues—or were such prolific slobberers.

Pant, pant, pant. Slobber, slobber, slobber. Scott did his best to keep the front seat dry with Kleenexes. He used up a whole box.

I tried to find Nita in my rear view mirror.

"You okay, honey?" I asked.

"I'm fine," she said, her voice cold as December. I shuddered.

We dropped Nita off at her mother's house and headed on down to the family's favorite camping spot on the creek. The weather was ideal.

Beautiful. Beautiful. This was going to be just great.

I began unloading our car, anticipating teaching my son how to set up a tent. But he was anxious to go swimming. I gave in and said okay.

He slipped into his bathing suit and ran and jumped into the creek. Mike didn't know what to make of it. After running up and down on the gravel bar and barking his head off, he finally plunged into the water himself.

I had trouble following directions on how to set up the tent, which peg went where, what hole to poke the tent pole through.

I finally got it up, however. It looked a little wobbly, but it was home—complete with a canvas floor. I called Scott to come see our weekend home. He came running, his wet dog on his heels.

As soon as Mike got inside, he shook himself vigorously, throwing cold creek water all over me and the inside of our "home."

I held onto my temper. After all, this was real camping, wasn't it?

I had a little trouble building a fire, the main reason was I'd forgot to bring any matches. Luckily, Nita and her mother showed up to see how we were doing.

They didn't have any matches either, but they went to the house and got some. Nita's sister and her husband came back with them.

They all helped me build a fire. By then, the sun was going down and Scott was cold and shivering—and hungry, too. Mike was off in the woods somewhere, chasing squirrels and barking up a storm. I knew he wasn't a squirrel dog. He'd probably found one he was wanting to play with.

I hurried to put on a pan of fried potatoes. The women watched me peel them and wash them in the creek. They had disgusted looks on their faces.

When I offered to fry enough for everybody, they said no. They were going back to town. Nita's Mom said she had some left-over fried chicken. She'd also cooked a pot of brown beans that day. Why didn't we just come into town and eat?

Well…since it was already fixed.

Scott didn't argue too much about going to town and eating. He didn't like smoke getting in his eyes.

We went to town. After eating, I couldn't help thinking how soft one of Mom's beds would feel. Her sheets were always so clean, you didn't ever want to get up once you crawled in between them.

Scott insisted we go back and "camp out." And take old Mike with us.

So back to the creek we went, me at the wheel dreaming about Mom's clean sheets, Scott over by the door about to go to sleep, and Mike in between with that long tongue hanging out and slobbering all over everything.

Mike acted disappointed about having to sleep outside. Scott pleaded to let him come in.

"No," I said. "Dogs sleep outside." Then I added, "They have to stand guard."

Scott's eyes got big. "Guard against what?"

"Oh, bears and things."

I'd said too much. Scott thought it might be better if Mike stayed inside with us.

"He's not a bear dog," he said authoritatively. "He's a bird dog."

He had a point. So we let Mike stay inside.

It was a good thing we did. It rained. And rained. And rained. Water was running in from everywhere, under our canvas floor, across the top of it, even dripping from the soaked roof of the tent itself.

Mike got wet, stood and shook himself, spraying everything and everybody with water that smelled like dog hair.

The rain finally slacked off enough for us to get some sleep.

Nita and her mother showed up at daylight and woke us up. They had come to see if we had made it through the storm all right.

What storm? I pretended that I slept so well that I didn't even know it had stormed.

But it didn't take much encouragement from Nita's mother for us to go into town where I could use her bathroom to shower and shave with warm water.

And it was so nice to sit down at my mother-in-law's table to feast on a breakfast of bacon and eggs with gravy and biscuits.

Mike? He was miserable being tied up on a strange porch. He kept whining and barking. But Nita's mother knew what to do for him. She gave him the left over biscuits and gravy and he settled down and went to sleep.

I lay down too—just to rest a bit. It was late afternoon when Nita woke me up.

"We'd better go home," she said.

I had to go back to our campsite, tear down and fold up a wet tent, and stuff it in the trunk of our car.

Mike got in the creek again. He was chasing a flying bird and didn't see the water. He fell in headfirst.

Not only did he pant and slobber in the front seat all the way back to Oklahoma City, but his coat was wet and stank to high heaven.

Nothing is as rewarding as taking your son on a real camping trip to teach him nature's beautiful ways.

The Cutting Edge of Technology

Paper and pencil was a part of my life my life, like my parents and my brothers and sisters and my best friend down the road a ways.

And Mom having to put pans at certain places in the house to catch drips from the roof leaking when it rained.

And the tree by the kitchen I loved to climb and look out across the country side, pretending I was a pilot.

Or the town nearby where school was.

All these things had always been there and, naturally, you assumed they always would be.

It was not until later that I realized what a great leap in technology for man it was when he came up with paper and a pencil.

No longer did he have to try and express himself by scratching marks on a rock inside a cave.

Or weaving beads into a wampum belt.

A pencil and a piece of paper, I sensed early on, would be a big part of my life.

You sit down with your pencil and piece of paper and chew on the eraser a few moments, mulling over how best to use words to convey your thoughts to another person before you write them down.

It was a beautiful release to do that. Sometimes I'd write for hours, describing sunsets I'd seen, what my friend and I did that day—even writing a few phrases of the novel I intended to write someday.

That's what writers did in the olden days—they wrote their manuscripts in long hand. There's a serendipitous relationship between the thought process, the movement of the hand, the soft whisper of pencil lead on paper. It's a sort of self-generating creativeness that's difficult to describe.

But you have to stay on the cutting edge of technology or get left behind.

The typewriter had taken over. It clattered incessantly in newsrooms. Publishers talked about typescripts. A whole new industry arose—the expert typist.

I would have to learn typing if I was going to be a writer. So I enrolled in Miss Chaffee's high-school typewriting class.

I was the only boy in the room, and I think Miss Chaffee resented my intrusion. She was a nice, quiet lady who kept her straight black hair combed back. I slid into a seat in the back corner and stared down at the black…thing…and its keyboard.

I labored over trying to master the thing. My fingers refused to work independently of one another. I struggled to get my assignments.

When Miss Chaffee started our speed drills, the room erupted into a wild chattering of typewriter keys. And there I was, clack-clacking away, making a key slap the paper ever minute or so, it seemed.

Miss Chaffee suggested strongly that I come in after school to practice. (And you know what a "suggestion for after-school work" means, coming from a teacher? It's a nice way of saying you're flunking.)

She sat in a seat nearby, coaching, as I clumsily fingered my way through the drills. Finally, exasperated, I exploded with, "Whoever came up with the idea of laying out a keyboard like this?"

"Like what?" she asked, a trifle surprised.

"Like this," I said, demonstrating. "Your left hand sets on the ASDF keys and your right fingers on the JKL semicolon keys. Why the semicolon? How often do you need a semicolon?"

She sniffed and said, "Just do your drills, and you'll learn. Everybody else does."

What she was really saying was, "All the girls learn how, why can't you?"

I felt humiliated. Maybe writing is, after all, a girl thing. It made no difference. I knew what I wanted to be. So, determined, I went through my drills, typing over and over, "ASDF" with my left hand and "JKL;" with my right hand.

As the drills advanced, I noticed my left hand also had the responsibility of other letters I used a lot, like e, t, r, c, and b. I'd look down at my right hand and get mad at it for just lollygagging around, waiting for a semicolon to come along.

By the end of each class, my left arm, from my fingers to my shoulder, would be aching from the strain. My right arm would be ready to—well, the only ache it had was to hug one of the pretty girls I was in class with.

But with Miss Chaffee's patient encouragement, I stuck with it and learned to type—sort of. I could do all right copying something, but I simply could not compose using a typewriter.

The noise bothered me—all that clackity clack and bells dinging to tell you when you were at the end of a line. But would they tell you when you came to the bottom of the page? No way! Just when you got going good, you'd look up and your paper would be slaunchwise on the roller and all your words would be going onto it in one big blob.

Besides the clatter that grew louder and louder the farther into the night you worked, keeping the family awake, other mechanics would conspire to overwhelm you.

Keys jammed up. Ribbons wore out. The ding at the end of the line came at the wrong time. Trying to figure out where to hyphenate a word has to be the biggest creativity-killer ever invented.

Newer models with added features, such as the ones that beeped at you when you misspelled a word, only added to the frustration, especially in weekly newspaper work where you have all those personals of Mr. and Mrs. Whosit visited over the weekend with their son and his wife, Mr. and Mrs. Whosit, Jr.

The beeper would go off at every name. It sounded like you had a drunk canary inside your typewriter.

Trying to compose on a typewriter, for me, was impossible. I tried and tried. I just couldn't do it.

To avoid that laborious mechanical nightmare, I kept writing longhand, and with a pencil.

I like the silence of writing longhand. The words seem to flow onto the sheet of paper. If you don't like the way a sentence is going, strike it out and jot in a correction over the top. You don't like a word, scratch through it and go on. You find a paragraph out of place, you bracket it and scribble a note in the margin to move it to page five.

You can write in the margins and make arrows to where you want the sentence inserted.

Sometimes my sheets of paper, when I finished with them writing longhand, looked like directions to find a secret buried treasure.

I compromised—compose in longhand with pencil and paper, and type it up later.

Giving impetus to this beautiful arrangement was the invention of the ball-point pen. No more would you have to interrupt your creativity by stopping to sharpen your pencil or go find another one when it was worn to a nub.

When I came to know about the ball-point pen, I was ecstatic. I thought they were a marvelous invention. They cost $12.50 each, a staggering sum.

By then I was in the army, and Nita and I were newly married. I felt like a fool for spending a week's budget for food on a ball-point pen. But Nita was supportive. She knew of my secret ambition. Being able to put your thoughts on paper was what writing was all about.

And just think, I argued with myself, you could carry it around with you, leaving its chrome top sticking up out of your shirt pocket—let the world know you were on the cutting edge of technology.

It had one major flaw. It didn't write well. It skipped so badly that you had trouble reading what you wrote. Banks often refused to recognize a signature written with a ball-point pen.

To be honest about it, I was ashamed to have plunked down so much money for a gadget that didn't work too well. But because I'd been suckered so badly, I had to keep using it, pretending all the while it was the greatest thing since God made little green apples.

Technology soon perfected the ball-point pen. Today I have them scattered everywhere about the house. Discount stores sell them in packets so large, it takes five years to use up a supply. Banks give them away. You can get them to write heavy, medium, or fine. In all colors.

For me, they've replaced pencils completely. I do miss chewing on an eraser, however, when I'm mulling over a clever way to phrase a thought.

Fortunately, down through the years, I had Nita to type up my longhand scribblings for me. Or sometimes I'd type them up myself, plodding along through the misery of ASDF and JKL semicolon.

The screwball way the typewriter keyboard was laid out was brought into even sharper focus for me when Nita and I got into the newspaper business and I began setting the reading matter on a machine called a Linotype.

When this machine was invented in the late 1800s, it revolutionized the printing industry. Its keyboard was obviously designed by a printer, a guy who had spent his life picking individual letters out of a type case to fit them into a sentence.

The most used letters in the English alphabet are E, T, A, O, I, and N. So the Linotype keyboard designer put all these in the extreme row on the left.

The second most used letters are S, H, R, D, L, and U. These were in the next row.

The rest of the alphabet, caps, etc., were scattered across the keyboard.

There were no "home keys" for your fingers on the Linotype keyboard. Your fingers just naturally hovered over these two rows on the left. It was made to order for the hunt-and-peck system.

Even so, you could set copy twice as fast as you could typing because you had most of the letters you needed all together. Your right hand did most of the work roaming over the keyboard picking up a consonant when you needed one.

I don't remember where the semicolon was. I didn't care. I don't use semicolons anyway. Nor does anyone else—except college professors who don't like, for some odd reason, to make sense when they write anything.

The Linotype, a seven-foot-tall, four-foot-wide mechanical marvel, revolutionized the printing industry, making the newspapers you read comparatively easy to publish.

Even though the Linotype made all kinds of racket, I found I could write copy on it without any trouble because of the keyboard arrangement.

As years rolled on, we sold our business and I turned to writing novels. I made another attempt to use the typewriter. I couldn't do it. I stubbornly continued writing longhand and Nita obligingly typed up the copy for me.

Eventually, however, my handwriting got so poor that she had trouble making out some of the words. Sometimes when she asked me to read it for her, I couldn't read it myself. This was discouraging. My literary ambition was losing its energy.

Then along came this wondrous thing we call a computer. While it made the Linotype obsolete and sent the typewriter into the dark recesses of household storage spaces, it literally saved my writing career.

I'd read all I could about the computer, how they came to be "invented" (by some college Joes playing with switches on electric trains), how computers could add, subtract, count words, correct your spelling, and I don't know what all.

But what got me excited was when I heard them called Word Processors. Since I was a writer, "word processor" meant processing words…didn't it?

Golly, I thought, all I would have to do is turn it on and it would process all my copy.

Remembering the ball point pen, however, I was leery. I'd sneak peeks at computers in stores and walk away in a cold sweat.

But the "keeping up with technology" pressure was on. I finally caved and went shopping for one.

The computer salesman was a goofy-looking young man with big head on a long neck. He wore faded jeans and oversized what we used to call tennis shoes, which cost us, probably, $1.99. His big shoes, I'd bet, cost him around $150.

I felt like turning away from this geek and walking out. But I knew I had to have a computer, since I couldn't write long hand anymore. The ovals and push-and-pull exercises we used to do in penmanship to train our muscles how to guide a pencil had lost their effectiveness. Sometimes my muscles would balk and do a "push" when I order a "pull," and my ovals looked like cracked walnuts.

But with a computer, you make an error, hit the delete key. Move a sentence, just highlight it and zap it in where you want it to go. Just like writing longhand. Almost.

I didn't want this geek kid to think I was too old to know how to use a computer.

"Tell me what this one will do," I asked pointing at one sitting on a desk with little birds flying lazily across the viewing area.

"What do you want it to do?" he asked.

"Oh," I shrugged, "write letters and things."

He smirked. I wouldn't have minded his impudent expression so much if he hadn't glanced up at my gray hair first.

"This model can do about anything you want to do," he said.

Oh, yeah. Can it do ovals and push and pulls like Mrs. Hubbell used to make us do in second grade penmanship class?

"It even has a thesaurus along with its spell check," my big-shoed salesman said.

Big deal. None of these whiz-bang spell checks, I had read, were as good as Zena Lee. We had a spelling test every day all through grade school and Zena Lee missed spelling only one word correctly in five years. When our teacher handed our papers back that time and Zena Lee made a 99 instead of 100, she laid her head down on her desk and cried.

"I see," I said and just for the hell of it, I said, "Go ahead. Make it write a letter for me."

He stared. His neck wilted and his goofy-looking head laid over on one shoulder. I had to lay my head over also, just so I could look at him even up.

He admitted it couldn't actually write a letter, but, he said, there was no need to do that anymore. Use the Internet to communicate with your friends.

To me, Internet messages are like written phone calls. Speaking and writing are not the same thing. There are rules you use in writing. If you don't know the rules, you can't write. Period.

Nor does the computer know grammar.

Besides, I always have the feeling when I'm using the Internet that the whole world is watching.

I didn't tell him, but we had Internets before the computer was ever invented. Only we called them window-peepers.

The young computer salesman with a limber neck obviously knew everything there was to know about computers. When he found out just how ignorant I was, he started at zero and told me all about them.

Most computer whizzes have developed their own language. They speak acronymese—like VCR, CD-ROM, ATM, DVD, things like that. And when he got into talking about gigabites and googles my eyes were beginning to glaze over.

His head had flopped over again and I was getting a crick in my neck just watching him so I said, "Okay. Write me up a bid on this one along with all the other gew-gaws I'd need to—" I started to say write a letter, but I didn't want to get into that again.

Sure enough, his limber neck stiffened and he hurried away so fast to find his bid sheet that he tripped over the long strings on his too-big tennis shoes.

He labored over writing the things down—using a ball-point pen, I noticed. He stuck out his tongue for balance like a second grader. He'd never even been taught how to hold a pencil, let alone how to make ovals and push-and-pulls. And he made a couple of mistakes adding it up—all in my favor, so I didn't correct him.

How sad. The computer had gobbled up his brain. He couldn't write, couldn't add, or even hold his head up properly.

I signed the contract with a ball-point pen that had a nearby bank's name on it.

At home, I took the computer out of the box and hooked it up. (I always think I'm smart enough to figure it out myself, so I never read instructions on how to do anything until I try to do it first and mess it up.)

I flipped a switch. I watched the screen flicker to life.

"Welcome to Macintosh!" it said.

Its friendly smile calmed my jitters somewhat.

I settled into a more comfortable position in my chair, fingers hovering over the keyboard. No problem there—it was the same old keyboard that the guy invented after he'd been hit over the head with a two-by-four a century and a half ago.

I went to work. Slowly at first, waiting for the ding at the end of the line. None. It even hyphenated so fast you couldn't believe your own eyes.

There were no ribbons to wear out. No more clatter—just soft little ticks, a comforting sound—like the pleasant clicking which the claws on your friendly Labrador makes when he trots across the tile floor in your kitchen to get a drink of water.

You make a mistake, just delete and redo. It even jumped to the next page without a hitch.

One of my biggest disappointments after buying my first computer was finding out how dumb they were.

I learned that a computer's vaunted and worshiped "spell check" program didn't know diddly-squat about the meaning of words—just as long as they're spelled right. Never mind that you spelled "had" for "hat," or "hip" for "ship;" your computer wouldn't know the difference. And substituting one for the other in a sentence would have devastating consequences.

Or in the case of the previous sentence, it would keep trying to throw out "diddly-squat" when you know darn well you know that's the word you wanted to use.

And ever since my eighth grade teacher tried to tell us the difference between who and whom, I could never get it right. I was disappointed in learning that computers don't know either.

In other words, computers were dumb, when you got right down to it.

The more I explored her virtues, however, I fell totally and helplessly in love with her. This new-found relationship reinvigorated my literary life. I'm anxious to get to my computer, turn her on, and see her smiling face.

Still…I can't help but wonder why all these brainy kids who developed these modern marvels failed to change the keyboard arrangement while they were at it. Looks to me like they could have come up with something more efficient—like the Linotype keyboard for printers—and we could have thrown the typewriter keyboard onto the junk rocket ship sailing off into space along with the typewriter itself and the Linotype.

I've owned three computers. Each one was so much superior to the last one that, I was told, I could do so much more work that I wouldn't believe how much work I could do.

Yes, you might turn out more material, but you keep on working the same amount of time you always worked.

So this new-fangled work-saver doesn't save you any work at all. And when you get used to how much you can get done with one, you're right back to where you started from.

Even though the computer I have now is five years old—that's fifty in computer age—I'm dragging my feet about getting a new one.

But you need a faster computer to cruise the information superhighway, the salesmen of today say.

I still haven't figured out where everybody is going on the information super highway.

You have all this information at your fingertips, they say. The information they are talking about is what we already have in our libraries, or you will eventually see in a *National Geographic* magazine.

Presidents tell us in their speeches that every school child should have access to the Internet so they can cruise the information superhighway.

I had an English professor once who liked to tell us: You could lock a monkey in a room with a typewriter and if you give him enough time, he would be able to recreate all the works of Shakespeare.

I suppose if a kid traveled on the information superhighway long enough, he would eventually read all the works of Shakespeare.

But I doubt it. There are too many distractions on the superhighway. Like sports stories, pornography, and the sex life of the African dung beetle. A kid would still need guidance to enjoy Shakespeare.

However, some would argue that knowing the sex life of an African dung beetle is of far more value than experiencing the grandeur of the Shakespeare plays.

No matter...I'd rather write and become immortal like Shakespeare than spending my time traveling the information highway to learn about African dung beetles.

Pickup Country

A big fuss is being stirred up in Tulsa over the police putting up cameras to catch drivers running red lights.

The camera gets your tag number. The police send you a traffic citation.

"What if somebody else is driving my car?" some protest.

Others claim such a tactic is an invasion of privacy. As one TV reporter commented, it will be only a matter of time when there will be TV cameras everywhere. People at a central monitoring station will be able to watch what people were doing on about any street corner in town.

I found myself agreeing with the television reporter because, as usual, he really wasn't delivering a news story, he was editorializing—his point being that invasion of privacy was a violation of a basic human right.

But the following morning I changed my mind because...

I was in my home office working at my computer when the phone rang. I picked it up. The man's voice asked, "Is Randy there?"

"No," I answered, hesitant because I wasn't sure whether or not this was a telephone solicitation. Yet, I thought I recognized the voice. I asked, "Is he supposed to be here?"

"I was looking for him. I drove down your street. I saw his pickup in your driveway. I just thought he might've stopped in to see you."

Then I recognized the voice and I laughed, calling him by name and teased, "That's my pickup, you knot-head. My truck is better than Randy's. His is just a six. Mine is a 350."

He apologized, laughing also at his own mistake. He then excused himself with, "Your pickup looks exactly like Randy's,"

I agreed, now that he mentioned it.

We chatted a while about other things then hung up to go about our own chores.

Only I didn't attack my "chore" immediately. I thought about last night's television story. What's the difference, I asked myself, between having television cameras monitoring your every move on a downtown street corner and human eyes monitoring you everywhere you go?

In small towns, the only privacy you have is the privacy allowed you by those living around you.

People can keep track of one another, for example, by where their pickup is parked. Also, when driving around town, you look at pickups, not at faces. The faces are hidden behind hard-to-see-through windshields and beneath ball caps pulled down low over the eyes.

But you get to know old Joe's scruffy pickup and can see him coming a mile away. You wave. Joe lifts a hand from his steering wheel and waves back. You feel good knowing Joe is out running around and that you and he had just completed a proper greeting.

When Nita and I retired and moved back to the small town where we lived as youngsters, so many people I didn't know waved that I got the notion I was being mistaken for someone else. After all, the area is now populated by grandchildren of our generation.

At first, I didn't respond to the waving. I didn't want anyone to be embarrassed when they discovered I wasn't who they thought I was.

I'd just drive on by keeping my eyes fixed on the road ahead. I'd tell myself the guy would know he made a mistake when we passed. If I don't let on I saw him wave, he won't be embarrassed because I wasn't who he thought I was.

Besides, I'd just moved here from a big city. There, you didn't wave at people you didn't know. If you started waving at people in a big city, you could wind up getting run off the road or in a fist fight or get shot, or all three.

But here, people kept right on waving. One morning when I felt in pretty high spirits on my way to the post office and got a wave from a guy coming at me in another pickup, I lifted one finger to let him know I was at least acknowledging his mistake. He grinned as he went by. I found myself smiling back.

That made me feel good. From then on, I started returning everybody's wave. Each time it made me feel super-good all day long.

Then when I did get acquainted with new friends, and reacquainted with old friends, one commented, "Saw you had coffee at Herman's Café this morning."

I knew darn well he hadn't been at Herman's place—at least not while I was there. Turned out, he'd driven by on the highway and saw my pickup parked in front.

Privacy? None. Zilch.

But that's all right. When you go to ball games, you don't have to get out and go in to see who's there. You just drive around in the parking lot and look at the pickups. You try to find a spot to park near a pickup that's friends with your pickup.

On the streets, you see a pickup go by and say to yourself, "There goes old Joe."

It might not be old Joe at all. It might be his wife or his boy or the guy who works his cows for him. That doesn't matter. It's old Joe's pickup. His pickup is a part of him—like an arm or a leg. Everywhere old Joe's pickup goes, old Joe goes, if not in person, then in spirit.

And it's even downright confusing when old Joe buys a new pickup, swapping in his old one. It's as if he died or left the country or something. All of sudden old Joe's pickup is nowhere to be seen.

Adding to the confusion, you notice a strange pickup running around town, driving up and down the streets old Joe always drove, parking in front of Herman's place, where old Joe always parked.

The strange pickup is shiny new, red and white with sporty wheels, tinted glass, and chrome tie-down rails on either side of the bed.

Then when you find out the new pickup is old Joe's, you laugh at him in the coffee shop and point with your thumb over your shoulder at his shiny pickup and say, "What's happened to you, Joe? You in your second childhood or something?"

Still, it's hard to fit the sporty new pickup to old Joe. Sooner or later, however, you will. It won't be long until deer season is here and old Joe will be scootching his new pickup through the timber on old logging trails where underbrush will be reaching out to make long scratch marks down the sides.

And after he makes a few trips across his place bouncing over washed-out gullies, hauling feed to his cows or throwing posts over his tailgate, the new pickup will take on some of old Joe's recognizable characteristics.

Then you get that comfortable "with friends" feeling again.

Like Merle Haggard said a few years back on Johnny Carson's show one night, "I'm from Oklahoma. That's where everybody drives a pickup. You can do anything to a man you want, even steal his wife, but you better not mess around with his pickup."

Yes, you get to know everybody by his pickup. You wave, even if it turns out not to be who you think it is.

It's like an elderly man said when telling about the time he came to the county seat to do business at the courthouse.

"I had to wait on some paperwork to get done," he said. "So I goes outside and finds myself a seat on a bench under a shade tree.

"I just get set down when I glance across the way and see this old man setting on a bench on t'other side of the walk.

"I guesses from the look on his face he must've knowed me. And to tell the truth, he looks sort of familiar to me. So when he jumps up and starts for me, I jumps up and start for him.

"We met up in the middle. I shake his hand and he shakes mine. We start talking and slapping one another on the back like old friends do.

"But you know, come to find out, it warn't neither one of us!"

So it makes no difference if you know me or not—just wave at my pickup and I'll wave back.

That way, we'll both have a better day.

The Perfect Editoral Job

No one plans a career in weekly newspaper work. It's slave labor with starvation wages.

After retiring, friends asked me to start yet another weekly.

I resisted at first, but finally caved in, especially when the committee ramrodding the effort promised me I wouldn't have to sell advertising. They would do it.

That pushed me over the edge. Why not, I told myself? I could spend my time writing stories about people instead of about the county commissioner's meeting last week, or who the drunk was that the police picked up and took to jail last night.

Oh, of course, you would have to have all that stuff, be the official recorder of local events, but instead of stopping there, you could tell about people whose lives weren't necessarily connected with "events."

Today's weeklies don't even have what we used to call personals, usually written by the editor's wife or some local lady who loved to keep track of what everybody in town was doing, where they were going, who was coming to visit them.

The more I thought about it, the more appealing it sounded. I finally agreed to give it a try.

One of the first delights was to name it. I ran through all the usual names for papers: *News, Journal, Times, Dispatch, Tribune, Herald,* etcetera.

I sat with the committee in the coffee shop discussing names when somebody, I don't remember who, suggested calling it simply the *Jay American.*

I knew immediately that it fit, not only the town but also what I had in mind—America. We in small-town America were the same all across the land. My stories could be read and enjoyed in small-town Wisconsin as well as in small-town Texas, in Vermont, or Arizona.

I knew also there were a zillion, probably, newspapers named something

American all across the land. But my American would be different, I vowed.

But what happens immediately when you become a "leading citizen" of a community, you are asked to help with the governing of that community.

Right away, the mayor asked me to serve on several Boards and Commissions. Retirees make good volunteer workers for Mayors because they are always available…especially when you're in a position to control what's to be published for public consumption.

Why not? It would give me something to do.

As Chairman of the Planning and Zoning Board, I saw my town in a new light. All property owners were linked, one with the other. What one property owner did with his property affected not only his neighbors, but his entire neighborhood.

There had to be ordinances to regulate this. And it had to be ordinances which we could all agree on.

We held hearings. Because of my position as editor, I wrote news releases to keep the public informed on what we were trying to do.

Our biggest problem, I learned quickly, was that generally people don't care what city hall does until it does something they don't like. Then they come charging in claiming individual rights. Or worse, pointing out that so-and-so isn't complying, then why should I?

It so happens that Old So-and-So had special rights because years ago he had sued the city and got a judge to concur with his so-called rights.

And on one occasion, the entire Board had to make several eighty-mile trips to Tulsa because we were sued in a federal district court for one of our new ordinances having to do with what used to be known as trailer houses, now mobile homes.

Sadly, we discovered this right was being abused by realtors. Some were purchasing not-very-good mobile homes, setting them up on lots, then registering their availability for rent with Oklahoma's welfare program. The state paid the rent for struggling families, the realtor got the money, the taxpayer got screwed.

I pushed for an ordinance to ban mobile homes all together, allowing those already located to remain so under a grandfather clause.

The National Manufactured Homes organization, through a local mobile home business, filed the lawsuit on the grounds that it discriminated against the local businessman.

This was a case of individual rights verses community desires.

Personally, I have always favored individual rights over social "goodness," but you simply cannot escape the fact that we are all affected by one another's decisions and must, therefore, get together to decide what is the best for everybody.

Unfortunately, there are abuses of the system, not to mention downright stupidity, shortsightedness, and inability to foresee the future by those we elect or appoint to arrange these community living standards.

But as long as we have corrective measures in place, democracy in action usually is the best in the long run.

I quickly learned when involved in community service, if you were too timid to set forth your own thoughts and ideas, you were of no value whatsoever serving on any community boards or commissions. Some people like to be on Boards and Commissions just for the honor. They never say anything. But you have to have them.

So, despite subjecting myself to criticism, when I was asked to serve on the Trust Authority to add onto and rebuild our courthouse, one of the first things I did was to submit a paper containing my ideas.

Turned out, most of my suggestions were adopted, giving me a feeling that I had "done some good."

A side issue of the courthouse renovation was to "do something" with our county's WWII memorial, which was nothing but a typed list of names, yellowing, tacked in a shadow box hanging in the hall.

Because I was a WWII veteran myself (and my name already on the list) I volunteered to not only update the memorial, but to raise money to have the names cast in place on a bronze plaque, which would enhance the decor of our new courthouse.

Members of the Trust Authority warned they could not use tax dollars for the project. I promised to raise the money by private donations.

I got estimates of cost, began a campaign to raise at least $10,000, and had our courthouse architect design an eye-catching plaque. It turned out costing $17,000.

Our goal was to include every name of every man or woman from our county who served, regardless of where they happened to be living when entering service. This took time and a lot of work, not to mention the agony of having to deny the wishes of some veteran's widow that her husband didn't qualify because he was a Korean veteran, not WWII.

But the worst was yet to come. The plaque maker demanded a fifty percent down-payment when I placed the order. They then went broke and another firm took over their business. The new owners were hesitant about completing the order.

I was heartsick. I would be accused of stealing the money unless I would make up the difference out of my own pocket. Lucky for me, the new owners finally agreed to honor the order.

No idea or commission set forth in community service, I learned, is ever perfect in its finished version. There are simply too many fringe areas which turn out to be an injustice one way or the other.

You just do the best you can.

Sounds of Joy

I'd gone out that day with my camera to get a story on a school for handicapped kids.

I was so affected by little five-year-old Holly—blind, deaf, mute—that I couldn't sleep that night.

Some time around three o'clock, I guessed because I couldn't hear a sound—no cars going by, no dogs barking—I lay there staring wide-eyed into the deep and silent blackness and asked myself, "How would it feel to be locked for life like this in a totally dark, totally soundproof room?"

Like Holly, I couldn't see a thing there in the dark of the night, but her image was still in my mind, her lightly freckled face, her soft brown hair rubber-banded back into tiny pony tails on either side of her head.

Image? How did images form in Holly's mind? Her eyes saw nothing, her ears heard nothing. How could your mind possibly form images?

Yes, the program director had said when I told her on the phone the kind of story I had in mind. And, yes, you may take a photo of one of our pupils.

When I got there, she guided me into a room where a teacher was giving Holly lessons. The program director introduced me to the teacher.

"Call me Miss Cora," said the teacher. "That's how I'm known to Holly."

Puzzled, I glanced down at Holly, alone at her table, her tiny hands busy with her lessons, her small, delicate fingers feeling about furiously, her touch the only message to her brain, and wondered how she could form a name in her mind.

Miss Cora told me she was proud of Holly's progress. For instance, she explained, Holly already knew that she was not alone in the world, that there were other beings like herself; beings who had arms, legs, hair, fingers, and hands.

But what names would Holly give arms, legs, hair, fingers, and hands? She had to develop her own words simply to communicate with herself. What, for instance, would she call a hand which might be holding hers? Would she

338

conclude that all hands everywhere were larger than hers? If so, why? Would her own hand always be the smallest hand in the world?

Miss Cora explained that Holly had just learned to separate beans from elbow macaroni. She was making little sounds as she plunged her hands repeatedly into a plastic container on the table before her, picking up a bean or a piece of curled macaroni. If the object was a bean, she placed it in a plastic dish to her left; if it was a piece of curled macaroni, she placed it in the dish to her right.

The little sounds she made had to be sounds of joy, for I could see the excitement in the way her fingers "talked."

Holly kept her head down, working fast to finish her assignment. She felt each object carefully before placing it in the proper dish. She did not make a single error. If either container got too far away because she inadvertently bumped it with her fingers, she immediately pulled it back to its proper place.

Holly's score for that lesson was an A plus, the teacher said smiling proudly. You can't get any better than that.

I prepared my camera for a photo, reluctantly, even though I had a written release from Holly's parents, the only stipulation being I would not use her last name.

Name? What is a name? Such a simple question as this, which you and I think nothing of, has no meaning in Holly's world. Yet, somehow, she had learned her name is Holly; that her teacher's name is Miss Cora; that her mother at home is Mother.

She might have other "names" for these words, but whatever words she has for them, they mean the same thing in her secret language as they do in ours.

As I attached the flash to the camera, I found myself fighting against the feeling that I was, somehow, invading Holly's privacy. There was no way she could know what I was doing, even know what a camera was, or the images it would make on film. Holly would never see a photo of herself, not even her own face in a mirror.

I framed Holly in my viewfinder. She still had her head down, busy with her lesson. Good journalism dictated that I get faces in my pictures. I asked Miss Cora if she could help with posing Holly so I could get a full view of her face.

Without hesitation, the teacher cupped Holly's chin in her hand and lifted her face for me. Then Miss Cora used her fingers, pressing a message into Holly's palm. Holly dutifully obeyed, smiled nervously, and held her head up to pose as her teacher had messaged.

She never knew when I snapped the picture. She heard no click of the shutter, saw no blinding flash of light. I could only guess that she sensed, somehow, by our movements, that her picture had been taken, because she resumed work on her lesson, making her excited sounds of joy.

I felt better now, knowing that she was happy over getting her lesson right. She had to be saying to herself, "Hey! This is a piece of cake. Why doesn't my teacher give me something more challenging to do?"

Miss Cora told me Holly was very bright, that she learned exceptionally fast, that she would roam all through the building if you let her go, feeling her way along the walls and through the open doorways.

Would I be that brave if I were like Holly? On the other hand, aren't there many, many such unknowns, even in a world of sight and sound? Aren't we all simply feeling our way down the long hallways of life, through open doorways?

Holly's limitations are not limitations. They are only parameters to be tested.

Although Holly existed in a different world, her emotions were like any other five-year-old. When she got tired, she pushed the containers of beans and pieces of cut macaroni away and lay her head on the table. She began sliding both hands around on the smooth surface, as if she were searching for something.

"She's like any other child in school," Miss Cora explained. "She's anxious to get out of here and go home."

Suddenly, Holly seemed to sense there was a stranger in the room. She lifted her head, slid from her chair and began searching about the room, hands out, fingers feeling everything.

"Don't move," the teacher told me. "Let's see what she does when she finds you."

It was difficult to stand still when Holly's tiny hands touched my leg. She appeared puzzled by the long trousers covering them. What was she "seeing" when her fingers "saw" me? I wanted so badly to lift her in my arms, hug her tight to let her know I was her friend, to apologize—for what, I didn't know.

Instead, I gently patted her head, then knelt and held her little agile hands.

She smiled, embarrassed by my strange presence, and hurriedly retreated to hide her face in Miss Cora's skirt the way any shy child might do.

I felt a strange mixture of joy and heartache: joy at the way Holly handled her handicap, heartache knowing how much happier she would be if she could suddenly experience the extensions which normal eyesight and normal hearing would give to her existence.

When I was leaving the room, Holly tried to follow me. Her teacher reached for her, calling out instinctively, "No! It's not time to go home, Holly!"

Then, embarrassed for having thoughtlessly used a voice command, she took Holly's hands and moved them through the signs for "not time to go home yet."

Holly understood. The expression on her face showed she was saying to herself the same thing all other five-year-olds might say as the day winds down, "Oh, golly! Will this stupid school day ever end?"

Even when locked in her dark, soundproof room, Holly is a total person...just different.

Lying there in the dark at 3:00 in the morning, I thought how exciting it would be to go through life again—next time like Holly. What an adventure it would be, learning things from a totally different perspective, without sight and sound, without distorted prejudices acquired from others.

But I can't. One thing I can do, however: When circumstances give me the feeling the world's against me, I'll remember Holly. You can overcome any problem by solving the simple parts of it first—like separating beans from cut macaroni.

And making little sounds of joy while you're doing it.

Boots and Books

The idea of having a garage sale to raise money popped up in one of our Delaware County Historical Society board of directors meeting one day.

I don't like garage sales. I kept quiet.

One enthusiastic board member bubbled, "We could have the garage sale on the sidewalk right in front of the museum."

Our young curator pointed out it would also bring new people into our museum that weekend.

I squirmed in my chair. We needed the money all right. Among other things at the moment, we were facing $8,000 for a new roof. Then there were the ongoing operating expenses and staff salaries it takes to keep the building open for the public during business hours.

Without a product to sell, we had to resort to other means of raising money.

But garage sales, to me, are too much of a hassle. You drag things out you don't use anymore or have forgotten you had and put them up for sale.

You set a time—commence at 8:00, quit at 5:00.

Then the professional garage sale shoppers get there before you get out of bed and start rummaging through your stuff before you've had time to get your coffee made.

They're looking for bargains. And because they are professional garage sale shoppers, they know a bargain when they see one.

I know, I know. The garage sale is a noble American enterprise. But I don't even like going to one because I always worry about paying too much for something I've found that I want, and I'm too timid to bargain.

And clothes—I wouldn't know how to buy anything to wear if my life depended on it. Mom always bought clothes for me until I got out of high school and left home. Then the army dressed me. Before I got out of the army, Nita and I were married and she took over—may God bless her beauty and tolerance.

Nita and I have been forced to have one or two garage sales ourselves when

we were making major moves.

I was just as uncomfortable selling things at our own garage sales as I was trying to buy things at somebody else's garage sales.

The first time we had one, we worked hard the day before, laying all our stuff out. The professionals got there at daylight. They caught me in my shorty pajamas when I stepped out on the porch to get the morning newspaper.

To keep them from carrying things away without paying, I sat down in our patio chair in my shorty pajamas to read the paper and peeked over the top to keep and eye on them as they hurriedly tumbled things about looking for bargains.

I even caught one old lady eyeing my pajamas. I was afraid she'd grab me and take them off. I was happy when Nita came out in her robe to relieve me.

My theory on garage sales is you have them to get rid of stuff. Nita's theory is to make money, to get all you can out of each item.

So when she'd leave me in charge, I'd operate on my theory—the "get rid of it" theory—and be delighted to see people carrying things away.

But I have to admit that when I'd leave her in charge and she'd operate on her theory—make sure you sold it for what it was worth—more money would show up in our cash box.

The thing I could never figure out is why we always seemed to have more to put away after our garage sale was over than we had when we started.

But the biggest trouble we had with having our own garage sales was we couldn't decide what to put out to sell and what to keep.

What seemed worthless to me always turned out to be a precious memory to Nita. And when she started emptying our library shelves of all the action-adventure paperback books I'd already read, I'd grab them and put them back.

The written word is precious to me, always has been. I have boxes full of my own stuff, bits and pieces, hand-written, and typed, going back to my high school days.

These bad memories about garage sales was why I kept a low profile when our historical society was planning its garage sale.

The board voted to do it. Fine, I thought. It's not my idea. Just leave me out of it.

Our young, energetic curator began working months ahead of time. She sent word out to all members—bring us your stuff.

Amazingly, Nita and I didn't have the trouble we usually had going through things trying to decide what to sell—probably because we didn't begin gathering things up until the day before the sale and were in a hurry.

No trouble, that is, until I reached back in the far corner of my closet and pulled out a pair of cowboy boots I haven't worn in twenty years.

She snatched them from me, saying, "No way are we going to sell those, especially in a community-wide garage sale. They're too expensive. Besides that, I bought them for you for a Christmas present. Remember?"

Yes, I remembered. And I loved her for doing it. I'd wanted a pair I could wear with dress-up clothes. Standing tall in them, I felt proud.

But that was then. This is now, I argued. I have a hard enough time keeping my balance walking spraddle-legged in flat-heel shoes. I'd probably fall over on my face wearing my expensive cowboy boots.

But fair was fair. She would let me toss my cowboy boots on the pile of things if I would get rid of all those action-adventure paperback books in our home library that I'd already read.

It was a tough decision on my part. I loved my books. When you've always dreamed of being a best-selling author yourself, you like to study the style of those who are.

We put our stuff, including my cowboy boots and a box of books, in my pickup and I took it to the museum.

Our curator helped us unload, then dragged out her work schedule, listing names of the volunteers and hours they promised to work during the sale. She'd already talked with Nita, and she promised to be around, off and on, all weekend.

With pen poised, ready to write down my name for a two-hour tour of duty, she asked me which days and what hours I preferred to work.

I picked the eight-to-ten shift on Sunday morning.

Anybody with any sense, I figured, wouldn't be garage-sale-ing that early on a Sunday morning.

Still, I had nightmares about them leaving me in charge when it was going on. I knew my "just get rid of it" theory wouldn't work because the main purpose of our sale was to make money for the society.

I guess I could say, I told myself, "You can have that armload of stuff for two bits, if you'll donate ten bucks toward our roofing project."

I did, however, make secret arrangements with one of those professionals garage sales shoppers to buy my books. I told him I'd buy them back later.

I didn't sleep the night before my Sunday morning shift began, for worrying about it. But I made it just fine—by keeping in mind I was raising money for the society.

With smug satisfaction, I noticed my books were gone. My professional friend had done his job. I noticed, too—with a twinge of regret—that my cowboy boots were also gone. I vowed to make it up to Nita some day for selling one of her cherished memories.

My shift over, I went home, relieved that as far as I was concerned, the dad-blamed garage sale was over.

However, when Nita went to help close it down that evening and came home and told me we had taken in over $1,600, I was ecstatic.

There was only one problem left—how to get my books from my friend and back in our house without Nita finding out.

But even that problem dissolved that night when I was getting ready for bed and got into my closet to get my shorty pajamas.

There were my cowboy boots—back in the corner where they'd been sitting for twenty years.

I had to laugh. Nita had bought back my boots. I'd bought back my books.

And the Historical Society got the money, so our garage sale was, without a doubt, a resounding success.

The Little Lewis Whirlwind Legacy

He just lived to be six.

Barely old enough to be deeded a rocky, ravine-sliced, 160-acre piece of land on the rim of the Spavinaw Creek drainage basin.

Then he died.

His name, translated from Cherokee, was Little Lewis Whirlwind. At the age of six, he had been old enough to be put on the Dawes Roll when the federal government broke up the Indian tribal governments before Oklahoma Statehood in 1907, taking each tribe's land held in communal trust and deeding pieces of it to each tribal member.

The boy died the following year. Whoever wound up owning the 160 acres of useless land probably got rid of it as soon as he could because our nation's wealth back then was based on agriculture. If you couldn't raise crops, you were poor.

Most Cherokees chose to sell their property for cash or trade it for goods and services at the nearest white man's settlement now springing up in Indian Territory.

So Little Lewis Whirlwind's land was forgotten—until Fred Baumgartner saw it. He'd flown here from Wisconsin to buy a piece of land for himself and his wife, Marguerite, to retire on.

He took one look at the Little Lewis Whirlwind place, signed a real estate contract, and caught the next plane out to Wisconsin to pack and bring his wife.

"I never saw the house until we moved," Marguerite said admiringly when I went out to interview them for a news story. "I trusted his judgment. It was perfect. We have a nice house to live in with enough acreage where we could enjoy our retirement and still carry on our work."

They lived in a neat, split-level home sitting high on a ridge. From our seats in the living room, we had an expansive view across the lush green hills of the Spavinaw Creek drainage basin. I spotted a portion of the creek itself in a cleft between a pair of tall pines. Was that the place we used to go swimming? Us kids?

Fred was a small man with narrow shoulders and unusually long arms. When he talked he peered at you over his dark-rimmed glasses, always wearing that perpetual smile which all retired teachers seem to have.

Marguerite was tall, too, and had dark, rapid moving eyes, a sharp contrast to her unkempt white hair.

After introductions were over, Marguerite simply could not stop talking. She was so proud of her work. She was writing a book, she said, about humming birds.

She showed me her specimens, each dead and well preserved in tiny boxes.

Soon Marguerite wandered off, forgetting we were there, to check a hummingbird trap in the far corner of their spacious yard.

Sadly, I learned from Fred, Marguerite was in the beginning stages of Alzheimer's. She was needing closer and closer attention. Her care was getting to be too much for Fred. They had decided to sell their lovely home on the "Little Lewis Whirlwind Estate," as they called it, and move to Georgia to live next door to one of their sons.

Marguerite was aware of her condition, he said. They hated more than anything to give up their new home, which they had purchased only fifteen years earlier—after both retired from professorships. They taught courses in ecology and ornithology at Oklahoma State University for twenty-six years before taking positions at the University of Wisconsin.

The Baumgartners called their nature laboratory the Little Lewis Whirlwind Sanctuary. Strangely, I learned, neither could quite seem to grasp the concept of land allotments to members of Indian tribes before our statehood.

Probably because Fred was from Indianapolis and Marguerite grew up in Rochester, New York.

"But when we retired, we wanted to get back to Oklahoma," said Marguerite in one of her ramblings as Fred stood by silently, politely, to let her have her say. "We also wanted to settle in an area where we could continue our work, studying birds in their natural habitats."

They told me then that had both been working on a book about birds for forty years. They were actively seeking a publisher. The University of Oklahoma appeared definitely interested.

The couple kept right on working after retiring to the Little Lewis Whirlwind estate on the rim of the Spavinaw Creek basin. Fred spent hours tramping the woods and ravines with his binoculars dangling from a strap around his neck, looking, always looking, for that rare bird he'd never seen before.

Marguerite had caught, cataloged, banded, and released over three thousand humming birds since living on the Little Lewis Whirlwind estate.

In addition to their own bird-watching, they arranged to be included in the ecology curriculum with nearby universities, converting their estate into a nature laboratory.

As their classes grew, they had transformed the unwanted land into a useful outdoor classroom of learning for college students, complete with wilderness cabins and a large meeting hall where young men and women could have a place to eat and sleep and study nature by living with her.

It was a pleasure just listening to Fred talk, a poetic kind of communication.

"We named our home for its first owner," he said. "We have dedicated it to the dream of a sanctuary where all the Lewis Whirlwinds, of whatever age, ethnic background, occupation, or inclination, may find inspiration and strength in the eternal values of the natural world."

This was such a rugged, beautiful land with such a rich variety of vegetation, he said, his blue eyes dreamy.

"There's the soft green, rippling water of Spavinaw Creek, flowing over white gravel between towering, pine-clad bluffs and grassy flood plains, on its way out of the Ozark foothills before joining other steams which empty into the Arkansas River."

His style of speaking showed up in the curricula literature they published for university students. It read: "In our residence school of outdoor classes, we seek an aesthetic approach to the wonder and beauty of our world, for personal enrichment, for deeper insights into the whole environment, and for appropriate research.

"This is your invitation to participate in classes, exploring and learning together, with opportunity to look, listen, feel, taste, breath, saunter, scramble, float, study, and absorb the rugged beauty of the Old Cherokee Nation, the endless succession of the seasons, each with its own special message."

And the universities which participated gave students credit for their studies in ornithology at the Baumgartner "laboratory."

Walking around Baumgartner's Little Lewis Whirlwind Sanctuary and listening to Fred and Marguerite talk, you couldn't help but be infected with their enthusiastic feelings for this area.

Instead of their acreage being nothing but 160 acres of useless ground straddling a flint-rock ridge with deep ravines plunging away toward the Spavinaw Creek, to them it was the most beautiful place in the world.

Listening to them talk, I could not help but think back…

Fifty years ago, you could buy most all of this land in the Spavinaw basin for $5.00 an acre. But there were no buyers, for nobody could raise enough to feed their families on these flint-rock, heavily forested hills.

On my way back to my office, I thought of the story of the Ugly Duckling—the one about the swan's egg that was hatched in a duck's nest. The swan was so different from his duck siblings that he thought he was ugly—until he grew up and found out he wasn't a duck at all, but a beautiful swan.

Over time, I forgot about the Baumgartners, except to wonder occasionally what had finally happened—did they sell their 160 acres of rocky land and move to Georgia to be near their son because of Marguerite's condition?

The answer came about five years later in a package from Georgia addressed to Nita and me.

There was no enclosed letter—just a book. It's title? *Oklahoma Bird Life* by Fred and Marguerite Baumgartner.

They had done it! Forty years!

On the fly leaf, in a flowing script that only a retired teacher could have written, were the words: "Finally!—Love. Bs."

In it the Baumgartners included a list of 282 species of birds in our state, ranging from the Common Loon, the American Wigeon, the Eastern Phoebe, the Yellow-Rumped Warbler, the Rufus-Sided Towhee, and, of course, to the ever present and worrisome House Sparrow.

I noted the Baumgartners even gave the Sparrow its just due along with all the many other exotic species nobody knew existed.

Fred and Marguerite Baumgartner had looked for beauty, and found it on an ugly piece of land in the Spavinaw basin nobody wanted.

And produced a valuable piece of literature on the science of ornithology.

The legacy of Little Lewis Whirlwind.

Old Speedy Me

I was late.

Late for me means not being where I was supposed to be at least five minutes ahead of time.

I promised the guy I'd have his pickup back before six. He had some hauling to do himself, he said. When he said that, I thought perhaps he didn't want to loan it to me. But when I told him I really didn't need to do what I wanted to do that day, especially if it meant keeping him from doing whatever it was he wanted to do, he insisted I go ahead and take it.

He jangled the keys in front of me.

I took the keys and promised him faithfully I'd be back before six.

I glanced at my wrist watch. Five-thirty. And still forty miles to go.

I pressed the accelerator. The speedometer needle climbed. Seventy. Seventy-Five. Eighty.

Sixty is my comfortable driving speed. I began worrying that I'd get caught. I honestly don't think I've ever exceeded the speed limit a time in my life that I didn't get caught.

The first time a highway patrol stopped me was when Nita and I and another couple were on our way from Tulsa to Claremore. A Hawaiian luau, the party invitation read.

We were all dressed for the occasion. I had on a colorful shirt and white shorts, tennis shoes. I was also wearing a *lei* around my neck. And, being young, we'd all had a drink or two before leaving the house.

Boy, did I ever feel stupid when the highway patrol stopped me and I climbed out from under the wheel wearing a Hawaiian *lei*. I talked to him out of the side of my mouth so he wouldn't smell any alcohol. He was nice, trying desperately to keep from laughing out loud. He asked me where I was going in such a hurry. To a party in Claremore—a Hawaiian luau party.

He smothered a smile and gave me a warning ticket.

The two other times I got caught were both on the same day. That was the day I learned traffic officers loved to stop Cadillacs. My sister's husband had died. She lived in Cushing. I was living in Oklahoma City. I borrowed Nita's car, a new white Cadillac, to drive up to spend the day with my sister.

I went sailing up I-35, fretting about my little sister's situation. I turned off at the Guthrie exit to take the state highway to Cushing. I hadn't gone two miles when I glanced up at my rear view mirror and saw the highway patrol come racing up behind me, lights flashing like mad.

I thought he was in a hurry to get somewhere. I dutifully pulled over to let him pass—like a courteous driver was supposed to do.

He pulled in behind me. Made me get out and come sit in the front seat of his car with him while he began writing me a ticket for speeding.

I knew darn well I wasn't speeding when he pulled up behind me. The only thing I could figure out was that he had been coming to meet me on I-35 and clocked me with his radar gun. I suspected he thought I had turned off the four-laner trying to dodge him. He wasn't going to let nobody driving a Caddy outsmart him, so he whirled off the four-laner himself and ran me down.

I wasn't saying anything as he wrote up the ticket. No use arguing. Finally, he couldn't stand it any longer and wanted me to admit I'd tried to get away from him by exiting I-35.

"Where were you going, heading this direction?" he asked.

It wasn't any of his business where I was going. But I told him the truth, that my sister's husband had died and I was heading for Cushing.

He acted ashamed. But he went on ahead and wrote up the ticket, handed it over, and I got out and went on my way.

Then on my way back to Oklahoma City from Cushing later that day, I rounded the curve just outside the city limits of the small town of Coyle.

I suppose there was a speed limit sign there somewhere. I usually don't pay much attention to speed limit signs when I'm entering small towns. I've got enough sense to slow down enough to keep control of my car in all situations.

Then I saw him. A local police car was sitting parallel to the curb on the other side of the street facing me. He and I were the only two cars in town that day.

Sure enough, he turned on his red light, made a U-turn, and pulled in behind me.

I pulled over, crawled out, and went back to get in his car.

"It must be the Cadillac," I said as he began writing the ticket.

"What do you mean by a crack like that," he said. His hostile tone told me that I had guessed right.

Then I told him how a highway patrol had chased me down after exiting I-35 that morning.

He acted embarrassed, then said I really was exceeding the speed limit when I came around the curve, but he was only going to give me a warning ticket.

I told him I appreciated it, got in my wife's Cadillac and drove on back to Oklahoma City—real slow.

That's why I was in a heap of trouble that day being late getting the borrowed pickup back—I was in a big hurry, but was afraid I'd get caught.

I made the next curve as fast as I possibly could. I had a piece of pipe in the bed, which I had forgotten about. When I turned the corner, the pipe rolled.

It scared the devil out of me and I glanced back to see what the heck was making all that racket. Maybe a cop was back there.

My eyes were off the road only a fraction of an instant. That was enough. The right wheels dropped off the pavement. Instinctively, I jerked the steering wheel to the left to get back on the paving. Before I knew it, the truck shot across the highway and into the ditch on the other side. I yanked back to the right.

It was too much. All I remember, about the roll over, was seeing the glass shatter on the driver's side window an instant before my shoulder crashed into it. The next thing I knew, I was lying down in the seat.

The pickup had rolled only once, coming to rest on its wheels. But the top was caved in, the windshield shattered and popped out.

Dazed, I sat up, then tried the door. It opened, its hinges complaining loudly.

I stared at the truck. How could so much damage be done in so little time? I seemed to be okay myself, but the borrowed pickup was…well, a wreck. I picked up the shattered windshield and lay it in the truck bed.

A passing motorist slowed and pulled off on the shoulder.

"Are you all right?" he shouted.

"Yeah," I said.

I was so embarrassed to have done what I did that I didn't want to talk about it to anyone. I climbed back in, tried the switch, and the motor started. It seemed to be running fine.

The motorist gave me a dubious look and drove on.

By now, I was trembling so much that I could hardly shift gears. I drove the truck on home. You never realize how much good a windshield does for you until you don't have one. At thirty miles an hour, it feels like you're doing a hundred with the wind beating you in the face.

Besides that, I was going to be late getting the truck back like I had promised.

And not in a very good condition. I did stop and have the gas tank filled up as a gesture of appreciation.

Naturally, I promised to have the pickup fixed. I got estimates. My insurance company said the truck wasn't worth that much. Okay, I said. Just find me another one of that make and model and bring it to me.

I won the battle. I got enough money to pay for the truck.

Turned out the guy I borrowed it from had a friend who fixed the pickup like new for a lot less than my estimates. The guy got his truck back and made $500 on the deal.

I stick to my sixty miles per hour any more when I go anywhere.

Nor will I ever drive a Cadillac again.

And I quit wearing Hawaiian *leis* a long time ago.

The Shotpouch Hog Fry

Not only do we have a run for governor and US Senator this year, we also have new congressional districts. Then there will be state legislators, state senators, and county officers.

Every one of the candidates needs to attend the Shotpouch Hog Fry. I went to the one in 1990, swore I'd go every year from then on, but never did.

I wondered: Do they still have it?

Although I was born and raised in Oklahoma, I'd never heard of a hog fry until I came to Delaware County.

I was young then. I thought hog fries were political rallies at the city park. I never found out what a hog fry was until Nita and I retired and moved back home.

After I had agreed to help start a local paper, the political season was just getting started. A very nice-looking woman came into my office. She had coal black hair, dark eyes, and carried a hint of a smile on her lips. Cherokee.

She said her name was Melvina Shotpouch.

"We're having our annual Shotpouch hog fry next month. It's always on the last Sunday in August. We'd like to have you and Nita join us," she said.

It was an event everybody in the county looked forward to, especially during an election year. All politicians were invited to come, including candidates for governor and congress.

For governor? Congress? I could understand why legislators and county candidates attended. But not those for whom the local vote would be minimal.

A political rally is not news, but people are. I might make it a people story somehow. I agreed to go. She gave me directions.

It was held where her parents, Mike and Jewel Shotpouch, lived, on their original allotment land in a hollow northwest of Jay. The annual event started as the first birthday party for their twin boys in 1953.

It was so hot, Nita decided not to go.

I thought I was getting there early. But I found that all close-in parking spaces were already taken. I had to park on the side of the gravel road a good distance from the Shotpouch home. I got out and began walking. A big Greyhound bus almost ran over me as it went by, billowing dust, its campaign banners flapping. A gubernatorial candidate.

I felt proud, hiking on down the dusty road. Here we were, one of the least populated counties in the state, on the lowest level economically. And yet they came, in person.

Topping the hill above the hollow, I stared in amazement at the people swarming the area, sitting in lawn chairs in the shade of trees. A spring bubbled from under a ledge, sending a tiny stream edging away along the foot of a low bluff.

Kids—blond-headed Caucasians and black-headed Cherokees—played in the stream, not caring, or even knowing, from which race they came. Many were cousins, probably, because nobody paid any attention to race, and when you fell in love with someone, kids followed. If the truth were known, most were mixed blood. I didn't even know my Nita was part Cherokee until years after we were married.

Ladies were busy spreading food across the long tables under an outdoor shelter.

Politicians milled about shaking hands and smiling. Great. It made you feel good, hobnobbing with the news-makers of our county, state, and nation.

The person I really wanted to meet, however, was the man who put this gigantic feed together every year. I found him stoking wood into the fires under the large iron pots full of bubbling grease.

Huge chunks of the freshly butchered hog lay on a table and men were busy dicing it into smaller pieces.

They dropped the bite-size morsels into the pots of boiling grease, allowed them to cook a few minutes, then ladled them out with a flat wooden paddle and dropped them into a cardboard box.

Two strong boys would carry the cardboard boxes to the food shelter, hoisting them up onto the tables, already seriously sagging under the weight of food.

In fancy French restaurants, they called this type of cooking "fondue." Same thing.

Mike Shotpouch agreed to let me take his picture. He was sweating profusely from working so near the fire, his eyes watering from the smoke.

He smiled as he wiped his face with a clean white handkerchief.

He was a big man, obviously a full-blood Cherokee, rugged face, broad shouldered.

"This is the biggest crowd yet," he told me after letting me take his picture.

He had to kill four hogs this year, he said. One hog weighed over four hundred pounds. The other three weighed almost as much.

He was beginning to get worried that he wasn't going to have enough. But his twin boys, busy working the pots, reminded "Pop" a lot of people had brought fried chicken.

A man came by, slapped Mike on the shoulder, and slipped him a twenty dollar bill. Thanks, Mike said and pocketed the money.

"People help out, ever how much they can," Mike explained. "It comes out about even every year."

Leaving him, I slipped him a twenty myself.

Not far away, Melvina and some of her sisters, along with a host of neighbor women, had their hands deep into large pans, working flour, water, and other ingredients into globs of dough. It was cut into squares and dropped in the bubbling grease. When ladled out, it became Indian fry bread.

Down at the far end of the shelter, a musical group got itself organized and began playing everybody's favorite country and western tunes. Old folks listen with smiles on their faces, patting their feet on the grass.

Somehow, it all came together at high noon. When a minister raised his hands, all talking ceased, parents shushed kids playing in the stream, and men working the pots of boiling grease removed their hats and bowed their heads.

The minister prayed in Cherokee. I had no idea what he was saying until he repeated it in English for dummies like me. He called on the Lord to continue blessing the Shotpouch family, to bless the food, and be with all those who may be in pain and grief wherever they might be.

He even asked the Almighty to watch over the political candidates and help them make the right decisions when elected. I wondered if any of them, especially those who would go to Washington, would remember this humble prayer said for them by a Cherokee minister in the hollow beside the Shotpouch home.

At his Amen, the talking resumed, punctuated by the kids' sharp cries of joy over being turned loose again.

Eventually, I worked my way to the front of the line and held out my paper plate so the ladies could pile it full of beans, potatoes, roasting ears, and condiments.

You helped yourself to the meat. I forked up a couple pieces of fried chicken just in case I found I didn't like the fresh hog meat. I eyed the dessert table loaded down with pies, cakes, and puddings. The huckleberry cobbler looked the best. I would return for it.

I found a rock ledge in the shade beside the stream where I could sit down and balance my plate on my knees.

The food was delicious, including the fresh hog meat. As I ate, the string band swung into one of my favorite tunes which Bob Wills had made famous— "Dusty Skies."

Life couldn't get any better than this, I thought.

I tried to imagine what it was like before statehood, here in the Cherokee Nation, when families like this gathered for reunions.

I could not help but feel as if I were an intruder. Welcome, but an intruder all the same. I had no idea of my own ethnic background. Just white, was all I knew. I did not want them to not like me because of the color of my skin.

I took refuge in the thought that Nita's father was listed on the famous Dawes Commission rolls.

That hog fry was twelve years ago. I knew Mike Shotpouch had died recently. I wondered if the tradition died with him.

I picked up the phone and dialed. Melvina is an old friend now. She works at the courthouse. She is also a member of the Cherokee Nation governing council.

Her voice was as pleasant as ever. I asked if her family was still carrying on the traditional hog fry which her parents began half a century ago.

"Yes," she said. I detected a note of pride in her voice. "We're still doing it— my four brothers, four sisters, and me."

That surprised me. "Same time, same place?" I asked.

"It'll be August twenty-fifth this year. Are you coming?"

"I have to," I promised. "It's the only decent place to be in the middle of a political campaign."

Where politicians get blessed.

Scat the Cat

Uh-oh.

I knew I had a public relations disaster on my hands when our granddaughter Dori Beth came riding her bike up to where I was sitting in my favorite chair on the carport, stopped, and pointed at the old gray striped cat crossing the corner of our yard and said, "Aren't you going to scat the cat?"

I didn't mind my neighbors knowing I scatted cats, but I sure didn't want Dori Beth to know her gentle, loving grand-dad scatted cats.

She loved animals, had two cats at her home in Tulsa, plus a hamster which I had teasingly called a rat one day, and I thought I'd lost the love of my grandchild forever.

I tried my best to explain to her why I scatted cats.

They persist in using my flower bed to go to the bathroom. I'd covered it with cypress mulch to make a place for Nita to set out her potted ferns and flowers.

And I love the view sitting in my favorite chair on the car port.

I admitted that cats think the field of mulch is for their convenience, but that doesn't make me feel any better each time I have to shovel up the mess and get rid of it.

Dori Beth seemed to understand and rode away on her bike.

I sulked. I've chased away cat after cat. Usually after three or four times, an intelligent, gentlemanly or lady-like cat will get the message and take his or her habits somewhere else.

But not that old striped gray cat. While he'll move when I stomp my foot and yell scat, he won't move very far. Then he'll look back at me as if to ask, "Do you mean me?"

If there ever was an alley cat, this is one. When I yell scat, he might go to the home south of us or to the one north of us.

It's very mystifying. How do you chase a cat away when there is no "away" to chase him to?

Just then Dori Beth came racing back on her bike.

"Grand-dad, come quick," she panted. "I found something."

She led me to the back yard and pointed. It was a dead mole.

"How did it get dead?" she asked.

Immediately I saw this as my chance to turn around the public relations disaster I'd gotten myself into for scatting cats.

"Old Scat the Cat did it," I said, not knowing for sure. But when you are in a war, a little fib here and there is necessary to win over public opinion.

"We need to bury him," she said.

"I'll go get a shovel," I volunteered, hoping to gain some PR points.

"And I'll make a tombstone," she said.

I got the shovel. She found a wooden stake and wrote on it with a magic marker: Here lies Chirpy the Mole—Died November 23, 2001.

Chirpy?

Why, of course. You bury a person, he's got to have a name, doesn't he? I started digging.

"Bury him deep," Dori Beth said. "We don't want a dog digging him up."

"Or Scat the Cat," I threw in—still trying to win her over to my side in my war with the gray cat.

I dug a real deep hole. I gently placed the limp Chirpy down into it. Dori insisted on covering him up herself. She didn't want any rocks in the dirt. Rocks hurt, she said.

After driving down the stake with Chirpy's name on it. I backed away, waiting for Dori Beth's approval.

To my surprise, she solemnly stepped up beside the marker and began speaking, "We are gathered here today on the twenty-third of November, 2001, in memory of Chirpy, who died—"

When she paused, I urged, "Fighting for his life with Scat the Cat."

She considered my suggestion for a long moment, finally agreed, and went on with her eulogy.

I knew then I had won my PR battle. I felt so jubilant that when Dori Beth finished her eulogy, I snapped to attention, whipped up a smart military salute, and made a sound with my lips as if I were blowing taps.

"Oh, Grand-dad —!"

She came at me, embarrassed over such foolishness. Realizing I'd almost lost her by overplaying the act, I apologized, pulled her to me, and hugged her tight.

She accepted my apology.

Now I was free to continue with my covert war. Every time I saw Scat the Cat lounging in the shade on my front porch, or under my pickup, I'd check around to make sure no neighbors were watching, and I'd sneak out to scat him.

Boy, he hated it when I woke him up from a nice nap, and he'd give me a dirty look as he moseyed off in the direction of one or the other of houses he belonged to, if either one.

Scatting the old gray cat is a very demeaning duty. Even Nita has told me I've gone off my bonkers scatting cats.

But each time I'd try to act civilized and ignore that old gray cat, I'd find a mess in the mulch in my flower bed and that evil being inside me would rise up and scream, "Catch that blankety-blank cat and ring his blankety-blank neck!"

Scat the Cat escalated our war by hiding behind a tree and trying to catch birds using my bird bath. I'd watch angrily out my window as the birds would come in after a hard day's work finding food and try to get a drink of water and take their daily baths.

They'd have to flutter around up in the trees, fussing at Scat the Cat, until I'd go out and scat him away.

I don't think it's right for somebody else's pet to come into my yard and mess around with my pets. This includes my squirrels.

I almost broke my leg one day when I glanced up from my computer and saw Scat the Cat stalking one of my squirrels.

The squirrel had bounded across the street to pick up some nuts under a tree in a neighbor's yard.

Old Scat the Cat had slipped out from behind a bush and ran to flatten himself below the edge of the paving, positioning himself right in the path which the squirrel would have to take coming back to his tree home in my yard.

I jumped up to go scat the cat and save the squirrel and tripped over the bottom drawer of my desk, which I had pulled out to get something and forgot to close.

I danced around holding my shin, and watched in agony as the squirrel got his nut and headed back for his home in the tree in my yard.

I just knew he'd had it, for there was old Scat the Cat lying right in his path.

The squirrel didn't seem to mind. Just as old Scat the Cat leaped, the squirrel ran under him in a flash and headed for home, his tail high, his nut in his mouth.

I laughed and applauded.

I finally got my chance to end the war once and for all one night when a storm came up. It was raining, lightning and thundering something fierce. I went the door to look out.

I flipped on the car porch light and there was old Scat the Cat sleeping on top of my car, snug and warm in out of the storm.

My internal being exploded with anger. If I catch him——!

I sneaked out the door in by bathrobe and made a mad dash to grab him.

Just as I lunged, Scat the Cat woke up and dodged under my grasping hands like the squirrel had done him. He ran off into the storm.

I almost broke a rib hitting the side of the car.

If it hadn't been storming so bad, I swear I would have chased him into the night and caught him at whichever neighbor's house he ran to.

Well, I consoled myself as I came back into the house, holding my bruised ribs, I bet I put the fear of God in him this time, and he wouldn't be back any more.

I was wrong. The next morning, I found a fresh pile of cat waste—not in the mulch in my flower bed, but right out in plain sight on my car port in front of my favorite chair.

That did it. Now it's open war. One of these days I'll be burying Scat the Cat beside Chirpy the Mole, and when I do, I sure won't be blowing taps with my lips, I'll be whistling and singing Happy Days Are Here Again!

Just Tiger and Me

When a voice on the phone told me about a ninety-year-old man who made fiddles using wood from sycamore trees, I was skeptical.

I'd seen a TV special once about the Stradivarius violin, how its wood, even its varnish, contributed to its exquisitely beautiful sound.

Still… making a violin, especially from an Oklahoma sycamore tree, is a story.

The caller told me the man's name. Harvey. I thanked him, then looked up Harvey's number and called.

"Hello," came the thin, but upbeat voice.

I identified myself and asked did he mind if I came out to interview him.

"Interview me? What for?" he asked, surprised. "I've never done anything."

"They tell me you make fiddles," I said. "Is that true?"

"Awww," he groaned in disbelief, then laughed and added, "Go ahead and come on out if you want to. There ain't nobody here but just Tiger and me."

Tiger?

My interest sky rocketed. Who was Tiger?

Harvey was standing in his front yard when I drove up. I hooked a finger in my camera equipment bag and got out. He came to meet me, a wide grin on his face.

He was a tall man, slender, lost in his roomy overalls. His alert, clear blue eyes fairly twinkled behind his rimmed glasses. You wouldn't guess he was ninety— eighty, perhaps, but not ninety. He brushed back his thinning white hair with one hand and motioned with the other.

"Come on in," he said, embarrassed but pleased, I could tell.

I followed him across the yard and kept looking around for something or someone who might be called Tiger. I saw no one.

Inside, he waved a hand toward an overstuffed chair. I settled into it, setting my camera bag on the floor. I glanced around for Tiger.

As in all interviews, you begin by getting acquainted—chit-chatting about backgrounds.

Harvey had lived all his life in the county. He grew to manhood farming. He met his wife, Violet, when haying for a neighbor. Courting her, he rode his horse through ten miles of wilderness to and from her house. He eventually asked her to marry him, and she accepted.

They worked their little farm until they had put all of their five kids through school. He retired at sixty-five. They sold their farm and moved to town.

He'd lost his beloved Violet ten years ago, he told me with deep sadness. He lived alone now—just him and Tiger.

I simply could not connect hard farm work with making violins. His love for music, perhaps?

"No," he confessed. "I don't know a thing about music."

This was unbelievable.

"I'd like to get a picture of you and one of your fiddles," I said.

He seemed pleased. He got up and disappeared through a curtained doorway into his bedroom. He returned with a fiddle cradled in one arm.

A striped gray cat was trotting at his heels. When the cat saw me, it arched its back and hissed.

"Tiger!" Harvey scolded, and reached down and stroked the cat until it calmed down.

So this was Tiger. The cat settled at Harvey's feet and kept throwing mean looks my direction. I could tell right off he didn't like me, an intruder.

As I prepared my camera, I asked, "So? How do you go about making a fiddle?"

He laughed softly and picked up the well-crafted instrument, saying, "I make mine out of native sycamore." Then he added, as if in apology, "Good fiddles are supposed to be made from maple."

"How do you go about shaping the wood, all those thin pieces and everything?" I asked.

First off, you have to have patience, he said. Believe it or not, the hardest part was carving the knurl at the end of the neck, the piece where the keys are that you turn to put the right tension on your strings.

The knurl he showed me did look—well, as if it had been carved by an old man with a slight tremble in his hand.

The "box" was fashioned from thin slabs of wood, very thin slabs. He said he would spend as much as a month or more scraping and shaping these thin pieces.

"Then you have to soak them in water and gradually mold them into the shape you want," he said. He shuffled out into the kitchen and brought back a long piece of thin wood, still dripping water. He showed me how far it could be bent while wet without breaking. Almost double, in fact, like folding a piece of heavy paper.

He told me how he'd carved the grooves for the narrow inlays. "But that's just for looks," he said bashfully. "All those pretty designs don't help the sound one bit."

What does he do with his fiddles?

"Give them away," he said. "Mostly to my family."

The one he was showing me, still unfinished, was the only one he had left.

As I fixed the flash attachment to my camera, I explained the kind of picture I wanted to go with the story—him playing.

"I'm not very good," he admitted.

"You got to be kidding! How can you make a musical instrument as complicated as a fiddle if you can't play? Why would you even bother to try?"

"It was just something I always wanted to do," he said.

He finally confessed he sneaked in a tune now and then. "When no one's here but Tiger and me," he said with a deep, body-shaking chuckle. He bent over to stroke the cat's back again and asked, "Ain't that right, Tiger?"

The cat swiveled his ears, looked up, and blinked his answer. I assumed Tiger said yes, by the way Harvey smiled down at him.

Then Harvey tucked the fiddle under his chin and poised his bow.

"Wait a minute," I said. "Let's be sure we get Tiger in the picture."

I could have sworn Tiger frowned at me. Harvey lowered his fiddle, and patted his thigh.

"Up here, Tiger."

The cat ignored the call. I know Tiger understood. His ears twitched, but he refused to budge. He swung his green, slitted eyes on me as if to say, "What do you want with us?"

Tiger and I weren't getting along very well.

Harvey reached down, hooked a skinny hand under the cat, and lifted him, limp as a rag, to his knee.

"He's getting a little old," Harvey apologized, then laughed. "Arthritis, I suppose. Like me."

Tiger kept his accusing eyes on me as Harvey put the fiddle under his chin and his bow to the strings.

The fiddle squawked. I focused the camera, careful to get Tiger in the frame, and fired. The flash blinded Tiger. With an angry yowl, he leaped off Harvey's knee and was just a gray blur disappearing through the curtained doorway into the bedroom.

Sorry, Tiger, I thought, wanting to laugh and apologize at the same time.

Harvey kept right on playing, his eyes closed.

Tiger was right. I *was* an intruder. I quietly broke my camera apart and put it away.

I was embarrassed for Harvey, the way he was playing. I didn't know beans about music, but I knew enough to know that wasn't beautiful violin music.

I didn't know what to do, say see you later, or what.

A movement at the curtain caught my eye. It was Tiger. He padded softly across the room and hopped up to land like a feather on the couch. He curled down contentedly against Harvey's thigh.

Suddenly, the harsh musical notes became softer, more mellow. I could not for the life of me place the haunting tune Harvey was playing. I glanced at him sheepishly, intending to ask.

But I didn't because his eyes were still closed, his bow gliding effortlessly across the strings, the notes filling the room with lovely music.

I knew that what I was hearing, while not a Stradivarius, was no ordinary fiddle music.

How could such a sweet sound be coming from a homemade box made of common old sycamore wood found all up and down the creek bottoms here in Oklahoma?

Harvey kept playing as I picked up my camera bag to leave. I hesitated. What should I do? Interrupt and tell him I was leaving?

Tiger's slitted eyes were fixed on me. His expression said, "Just go."

Then I understood.

"There's nobody here but just Tiger and me," Harvey had said.

I left quietly, knowing that what I was hearing wasn't fiddle music at all.

It was the sweet sound of two lonely souls in love.

The Root Canal

Our Planning & Zoning Board met the other night. They weren't enough for a quorum—only two members, our chairman and me, besides the mayor, our secretary, and guest, who was the new president of our bank. He was there because he had volunteered to serve on the board.

One of the items on the agenda was to recommend to the city council that the young man be appointed to fill the vacancy on the board.

But without a quorum present, we couldn't even do that.

While we waited for at least one more member to show up, we talked about really important stuff—root canals.

The mayor started it. He said he'd just had one and couldn't talk very well.

Our chairman said he'd had one some time ago and wondered how much they cost today.

I was proud to report what they cost because I'd just had one recently myself.

The young bank president maintained a pleasant smile during this brilliant conversation. He is a young man. He doesn't understand about root canals. Once you have one, you're a veteran. You can discuss the procedure in detail with your fellow root-canalites.

I didn't believe it when my dentist said one of my back molars needed a root canal. I'd already had one on another tooth, and it wasn't any fun.

My dentist is a tall young man, strong and likeable—if you could like a dentist.

"It won't hurt," he explained, patting me on the arm. "I'll deaden your gum and you won't feel a thing."

He didn't know me. It made no difference how much novocaine he shot me with, my imagination went into high gear when he started drilling. It felt like he had a jackhammer and I felt it all through my skull and down my back bone.

"It's not the pain I'm afraid of," I told him. "It's my imagination. Can you do something to deaden my brain?"

"Nope," he said. "Your brain is about as dead as it can get already."

We were friends. But he didn't understand about my imagination.

Like when his nurse yanked on a lever on the side of the chair, flopping me backwards. I felt like I was going to be executed, stretched out and defenseless. Then when the dentist came at me holding his needle, it looked a mile long with poison dripping out the end of it.

"There'll be just a little stick," he warned.

"Heck, I know that," I bragged. "I'm not afraid of needles."

He nodded knowingly and said, "Open wide."

I shut my eyes and opened my mouth.

It stuck and I flinched. I thought I heard him snicker. He jabbed here. He jabbed there. He jabbed everywhere.

"Okay," he said, patting my arm again. "We'll wait a few minutes so the medicine can numb the area."

He said something to the nurse and left the room. I peeked up at the nurse.

"I hope he has an emergency in Dallas," I wished out loud.

I don't think she thought that was very funny. I was in big trouble, I thought. I felt my face getting numb.

About that time the dentist came back. Just the sight of him made me tense all over.

"Open wide," he said.

I did. The nurse hung a crooked suction tube over my lower lip. It made a hellacious noise, sucking stuff out. It even tried to get hold of my tongue and suck it out. I didn't care if it had—my tongue was so numb I didn't think I'd ever be able to use it again.

The dentist came at me with his singing drill. The water squirting out of it was for my benefit, I knew, but I imagined that without it that singing drill would get so hot it would burn my dead tongue.

The drill sang. The water squirted and splashed and filled my mouth and ran down my chin. The nurse tried to keep it mopped up. I couldn't keep from swallowing a bunch of it.

I became rigid. My toes curled up. I imagined that drill going deeper and deeper. I knew there was a nerve down there somewhere.

My imagination brought back the picture of the time when I worked with my Dad on an oil well drilling rig. The heavy bit would grind up rocks down in the hole so it would wash out with water.

I just knew my dentist was going drilling for oil down underneath the roots of my tooth.

"That's odd," he mumbled, pausing to take a closer look.

What! What! What! I wondered. Had he hit oil?

"That tooth of yours has three roots instead of just two."

Oh, mercy! Does that mean it'll cost a third more? I'd had sense enough to get an estimate before we started. But he never said it depended on how many roots your tooth had. I tried to remember how much money I had in the bank.

"What do you think of the war in Afghanistan?" the dentist asked.

It took my mind off my bank account.

"Wug gook woogy gaa—" I said, but stopped because just then he rammed both fists into my mouth.

I regretted not being able to tell him about the war in Afghanistan, because I'm an expert on it. I listen to all the news on television and read two papers every day and I don't know as much as anybody else doesn't know. That makes me an expert.

"Put your hands down," the dentist said.

I didn't know I had my hands up. I guess I was trying to push him away.

"Oog ah," I apologized and dropped my hands down out of the way.

The dentist pounded and pecked, poked and pulled. I stiffened even more. I didn't want him to roll me off the chair I was lying on.

And all the while he and the nurse were chatting away about their kids and school lessons and how nice SUVs were. I wanted to get in the conversation. I thought it would help me relax.

"Ah guggle uh ochk," I said, swallowing another mouthful of water.

"I agree with you one hundred percent," the dentist said.

Then he ignored me and went back to work. When the drilling was finished, I closed my eyes and tried to relax and uncurl my toes.

Then he started the hard part. He picked up a steel wire roughed up like a wood rasp and began jabbing it up and down in the holes in my tooth, trying to get all the old nerves out.

You think it's old nerves. What else could it be down in that hole?

Once Dad and I lost a bit in the hole when we were drilling that oil well. We had to fish it out. Dad made a contraption about twenty feet long, with prongs on it that weighed no telling how much. We dropped it down in the hole, snagged the lost drill bit, and yanked it out.

That's exactly what I thought of when the dentist was standing over me jabbing that wire rasp up and down into the hole in my tooth.

Then he got it caught and began tugging on it. I was so stiff, I thought he raised my entire upper body with only my heels left touching the couch.

Then whatever he was after came out. I plopped back down on the chair. The water in my stomach gurgled.

"There," he said. He sounded relieved.

What did he mean "there"?

Was he giving up? Was he going to drag out the jackhammer again? I prayed. Oh, please, God. Don't let him do that again.

He didn't. He simply filled the tooth and put a crown on it.

Finally, after two and a half hours, the dentist ordered X-rays, looked at them, and said, "Perfect. You can go now."

If you've never seen a body stiff as a log try to stand up, you should have seen me struggle to get out of that chair. I finally wound up rolling off.

They handed me the bill.

I didn't even look at it twice. I would have paid anything—any amount at all—just to get out of there.

When I got home, Nita asked, "How'd it go?"

I rubbed my numb cheek and said, "I'bb oobed ga buh."

Then she petted me a little. So everything came out all right.

It was an excellent Planning & Zoning Board meeting that we didn't have, talking about the misery of having root canals.

A Lovely Gray Dove

There was no mournful music being piped in. I'd never been alone with a dead person before. I didn't know what to expect of my emotions. I closed the door softly, muffling all exterior sounds. I selected a place on one end of a nearby sofa to sit down.

With the briefest of a glance at the body with soft gray hair lying in the coffin, I made a quick scan of the unusual number of flower arrangements sitting about the room, on the floor, on tables, across the casket.

That was understandable. Mazie had many friends. Fact was, I doubt there was a single solitary person in her whole life who ever had the slightest dislike for Mazie.

Of course I thought the dozen peach roses Nita and I sent in the name of our family were the prettiest. And the most appropriate.

I smiled, knowing Mazie didn't have to worry anymore about how flowers sometimes triggered her asthma, sending her rushing to the hospital in an ambulance.

Odd. Instead of sadness, I felt an undefinable peace, being alone with Mazie.

When you're growing up, big sisters are sorta up there somewhere on the same plane with your mother.

You don't ever really know them. They're always in the kitchen helping Mom fix a meal when relatives come and kids are outside playing.

You aren't even aware of her at school because she is so many grades ahead of you.

But I was always proud of her because she was so pretty— coal black hair, smooth complexion, a fully developed body. Even though she was studious and serious almost to a fault, her quick smile and infectious laughter could spread joy in an instant.

I felt sorry for some of the more popular boys who flirted with Mazie but got nowhere. They didn't fit.

When the superintendent announced at Mazie's graduation that she was valedictorian, I whispered to Mom, "What's valedictorian?"

She shushed me up. You're not supposed to talk in church and at graduation exercises.

So I waited until after it was over and asked Mazie, "What's a val—"

By then I'd forgotten how to say it.

"Valedictorian?" she finished for me, smiling and patting me on the head. "That's just a person who studies hard and gets their lessons."

But I knew by the way all the other kids in her class kept coming up and congratulating her that valedictorian was more than just getting your lessons.

That's when I first began to realize, I suppose, that my big sister was somebody special.

So I wasn't too surprised when she walked right out of high school and into Doc Phillips' clinic to become his much-needed nurse.

There were many in the community who felt more comfortable confessing their ailments to Mazie than to old Doc. But Doc understood and contentedly stayed in the background and let Mazie do the "doctoring" in cases like that.

From her meager salary, Mazie would find a dime almost every Saturday and slip it to me so I could go to the show and not miss important episodes of the exciting serial.

Then it just seemed that all at once, Mazie was gone. Doc Phillips thought she had too good a mind to waste bandaging bruises and cuts in our small town. He urged her to take nurse's training at a hospital in Tulsa.

Nurse trainees lived in dormitories. They took classes during the morning, did slave work janitoring and performing hygienic duties for bed patients in the afternoon, and studied at night.

Mazie came home with a friend once in a while. Her name was Thelma. Her folks were rich and Thelma owned a brand new '36 Ford coupe. It had yellow wheels.

Thelma would take us riding in her new car that smelled good and rode smooth.

I simply couldn't understand why Mazie wanted to be a nurse, especially after she told me about having to scrub the floor in the morgue where there were a lot of dead people around.

But Mazie stuck with it for three years. She made the highest score ever recorded in state history on her final nurse's exam.

She never boasted or bragged about it. Her friend Thelma was the one who told us. With a score like that, Thelma said, Mazie could go to work anywhere for anybody and get the highest pay.

Then war came and turned everybody's lives upside down, separating families.

I had been in the army and away from family for months before I got to go home on furlough. Nita and I decided to get married. I announced it to Mom and Dad and wrote letters later to others in the family.

I don't remember ever writing Mazie and telling her.

Thinking back, that puzzles me. Why didn't I write to Mazie telling her about Nita and me?

Maybe it was because I didn't want to hurt her feelings. She didn't even have a boyfriend yet and here I was, her baby brother, getting married.

I suspected one of the reasons she didn't have a boyfriend was because she had started having asthma attacks. Knowing Mazie, if she couldn't be a perfect girlfriend for a boy, she wouldn't be one at all.

When Mom wrote and told me Mazie was getting married and going to New York to be with her new husband, I was so stunned that I studied the letter a long time, trying my best to picture Mazie being in love like any other mortal.

And the guy's name was Zeke. Well, that wasn't his real name, I was to learn later. His real name was Matthew. But Zeke fit him better.

I didn't get a chance to meet Zeke until after the war. In an instant, I knew they were the perfect couple—he was so kind, gentle, understanding. But most of all, he was obviously deeply in love with my big sister.

Mazie had done it again—she brought me a perfect brother-in-law, a cherished friend, another big brother to love and adore.

Well, would you expect anything less from Mazie than to get a perfect husband?

We tried our best to return to normal life after the war. I enrolled at Oklahoma University. Mazie went back to work as a nurse. Zeke was a master electrician, the kind contractors pay premiums just to have on their jobs.

I had to have an expensive operation while I was at Oklahoma University. Mazie was so well respected in the medical community where she worked, they waived all fees just for her.

I was humbly grateful, and my love for my big sister deepened.

But I thought she and Zeke made a terrible mistake when they bought an acreage south of Claremore with a small fixer-upper ranch home on it. Zeke had a dream—he wanted to raise cattle. They would commute to their jobs in Tulsa.

I thought country living would aggravate Mazie's asthma, especially living in an older home and helping work cattle.

With their two children, they struggled like all young couples do, trying to raise a family, get ahead financially, make their dreams come true.

Their cattle enterprise did grow. They purchased more land. Mazie kept books as well as pitched hay to help the man she loved realize his dream.

As the years slipped by, Mazie's hair turned from solid black to a soft gray.

They never spent lavishly fixing up their little ranch home. It was comfortable, which I thought fitted Mazie's personality perfectly. She was never one to show off.

Mazie never complained, even when arthritis attacked her joints. As her health worsened and she was unable to meet the rigors of the nursing profession, she did volunteer work for the church, serving in its nursery and teaching Sunday school classes.

I was to learn from her associates in church that Mazie was the sweetest, kindest, most unselfish person they ever knew.

I have never in my life enjoyed fifteen minutes alone with Mazie as much as I did that morning in the funeral home.

For I knew that now she was free of those severe asthma attacks, of painful arthritis that distorted her joints. She was free of worrying about her loved ones, free from all the troubles in the world.

After the funeral service, and the family gathered for one last time at their modest ranch home, I noticed a lone gray dove that came circling down to land on the front lawn.

It was too late in the season for birds. But there it was. The kids, laughing, ran to try and catch it. It fluttered upward, untouchable, I knew, as it circled slowly before flying away.

I watched in silence as the speck disappeared in the darkening sky. I knew it was Mazie.

A lovely gray dove, leaving, her final goodbye.

Community Achievement Award

Mr. Chamber of Commerce President—

Honored Guests—

I have been asked to make this presentation, the Community Achievement Award. It will be given posthumously, for Anna Mae Kelly is not here tonight.

But I can imagine seeing her—that quick, shy smile, those attentive blue eyes. When Anna Mae looked at you, she gave you her full and undivided attention, filling you with a sense of worth no matter who you were.

I've known Anna Mae—we all called her Ann—for half a century. A few short months before she passed away, I went into her clothing store to discuss business with her. She was behind the register, sitting on a high stool. She apologized for not getting to her feet.

The apology shocked me. It also brought my attention to the fact that I had seldom seen her sitting down—especially when she was at work.

I knew she wasn't seeking pity. She would never do that. But she knew I would understand. She and I were patients of the same lung specialist in Tulsa. We often exchanged comments about our symptoms—mostly joking about not being able to run around the block anymore.

When I left her that day, I couldn't help thinking: We all die sometime. But I simply could not visualize Jay without Ann Kelly.

This unique person was born in the Zena community on December 9, 1921, the daughter of Ollie and Leila Praytor.

She attended local elementary schools.

And it was there she saw this tall boy in the class ahead of her. He had a slow smile every time he looked her direction. His name was Clyde Kelly. They became childhood sweethearts.

I wasn't there when, later, Ann and Clyde first realized they were in love.

But I can imagine it.

It happens to all of us.

There's the thrill of that first touch, of holding hands. You walk together, talking about silly things—cloud formations in the sky, if it's daytime, the moon and big dipper at night.

They both graduated from Grove High School. Clyde first. He went to California to work.

Did Ann ever dream about building a life outside Delaware County?

Perhaps. But I doubt it.

She did go away in 1940 to attend Tulsa Business College. But she brought her new skills back to Delaware County and became a court reporter in our courthouse.

Then the unthinkable happened—our country was drawn into the most devastating war that ever happened. It ripped apart unions bound by love when young men rushed with eagerness to get in the fight, literally throwing their lives away.

Clyde returned home and volunteered for duty in the navy's Construction Battalion. He would be sent to the South Pacific.

I wasn't there the night Clyde had to leave.

But I can imagine it.

It happened to millions of us.

You stand close to the one you love, sharing your warmth. You're too old to cry. You fight against weeping, even. Both of you talk about everything and anything to put off saying that final goodbye.

She promised to wait for him.

Then there was a final kiss that you would remember, and remember, and remember as the days turn into months, the months into years.

He wrote letters home, telling her what he was doing, what he had seen, and, most of all, that he still loved her.

Ann waited for him, sustained by his letters, his declarations of love. When he returned to the states in 1944, she hurried to California to meet him.

I wasn't there at that reunion.

But I can imagine it.

It happened to millions of us.

You rushed into one another's arms. You held tight. It made the world right again. There was no greater joy, no greater happiness.

Ann and Clyde were married in 1944 in California. When Clyde was eventually discharged in 1946, the young couple returned to Delaware County.

You think home is going to be the same as always. But it's not. It slowly dawns on you that you've lost your most precious young years. Someone has knocked a hole in your future. You have to get on with your life, and in a hurry.

Ann and Clyde decided they would go into the grocery business.

For thousands of years, merchants in stores kept their wares on shelves behind their counters. If you wanted something, the clerk got it for you. You paid for it. He put it in a sack for you. You carried it home.

All over the country there was a new concept being developed in grocery sales. It was called the supermarket.

They would put in a supermarket in Jay.

What a wild idea. They could have gone to Tulsa, or some other metropolitan area, where the supermarket idea was being accepted.

Instead, they chose their own home town.

If you've never been in business, you have no idea what it's like. No matter how big the business gets, it seems you're always having to scrounge for cash.

It's certainly not the same as getting a check at the end of the week which you can use to pay bills with, then set back and wait for the next check to come.

In business, you're on the other side of that weekly check. You know the money has to be in the bank when you write it, no matter what.

You never know if a business is going to succeed. If you're real careful. If you watch your expenses. If you work twelve and fourteen hour days—if you do all these things, you might succeed.

To conserve expenses, Ann and Clyde tried to do most of the work themselves. They lived in a makeshift apartment in the back of their store. They hung a quilt over the opening.

Instead of squandering their profits, the young couple kept reinvesting the money in their business, their belief in the future of Jay unshakable.

They added an appliance department, then a ready-to-wear.

They became involved in every phase of community development.

They promoted Saturday drawings for cash. It drew large crowds. People went home feeling good about the activity in town, agreeing with one another that perhaps our little town of Jay wasn't such a bad place to live after all.

The Kellys worked hard promoting their home town, making it a bigger town, a better town, a town we could all be proud to live in.

One time they even drained their meager bank account to back a risky chicken business. It is still here providing jobs for families—for parents who buy food, clothing, and toys for their kids.

When customers needed credit, they gave it—sometimes at great sacrifice.

They also knew personal tragedy. Their seven-year-old, Joe, was struck down in an accident on the streets of Jay. He died on the road to a hospital in

Vinita.

Ann and Clyde did not want others in Jay to suffer the trauma they did. They began a campaign to build a hospital here.

They succeeded. Today that hospital has been taken over by the Cherokee Nation, dispensing free medical to Native Americans.

Ann's and Clyde's personal sorrow was partially alleviated when Ann gave birth to a second child, a daughter, Mary Ann, who, we believe, is extending and reinforcing her parents' belief in, and commitment to, the future of our town.

Ann was a prime mover getting our now-famous Huckleberry Festival underway.

She was a charter member in the Delaware County Historical Society. She was a very active member in the Business & Professional Women's Club. The Garden Club.

She reinvigorated the Chamber of Commerce.

She was a strong supporter of our First Baptist Church.

Then there were the civic responsibilities which Ann accepted.

The Park Board. The Industrial Board.

Any time city officials needed help, they'd call on Ann. She always responded. Always. Without complaint. And, most of all, without bringing along a basketful of negatives.

Anna Mae died on June 15 in the year 2000. Clyde preceded her in death December 9, 1998.

This time HE was at home waiting for HER.

I wasn't at this final reunion.

But I can imagine it.

I know they are now sharing the happiness and joy of being together again. And this time forever.

Mr. Chamber President, Members of the Board of Directors—It is with great pride that I nominate Anna Mae Kelly tonight to be the recipient of our Community Achievement Award.

I would also ask that their daughter, Mary Corn, accept in her mother's honor.

Sir Edward the Great

You know how it is when you see something going on in the neighborhood that is—well, sort of improper.

You love watching it unfold, episode by episode.

Fact was, I'd watched these three young chicks grow up, dashing about in my neighbor's yard, venturing out onto the street as they got older, then into other yards, including ours.

They were so full of life, racing this way and that, scratching and pecking, scratching and pecking.

It wasn't until they got a little older that I could tell one was going to be a rooster and the other two hens.

I laughed when the young rooster first tried to teach himself how to crow. He stretched his scrawny neck, flapped his skinny wings and went, "Er er errr!"

The final syllable ended in a high pitched squeak. I immediately gave him the name Sir Edward the Great.

During adolescence, the hens wouldn't pay any attention to Sir Edward—just kept on chasing after a flittering grasshopper, or making themselves dizzy watching a butterfly flip-flopping its way through the air over their heads.

In no time at all, it seemed, both hens shed their baby feathers and grew new ones. One turned out to be a plump dominecker. The other was a trim, beautiful light brown.

Sir Edward? Well, he dressed himself in about the prettiest set of feathers you'd ever see. His plumage from the head down to his body was a rich golden brown. The gold mixed with darker feathers on his body and a proud flurry of black tail feathers arched upward as high as his head.

He fit the silhouette image of every rooster you ever saw on weather vanes around the world.

I knew Sir Edward had fully matured when I saw him stretch, flap his beautiful wings, and let go with as lusty a "Er er err!" as you ever heard.

Then tragedy struck. From somewhere—about a block away, I judged—there came an answering, "Er er err—err!"

Sir Edward looked shocked. He twisted his proud head this way and that as if to say, "Who—?"

I knew who his challenger was—the rooster running with a wild bunch of game chickens living in the brushy fence rows down on the other end of our block.

The rooster was a tall rangy thing with scrawny tail feathers and a fierce-looking head and beak. For the past year or so, he had reigned as lord and master over six or seven game hens, all full of life, with brilliantly colored plumage. Every so often, you'd see one of the hens dash across the street with six or seven babies trailing.

Sir Edward decided, finally, not to answer the call from the wilderness a block away. He returned his attention to his two ladies, helping them search about in the grass for something to eat. He had to do an extra amount of scratching for the brown one because she was either too lazy to do her own scratching or simply took pleasure in pretending not to know how.

But I knew this was not over, not by a long shot. I recalled how neighbors would swap roosters when I was growing up. I didn't understand why. I asked Mom once. She turned her back, saying only, "Just because."

Nature has a way of doing its own "swapping." The males battle for the right of flock ownership.

Sir Edward, I knew, wasn't old enough to be aware of the danger he was in. He and his two ladies kept on pecking and scratching the day away. Then he'd lead them into the backyard where they'd grown up and find a place to roost in a vacant garage.

The rangy old game cock would herd his mistresses into the undergrowth and keep them hidden there until dawn.

It was just a matter of time, I thought, before nature forced the issue. And sure enough, I heard the rangy game cock call one day, and saw Sir Edward's trim brown lady sneak away to go join the game hens living in the brush.

For days afterward, Sir Edward wandered around not knowing what to do, not even taking time to scratch and peck. He called. There was no answer. But he was suspicious. He'd run down the street a short distance toward the bushy fence row, stop, stretch, flap his wings and fling loud insults at the rangy game cock.

The rangy game cock ignored him. This would infuriate Sir Edward. He stomped the ground in helpless anger. Then, still angry, he whirled and ran back across the road to strut around the plump dominecker as if to say, "You'd better not ever try to run away."

But Sir Edward wasn't about to give up. One day he spotted his beloved brown one away from the flock of game hens. He made a mad dash down the street, circled her, stomping his feet and fluttering his wings.

"You come home," his body language said. "And I mean right now!"

The brown one tried to get around him to get back into the brush with Old Rangy and the flock of game hens. But Sir Edward kept blocking her way. She finally gave up, and Sir Edward herded her back home.

Mission accomplished, he stretched his beautiful neck and let Rangy the game cock know he'd won his beautiful brown one back.

I heard Rangy answer. He sounded angry. I knew this was heading for a showdown—and all over a female's infidelity.

Sir Edward and Rangy kept making long distance challenges for a few minutes, then both shut up to resume their scratching and pecking.

I considered helping Sir Edward by reporting the flock of game chickens to our city's Animal Control Officer. I had served on the Board of Animal control when we wrote the ordinance a few years ago.

Our intent was for folks to keep their dogs penned up—not because of any danger to our citizens, but because when they ran loose they killed too many rose bushes in people's yards by sniffing and marking their territory.

We'd included cats in the ordinance. But since nobody could catch a cat, it didn't make cat lovers mad.

But chickens? I wasn't sure if chickens were on the list or not. So I decided to stay out of the domestic squabble.

It was all up to Sir Edward.

Would he be able to keep his sexpot home? Would he have to take on Rangy the game cock and fight to the death?

Or would the scandal blow over and peace return to the neighborhood of its own accord?

Peace did return of its own accord. But not without a little skullduggery by the two leaders.

One day when Sir Edward and his two ladies were scratching and pecking, I saw old Rangy come sneaking up the road, darting from bush to bush.

When Sir Edward and the dominecker disappeared around the corner of the house, Rangy made a mad dash across the road, circled the brown hen twice, and ran back toward the bushy fence row with the brown one jogging along behind.

I was disappointed the way Sir Edward went about his business for a day or two, scratching and pecking contentedly with his dominecker. He didn't even make any effort to crow and call the brown one home.

And then one day I saw him racing toward the vacant lot behind our house. I dashed to our rear window, expecting to see a real old-fashioned, feather-flying cock fight.

A couple of Rangy's game hens had wandered away from the brushy fence row and were out in the open by themselves.

Sir Edward ran up to them, circled them repeatedly, feet stomping, wings out and quivering, coaxing in a low rooster language.

The game hens were impressed and, when Sir Edward pranced back toward his home, the game hens followed.

Once Sir Edward had them safely in his own yard, he stretched his beautiful neck, flapped his wings, and let out a victorious, "Er er a errr!"

Rangy came running, but scooted to a halt when he saw Sir Edward racing to meet him, head low, his feathers fluffed, his wing tips dragging the ground.

Rangy took one surprised look, then turned and high-tailed it back to the sanctity of the brushy fence row. He did, after all, have the brown one.

But Sir Edward didn't care. Two for one was a pretty good deal—especially when you get two feisty, brilliantly colored game chicks who loved you in exchange for a drab-looking unfaithful one.

It was nature's way.

Miracle of the Hen

"Dear Mr. Newspaper Editor," the note began. "I want to run an obituary on my pretty white hen. Her name is Daisy. She came into this world on June 6th and disappeared October 11. That was the day I went out to feed her and she was gone."

I recognized the signature. I'd known Lettie for several years. And she certainly was no kook. Used to be involved in a lot of civic activities. However, it had been some time since I'd had any close contact with her. Had the added years affected her sharp mind? Or was she pulling my leg? If not, how do you write up an obituary on a white hen? Nor do you want to mock legitimate obituaries. This needed looking into.

I rose from my desk, lifted my hat from its rack and went to investigate. Lettie lived in a little brown house that had been added onto over the years by her long-dead husband. What was his name? Alzie, I remembered. The house set in the middle of the block, not far enough from the street to have a very large front yard—just enough room for a small lawn and a bed of roses—but far enough from the back alley to have one or two out buildings. I parked, went to the door and knocked.

She opened the door. "Lettie?" I asked. "It's me. Denney. The newspaper editor." There was a blank look on her face and I added quickly, "You wrote me a letter...about Daisy."

Her sudden smile put even more wrinkles in her face. She tried to fluff her snow-white hair, then straightened her brown woolen sweater, the one she always wore, summer and winter. "Come in," she said, opening the door wider. I noticed the sparkle in her dark eyes. She had been spoofing me, I thought as I walked in. I respectfully removed my hat.

"Oh, my," she said, hurrying about picking up scattered newspapers, "I didn't expect company."

Embarrassed for her, I apologized. "I should have called."

"Oh, no. That's all right. Here. Sit in this chair."

I eased myself into the soft chair. It had been sat in so many years that I could feel the springs pushing against my bottom.

She settled onto the couch across the cluttered coffee table from me. "Which letter was that?"

Then I knew I shouldn't have done this. "The one about…" I gestured helplessly, "Daisy's obituary," I finished with a rush.

Her face lit up. "Oh, my. Then you didn't get my other letter—the one about the miracle?"

"No…"

And she told me the story of the miracle.

"I got up that morning and went out to feed my Daisy the first thing. Like I always do. She was so pretty and fat and had a pretty red comb. She'd fluff her white feathers when I opened the door, cock her head like this—she'd cluck. Like this: *Cluck. Cluckety Cluck.* We'd always have a nice little conversation about things when I fed her. But she wasn't there. I looked around the yard. There was no sign of her anywhere. I called for her. I didn't even get one single cluck back.

"I was frightened. I hurried to my bedroom and pulled on my sweater—this one here—over my nightgown and walked around the block searching for her. I didn't find her nowheres. I was crying by the time I got back to my house. I just knew she had probably scratched herself so far away from my backyard that she got lost and couldn't find her way back. And somebody got her and et her.

"I never fell in love with a hen before. I had two roosters once. But they didn't have no pretty feathers. Besides that, Daisy laid such pretty eggs. I found out one day that she wanted to set. I put two or three boiled eggs under her. That made her happy. She set on them for a few days, then gave up that idea. She went back to scratching in my backyard and clucking on my back porch until I came out to feed her.

"I thought about calling the police to help me find Daisy. But you know what they'd think of me if I did that. They'd be nice and promise to help and laugh about it when they hung up their phone. That's when I wrote you about her obituary. I just couldn't stand it no longer. The very next day I decided I would drive around and look for Daisy myself. I hated to. I know how people in town complain about my driving. That's why I mostly keep my car in the garage all the time. But I loved my Daisy, and I knew she loved me. I had to try to find her.

"I got dressed, something I don't do every day. You don't know how hard it is to push buttons through button holes until you get arthritis. I took a quick peek at myself in the mirror before I went out. And it's a good thing I did, too.

My sweater was on slaunchwise. I had to unbutton it and do it all over again. I
scrunched up my hair a little and pinched my wrinkly old cheeks to try to squeeze
some life into them. Before I went out, I got down on my knees where the rug
is worn beside my bed and prayed real hard. Dear God, I prayed, if my Daisy is
lost, help me find her. I don't want her to be et. I always tried to do the right
thing, Lord, so please bring Daisy back to me. And, Lord, don't let me run into
anybody with my old car. I don't want to hurt nobody.

"It wasn't much of a prayer, and I just threw that in about driving my car. But
I figured I needed help there. I didn't drive much at all until my Alzie passed on.
Our kids told me not to drive no more, but a body needs to go get groceries.
How do they think I'd get groceries in the house? I just don't say anything about
it when they come home. The kids, I mean. If they think groceries get in this
house by magic, let them think it.

"I found my car keys and headed for the back door. When I opened the door,
there she was! Standing on my back steps, with her pretty red comb standing so
proud. She looked up at me and clucked a hello. I couldn't hardly see her because
of the tears in my eyes. First thing I did was thank the good Lord for answering
my prayer! And that's when I wrote you the last time and told you about the
miracle."

I picked up my hat and got up to leave. "All right, Lettie." I said. "I'll
probably get your last letter —the one about the miracle—in the mail tomorrow.
That's the one we'll print." Didn't hurt to promise. She'd probably forget about
it tomorrow.

"You're such a nice man," she said. "Would you like to meet my Daisy? She's
such a sweet hen."

"Well…okay."

Lettie led me through the house to the back door. She opened it. "Here,
Daisy," she called, and clucked.

Daisy waddled from behind one of the outbuildings, answering Lettie's
cluck.

I'd like to write that Daisy and I had a nice visit. But I didn't understand the
language. I did squat on my haunches, however, and said Hi. But when I reached
to stroke her pretty white feathers, she pulled away, clucking angrily.

"Don't you think that was a nice miracle?" Lettie asked. "Letting me have
Daisy back?"

I agreed, and left.

Driving back to town, I felt a stinging sensation in my nose. My vision
blurred. Lettie wasn't like she used to be. All alone, even the police laughing at

her, with only Daisy to keep her company. I made up my mind to publish the letter about the miracle of the hen. If it would make Lettie happy, why not? Who cares what other people think?

After all, it was a real miracle, wasn't it? All the world knows nobody "et" Daisy; that she really hadn't scratched herself so far away from her backyard that she couldn't find her way back; that the poor old lady simply overlooked Daisy when she went out in her pajamas to find her beloved hen, and that her praying really didn't make things turn out like they did.

And yet…Daisy did come home, didn't she? So who's to say what a miracle is? Is it a happening after a prayer, or a prayer before a happening?

A Good Seconding Man

I think I'm about the best seconding man around.

You know—the guy in a meeting who is always alert to what's going on and is ready to say, "I second the motion," without any dilly-dallying around.

I sit in on a lot of meetings these days.

We talk about things, then after we pretty well agree on what's to be done, the guy who's running things asks, "Do I hear a motion on that?"

The one who has done the most arguing for it, whatever it is, says, "I make a motion we—"

That's my cue. I take a deep breath, and as soon as he is finished with his motion, I do my thing.

"I second that motion," I say.

The actual vote is just a formality. Those who were against the idea know they've been whipped. They just keep their mouths shut.

Sometimes I've thought about voting no after I've already seconded the motion, just to see what would happen.

But you can't do that because it's not allowed in the *Robert's Rules of Order,* so they tell me.

Don't ask me what the *Robert's Rules of Order* are. I've never read them. When I first got involved in civic work, I swore I'd read the *Robert's Rules of Order* someday. But I never did. I wonder now if there is such a thing?

I didn't feel I needed to read them anyway as long as I just stuck to being the seconding man.

I got in big trouble once when I agreed to be the original motion-maker instead of sticking to being the seconding man.

It was at a political convention in Oklahoma City. Our group was an organization of young people of our state's political party.

I got dragged into it because of an editorial I wrote shortly after going into the weekly newspaper business. A young banker from my county who said his name was Alford read the editorial and called me on the phone.

He thought my suggestion to change our political party's position on a controversial subject made a lot of sense. He invited me to attend their upcoming young people's convention in Oklahoma City.

Delighted to be recognized, I promised to attend. Nita said I was wasting my time, but I argued that my writing was bringing me fame and it was calling.

She agreed to keep the business going and I took off for Oklahoma City.

It was exciting going to meetings and rubbing elbows with up-and-coming young people you'd been reading about in the newspapers.

However, I was sort of disappointed when I met banker Alford.

Oh, he was all right, I guess. He combed his black hair straight back, looked sort of smart, and had on a nice suit. But the black leather shoes he had on must have been nine days older'n God—they had so many cracks in them his white socks showed through.

He told me they had used my editorial as a basis for their controversial resolution and they wanted to get it passed the next day.

Boy, was I ever proud. I was even more proud when he said, "And we want you to make the motion to pass it."

Man, this was heady stuff. Not only were they building a philosophy out of something I wrote, I was being promoted from being the seconding man to being the man who makes the motion.

I was told reporters from the state's prestigious *Daily Oklahoman* would be there to cover the event.

I called Nita that night to tell her how important I was. She couldn't talk long, she said. She was getting ready to go play bridge.

No matter. I was still excited. The only time I'd ever been brave enough to make the original motion was the time there were only three of us council members at a meeting one night and old Tom Spradlin refused to do it.

Old Tom was a tall, lanky man with a deep voice—ideal for making motions in a meeting. But he was against whatever it was we were arguing about.

That left me and a lady. Ladies hardly ever made motions back then. So it was up to me.

All eyes swung on me. I had no choice but to speak up. I cleared my throat a couple of times to make sure my voice wouldn't be off-pitch when I spoke, and boldly announced, "I make a motion that we —"

The lady seconded—which ladies were allowed to do—and we voted Old Tom down two to one.

But after that, I reverted to my slot in life—that of just being the seconding man.

However, I felt I was up to the responsibility of being the original motion-maker on a state level, especially since it was my editorial that stirred up the state fuss in the first place.

Alone in my hotel room that night, I stood in front of the mirror and practiced saying, "I make the motion that we —"

It wasn't as simple as making the motion like old Tom did back home. In home town meetings, all you have to say is: I make that motion.

Everybody there knows what it is you're making the motion to do, so there's no need going through all that rigmarole about what it's all about.

But making the motion to pass a resolution that goes against the policies of your senior political party calls for saying distinctly what you are making the motion to do.

My banker friend with the cracked shoes and his cohorts had written out on a piece of paper the way I should make the motion. But they cautioned me against reading it because the reporters would be there.

The fact they had already released a draft of the resolution to the press was beside the point. They did that to excite the press people and make sure some of them would be present at the moment it happened.

I studied myself closely in the mirror as I recited my lines, trying hard to make them sound unrehearsed. Since it would get a lot of state-wide publicity, maybe even a picture of me actually at the moment of making the motion, I wanted it to be a very dignified affair.

I also wanted to be sure I got credit for what I was doing. I decided to start off with, "I, Dale Denney, make the motion to —"

By the time I went to bed, I thought I had it pretty well under control.

I spiffed up real good the next morning, just in case they did take a picture of me actually making the motion. You don't get your picture in a state-wide publication but once in a lifetime—especially as a motion-making man—so I wanted it to be just right.

The banker with the cracked shoes opened the meeting by whacking a gavel on the table.

And for the benefit of the reporters, he went to great lengths explaining how, prompted by my editorial, we came to this point of passing such a controversial resolution.

He asked a young woman to read the resolution in its entirety. She was a little nervous, but she got through it okay.

When she finished reading it, banker Alford glanced at me to make sure I was ready and asked, "Do I hear a motion that we pass this resolution?"

I wanted to dramatize it all I could. I pulled in a deep breath and rose slowly to my feet.

Just as I opened my mouth to speak, a guy on the other side of the room sang out, "I make the motion that we pass the resolution as read."

All the reporters rushed to get his picture. He wasn't even standing up.

Evidently the banker and his friends hadn't clued him in on the script.

That left me standing there with my mouth open and nobody paying a darn bit of attention to me.

Quick as a flash I thought of reverting to my old status—that of being the man who was an expert at seconding motions.

"I—"

That's as far as I got before the nervous girl who had read the motion said, "I second the motion."

As the banker with the cracked shoes called for a vote, I wilted down into my chair, now just a plain old nobody.

I didn't even bother to vote. Once the motion is made and seconded, it's all over. The vote is immaterial.

Yes, it's a silly way to govern ourselves. But it's a heck of a lot better than not even having a chance to make motions and having a good seconding man around to wrap things up.

I'm proud to be a reliable seconding man.

Death of a Sparrow

The hunter was a big man who wore a camouflage outfit. He didn't look much over thirty. A wide smile creased his tan face underneath his ball cap, pulled low when I drove up and got out, dragging my camera.

It was deer season in Oklahoma. The story would be appropriate. A photo would dress up the article, catch the reader's eye.

The eight-point buck lay tongue-out in its own blood in the back of the his pickup.

I asked him to pose with his kill. Proud, he hopped into the back of the pickup, kneeled, grasped the deer's antlers, and held the head up.

After I snapped the picture, I tried to find a spot on the bloody tailgate where I could lay my camera to free my hands so I could take notes.

He'd downed the 123-pound deer with one shot from his 30-30 Winchester, he said.

Those powerful guns are fun to shoot. *Ka-Wham!* They kick against your shoulder. *Thwop!* The bullet hits flesh a hundred yards away and the game falls.

I only half-heard his excited talk because there was one question I wanted to ask.

Was the world all quiet when you walked up to your kill?

Did you cry?

But I wasn't quite sure how to ask it. Or even if I should.

I've been wanting to ask that for a long time, just to see what one of these young men in their camouflage outfits with high-powered rifles driving the back roads in their pickups would say.

We talked about how our state's re-stocking program and hunting regulations were so successful that without our annual deer harvest, these pesky creatures would proliferate to the point that they'd run out of food. Then the weakened animals would become diseased and die. It's nature's way. Our hunting laws dovetail with nature's way.

The hunter had made a good kill, and was so very proud.

Should I ask him? Or not?

Maybe it is different killing deer.

I've never hunted deer. When I was a young man there were; (1) No such things as camouflage outfits (these were created for jungle wars), (2) You could drive the back roads all day and all night and not see a deer because there were no deer in Oklahoma; and (3) We did not have high-powered rifles.

We hunted rabbits mostly, with shotguns.

The thing I liked about us boys hunting rabbits was that we never went alone. About seven or eight of us boys, our shotguns ranging from .410s to ten-gauges, would tramp through the woods with our dogs. We kicked on brush piles.

Whenever a rabbit scooted out, running for his life, the one who saw it first would shout, "There he goes!"

Our dogs would take after him yapping and barking. We'd all start blasting away with our shotguns.

It sounded like a war. It was fun, shooting guns like that. Sometimes the rabbit would get away. We'd cuss and pretend we were mad, but at the same time we'd be laughing.

Sometimes the rabbit would go rolling head over heels, a furry mess. Since so many of us shot at him, the one who yelled first, "I got him!" got the rabbit. He'd pull its head off, punch a stick through a hind leg, and hang his kill from his belt.

I hardly ever was the first to shout "I got him!" because my sympathies were usually with the rabbit. I'd just shoot because all the others were shooting.

Sometimes I'd carry the rabbits for Jake. He was the best shot—at least he'd shout, "I got him!" before anybody else did.

I felt like I was doing my part walking along with two or three of Jake's rabbits dangling from my belt, blood from their necks spotting my pants leg.

If it sounds like I was squeamish about killing things, I was. I never told anybody about my first kill—until now.

It was with a beanie flip. Some people call them sling shots.

Whichever. We made them ourselves. You take a rubber inner tube, cut a couple of thongs about one foot long, tie the ends to a forked stalk and the other ends to a piece of soft leather, preferably a piece cut from the tongue of an old shoe.

You use any hard object for a missile—rocks, bolts, even marbles. Rocks where I lived were predominantly sandstone.

Since the softer pebbles would break into a thousand pieces under impact, sometimes you had a hard time finding ones hard enough to kill anything when you did hit it.

I usually found my "ammunition" for my beanie-flip along a creek when I went to look for the cow and bring her home for milking.

I'd check them for hardness by pressing them between my thumb and forefinger. If I couldn't break them, I'd drop them in my pocket.

We shot at everything with our beanie-flips, tin cans, knots on logs, telephone poles, birds. We never hit anything, but it was fun trying.

The power of throwing a missile was exciting, like shooting a gun. You'd finger a rock into the leather pocket, stretch the rubber bands tight, take aim, and let go.

The rock would sail away at the target, chinging off a tin can, or ticking through the leaves of a tree and scaring the bird enough to make it fly, or making one heck of a splash in a water pond six inches from a frog. The frightened frog would let out a loud croak, give a mighty leap, and disappear under water.

I usually hunted for the cow alone, entertaining myself by shooting rocks with my beanie-flip at everything in sight.

One time, I spotted a sparrow in a hickory nut tree. I pretended I was a big game hunter in Africa. I stalked the sparrow, moving silently through the buck brush underfoot to get a better shot.

I slipped a well-rounded rock in the leather pocket, never taking my eyes off my quarry. I stretched the rubber bands tight, took careful aim and let go, fully expecting the sparrow to fly away.

Thwack! The sand rock hit and broke into a thousand pieces, and the sparrow tumbled into space, a ball of feathers fighting for flight. It fluttered downward and disappeared into the buck brush.

I hit it! Elated, I hurried to find my kill.

As I approached the spot where the sparrow fell, my elation dissipated, replaced with deep sense of regret.

I didn't mean to hit him. Maybe he was just stunned. Yeah, that's it. In a second, he'll come fluttering out of the buck brush and fly away.

My scalp tightened when I heard his pitiful chirping. I felt a chill. I crept closer. I saw him flopping about, afraid of me, his wing horribly out of shape. He tried to get away, trying to hide in the buck brush.

I panicked. I couldn't let him get away, to die in pain and starvation even if he lived. I chased him through the buck brush, trying to stomp him. I missed and missed again. I was crying by the time I was finally able to stomp the life out of him.

Suddenly, the world was silent. No sound anywhere, except my own sobs. I stared at the dead sparrow, wiping away tears with the heel of my hand. I never felt so alone in my life. No one knew what I had done, nor would I ever tell.

The deer hunter detailed his kill to me again, describing how the buck had come out of the brush, how he'd raised his gun to his shoulder, how he'd waited until he could get a good clean shot before he squeezed the trigger.

He told me the deer tried to run, but collapsed in the brush. He felt sure he'd killed him, but he threw a fresh shell into the gun's chamber, just in case, he said, as he walked up to his kill.

I couldn't keep from wondering if he had felt the way I had felt that day when the world was suddenly silent and the deer lay dead at his feet.

And did he cry?

But I never found the courage to ask. There are things in each of our lives which we would rather keep to ourselves.

I thanked the hunter, got back into my own pickup, and drove away.

Keeping the secret of my kill to myself.

Shingles

Lor-dee! It hurts.

The doctor called it shingles.

I'd heard about it. I've even seen one or two people who showed me the skin rash that it causes. But I thought they were just putting me on when they told me how it hurts.

How in the world can a little old skin rash hurt? You can understand it burning and itching, maybe, like poison ivy. But real pain? No way.

Now I know.

Every time you move, it hurts. Besides the skin eruptions around my side, all the muscles in my torso hurt.

You wonder how in the world such a complicated thing has such a stupid name. Shingles.

Shingles is a name for things you roof your house with. An ailment that hurts so bad that you cry yourself to sleep ought to have a name more sophisticated than shingles. For crying out loud, the medicine they give you for shingles has a more sophisticated name than the ailment itself does.

The doctor said it comes with chicken pox—you know, the chicken pox you had when you were a kid that you don't even remember having?

A variant of the chicken pox virus, the doctor explained, hides itself in the big nerve running up and down in your spinal column. Through the years, it keeps trying to break out, and your immune system keeps beating it back.

Then one day when your immune system is weak or worn out—like when you get older—the shingle virus breaks out and attacks.

Its favorite target is one of your nerves branching out from your spinal column—usually the one that wraps around one side of your body just below your rib cage.

Mine started with a pain in my left side—kinda like when you were a kid and played so hard that it caused your side to ache.

And, naturally, you always get sick Friday night when all the doctors go home and all the nurses and everybody shut the doors on all the clinics. So, naturally, I had to jump in my pickup and go to the hospital emergency room.

With a side ache?

Hey, when you get older, every little pain and ache becomes an emergency, because your imagination runs away with you. When you're young, you know you're going to live forever, so aches and pains are simply that—aches and pains that'll go away.

But when you get older, you come to realize that you've just been fooling yourself all your life because you're going to die one of these days, sure as shootin'.

It shocks you how death sneaks up on you when you're not looking. You start finding more and more of your friends' names in the obituaries. What's even more startling is when you start noticing a lot of the names of these "older" folks are younger than you.

So you don't fool around about "little" aches and pains anymore. You high-tail it to the doctor to get some help.

The closer I got to the hospital, the sillier I felt. I could just see the emergency room doctors and nurses looking at one another and grinning when I walked in and told them I had a pain in my side.

This thought made me want to turn around and head on back to the house. Surely we had some Motrin somewhere in that jar full of pills we keep handy on a kitchen shelf. A couple of Motrin would probably take care of it.

That's all they do at hospitals anyway—give you a Motrin and send you home.

But then I recalled a story about old so-and-so who had this little lump come up under his arm and he was dead within six weeks.

And there was this other one about a lady who thought she had the flu. She took a couple of aspirin and went to bed. She never got up again.

To heck with what the emergency room doctors and nurses thought. Let them laugh. I wasn't going to have people be saying in two or three months, "You won't believe this, but old Denney had this pain in his side and six months later he was gone. He wouldn't go to the hospital because it was Saturday."

Why do people need a doctor most on Friday nights and Saturdays?

I parked in the hospital parking lot and headed on into the emergency room.

When I walked in, there were all these young people sitting around with happy looks on their faces.

How could they be so happy? Didn't they know a dying man when they saw one?

I bent over and held my side as if I might have been kicked by a mule and muttered, "My side hurts. Is there somebody here who can make it go away?"

The whole crowd went into action. One began clacking computer keys. One began shuffling papers. Two who had been eating donuts put their donuts down, took quick sips of coffee, and headed off to get the emergency room bed ready.

The one clacking the computer keys asked me a bunch of questions.

A nurse led me into a bathroom and instructed me how to do a urine sample. For a second there, I didn't think she was going to leave. I assured her that I knew how to do that and she left, finally.

Back in the emergency room a young man in a green scrub suit had me pull up my shirt and show him where it hurt.

I didn't think he was old enough to be out of high school, let alone be a doctor. But when you're in pain, you'll take any kind of doctor you can find and be darn glad you got one.

I pulled out my shirt tail and showed him my side.

"Yep," he said. "Just as I thought. You got it, and got it bad."

Got what, for gosh sakes? How could he see a hurt inside me? Maybe he was just a high school kid, after all.

He punched around on me. It hurt and I jerked away from him.

"It's the worst case I ever saw," he said.

"Worst WHAT you ever saw?"

"Shingles," he said.

Awww, I thought. This hurts, kid. And I mean HURT.

That's when he explained all about chicken pox and viruses and shingles to me. And while he was talking, he held a mirror so I could see my side. I was horrified. I hadn't had all that breaking out when I left the house.

"All right," I conceded. "What do we do to fix me up?"

"We don't," he said. "I'm going to give you a shot and prescriptions for a couple of things. One is an anti-viral medication to fight the virus. The other is to help with the pain."

"Will that cure it?"

"Nope."

"You mean I'm going to have to put up with this pain the rest of my life?"

The kid looked at me as if to say: So what's so long about the "rest of YOUR life, old man?" But at least he didn't say, like a lot of doctors do when you tell them about your aches and pains, "Let's see—how old did you say you were?"

So I got my shot in my you-know-where, stuck the prescriptions in my pocket, and headed on home.

Luckily, the drug store stays open on Saturday, and I was able to get my two prescriptions filled.

By Sunday morning, my left arm and left leg began hurting even more than the place where my skin had broken out.

My first thought was that the kid doctor had diagnosed me wrong and gave me the wrong medicine.

So first thing Monday, I got hold of my own doctor. He's an older man. I hoped he would change the diagnosis. But he only verified it.

I made him tell me more about shingles, especially after he said what the kid doctor had said—that mine was the worst case he'd ever seen. Since he was a lot older than the kid in the emergency room, that didn't sound so good.

He reassured me that the breaking out would heal in two or three weeks.

"Then the pain will go away?" I asked.

He shook his head.

"When, then?"

"Three months...if you're lucky."

Damn that chicken pox! It got me, after all.

But it wouldn't have if I hadn't lived so long.

Which brings me to this thought: We all work so hard on health and spend so much money on it, and what do we get?

A body that requires even more attention and more money to take care of.

No matter—it still hurts.

And it's time to take another pain pill.

Attack on America

September 11, 2001 will be a new date in the history of the birth and survival of America which kids in future generations will have to remember.

Like dates in 1492, 1776, 1812, 1862, 1918, 1941.

This new date is yet another attack on America. Nobody knows why. Most of us spent the week watching our television sets in horror and disbelief.

I had my week planned. Ironically, the most important thing I wanted to get done was to make arrangements for how best to display a new World War II Memorial plaque in the Delaware County courthouse.

I wanted it done just right because not only is my own name on the plaque, along with 1,755 others from Delaware County who went into service during World War II, I was personally involved in raising the $17,000 for the project.

I am so proud of each and every name on the plaque. The total represents over ten percent of the population of the county at that time. Sending ten percent of your total population off to war is quite a contribution.

And they are names close to people living in this area today: a father, possibly a mother, an uncle or aunt, perhaps a brother or sister, a close friend.

But all my plans were changed when the phone rang the morning of September 11. I picked it up.

A friend asked if we had our television turned on. I told her no.

Turn it on, she said, explaining why. The twin towers of the World Trade Center had been hit and were down, and the Pentagon had also been hit.

I flipped on the television and collapsed in my chair, watching in disbelief as the replay showed an airplane crashing into one of the buildings. In seconds, it fell. Soon, the other one crashed to the ground. The dust cloud rolled up the street, enveloping the fleeing people.

I forgot about my own personal plans. Along with everybody else in the nation, I watched the replays over and over, hungry for news: What was going on? Who? Why? How did they do it?

Nothing made sense.

As the information trickled in, it soon became obvious that four jetliners, loaded with fuel for a cross-country trip, had been hijacked, all at the same time, or nearly so.

The hijackers obviously took control of the cockpits and turned the fuel-laden planes, with their entire load of passengers, into guided missiles.

Even worse, it had obviously been planned to be a suicidal mission from the start.

My mind was filled with flashbacks of the Japanese *kamikazi* attacks on our naval fleets at the tail-end of World War II.

There is no defense against a suicidal attack—except shoot them down before they hit the target. Just killing the pilot is not enough, especially if they are in their final dive.

Each has to be totally destroyed in the air, and at a distance from its target.

This is as difficult, militarily speaking, as trying to intercept intercontinental ballistic missiles with a missile of your own.

Oddly enough, I had heard about the Pearl Harbor attack in 1941—sixty years ago this December 7—also from a friend.

A bunch of us kids—mostly high-schoolers—were sitting in Smith's Drug store here in Jay, having fun, cutting up, laughing, probably flirting while pretending not to.

A close friend came in and, instead of sitting down to have a Coke with us, told us the Japanese had bombed Pearl Harbor.

That was the day our generation quit laughing.

We had no television to show us the planes flying over, the bombing, the fire balls, our battleships rolling over with billows of black smoke pouring from them.

Many of us didn't even have access to radios. We got our news from others—little groups huddled in front of stores on the street talking.

It wasn't until twenty-four hours later that we were able to hear our president on the radio, telling us what we had to do and, most importantly, reassuring us we would win the war.

He sounded strong, and angry, when he vowed that we would retaliate, that we would ultimately prevail.

We liked that. So we, individually and as a nation, dedicated ourselves to defeating the people who did this to us.

In contrast, after this attack on America, television showed it over and over in graphic detail, from multiple angles.

I watched our president, senators, and people in the street expressing anger.

All were in agreement: Let us find out who did this—and we will—and bring them to justice.

To me, "bringing them to justice" sounded weak.

There was no talk after the attack on Pearl Harbor of bringing anybody to justice.

We simply declared war. We didn't have anything to fight with—no tanks, no planes, no army, no navy—especially after most of our fleet had been destroyed in the bombing.

But we declared war anyway.

We had to remake ourselves into a warring nation before going out to meet the aggressors.

That meant retooling our factories to make tanks instead of automobiles. It meant cutting the time from building ships from months to weeks.

It meant buying farm land and building new facilities like the Powder Plant between Pryor and Chouteau to manufacture powder for ammunition and bombs.

We had to build bomber plants from scratch like the one in Tulsa and set up assembly lines to turn out planes faster than the enemy could shoot them down.

In fact, we didn't even have a command center, and we built the Pentagon— the very one which was bombed in this attack—in the incredibly short time of eighteen months.

We had to take men and women by the millions into service, equip them, and train them. In many cases, we trained men using broom sticks for guns, soup cans full of sand for grenades, and junk cars for tanks as our targets.

In the meantime, what pitifully few fighting men and women we did have fought back, holding off the enemy until we were able to match them bomb for bomb, ship for ship, plane for plane, life for life.

In the incredibly short time of four months, we organized a bombing group, put them on one of our few remaining aircraft carriers, and ferried them as close to Japan as we dared before sending them off on a retaliatory raid over Tokyo.

Within a year, we went from being on a crippled defense to roaring out on a world-wide offense.

And we won—finally.

The most remarkable thing about winning that war, however, is that we occupied the country of both enemies—Germany and Japan—and not only helped them rebuild, but also taught them how to govern themselves, how to be free from Emperors and self-proclaimed leader-gods.

Nor did we demand that they give up their religions or their cultures.

Today, these former enemy nations are among the strongest in the world.

And, today, they are our friends.

You would think this would tell everybody everywhere that America is not a people.

Instead, America is an idea—the idea that man can live free. It makes no difference whether you are black or white, red or yellow, believe or don't believe, can speak English or not.

If you want to live free, you are an American.

This week we have been attacked again—not unlike our first Pearl Harbor sixty years ago.

And we're told the forces who did it are going to be difficult to conquer, because they are not of a defined country.

They are individuals who hate us, for whatever reason, who are willing to die to do something, anything, to disrupt our way of life.

They are the *kamikazi* pilots of my war.

What they do not understand is they could destroy all of us and still not destroy America.

For America is an idea.

We created it. We offer it to the world.

It will never be destroyed. It is here to stay.

And the amazing thing about this strange war we are facing today is that when we win it—and we will—we will probably move in to rebuild their homelands and teach them how to govern themselves and keep their own religions, their own cultures.

Then they, too, will be able to enjoy being free, enjoy being an American.

No matter where on this planet they choose to live.

For the idea of America is here to stay.

Hats on Crooked

A lady once described the American Legion group as "Old men with their hats on crooked."

The lady meant it as a fun joke, and I laughed with her because it was such a graphic description.

I still think about how the lady described us every time I put on my legion cap to attend some public function, or a Legion meeting.

We're not so formal about wearing our caps at legion meetings. But marching in parades or at other public functions, we try to spiff up a little and wear our caps properly positioned on our heads.

And properly positioned means being "on crooked." Getting your first one was a big thing.

Before World War II came along, guys never wore a head covering of any kind—no, not even a ball cap. Only ball players wore ball caps.

Having a cap thrown at us as part of our uniform when we arrived at Fort Sill near Lawton, Oklahoma was a culture shock.

But we hurried to get into our new uniforms. We'd go stand in front of a full-length mirror at the end of the barracks to make sure our ties were tied properly and tucked in neatly between the second and third buttons of our shirts, our belt buckles shiny and positioned exactly where they were supposed to be, our pants the right length and our high-topped GI shoes polished.

I was a little embarrassed by my size-twelve shoes because they looked like boats at the bottom of my long skinny legs.

The last thing we put on were our caps, not sure how we'd like them. It was a collapsible thing and made of cloth. They called it a field cap. It was supposed to sit on the right side of your head and forward, its bottom edge on your forehead exactly two finger widths above the right eyebrow.

I liked the jaunty angle. I measured mine with two fingers above the right eyebrow several times so I could get the feel of it without having to look in a mirror.

You were supposed to take it off whenever you went inside anywhere, out of respect for the general public—to the movies, in a restaurant, church, your girlfriend's home, at dances.

But the army didn't have to tell us that. Our generation had been raised to respect women, our elders, others' homes, and property rights. That came naturally for us.

You slipped your cap on again the minute you got outside. You sure didn't want to be stopped by an officer or military policeman somewhere on the street and told you were out of uniform because your hat was not sitting properly on your head.

I came to like my cap. You could slip it off easily and quickly without mussing up your hair and it'd collapse as flat as a folded handkerchief. You could quickly slip one end under your belt. There, it was tucked away, always handy, and not laying around somewhere where you might walk off and forget it.

When we got beyond the recruit stage, all the guys began customizing their field caps. Some would keep them in perfect shape, sharp as a knife on top; others would tuck down each end of the crown.

To impress the girls, some would keep their caps scooched back so their cute curly hair would show. Since I didn't have any pretty curls to show, I always kept my hat on exactly like it was supposed to be.

Besides, I had no reason to impress girls. I had Nita at home waiting for me. Well, not exactly at home—she'd gone to California to stay with an older sister that summer.

Even so, I was proud of my new uniform and was anxious to get my first three-day pass after basic training so I could go home and strut around town showing off my new clothes and the neat hat I was wearing.

At the bus station, the only ticket I could buy was standing room only on a bus going through Tulsa, heading for St. Louis.

"Just get me to Claremore," I said, and laid out the money. "I can hitch-hike from there."

It began pouring rain before we got to Tulsa. I got sleepy. I would have given anything to take my hat off and lay my head on a pillow. To stay awake, I focused my thoughts on Nita in California. Would home be the same without her? Would she ever come back? How long would a love last sustained only through letters?

I could detect a subtle change in her letters already. It was an exciting new world for her in California, meeting new friends, running into old ones from

403

home, seeing new sites.

And it had been only three months since our final tearful goodbye. But three months is forever when you're in love and apart, so short when together.

I managed to stay awake and got off in Claremore.

The rain had let up, but by the time I had walked to the east edge of Claremore to start hitch-hiking, it began coming down again. I stood under the portico of a church to keep dry. When I saw a car coming, I'd run to the edge of the highway and hang out my thumb.

My cap got soaking wet. It dripped water down my face. I had to take it off several times and wring it dry.

I finally caught a ride. I felt like a wet chicken looked coming in out of a rainstorm, all its feathers drooping, by the time I got to Jay.

After I dried out, my sister-in-law tried to iron my cap for me. I wasn't too happy with it, but I slipped it on—its lower edge exactly two fingers above my right eyebrow—and wore it anyway.

I didn't do much strutting on the streets. I stayed mostly out of sight. Home just wasn't the same without Nita being there.

Having to wear that type of cap was real handy when the army sent me to study engineering at a university in Maryland. You could slip it on quickly, march with your platoon to class, slip it off and tuck it away while sitting through a professor's boring lecture and writing a letter on notebook paper to your girlfriend back home.

Writing the letters paid off. When I came home the second time, Nita was here. We decided to get married. I felt dressed up for my wedding wearing my army uniform. As we entered the church together, I slipped off my cap and tucked it away to walk with her down the aisle.

After it was over, I slipped my cap back on, feeling as well-dressed as any man wearing a tux.

When taking advanced training exercises deep in the heart of Texas, we guys couldn't wait to get back to the barracks, unload our helmets, shower, dress, and slip on our neat little field caps before catching a bus to town.

Nita was with me then. We'd go to movies and see the sights in downtown San Antonio. My field cap was so handy to slip on and off and tuck away when we went in and out of stores.

The only time I failed to uncover properly was when we decided to tour the Alamo. Just inside the door was a place to sign in. Before the lady let me sign the book, she told me in no uncertain terms, "You cannot wear your hat in here."

Hat? It was a cap! And part of my uniform! She made me so angry I felt like telling her us Okies NEVER removed our hats for Texans.

But I didn't. I slipped off my cap, tucked it under my belt, signed in, and took the Alamo tour with Nita.

My field cap was one of the first items of my uniform I discarded when they gave me my discharge papers. Although we were supposed to remain in uniform until we got home, I slipped my field cap off and tossed it in the back seat of our car when Nita and I headed for Jay.

So you see, dear lady, those caps were a big part of our life when we were all young—when so many of us did what we were told, went to war without complaining, won it, and came home to try and learn how to be young all over again.

And now, those of us who are left, are just as the lady described us—old men with their hats on crooked.

Grandma's House

I loved walking underneath the rose bush arbor at Grandma's house. And it would be even more special today because this was the first time Mom was going to let me go by myself.

"Now you look both ways before crossing the highway," she cautioned for the umpteenth time, it seemed, as she kept trying to get the wild sprigs of hair on my head to lay down.

"Awww, Mom," I groaned.

I was eight, wasn't I? I could run fast, couldn't I?

I knew what she was worried about. They'd just finished building the new highway through town last year. We had to cross it going to Grandma's house. Sometimes there'd be as many as two or three cars going by within ten or fifteen minutes, a lot of them doing thirty, at least. You had to be careful and not get run over, with them whizzing by like that.

She even warned me again as I went out our gate and started down the lane toward town. I walked fast, strutting importantly in my clean striped overalls and hair plastered down.

I stopped at the newly paved highway, looked both ways. There were no cars in sight, but I waited anyway.

I was hoping one of those beautiful new Model A Fords with yellow, wire spoke wheels would come by.

Wooden spokes like on a wagon wheel made sense. They were strong and held the axle up when the wheel rolled.

But wires? It was a real puzzle to me.

I sighed, giving up finally, and hurried on across the concrete strip. I was anxious to get to Grandma's house. She'd have a fit, I knew, when she'd see me come through the front gate all by myself and come walking underneath her rose bush arbor up to her front porch. No telling what she'd say. I bet she would make twice as many cookies though, now that I was grown-up—well, almost.

And she'd go digging in her trunk again to find some more grown-up type toys for me to play with—ones she'd stored away after her own kids grew up and left home.

All I knew about Grandma and Grandpa was that they were from far-away place called Kentucky. They were born there, Andrew Jackson New during the Civil War and Margaret Ann Pendleton a few years later. People called Grandpa "Jack." But *everybody* called Grandma "Grandma."

They had grown up together deep in the hills of Kentucky, got married young, and had their kids. Grandpa provided for his growing family with income from his little country store. But after all their kids had moved to Oklahoma to get in on the oil boom, Grandpa sold his business and came here too.

This was a strange land to them, barren and bleak, overrun by people without a past.

Grandma hated Oklahoma. Her only comfort was her roses. She had brought some cuttings from her favorite wild rose bush that grew on the back fence of the far pasture. They thrived here. All you had to do was poke one in the ground and it'd grow like mad.

Grandpa tried oil field roustabouting, but found the work too hard for a man his age.

Grandma wanted to go home. But when she went near blind (cataracts, Mom told us) Mom and the others wouldn't think of letting them return to live alone in the hills of Kentucky.

They all chipped in and bought them a small two-bedroom clapboard house in town.

Grandma was happy when Grandpa and my dad built an arbor over the front walk out of steel rods they used in the oil fields. They covered it with chicken wire. Grandma planted some of her new cuttings along the base, and in no time at all, the whole arbor was covered with the wild rose vines.

The small pale roses had a certain unexplainable, mystic beauty about them—as if every single one of them was looking at you as you walked beneath them and saying, "And how are you today, kind sir?"

Every Memorial Day, people from all around would drop by—often unannounced—to get some of the little roses from Grandma's arbor to take up to the cemetery to decorate the graves of their loved ones.

Even as blind as she was, Grandma would help them clip the little roses, which was awkward sometimes because she still chewed tobacco and didn't like to be caught doing that here in this strange land.

Even in front of us, her very own family, Grandma tried to be discreet about chewing. She'd turn her back when she'd dig her plug of cotton bowl twist out of her apron pocket and bite off a chunk.

We all knew about the coffee can on a shelf beside the stove she used to spit in when she was fixing something to eat for Grandpa. We all respected her right to chew tobacco if she wanted to, because that's the way her mother did back in Kentucky and her mother's mother before that.

Grandpa never talked much—just sat gently fingering his moustache, his watery eyes staring into space. Grandma treated him like he was a king. It was their way.

Grandma always cautioned Grandpa to "be keerful" when he left for his daily walk to town. He'd get the mail and stop in to play a game of checkers with Paul the undertaker.

The undertaker never won. Whenever Grandpa would make his final leap to wipe the undertaker's last man off the board, he'd lean back with a triumphant gleam in his eye and sly smile underneath his moustache.

Then, angry as all get-out over being beat yet again, Paul would start slapping the checkers back on the board for one more game. And Grandpa would oblige.

By the time Nita and I finished our studies at the university and moved back home to buy the local newspaper, Grandma wasn't getting out anymore at all because the cataract growth had taken away everything but shadows. But she still kept trying to cook to take care of Grandpa.

Sometimes after beating Paul again playing checkers, Grandpa would come to the newspaper office. He liked to read the grocery ads, shaking his head in wonderment and disbelief over how much prices had increased since he'd been in the business.

Grandma came down "feeling poorly" one day. The doctor said it was the flu, and wasn't very optimistic about her overcoming it at her age. More and more of our relatives kept coming to "sit up" as Grandma got weaker and weaker.

She fought her illness like a tiger. Although bedridden, she kept calling for Jack. When he'd get up out of his rocker and shuffle into the bedroom to hold her hand, she'd start giving him orders, like who was to sleep in which bed, what to fix for supper, finishing with, "For heaven's sake, Jack—put on a clean shirt. Can't you see we got a houseful of company?"

She even tried to cheat death when it stole into her bedroom late one night by calling out in a strong voice, "Jack! Oh, Jack!"

Grandpa struggled out of bed and shuffled into her room.

"I'm right here, Margaret."

Grim faced, she reached for him. He bent over the bed, slipping his arms under her now bony body. She lifted her arms about his neck, hugging him tight.

The strong voice turned plaintive before disappearing into a whisper, "Jack! Oooo, Jack!"

A heavy sob jerked through Grandpa's body. He held her tight as her limp arms slipped from around his neck. After several minutes, he laid her down gently and shuffled out of the room, fingering tears from his damp moustache.

We buried Grandma in the local cemetery in this strange new land. And within a few months, Grandpa died—with a broken heart, I knew. We placed him beside Grandma. Dad and I built a small arbor over the two graves, tying them together. We planted Kentucky cuttings from the tiny pale roses. They flourished.

Paul the undertaker struggled to keep his voice from breaking when he told me later how he could never beat Grandpa playing checkers.

"But we'll continue the game when I get up there," he said, "Because I know in heaven you get to do all the things you like doing best."

Not too many years later, Nita and I placed both Mom and Dad beside Grandpa Jack and his beloved Margaret. Family survivors deeded the old home place to the home town public school system. They built a new high school on it with a bronze dedicatory plaque at the entrance acknowledging Mom and Dad's (George and Lula Denney) generous gift.

Mom would be so proud. She'd given up her desire to be a school teacher, married her young love, and followed him to Oklahoma where she became a hard working housewife, bearing seven children. Now her long-held dream of being a school teacher has become a reality, a gift that will go on teaching kids forever.

A few rows away are three of my brothers.

It's a beautiful cemetery, a home cemetery.

Nita and I have reserved a couple of spots here in Jay, Delaware County where she grew up and where I came to maturity.

And we've made a secret vow: When all the people go home after the funeral held for the last one of us and we're alone, we're going to reach out and hold hands—just like we did on our first date when I walked her home in the dark that night.

Generation P

Tom Brokaw, the NBC evening news anchor, called us WW II veterans and our families "The Greatest Generation" in his book a few years ago.

That made me feel so proud. I've never been "The Greatest" of anything. It feels good to be one, even though I have to share it with the sixteen million of us who were in the services during that time.

Sad to say, but we've become Generation P today.

We have a Generation X (sixties crowd) and a Generation Y (the latest group).

We of Brokaw's "The Greatest Generation" have become Generation P.

The P stands for pill.

I never saw a doctor or dentist until I went into the army in 1943. I was twenty.

Now I have so many doctors I can barely fit them all into my appointment schedule.

In fact, my foot doctor (he keeps my ingrown toenails trimmed back) was running so far behind the other day, I had to put my shoes back on and limp out so I could get on over to see my ear doctor.

My ear doctor had a higher priority that day. I was wearing Nita out making her repeat everything she said. I knew that if I didn't get some ear doctoring done soon, she'd stomp on my ingrown toenails.

Besides that, my foot doctor grew up in Philadelphia and is a Philadelphia Eagles fan. There are a lot of professional football teams besides Dallas I kinda like, but not the Philadelphia Eagles.

I kept calling my foot doctor a damn Yankee. I may not be able to get back in and see him after walking out on him the other day to go see my ear doctor.

I found out my regular ear doctor had retired. A young man had taken over his practice. My old ear doctor always knew what to do: get his poking instrument, dig out the globs of ear wax that always collect in my ears, and send me home.

But this new guy sat down with his pen poised over some kind of chart and began asking me about my medical history.

"Before fifty or after fifty?" I asked.

"Both."

"Before fifty, I don't have a history. After fifty…"

I couldn't fill in the exact dates. I'd say this or that happened about thirty years ago, or twenty-five years ago, or forty years ago.

"Any current medications?"

"Naw," I started to brag.

Then I remembered the acid-reducing pill I was put on thirty or forty years ago to keep my stomach ulcers in check.

"That all?"

"Well… no. I'm taking an antibiotic."

"What's that for?"

Well, it's a long story, Doc. Right after taking chemotherapy treatments to get rid of the cancer cells—"

"You've had cancer? What kind?"

I had to explain all that. How the doctor found a lump in one of my lymph nodes, the chemotherapy treatments and stuff.

"Is it cured?"

"No. my oncologist says you don't cure cancer. It goes into remission."

"It's in remission then?" he asked.

"I guess so. It's gone somewhere. If it's planning on coming back, it'd better hurry or I might not be here."

I watched him write all this down. Then I added, "After my chemotherapy treatments, I started getting these little bumps come up in my hair and sometimes on my face."

I told him that my regular doctor (we Greatest-Generationers have to have home-town doctors so all the specialists will have somebody to send a copy to) said it was adult acne.

I laughed at him and said you got to be kidding. I got rid of acne before I got out of high school.

He put me on the antibiotic. I didn't want to be taking pills the rest of my life for acne.

So I went to see a skin doctor—dermatologists, we call them. I wanted a specialist to tell me my regular doctor didn't know what he was talking about.

Instead, the minute he walked into the examining room and saw the bump on my face, he said, "Rosacea." And it's incurable. In fact, nobody knows what causes it.

He prescribed the same antibiotic medication my regular doctor did. I didn't want to make him feel bad by telling him I already had some of that.

I was somewhat relieved I wasn't having to go through that teenage misery again, back when you'd get a pimple on your face at the wrong time.

You'd be so miserable, you'd say to yourself you'd rather die than to go to school with that thing on your face.

But we members of Generation P don't dare say today we'd rather die than do something—it just might happen.

Back to my new ear doctor. I could see I was boring him. But then he asked, "Is that all?"

The chemotherapy had disturbed my sleeping chicken pox virus, I told him, and I had a bad case of shingles. It hurt so bad I did want to die.

"Hmmm."

And there was my bone doctor, I continued. You see, I had this back pain and it kept getting worse. The bone doctor ordered X-rays.

It didn't show much, "Except some deterioration."

"Deterioration" had an ominous ring to it. You might be able to take pills to dull the pain of arthritis, or get an operations to relieve pressure on a nerve, perhaps even fuse a couple of vertebrae together to keep them from moving so they wouldn't cause any pain.

But how can you fight "deterioration"?

Deterioration is like getting old. It's irreversible.

I gulped down my disappointment and asked what we could do about it.

Doctors love to hear that. He whips out his prescription pad and makes a lot of chicken tracks on it and tells you to "try" this.

Off you go to the pharmacist. He can read anything—or at least pretends to. You really don't know if the pill he gives you is the one the doctor ordered, or something else.

You have to make room for another bottle of pills in your medicine cabinet. Or if your medicine cabinet doesn't have any more room in it, you find an unused corner in one of your kitchen cabinets.

Sometimes I find myself chasing all over the house at bedtime trying to round up all the pills I'm supposed to take.

My bone doctor's pain pills made me itch all over—just like having the itch. And I know what that's like because I caught the itch when I went into the service. It's miserable. You have to scratch, even though you know scratching only makes it worse.

The army doctor called it scabies. He didn't explain. But the look on his face when he said it told me it was man's version of the dog mange.

I don't remember if he prescribed any pills for my itch. But I do remember him sending me to an isolation ward in the base hospital. I had to smear sulfur grease all over me from head to toe and keep doing it for two weeks.

So when I called my bone doctor and told him the pain pills made me itch all over, I knew what I was talking about.

So he ordered another pill to stop the itching caused by the pain pill.

That anti-itch pill made me so drowsy that I'd fall asleep at my computer trying to write a story.

I liked feeling drowsy, so I didn't complain about that to the doctor.

I saw I was boring my new ear doctor, and he'd run out of space in which write on the form he was using to write on, so I shut up and asked, "I can't hear too good. Can you get the wax out?"

He did, and I could hear a lot better. But he had his nurse run a pressure test. They found out one ear was filled with fluid.

"What causes that?" I asked.

You get water in it, he said. A brilliant answer, I thought.

And—you guessed it. He gave me some pills to take to get rid of the fluid build-up.

They were kinda cute—not the pill itself, but the directions.

You started off with eight the first day at specified intervals, seven the next, six the next, and so on, down to one on the last day.

Wonder of wonders—when I had taken them all, I still couldn't hear any better.

What us Generation P people need is an assembly line of doctors: you go in one end of the building and come out the other all in the same day and come home with a fistful of prescriptions to keep you going another six months.

My trouble is, I always revolt, especially on the pill I'm supposed to take for the rest of my life.

Until the pain comes back. Then I go running around the house looking for the pill that's supposed to fix that.

The Man in the Mirror

I swished my razor through the water in the sink to clean off the accumulated shaving soap, then lifted it again to resume shaving.

But my arm with the uplifted razor froze as I stared at my reflection in the mirror, face partially lathered, uncombed hair awry.

Who is that man? I thought, startled. He definitely wasn't me.

I was tall and handsome—well, maybe not what you'd call handsome, but at least a decent, dignified-looking guy. That man in the mirror was just plain ugly. Bald. Big ears. A red nose. Wrinkles everywhere.

If that was the man the people of the world saw every day and thought was me, then they'd never seen me at all.

So if they don't see me, who do they see? I didn't know the man in the mirror myself, and we'd been shaving like this every morning…for how long? Over half a century. Good Lord!

I laughed at the man in the mirror and continued with my shaving.

The more I stared at him, the more I was convinced that he wasn't me. He tried to pretend he was me from the first time we started shaving together that Sunday morning so long ago.

I'd stayed home from church—because, I told Mom, I had a belly ache.

When she gave me that don't-you-lie-to-me look, I doubled over and held my stomach and really put on an act.

It worked. And as soon as everybody got out of the house, I bustled around to get a pan of water heated and Dad's straight razor out.

I stropped it good, just like Dad always did. I sure didn't want anything to go wrong with my first time shaving.

While waiting for the water to heat, I hung Dad's little shaving mirror on the nail between the two south windows in the kitchen like Dad always did. Even with a bright sunlight shining in, I had to lean close to see the dark fuzz over my upper lip.

As I was fingering the fine fuzz, that's when I first noticed that other man.

Gee, he looked young—even though I knew he'd just turned seventeen and was graduating from high school that year. He had lots of black, unruly hair on his head. There wasn't a wrinkle in his face, except when he smiled back at me.

As we sized one another up—the man in the mirror and me—the water in the pan on the stove began boiling. I rushed to turn off the fire and carried the pan back to the bench under the mirror.

I got Dad's shaving mug, dipped the brush in the hot water, whipped up a nice foam, and began lathering my face.

The other man did too, only he was left-handed. That confused me at first. But he seemed as happy as I was, getting his first shave, and kept lathering.

Once we got our faces lathered good, I got Dad's straight razor and held it up. The other man did too, left-handed. Every time I tried to move the razor according to what I saw in the mirror, my hand went the other direction.

I panicked. The man in the mirror was going to cut my throat, sure as shootin'.

I stepped to one side to get rid of the man in the mirror and practiced moving the razor in the direction I wanted it to go.

Without looking in the mirror, I tried sliding the razor on my cheek since that was the smoothest part. Soon's I got the hang of it, I scootched back over in front of the mirror and went to work on the fuzz over my upper lip.

I had a terrible time handling the razor. When I kept moving my hand one direction, the man in the mirror moved his the opposite way. I finally learned I had to let my mind tell me which way to move my hand and only use the mirror to see the results.

This is tricky thing to do. I didn't even dare attempt to negotiate around my chin and neck with Dad's straight razor. I simply didn't trust that other man in the mirror to show me how to make the right moves.

I had everything put away by the time the family returned from church. I hoped Dad's shaving brush would be dried out by the next morning and he wouldn't notice.

I was so proud of what I'd done, I forgot about my belly ache. Mom noticed the way I was prancing around and asked if my pain was gone. Startled, I said yes, most of it, anyway.

When she continued to eye me suspiciously, I held my hand over my upper lip, pretending to scratch my nose, so she wouldn't notice that all my dark fuzz was gone.

Not long after that, I left home. Even though I didn't have to shave but once every two or three weeks, I bought myself a safety razor, some blades, and my own shaving mug, soap, and brush.

I discovered that the left-handed man in the mirror wasn't such a bother with me using a safety razor. Besides, I was getting to where I mostly ignored him—I had something now that he didn't have—a girlfriend.

That changed our relationship forever. I knew love. The man in the mirror didn't. That's when I first realized he didn't have anything inside him at all. He was just what you see—and left-handed besides that.

I could stand there and look at him and be brimming over with love and he just looked the same as always, dark unruly hair, eyes that never moved—even when you turned your head this way and that.

I mostly ignored him when I went into the army. It was easy to do. We had no mirrors. All we had were little squares of polished metal lined up along one wall in the communal latrine.

Even though I still wasn't needing to shave every day, I pretended to because all the other guys did.

When you stood in front of one of those polished metal plates, the man in the mirror was so distorted you couldn't tell who he was.

You darn sure couldn't tell whether you needed a shave or not.

I found that out the hard way. I got gigged for not being clean-shaven one Friday morning during inspection, and spent the rest of the day picking up rocks around the barracks.

I had to do something to bring back my left-handed man in the mirror.

That night I went straight to the PX and bought a small mirror that I could keep in my shaving kit. I kept a closer watch and, sad to say, I had to start shaving two, sometimes three times a week.

I really didn't start needing to shave every day until after Nita and I were married and were living in our own little apartment off base. And the man in the mirror was so sleepy-eyed that I quit paying any attention to him.

I'd have to be on duty at the base by 6:00 AM. I'd get up at 4:00 so I'd have time to shave, dress, and hurry uptown to catch the base bus before it left for its forty-five minute drive to the base.

Shaving became so routine over the years that I mostly just went through the motions, especially after they came out with lather in a can. You could shave in your sleep almost—just slap some canned lather on, drag a safety razor around over your face, rinse, towel, and hurry on out the door so you wouldn't be late to work.

Suddenly one day I paused and took a good look at the man in the mirror. I was shocked to see that his hair had turned gray and lines had begun to form at the corners of his eyes and around his mouth.

Then I knew for sure he wasn't me, because I wasn't a day older than I was when I first started shaving.

And today, years later, when I looked at the man in the mirror, I had to laugh when I saw that old, overweight, bald-headed man with a wrinkly face in the mirror.

He just keeps on growing older—but I don't.

And someday, I know, when I look for the man in the mirror, he'll be gone, but I'll still be here—because I knew love in my lifetime and he didn't.

My Morning Newspaper

Something was terribly, terribly wrong.

I kept peeking out my kitchen window to see if my *Tulsa World* had mysteriously appeared on the driveway.

It hadn't.

I poured another cup of coffee, my hands trembling.

I simply could not believe our newspaper carrier had taken upon himself to not deliver our paper. Carriers can't do that—can they?

He (or she, American, or whatever nationality) had missed leaving our *Tulsa World* the day before—Sunday, of all times. The biggest, best paper of the week.

You don't have anything to do on Sundays. You can lounge around in your pjs and robe and drink coffee and read until the coffee pot runs dry.

Instead, I had to dress, go out in the cold, climb in my pickup, and drive to town to pay a buck-fifty to get a newspaper out of a vending machine.

I immediately emailed the *Tulsa World* to deduct a buck-fifty from my bill that month.

A man called. They were sorry, he said. I'd have my paper in the morning.

Yet there I was, slurping my morning coffee and peeking out the window between every slurp to see if my paper was there.

No paper.

What good is there to go on living without a morning newspaper? We'd gone through so much together. I learned to read by reading the comics in the *Tulsa World* in 1929—Buck Rogers, Little Orphan Annie, Joe Palooka, Skeezix, Dick Tracy, the Katz and Jammer Kids.

As I grew older, its pages expanded my knowledge of geography, explained American politics, told me what was going on in foreign lands.

It kept me informed about the war raging in Europe whether I was interested in it or not, and brought the horrifying details about the Japanese bombing Pearl Harbor.

I couldn't remember life without the *Tulsa World*. The morning dew would still be heavy in the air when Mom or Dad would tell one of us kids to go get the paper. And it was always there—in the little white tube on top of a post beside the road that ran by our front gate.

Ours was a large family, all of us readers. Dad would take charge when the paper was brought in, giving each of us a section. Your age and family seniority determined what section you got.

I don't remember exactly when I learned the morning paper didn't just magically appear in our mail box, that somebody brought it—every morning, seven days a week, fifty-two weeks a year, year in and year out.

It was like coming to realize babies were born of women. You don't know how or when you acquired this knowledge, you just did.

My first suspicions of the *Tulsa World* being delivered by a person came when Dolphus James would stop by every once in a while and Dad would give him some money.

Or a bushel of peanuts, whichever Dolphus wanted most.

Dolphus was the best carrier there ever was. He was a quiet but determined young man, a gaunt, hatchet-faced redheaded. His family was even poorer than we were.

Dolphus began delivering our paper when he was a freshman in high school, and was still delivering it when he graduated. He saved enough to pay his way through law school at Oklahoma University.

Just before Dolphus had to leave to go to college, he asked me if I wanted to take over his route. It sounded like fun.

But at four AM you get other ideas. You don't know how early four AM is until you have to get up that early no matter the weather, whether it is thundering and lightning and raining outside, or colder than blue blazes and blowing snow.

But it was a fine summer morning that first day when I met Dolphus uptown in front of the post office. He was already busy folding papers when I arrived. It is eerie being uptown at that hour because without people in it, a town isn't a town at all, just a bunch of hollow buildings.

Dolphus taught me how to fold papers and the art of throwing them. And until I learned how to do it right, he made me dig my misses out of the flower beds or from under parked cars and place them on the porch, out of the weather, like they were supposed to be.

There is nothing more disgusting, he pointed out, than unwrapping a wet morning newspaper.

Dolphus taught me that the best way to calm a barking dog was to be nice to him instead of kicking him for snapping at your heels. Before we finished our route, we'd have a large pack of dogs following us, all wagging their tails and having a good time.

I couldn't have had a better paper delivery professor than Dolphus James. He lectured constantly as we made our rounds, who paid promptly every month (that was when the carrier did the collecting and paid the newspaper publisher), whom you had to catch up with and dun him in the domino parlor to embarrass him into paying, who tried to cheat you, who wrote bad checks, and on and on and on.

I loved delivering papers, but I hated collecting. Who would have thought, for instance, that my English teacher would try to cheat a paper boy?

And it was a clipping from the *Tulsa World* that Mom sent me when I was in the army that told me what happened to Dolphus. A local hero, the story said, killed in action. He was a tank commander whose outfit had been attached to the British.

They drove Rommel across northern Africa, invaded Sicily, fought up the Italian boot to free Rome, and were in the group that invaded southern France and raced north to join Eisenhower's armies fighting on the German front.

Dolphus, the story said, was sitting beside his tank reading a newspaper somewhere in Germany when a sniper shot him through the head.

After the war, my morning newspaper kept me abreast of the birthing of television, and even took me on a space voyage to the moon and back.

And now my carrier had quit bringing the *World* to me. I was suffering from a terrible withdrawal agony.

One of the more pleasurable hours for Nita and me is the time we spend together—usually before daylight—reading the paper and discussing current events as we sip our morning coffee.

How can I possibly adapt to not having a morning paper?

The loss was overwhelming. Why did this happen to me? Why had I been so arrogant over a measly buck-fifty?

Nor did he (or she, or whoever) come the next morning, or the next.

I'd already called the Tulsa World three times, sent two email messages, and even promised to pay the buck-fifty for the paper I didn't get.

He promised me faithfully there'd be a paper on my driveway the next morning.

It wasn't there.

I sat brooding in my chair: What was this world coming to? Have I outlived my time? When you had to pay the carrier, you at least had someone to gripe at.

This new-fangled way of paying the paper and them paying the carrier takes all the person-to-person relationship out of it.

Would I have to spend the rest of my days in this old world without a morning paper to browse through as I sipped my morning coffee?

The mere thought was almost more than a man could stand.

Late that evening, the phone rang. She said she was the new carrier for the *Tulsa World*. She apologized profusely. She and her family had only recently moved here from Mexico. She hadn't learned enough English yet to read house numbers. She went by colors. She'd been leaving my paper at my neighbor's house up the street. It was a brown house too.

You mean——?

Yes, sir, she vowed. You'll get your paper in the morning, before 6:00, and tossed onto your carport, out of the weather.

Oh, joy, joy, joy!

Life isn't over after all…I went to bed early—like a kid on Christmas Eve—so I could get up before daybreak and run out to get my morning paper.

And enjoy yet another pleasurable hour with Nita discussing what went on in the world yesterday as we sip our coffee and rustle our way through the *Tulsa World*.

We've never met the lady from Mexico who can't read English but memorizes the colors of houses she delivers papers to.

But she's the best paper carrier I've ever known.

Besides Dolphus James, of course.

Autumn Leaves

Leaves are like people, I think as I look out my study window at the fall leaves swirling down. Each different but all alike. Is there one perfect?

I sigh heavily and go to the shed to get my leaf rake.

I don't know where to start. They're falling all over the place, covering the dead and dying grass, skittering across the driveway, filling the roadside ditches. They run up the street, scooted along by a strong south wind; tomorrow, the wind will be out of the north to send them scampering the other direction.

Leaves pay no attention to property lines. They rustle this way and that, go anywhere they want. I get my neighbor's leaves. He gets mine.

I begin raking and bagging, keeping a sharp eye out to find the perfect one.

There's something sad about watching leaves let go of a tree and flutter to the ground. Their departure, one by one, from a spot they'd been clinging to since spring strips the tree of its majesty. Bare limbs have no meaning; they support nothing, become only naked arms and fingers probing about aimlessly in a wintering sky.

Scientifically speaking, leaves are the lungs of a tree. They have microscopic openings on the underside—stomata, they're called. The leaves take in carbon dioxide through these stomata and use it in the manufacture of sugar for the tree. Then the leaf exhales oxygen, reversing the process I use when I breathe. I know that if there were no leaves on this globe we call Earth, we would soon use up all of our oxygen and smother under a blanket of carbon dioxide.

And there are so many different species of trees in the forest that you can't count them. But each leaf on each tree has the same assignment. They are different, but the same.

In concert, leaves toil during the summer, fueled by the sun's energy to balance the earth's gases for animals. When their work is done in the fall, they change colors, giving the hills a breathtaking beauty which is both sad and exhilarating at the same time.

During my daily walks, I saw one house where the people living there had cut down all their trees. I could understand. Yet the violence against nature was severe. I stopped to count the stumps.

Eighteen! Eighteen times X number of leaves equals how many? One thing for sure, they didn't have any leaves to rake come fall. But the animal kingdom lost a little bit more of its oxygen supply. Not enough to affect those of us living here now. But what if each of us cuts down eighteen trees? Will our grandchildren have enough oxygen to breathe?

I continued with my walk, forgiving the people for cutting down eighteen fine trees so they wouldn't have to rake leaves come fall.

I cannot solve the problem. But I do know the tree is my friend.

I have to thank the tree for the job it has done the past summer. Its leaves have taken my waste, made something useful from it, and have given me more oxygen to breathe. Thank you, tree.

A gust of wind whips by. More leaves flutter down, come swirling around the corner of my house, rustle mischievously across the concrete drive and try to find hiding places in the corners of my car port, under my charcoal cooker, behind my trash can.

So many. I feel guilty in my search for the perfect one because I'm in a hurry to get them all raked up. But I try, even as more leaves come swirling down from above.

Falling leaves is nature's way of recycling itself. When there are no leaves in the spring, the tree dies. Where time does not matter, the tree topples, decomposes and becomes nutrients for yet another tree—filled with leaves.

I know I have excluded myself from nature's way of cycling itself. We humans refuse to live with nature. We fight it. We do not even acknowledge there's an end to the life we're living; that one day we, too, will have to let go of our mother tree. Instead of recycling, we consume nature's products and give nothing in return. We, the noblest of all the species, violate one of the most unforgivable of all of nature's laws—we foul our own nest with our own waste.

I resume my search, raking, raking, raking. They cover the ground, ankle deep in places. More are falling. I pause and lean on my rake. Why bother? I glance up. One lone leaf on a limb waggles at me.

I study it closely, waiting for it to fall. It's a good leaf—well shaped, healthy looking. The perfect one?

I laugh softly. We have one thing in common, that leaf and me. I, like it, am barely hanging on with my four score years.

During my time on the tree, from a sickly green bud to a full blown leaf, I've collected a few rust spots here and there. And I could remember many times when I had shut down some of my stomata because I didn't think any of the other leaves would notice me slacking off in my assignment to exchange good for the bad. They probably didn't. Nor did they care, probably. They were busy with their own space.

Suddenly, there was sense to the nonsense I have been living, fluttering in the wind, thinking my spot on the tree was the most important spot of all when all the time I was nothing but a tiny part of the whole.

During my turn on the tree, I had listened to the lessons of the elders, yes, but I insisted on shaping others to think like me.

But wasn't that what I was designed to do? Help, somehow, to purify the space allotted to me? Or did I do too much fluttering around in the shade thinking nobody would notice me?

I drop my attention back to the leaves at my feet and begin raking again. My enthusiasm to find the perfect one wanes. I have to get them stacked and burned. The rains will come soon and turn them into a useless, soggy mass.

The south breeze teases me, taking some of the leaves and running off with them. I keep raking. They all look alike. They are my enemy.

I pause again and remove my baseball cap and wipe the perspiration off my forehead with my sleeve as I survey the area of my yard I'd cleared. I'm almost finished.

I glance up again as the south breeze twists that one last leaf on the tree this way and that until it finally lets go. It floats gently down and comes to rest in a bare spot near my feet.

I stare at it, wondering. It wasn't a part of the pile beneath my rake. It was an existence in and of itself. Its shape was like a fingerprint—none other like it on the tree, perhaps none other like it in seasons past or seasons yet to come.

Isolated from the others, that particular leaf had meaning. It still carried some of its red-orange coloration which had contributed to the beauty of the fall foliage I had enjoyed so much a few weeks ago. I did not see that leaf then, for I was looking at the beauty of the tree.

I pick up the fallen leaf, twirl its stem as I study it thoughtfully.

The lines from Joyce Kilmer's poem, *Trees*, came out of my past. *"I think that I shall never see / A poem lovely as a tree / Poems are made by fools like me, / But only God can make a tree."*

It is so oddly shaped—

And then it dawns on me. How can any one leaf be oddly shaped when they are all oddly shaped? And if they are all oddly shaped, then none are. And if none are, then each is perfect.

I found what I was looking for—the perfect leaf! Smiling, I drop the leaf onto the pile at my feet and continue with my raking.

Its work was done. As God had intended.

Me? Not perfect. Yet none of us are. And if none of us are, then each is perfect.

As God intended.

Printed in the United States
28269LVS00003B/37-111

9 781413 752915